Ellie suck~~ed~~
She patted her ~~curls and straightened her uniform.~~

"Great." Simon hoped he'd drained all the enthusiasm out of the word. As Ellie waited for their colleague to arrive, he noted with deepening gloom her heightened color.

Thad came to a skidding halt at the top of a small rise, which allowed him to stand nose to nose with the taller man. His regulation tie was askew, and his regulation shoes were untied. Ellie seemed at a loss for words, so Simon asked—keeping his animosity on a short leash—"What brings you here so early, Farnsworth? I thought your shift didn't start until two."

"Hiram…called…me…in." Thad fanned his red face with a massive paw while his broad chest rose and fell in rapid heaves. "Sent me…Needed…needed his best man on the ground…I dropped everything…He…"

What a piece of work. "He sent you to find us?"

He nodded, sending a shower of sweat flying. "I'm here…about…the body."

Simon's jaw dropped.

So did Ellie's. "You heard about it already? We only just called 9-1-1."

"You did? Why?"

Ellie pointed.

Thad looked down and emitted a high squeal. "Oh my God, is that another one?"

Flotsam and Jetsam:
The Amelia Island Affair

by

M. S. Spencer

This is a work of fiction. Names, characters, places, and incidents are either the product of the author's imagination or are used fictitiously, and any resemblance to actual persons living or dead, business establishments, events, or locales, is entirely coincidental.

Flotsam and Jetsam: The Amelia Island Affair

COPYRIGHT © 2018 by Meredith Ellsworth

All rights reserved. No part of this book may be used or reproduced in any manner whatsoever without written permission of the author or The Wild Rose Press, Inc. except in the case of brief quotations embodied in critical articles or reviews.
Contact Information: info@thewildrosepress.com

Cover Art by *RJ Morris*

The Wild Rose Press, Inc.
PO Box 708
Adams Basin, NY 14410-0708
Visit us at www.thewildrosepress.com

Publishing History
First Mainstream Mystery Rose Edition, 2018
Print ISBN 978-1-5092-2334-3
Digital ISBN 978-1-5092-2335-0

Published in the United States of America

Dedication

To my grandfather, James Douglas Brown,
a descendent of James, the Black Douglas,
comrade-in-arms to Robert the Bruce,
first king of Scotland.
Every family needs a swashbuckler!

Chapter One
The Corpses Danced at Midnight

Fort Clinch State Park, Sunday, April 15

"Simon, I think you'd better call 9-1-1."

"Ya think so, Ellie?" Simon dunked his head in the briny water again and shook the drops free like a winter-weary brown bear rising from the icy Yukon River. He loosened the collar of his park ranger uniform and turned his eyes, the thick lashes dripping, on Ellie. "Shouldn't we just leave the carcass here for the vultures to pick clean? I thought you were soooo into recycling."

"Your flippancy is totally inappropriate, Simon. If you won't, I will. I'm calling Mother."

"Oh, is she on duty?"

"Yes." Ellie set her campaign hat on a log and pulled out her phone. Simon couldn't help but admire her slim fingers as she touched three numbers on the keypad. *They fit so beautifully at the end of her perfectly shaped arm, which flows ever so gracefully into that ravishing shoulder, currently obscuring those beautiful billowy breasts…Ulp. Where was I?*

A voice like a rutting peacock blared. "You've reached 9-1-1 Fernandina Beach Dispatch. Please state the nature of the emergency."

"Mom? It's me, Ellie."

The voice came down a notch but took on an ominous growl. "Ellie, you know how I feel about—"

"Mom, it's an emergency."

"Oh? Tell me."

Simon moved a little closer. *Just so I can hear better.*

Ellie rotated the phone to allow them both to listen. "Simon and I are at the fort. There was an event here last night, and Hosea sent us to check out what, if any, mess the participants left before we reopen to the public tomorrow."

"Oh, right. Betty Lawrence told me it was some sort of cult initiation—torches and secret handshakes and masks and stuff. I doubt they'd leave anything behind. Wouldn't want to divulge any clues to their Circean rituals."

Simon whistled. "Did she just say 'Circean'? Cool!"

Ellie put a palm over her phone. "What on earth are you talking about?"

"Circe. You know. Greek goddess of sorcery. Well, minor goddess to be precise, but she did land a pretty good gig in *The Iliad*. When Odysseus and his men…" Simon petered out in response to the look on Ellie's face.

She took her hand off the phone and spoke into it. "We're not sure our little emergency has anything to do with the attendees. The inside of the fort was reasonably tidy, but outside the walls—"

"Get on with it, Ellie. You're just like your father. What have you found?"

Ellie brushed the criticism aside with a wave of her hand. "A bit of unexpected flotsam washed up on the shore."

"Where?"

"You don't want to know what it is first?"

"I need coordinates if I'm to send out reinforcements."

"Okay, the *body* is on the stretch of sand facing St. Marys River. Northeast of the fort."

"Body, huh. Dead?"

"I'd probably call it a man if it wasn't."

"Good point. Does it look pruny?"

Ellie checked out the corpse, lying supine on the sand. "Not really. So that means he died recently?"

"It means he wasn't in the water long. Stiff?"

"Stiff, vic, cadaver—whatever you want to call him, he's dead."

"Ellie…"

Simon sensed the increasing threat level and, on the off chance Ellie didn't, intervened. "Hold on a sec." He prodded the dead man's jaw, then tried to lift his arm. "Tell your mother rigor mortis has set in. Body's cold. I'd say he died maybe eight to twelve hours ago."

Ellie stared at him. "How did you know that?"

"Elementary, my dear. Rigor mortis usually presents first at the eyes, neck, and jaw within two to six hours of death. From there, it spreads to the rest of the body. His arm is stiff, so I'd guess he kicked the bucket around midnight last night."

Ellie continued to stare. "And where did you come by all this medical knowledge?"

"Me? One of my majors in college was criminology."

"Majors? As in plural? How many did you have?"

Let's see…if I tell her, will that confirm that I'm a

colossal nerd and ruin any chance I have with her? He regarded the woman who drove all his favorite romantic heroines off the pages and into the back alleys of his memory. *Simon, you have exactly zero chance she'll ever think of you as anything but that awkward colleague whose claim to fame is he can beat everyone at Trivial Pursuit.* His lips formed the lie, but one glance at her dark golden ringlets and eyes the inky blue of a tropical twilight and he had to risk it. *I've got to be me, warts and all.* "Only two. Two undergraduate majors, that is. The other was linguistics." He added lightly, "The minor in poetry was just for fun."

Ellie paused a moment, eyes glazed, before rousing herself enough to say sternly, "I don't think you're supposed to touch anything."

The dispatcher's voice interrupted. "Eleanor? Hel*lo*? I'm waiting." Ellie gave her mother the particulars. "Okay, I'll notify Amos. Iggy and Virgil will bring the ambulance."

"Thanks, Mom." Ellie hung up. "Help's on the way."

"I heard." Simon sat down on the log and studied their new acquaintance. Mid-thirties, he guessed. Close-cropped hair, thick lips, dark brown skin—pale now. "See how wan he looks? It's because the blood's pooled in his back and butt." He nudged him with a foot. The head rolled an inch, and something sparkled at his throat. Simon looked closer. "That's a crucifix. Maybe he's a priest."

"So why is he in civilian clothes?"

"He left the priesthood. Or perhaps he was working in a dangerous neighborhood and didn't want to be too conspicuous."

"For heaven's sake, Simon. This isn't getting us anywhere." She moved a step closer and peered at the body. "How do you think he died?"

"Most likely a horrible hazing accident during the arcane ceremonies last night." A corner of his mouth turned up. "I believe druids are known for that."

"Don't be ridiculous. I—"

"Hellooo! Ellie! Simon!"

With a sinking feeling, Simon stood up to see a brawny young man with a thatch of luxuriant yellow hair loping toward them.

Ellie sucked in her breath. "Oh, look. It's Thad." She patted her curls and straightened her uniform.

"Great." Simon hoped he'd drained all the enthusiasm out of the word. As Ellie waited for their colleague to arrive, he noted with deepening gloom her heightened color.

Thad came to a skidding halt at the top of a small rise, which allowed him to stand nose to nose with the taller Simon. His regulation tie was askew, and his regulation shoes were untied. Ellie seemed at a loss for words, so Simon asked—keeping his animosity on a short leash—"What brings you here so early, Farnsworth? I thought your shift didn't start until two."

"Hosea…called…me…in." Thad fanned his red face with a massive paw while his broad chest rose and fell in rapid heaves. "He…sent me…Needed…needed his best man on the ground…I…dropped everything…He…"

What a piece of work. "He sent you to find us?"

He nodded, sending a shower of sweat flying. "I'm here…about…the body."

Simon's jaw dropped.

So did Ellie's. "You heard about it already? We only just called 9-1-1."

"You did? Why?"

Ellie pointed.

Thad looked down and emitted a high squeal, reminding Simon of the time the fellow found a weevil in his sandwich—a cross between a startled marmoset and a fifteen-year-old girl. "Oh my God, is that another one?"

Ellie sat down abruptly. "What do you mean, 'another one'?"

"They found a body washed up on shore just south of the fort. Hosea sent me to fetch you."

"Well, we've got our own corpse, thank you very much. You'll have to deal with the other one yourself," Simon said crossly. He couldn't help it; he resented Thad's intruding on his precious time with Ellie.

Farnsworth's ruddy cheeks went ashen. "But…but…I can't…You have to…I don't…"

Oh, for Christ's sake. The fathead gives new meaning to the phrase "all hat and no cattle." "You can't handle it yourself?"

Thad took a step back. "Sure…sure I can."

"Good. Why don't you tiptoe on back then?"

"All right, I will." Lower lip protruding, he swung around and headed toward the fort.

Ellie made a snuffling sound, like a plucky rabbit. "Now, Simon. You'd…um…you'd better go with Thad. I'll stay here and wait for the ambulance."

"No, no. You go." *Shut up, Simon. Why do you always have to make it easier for her?*

"Okay." Ellie lobbed him a joyous smile and took off after Thad. A siren blared in the distance.

Simon trudged back up the bank and around the fort walls to the road. *Am I ever going to drum up the nerve to ask her out?* He watched Ellie racing to catch up with his rival. *The man's a nitwit. What the hell does she see in him? Not the broad shoulders and cleft chin, surely. Nor the blow-dried coiffure.*

An ambulance, followed by a police cruiser and a white van marked Nassau County Crime Scene Unit, roared up to the fort entrance and stopped. Two men in shirts emblazoned with "EMT" in bright yellow letters pulled a gurney out of the ambulance and began to set it up. From the cruiser emerged a policeman, a sergeant's chevrons embroidered on his sleeve. Two others—a short, swarthy woman and a stocky man, both wearing CSI ball caps—fished equipment out of the van and trudged toward Simon.

"Alice. Maurice." As the sergeant approached, Simon nodded in greeting. "Hey, Tommy."

"Simon." He wiped his brow. "Where is it?"

"It's down on the sand. Follow me." Simon led the others to the dead man. Maurice stuck stakes in the ground and attached yellow tape to enclose an area eight feet square, then proceeded to snap photos from every angle. Meanwhile, Alice searched the ground on her hands and knees, now and then picking up something minuscule with tweezers and dropping it into a plastic bag.

When she stood up, Simon asked, "Find anything?"

She patted her satchel. "Not much. Cigarette stubs. Coupla quarters. Empty Pabst can." She looked hard at Simon. "Not one of yours, I hope."

Before Simon could defend himself, the two medics arrived with a stretcher. One said, "Hey, Simon,

7

grapevine says you got yourselves a mess o' corpora delicti." He grinned.

"So you heard about the other one, Iggy?"

"Yeah. Yulee boys are handling it."

Maurice unsnapped the lens cap off his camera. "Hello, Iggy." He tipped his hat at the second EMT. "Yo, Virgil, my man. How's tricks?"

"Happy in our work, as my old pappy used to say." Virgil turned to the other field investigator. "You about finished, Alice?"

She nodded. Iggy knelt down and examined the body. "Dead probably a day, not more'n two." He touched the chest with gloved hands. "Wet shirt." He sniffed his fingers. "Smells like blood." He raised his head. "Know him, Simon?"

The ranger shook his head.

"Mo, is it okay to remove the body?"

Alice's partner nodded, and the two medics hoisted it onto the stretcher. "Come on, Virgil. We can drop him at Lime Street."

"We don't have to schlep the body to the morgue?"

"No. Kenny had to come up from Jacksonville to sign some death certificates. He'll be there shortly."

Maurice and Alice headed toward their van. "We'll take the evidence bags back to the lab."

Simon trickled after them. "I gotta report to Hosea. Tell the ME to buzz us when he's got some answers."

"Will do."

Simon dropped his hat on the car seat and drove down the canopy road, a lane tented by live oaks shrouded in Spanish moss. He liked to picture the eerie veils of living epiphytes as a squadron of hoary-haired witches flying overhead. At the park headquarters he found his boss—a chubby, balding man with a persistent dribble of perspiration on his temple and coffee stains on his shirt—talking into the phone. "Yes, Kenny. I know, Kenny. Sometimes shit happens on Sunday, Kenny. Now, are you at the Fernandina station?…Good. Amos has two stiffs on ice, and we both want answers…Me? Because they washed up on park property, that's why. Technically, I have jurisdiction, but I'm generous enough to share the glory with the police department." He looked up, saw Simon, and raised an eyebrow.

I'm betting brother Amos won't see it that way. The friction between the twins—park superintendent and police chief—was longstanding and frequently explosive.

Hosea continued to listen. "State police? Yeah, I'm sure Amos called them. See you in five." He got his hat. "Come on."

The two men took the superintendent's car and followed the park road to Atlantic Avenue, turning right. "Where are Ellie and Thad?"

"They went to secure the other victim. Should be along soon." The car phone beeped. Hosea put it on speaker.

"Superintendent Barnes? It's Thad."

"Thad? Didn't I tell you to call me Hosea?"

"Yes, sir. But Dad says it's important to maintain the chain of command."

"Well, Judge Farnsworth is not on my staff." Simon knew Hosea wished the judge's son wasn't on his staff either. "What is it?"

Thad took a break to sulk before continuing. "We've hit a snag."

"The Yulee ambulance didn't arrive?"

"Oh, it's here. It's just that they only brought one gurney. And we need two."

"What are you talking about?"

"For the second victim."

Ellie's voice rang hollowly from a distance. "He means the third victim."

"What? Where is it?"

"First one's just south of the fort, like Rosie said...but Mr. Turley...You know him? He lives over there on Ladies Street. Anyway, he was walking his dog—"

Ellie interrupted again. "It's that huge St. Bernard. Friendly, but boy, what a drooler."

"Thad? The third victim?"

"Turley found him just up from the mouth of Egan's Creek."

"Within the park?"

"Barely."

"Um, well, hang in there. I'll tell Amos to send Virgil back out as soon as I get to the station." He hung up. "They seem to be dropping like flies. What is this, the eighth plague?"

"Locusts aren't due for another two years."

Hosea shot Simon a dry look. He turned into the police station parking lot on Lime Street just ahead of the second ambulance and Ellie's squad car. The lot was nearly full. "Why are all these people here?"

Simon surveyed the license plates, which ranged from Ohio to Massachusetts. "Snow birds. Either looking for drowned relatives or too cheap to pay the beach parking fee."

"*Hmmph.* Amos needs to crack down."

"He would, except due to all those tourist dollars pouring in during the season, his salary is twice that of the Nassau County executive."

"Doesn't compare to what Fort Clinch visitation shovels into the coffers of the state park authority."

"Which is why your salary is also twice that of the Nassau County executive."

Hosea's lip curled up. "A bit cynical for one so young, aren't you?"

"Me? Young? Yeah, I guess thirty-five is young." He stretched out a long leg. "How come my joints ache in the morning, then?"

"Not enough sex."

Simon gaped at his boss, who ignored him and pushed through the swinging door into the building. Ellie and Thad followed him while Simon waited for the men from the Yulee ambulance. They rolled two bodies covered in sheets down the ramp. "Where'd you get the second gurney?"

"Found a folding one tucked under the driver's seat."

He followed them inside. They pushed their cargo through a steel door marked Autopsy, returned with the empty gurneys, filled out some forms, and left.

Thad had been muttering and shooting glances at the door. "Superintendent Barnes—Hosea—you want me to head back to HQ?"

Hosea cocked his head. "Why? Is there something you need to do?"

"Er…no. That is…I didn't get any lunch, seeing as how you made me come in early and…I…"

His boss scrunched his nose up as though he'd just dropped a rotten egg on his shoe. "All right. Go get

11

something to eat. And meet us back here in half an hour, okay?"

Thad was gone before the door swung shut on Hosea's last words.

Sheesh.

A man in a white lab coat who could only be described as petite, his pinky blond hair curled fetchingly around his ears, trotted in and picked up the clipboard. "Hey, Iggy. Virgil. Thanks for coming in on such short notice." He looked past the two paramedics to the park superintendent. "Hosea. My bad luck I was on call today, huh? Whatcha got for me?"

"Congratulations, Kenny, as our millionth customer you have won three—not one, not two, but *three*—prizes."

"Three? What is this—bring-a-body-to-work day?" Kenny took the clipboard into the autopsy room.

Just then the police chief came out of his office and walked over to the desk sergeant. "Have you seen the medical examiner, Tommy? Fred told me he was on his way from the morgue."

"Mr. Mathews is with the new arrivals, Captain."

"Ah." The chief noticed the three rangers standing in a clump by the entrance. "There you are. Ellie. Simon...*Hosea.*"

"Amos." Hosea spat it out with barely disguised malevolence.

Ellie knew them well, but she never failed to marvel at the brothers, carbon copies of each other, from the belly to the wispy ring of white hair. Though identical twins, they were always one jab short of a pitched battle. "Um, hello...Amos." She cast a timid glance at Hosea.

The chief curled a finger at the group. "Shall we?"

He knocked at the room Kenny had entered. The medical examiner stuck his head out. "What? Oh, it's you, Amos."

"So, what've we got?"

Kenny came out, pulling his latex gloves off, a sour look on his face. His voice was thin and a bit shrill. "What a day. Three! Good thing both Iggy and Virgil were available."

The two techs locked arms. Virgil chirped, "No problem!"

Iggy said cheerily, "Overtime!"

Hosea gestured at the door and asked, "ID?"

Virgil shook his head. "Nothing on any of them."

"*Hmm*. Accidental death?"

"Possibly. All three were found on the shore. They might have been passengers on a boat."

"And fell overboard?" Hosea scratched the top of his head. "I can see one. But three?"

"Suicide pact?" Amos must have been joking, but Simon wasn't sure.

Virgil ventured, "Maybe a robbery gone bad?"

"Could be." Iggy patted his partner's shoulder. "If pirates attacked a boat, they'd have to get rid of the victims somehow."

Ellie laughed. "Are you suggesting brigands are marauding in St. Marys River?" When no one responded, she stopped and regarded the others. "What? Is that even plausible?"

Simon murmured, "Considering Amelia Island's lurid past, pirates are not beyond the realm of possibility."

"Lurid past? What are you talking about?"

Kenny spoke condescendingly. "That's right, you're not a native, Miss Ironstone." He gave Simon a meaningful look. "This coast swarmed with privateers during the formative years of our young country. In fact, Amelia Island was once ruled by a French buccaneer."

"French, yes," Simon conceded. "But he raised the Mexican flag over us. And he only lasted a month."

The desk sergeant put his phone down. "Iggy. Virgil. That was Dispatch. You need to head over to the elementary school. Some kid broke his leg."

The EMT men saluted and, grabbing a gurney, pushed it out the door.

"So…" Ellie spoke thoughtfully. "If these three were killed by pirates and then thrown overboard, how do you explain why they were found so far apart?"

"Rip tide?"

"Or—what about this? They were killed at intervals and tossed in the drink while the boat was moving." Amos turned to Kenny. "Have you examined them yet?"

"Are you kidding? They came in five minutes ago. Wait here, and I'll do a quick inspection."

Kenny closed the door, leaving the others to pace the small lobby. The two CSI agents passed through.

Simon called, "You guys going back to Yulee?"

"Yeah, heading to the lab. What's up?"

"Did you find anything at the other sites, Alice?"

The woman stopped. "Nothing that jumps out. Styrofoam take-out box. Somebody's flip-flop. Cigar stub. Another beer can." She paused as if waiting for him to fess up. After a minute, she went on. "Maurice picked up a lighter and some black fibers—he thinks they're silk."

"Anything on the victims?"

She shrugged. "Female had one shoe missing. Not the flip-flop. Male had a partial news clipping in his pocket. Funny, the other male—the one you found, Simon—was totally clean, stem to stern. Not even a handkerchief. Mo thought that was kinda weird. I mean, *everyone* has something in his pocket, right? Even if it's a mint."

Simon found himself at a loss to answer. Hosea stirred. "The first male had a news clipping? Of what?"

Alice shook her head. "Pretty soaked. Mo found it."

"Was it legible?"

She called to her partner. "Hey, Mo, could you read the clipping we found in the vic's pocket?"

The CSI agent turned around. "Not much. It disintegrated as I put it in the evidence bag. I could only make out one word in the headline."

"Which was?"

"Sanchez."

"*Hmm*. Could be his name."

"Yeah, but it's not much help. How many Sanchezes do you think you'll find in a Florida phone directory?"

Amos shrugged. "I'm sure we'll identify him soon enough."

"Well, good luck with that. We have to get this stuff to Yulee." Maurice held the door for Alice, and they disappeared into the parking lot.

Half an hour passed before the medical examiner reappeared. "I've got some preliminary findings. Follow me." He led the way through double doors into an icy chamber. Ellie shivered. Simon took a step toward her, the urge to wrap his arms around her stronger than he cared to admit. The room, lined with sinks and cabinets, held three long stainless-steel tables. Three forms hidden under white sheets had been laid out on them.

Mathews went to the first and pulled the covering down. Simon saw a man in his forties, his pinched face and snub nose reminding him of a Boston brown terrier. He had black hair and thin lips. His rumpled gray suit could have come off the rack at Goodwill. "Hispanic male, middle-aged, in poor health."

"You mean because he's dead?"

The medical examiner said something under his breath that sounded a lot like "asshole."

The man has no sense of humor.

Kenny moved to the next table, where the person Simon and Ellie had discovered lay.

Simon spoke again. "I'm guessing priest."

Ellie frowned. "Wearing a cross could just mean he's a good Christian."

Simon shrugged. "I dunno. Alice said there was nothing in his pockets. Who but a man of the cloth would go anywhere without his wallet? Anyway, there's just something…upright and honest about him."

She laughed. "And you think in this day and age the only man with those qualities has to be off limits to women?"

For the second time that morning, Simon gaped. "Um…er…"

Hosea hastily intervened. "Not at all. On the other hand, a missing wallet does give greater credence to the robbery motive." He moved to the last table.

When Kenny bared the face of the third victim, Ellie gasped. "It's a female!"

"Nothing unusual in that. Fifty-one percent of the population is female. Stands to reason one out of three corpses would be from the distaff side."

Amos pressed his lips together. "Yes, but this one's *huge*."

Hosea breathed, "And *old*."

Mathews nodded. "I'd say in her late fifties, early sixties. Her facial features hint at Caribbean, maybe Haitian."

"Not American?"

"No. Bone structure shows African, Spanish, and some native traits."

"Illegal alien?"

"Don't think she came by coyote, if that's what you're thinking. Her clothes are high end—designer label."

Ellie asked Kenny, "Why do you think her head's shaved?"

Hosea mumbled, "I believe that's the fashion nowadays."

In the rather uncertain silence that followed this statement, Kenny pulled the sheet all the way back, revealing tight black silk pants. One foot was encased in a yellow, rhinestone-encrusted sandal. The other was bare.

All five gazed at the person lying on the table. Finally, Ellie murmured, "She really is a big woman, isn't she?"

Simon pointed at her pants. "Look, there's a tear in the hem."

"Maurice's silk fibers?"

"Likely."

Kenny lifted the unshod foot with a gloved hand. "Only unexplained marks are these abrasions around her ankle."

"An ankle bracelet?"

Amos fingered his police revolver. "More evidence of robbery?"

Hosea sniffed. "Hold your horses, bro. We don't have near enough information yet."

Ellie waved at the tables. "So…how did they die?"

The ME wavered. "I'm not ready to make a determination until I've done a complete analysis." When this pronouncement was met with general dissatisfaction, he said cautiously, "What I *can* say is the priest guy was stabbed in the chest. That one over there"—he gestured at the woman—"likely drowned. The other man…"

"Well?"

"I'm not sure yet. From the looks of him, he bled out. He may have been stabbed as well."

Simon whistled. "Could be gang-related."

Hosea pursed his lips. "Here in sunny, peaceful Amelia Island? Ridiculous."

Amos looked down his nose at his brother. "You park service people are such hicks. Jacksonville police just arrested two MS-13 members last week. On their way north on A1A." He turned to Kenny. "Any gang tattoos?"

"Don't know yet." He looked pointedly at the door. "I'll let you know when I've finished the autopsies."

Hosea, still fuming at his brother's jibe, shoved him toward the door. "Come on, Amos. You're in the way. Let the man do his job."

To his credit, Amos went quietly. The four trudged out to the hall. Thad had been pacing the lobby, pretending to talk on his cell phone. "There you guys are! What's the scoop?"

Simon answered him. "We may be looking at two murders. At least."

Hosea asked Amos, "What about the state police?"

"I have a call in. Christ, I hope they didn't die in Georgia. What a pain in the neck that would be."

Ellie interjected, "Then it would be Georgia's problem though, wouldn't it?"

"Only half of it. Do you have any idea of the paperwork involved in transferring a John Doe across state lines?"

Simon tapped his lip. "Nonetheless, they must've arrived by boat. The park gate was locked. The killer would have had to drag them through the wetlands to get to the fort. Someone would have seen him."

"If the gators didn't get him first." Hosea nodded sagely.

"And why take them all the way to the shoreline? Why not dump them in the marsh or the mangroves?"

"He could have carried them up from Egan's Creek." Thad rubbed his jaw, probably to add gravitas to his words.

"Who's he?"

"The killer. Natch." He looked at Simon as though the latter were a bit of a dim bulb.

Ellie coughed. "Um…do the victims have to be related?"

The men stared at her. "They were simultaneously off-loaded here by three different people? That's pretty incredible."

"No, wait. Only one of them drowned. The other two may have been dropped at the fort at the same time the woman washed up on shore."

"Like I said," put in Thad eagerly.

"Two if by land, and one if by sea?"

Thad piped up in the kind of voice he likely used when reciting "The Charge of the Light Brigade" to his parents' friends. "It's *one* if by land and *two* if by sea, Simon." He held up a pedantic finger. "Paul Revere."

Does he expect a round of applause for that? Simon really, really wished he had a gold star. *I'd glue it on his forehead.*

"It's worth pursuing, Ellie." Hosea opened the door. "Let's head back to the park and—"

Ellie laid a hand on his arm. "It's almost four o'clock, sir. And Sunday to boot. Add to that I'm on duty tomorrow at eight. Do you mind if I head home?"

The superintendent's normally genial face blanched. "Oh, dear me, I wasn't paying attention. Since Cornelia passed, I sometimes forget the time. No one to badger me about supper." His shoulders sagged. "Run along, child."

Thad straightened his shoulders. "I'll accompany you to HQ, Hosea. I've got my second wind!"

Not to mention two more hours on your shift.

"Oh, but…Thad." Ellie gave him a pleading glance, which he missed entirely. "Didn't you say you'd take me home?"

He gazed over her head. "I did promise you a ride, but…but…someone's got to be available in case…in case of anything…er…happening." The thin layer of bravado failed to mask the fear that something might indeed happen.

Simon looked from him to Ellie and shrugged. "I can drive her." *He really is a boob. But how to turn his boobness to my advantage?* The intricacies of courtship had never been Simon's forte. He thought furiously as they threaded the streets back to Atlantic Avenue and turned right. Just before he reached the circle that would take them to Fletcher Avenue and Ellie's house, an idea finally wormed its way through the haze of desperation. "You know, it's happy hour at Sliders—want a beer before you head home?" *Too forced? Too needy?*

Ellie shrugged. "Sure. Let's sit outside, okay?"

They wended their way through the dark restaurant and out into the waning sun. The wooden tables sat precariously on the low dunes, umbrellas tipped toward the south wind. Beyond them lay the leaden ocean, quiet now at the end of the day. A woman with hennaed hair and impish eyes skipped over. "Hey, Simon. Ellie. Still in uniform? You rangers put in awful long hours."

"We did not have what you'd call an ordinary day, Gretchen." His lip twisted.

The waitress paused, holding the menus close to her chest. When it became clear that he wasn't going to elaborate, she sniffed. "All right, keep it to yourself if you want. Debbie Daugherty and Glenda Slocum are coming in later—I'll get the scoop from them. Now, what can I do you for?"

Ellie scanned the bar list. "I feel like a local beer. How about this one from Werewolf Brewing Company—Arwen's Brown?"

"Good choice." She gave her a menu. "Pabst for you, Simon?"

"Yeah, I guess." He held out his hand. "Don't I get

21

a menu?"

"You? Uh…sure thing."

Now why did she giggle at that?

While Ellie read the specials, Simon permitted himself to inspect her features. Short curls of honey hair crowned her small head. Long lashes covered what he knew were the biggest eyes he'd ever seen—tinged the stormy blue-gray of a squall over the Atlantic. Once when she'd been furious at him, he had glimpsed streaks of platinum in them, exploding like fireworks in the frigid indigo depths. He shivered at the memory. *I never want her that angry at me again.*

"What's the matter?"

"Um…er…just thinking about the victims. They don't seem to have much in common."

"Other than all appearing on the same morning?"

" 'Of all the gin joints, in all the towns, in all the world, she walks into mine.' "

Ellie laughed.

She liked it! Maybe I'll try my Rodney Dangerfield impression. He peeped shyly at her. *Nah. Save it for a special occasion.*

Gretchen brought their beers, Ellie's in a frothing mug, Simon's in a can.

Ellie took a long pull. "So…" Her pale skin suffused with pink. "Did you have that talk with Thad about me?" She didn't look at him.

Damn. "Not yet. He's been busy er…working with Hosea." *Fawning over him is more like it, but she wouldn't agree.* "Thad has…ambitions."

"I know!" Her eyes lit up. "He really wants to make good, you know—prove himself to his father." A spasm of pain flitted across her face. "Judge Farnsworth has always been so hard on him. I don't think he appreciates his son's potential. Thad says his father always liked his older brother best."

Simon reflected that, in fact, the good magistrate appreciated only too well his second son's lack of talent. He'd done his best—sent him to Exeter and then to Princeton (eased by a generous endowment). He couldn't help it that the poor lad suffered from an acute shortage of brain cells. *But he'd make a great statue of David.* Gorgeous to look at—the shoulders of a linebacker, the slim hips of a champion swimmer, a mane of thick, butter-colored hair. *And the vacant stare of a particularly fatuous mullet.* Simon took a healthy swig of beer. *If only he* were *a statue—that way we'd never have to listen to him.* He noticed Ellie's drooping expression. "He helped him get the ranger job. That shows he has some faith in him."

Ellie checked, her mug halfway to her lips. "I thought Thad did that on his own."

Oops. "All I mean is, I don't think it hurt that Thad's father sits on the district court. He's—*urk*—done a bang-up job at Fort Clinch. Really."

Gretchen came by. "Want something to eat?"

"Just something to munch on. How about the fried pickles?"

She wrote it down before turning to Simon. "And for you?"

"He wants the hamburger."

Simon blinked. "I beg your pardon?"

Ellie smiled fondly at her companion. "Sweetie, you always have the hamburger."

"Oh. Okay—I guess you know how I like it then." He did not expect the ready answer.

"Yup. Medium well, no lettuce, no tomato, no onion. Large fries."

"Er…" *Okay, so maybe I* am *in a rut, what with Mother…* He sneaked a peek at Ellie. *That's not the reason and you know it, my lad. If you could stop obsessing over someone who thinks you're wallpaper, you might have time to try something new.*

Ellie watched Gretchen head toward the kitchen. "I don't know how you stay so thin, Simon. Your idea of health food is low-salt Cheetos."

"I beg to differ. In fact, my nickname in high school was Nero Wolfe."

"Wasn't he a fictional sleuth?"

"And a gourmet." His cell phone buzzed. "Simon Ribault." He listened intently. "Okay. See you first thing."

Ellie put down her beer. "What is it?"

"They found the knife used to kill the priest."

"Where?"

"In the other victim's back."

Chapter Two
Shipping News

Park headquarters, Monday, April 16

"So, have they identified any of the victims yet?" Simon filled his mug from the office urn.

"Haven't heard." Hosea poured sugar into his coffee with a generous hand. "Amos better not try to pull his usual stunt."

"You mean, keeping you out of the loop?"

The superintendent slammed the cup down, splattering drops of coffee everywhere. Reaching for a doughnut, he knocked it off the plate, spewing crumbs into the puddles on his desk. Oblivious, he jumped up to pace, angry words burbling through his lips. "He can't get away with it this time. The events occurred on my turf—he *has* to share any evidence he finds."

Simon grabbed a wad of napkins and wiped up the mess. "Hey! Can't you multitask? I need a little help here."

Hosea gazed unseeing at Simon, his mind on his twin. "Presumptuous SOB. Don't know where he gets his attitude from. A state park superintendent way outranks him."

Simon kept his comment to himself. Hosea and Amos had been feuding for years. It had started—as it usually does—over a girl. The two brothers had been inseparable all their young lives, but when Beulah May Bradford showed up that first day of school at Fernandina Beach High, her rosebud mouth pursed, her soft brown eyes blinking, they were both goners. It didn't matter that Beulah May's mouth was pursed because she was in a perpetually foul mood, nor that she blinked because she'd never figured out how to insert her contacts properly. It didn't even matter that her heart immediately fixed on Thad Farnsworth's older brother, Wesley. And when said Wesley, an even dumber version of his sibling, swept her off her feet and eloped with a visibly pregnant Beulah May their senior year, the conflict only intensified. Hosea and Amos were convinced their rivalry had doomed any chance at romance with the lady and barely spoke for a decade. It took two happy marriages—Hosea's to Cornelia and Amos's to Sylvia, to bring them back together. Still, blasts of ash as if from still active volcanoes were sometimes observed in high stress situations.

Ellie came in, Thad trailing behind. "So, have they identified the victims yet?"

Simon hiccupped. "My exact question."

Hosea retrieved his mug. "Nope. Puzzling sort of trio. A young, dark-skinned man, a middle-aged Latino, and an older black woman. How could they possibly be connected?"

"Well, the men have the knife in common." Ellie thought back. "Didn't Virgil suggest they all fell off the same boat?"

Thad clearly wanted to stick with his theory. "Or, like I said, they could have been dropped on the shore."

Simon wasn't sure. "That would be awfully risky. That's a busy channel."

"Then we're back to the killer transporting them through the park."

"Nah—like you said, Hosea, why lug them all the way to the river?"

"Okay, okay." Hosea seemed put out. "He could have driven them."

"Then there would have been car tracks."

Ellie added, "And anyway, how would he get around the gate?"

"Damn."

"Maybe…" Thad had evidently decided to add two more cents. "The killer could've come by boat and met them on the shore."

Simon thought this over. "So the three victims were alive when they arrived at the river?"

This had the unfortunate effect of encouraging the lad. "Yes! They snuck into the park and followed the trail to the fort."

The idea has promise.

"Why were they all wet then?" Hosea shook his head.

"And why were they found so far apart?" Thad squirmed under Ellie's gaze.

Never mind.

When Thad didn't answer, Hosea stopped pacing. "How about this? It was part of a satanic ritual conducted by that secretive bunch that rented the fort."

Simon eyed him. "What do you know about them?"

"Not much. A private company handled most of the arrangements. I only skimmed the file they gave me. Fellow named Carson Gregory filled out the paperwork. Said it was an organizational meeting of the

League of the Green Cross."

"Green, huh. Enviros?"

"No idea. He told the event planner there would be about a hundred attendees. They needed tiki torches around the yard and on the battlements, plus a tent and tables. Requested a band and a couple of barbecue grills."

Simon spoke up. "Maybe Amos should go have a talk with this Gregory."

Hosea harrumphed. "No, this is park business. I want you and"—his gaze passed over Thad to Ellie— "Ellie to go."

Before Simon could respond, a uniformed woman bustled in with a sheaf of papers. "FBI just faxed this wanted poster." She handed copies around.

Simon took one. "Thanks, Rosie. Who is it?"

"Escaped convict, name of Miguel Alvaredo. Tunneled out of Miami Correctional Facility."

"What was he in for?"

Rosie said heavily, "Murder. Killed five members of a rival gang in an ambush. Also racketeering and drug dealing. Real nasty piece of goods."

Ellie glanced at the photo and dropped the paper. "Oh my God."

"What?"

"Don't you…don't you recognize the fellow?"

Hosea looked at it and shook his head. Simon's eyes opened wide. "Well, hello. It's one of our victims."

"Which one?"

"The older fellow. The one who washed ashore down near Egan's Creek."

"So…he's a murderer. He must have killed the

other two then."

Ellie raised her hand.

"What?"

"Except…er…he was the one with the knife in his back, wasn't he?"

Hosea stood up. "That's right."

Simon brushed his fingers across his brow. "Scenario number two hundred fifty-three: Alvaredo stabbed the priest, who then managed to pull the knife out of his own chest and kill his attacker."

Only Thad seemed to consider this seriously. Finally, Hosea relented. "I'm sure the lab is checking for DNA on the handle."

Ellie persisted. "What about the woman?"

"Her? Kenny thinks she drowned. Probably just serendipity. There's nothing linking her to the other two."

"That we know of." Hosea picked up his hat. "I'm heading down to the police station. Aren't you guys on duty? Girl Scout troop set up last weekend at the Amelia River campground. You'd better read them the riot act."

Simon snickered. "Right. Remember the last time?"

Ellie did not approve. "That food fight meant days of trapping raccoons and driving off importuning squirrels."

"Right. Plus those little girls left more hair behind than a twelve-pound Persian cat. Every drain had to be reamed out."

Thad ignored the titters and focused on his boss. "What's up for today, Chief?"

"You come with me. I want to see Amos." Hosea

waved at the poster. "This should be good for twenty points."

Ellie watched Thad leave, a wistful expression on her face.

Simon took a stab at jovial. "Shall we go? We can ask the girls if anything caught their attention while they were making camp. And after the Girl Scouts, we could tackle that contingent of Red Hat ladies."

"Oh?"

"They want to rent the fort for a quilting bee."

"The whole fort?"

"Well, they need space for the heavy metal band and the open bar."

The rest of the day was spent in pursuits that never came up on the park ranger exam.

****

Park headquarters, Tuesday, April 17

The park superintendent was at his desk when Simon arrived the next morning. "Anything from the Girl Scouts?"

"They were off on a day hike. We'll have to catch them another day. What did Amos say?"

"About what?"

"Hosea!"

"Oh, you mean the convict." He frowned. "Claimed he'd already identified him and had been in touch with Miami-Dade."

"Are they coming to get it…or rather, him?"

Hosea put down his newspaper and got his hat. "I suppose they will. Hadn't thought of that. Yes, we'd better get cracking."

Ellie picked up her keys.

Simon eyed her. "Where are you going?"

"I…uh…thought…" She trailed off.

Hosea spoke for her. "What she's trying to say is, we have yet to figure out the connection—"

"If any."

"If any, between the three bodies. So…if they take one away…"

"Okay. You want us to postpone the interview with Gregory and work on this?"

"Yes." Hosea rapped his ruler on the desk and said firmly, "Top priority is to retrace this Alvaredo's trail. He was last seen near the Port of Miami. Probably stowed away on one of the cruise ships."

Ellie wasn't convinced. "How would he end up on Amelia Island then? I doubt if those big ships dock at Fernandina Beach."

"True." Hosea thought. "Let's say a ship is heading back to port, and this Alvaredo jumped or was pushed off near the mouth of St. Marys River and floated to shore."

"Bit of a stretch, especially considering he managed to wash up two miles south in the Amelia River." Simon rubbed his chin. "But it might work for one of the other two victims. I'll go down to the port authority and ask Clem."

"Take Ellie with you. She needs to broaden her acquaintance with our local officials."

They found the port director in his shiny new office.

"Hey, Simon. Miss Ironstone, isn't it? What's up?"

Simon spoke first. "We were wondering if you ever have cruise lines dock here. You know, like the Celebrity or Princess."

"Cruise ships? Nah. They all go through Miami or

Fort Lauderdale. We're strictly a shipping port."

"Damn. How about those small ones? You know, like the river boats or mini cruise ships."

Clem scratched his head. "You know, I think I've seen one of those out in the river—they may stop in at the marina."

"Thanks." Ellie led Simon out to the car. "Marina?"

"My thoughts exactly."

They found a parking spot only six blocks from the Fernandina Harbor Marina. The sidewalks teemed with red-faced, white-legged tourists. Ellie pointed at a couple in shorts and down jackets. "Rather early in the season for crowds this big, isn't it?"

"It's those bad winters they've had up north. My friend Donald says the Gulf Coast is even worse—more and more people are moving there and staying year-round. Traffic's horrendous."

Ellie zipped up her jacket and checked the overcast sky. "Well, it's pretty darn chilly here."

"Hey, this is bikini weather for a Mainer."

They passed a large gathering on the sidewalk. Many were pointing and taking pictures. Ellie stopped. "Must be something going on."

Simon stood on tiptoe to peer over the arms brandishing cell phones in the air. "Why, it's the Wienermobile!"

Just then the pack parted, revealing a red hot dog in a bright yellow bun the size of a blue whale sitting on top of a souped-up station wagon. Simon turned excitedly to Ellie. "I drove one of these back in college. Great summer job."

"You're kidding." Ellie looked at her companion

with a mixture of awe and mirth. "You have hidden depths."

"Aw, shucks. Actually, I think that's how I landed the job in the park service."

"I guess it really stood out on an otherwise humdrum resume."

"Your mockery is not appreciated. How did *you* pay for beer and pizza in college?"

Ellie mumbled something.

"What's that? Pole dancer?"

She raised her voice. "Minnow counter."

"Minnow? As in small fish? Yup, sounds like something the bureaucrats would spend our taxpayer money on."

Ellie pouted. "It was in fact a crucial part of the Virginia Game and Inland Fisheries research. Sort of like the annual Cornell backyard feeder watch. We had to count the number of fish running through the Potomac watershed in the spring run."

Simon stopped short. "How on earth did you do that?"

"Weell, it was really more of an estimate. I'd fill a bucket with fish and count those, then extrapolate."

"Using rate of water flow and speed of the little fingerlings?"

"Something like that."

"Well, I hope you got a Girl Scout badge for it."

"Better. It counted as credit toward my biology degree."

"And the dumbing down of the American education system continues."

"Ah, here we are."

They found the dockmaster eating his lunch. "Hey,

Simon. Miss."

"Hey, Bert. May I introduce Ellie Ironstone, my partner?"

Bert condescended to rise a few inches from his seat.

"Got a minute?"

He put down his sandwich. "Is this a shakedown for the park rangers' benevolent fund? If so, you'll have to talk to my wife."

"No, no."

"Okay, then. Have a seat."

"You heard about the bodies that washed up at the fort?"

"Have I! Everyone's talking about it. Heard they've only identified one."

"Yes. Name of Alvaredo. He escaped from the Miami Correctional Facility."

"So how did he get to Amelia Island?"

"That's what we're aiming to find out. Since he washed up on shore, he may have come by boat."

"And you want to know if any of the vessels in my marina reported a missing passenger?" He riffled through the pages on a clipboard. "Nope."

"Er…he might have stowed away. He was an escaped prisoner after all."

"Well now, how could they report him missing if they didn't know he was on board?"

"Ah…er…" Simon perked up. "Maybe the owner killed him."

"In which case, the killer would be long gone. Of the fifteen slips we keep available for transients, only one has been here since Saturday."

Ellie took another tack. "Could we search the boats

that are still here?"

Bert shook his head. "You'd have to get Amos to do it—not your jurisdiction."

Simon made a note. "Okay." He stood.

Bert finished his iced tea. "Of course, he could have been on the cruise ship."

Simon sat back down. "Cruise ship?"

"The Southern Coast Cruise line makes a couple of runs between Jacksonville and Charleston. Usually calls in at Amelia Island."

"Any come through recently?"

"Yeah."

"When?"

"Saturday."

"Is that typical?"

"Uh huh. They're on a regular schedule."

"And that is?"

"Once a week until May."

It's like pulling teeth. "Did the company report anyone missing?"

"Well, now, number one, they wouldn't tell me unless they had to—bad publicity."

"If a passenger falls off one of their ships, I'm betting they have to tell *someone*."

"Not me. I hate to repeat myself, but if he was a stowaway, they wouldn't know they'd lost him anyway, would they?"

Simon put a hand on Ellie's arm. "Come on, we're not getting anywhere here. Thanks, Bert."

"Sure—tell Amos if he wants to search the boats, he'll have to get warrants for every single one. We currently have twenty moorings."

Simon muttered as he steered Ellie out, "The

wheels of American justice grind to a halt."

"Okay, my man, what now?"

"Lunch."

He indicated a restaurant in the middle of the marina, its distressed shingles and plastic life preservers emblematic of the seafaring life, at least for wide-eyed Nebraskans. "Salty Pelican okay?"

"Fine."

They found a table by the window. After a few minutes' wrestling with his natural inclinations, Simon admitted defeat and ordered a hamburger. Hoping to wipe the smirk off Ellie's face, he announced, "Tomorrow, I shall eat pie."

"I—" *Giggle.* "—expect it will be hamburger pie."

Simon refused to talk after that and defiantly poured extra ketchup over his burger. He called for the check before Ellie had finished.

"Hey!"

"Got to get going."

"At least let me finish my drink." As Ellie raised her glass to her lips, she stared over Simon's shoulder. "Who's that?"

He twisted around. "Couple of tourists—from the looks of them, blessed with hearty appetites."

"No. Out on the dock. Isn't that old Salvatore Poli? Rosie told me he'd retired."

"Poli? Nah. He'll go down with his ship. Doesn't make enough money shrimping to retire."

She gazed at the man speculatively. "I read that shrimping used to be big here. There doesn't seem to be a lot left."

"It's true. Amelia Island was the center of the industry in the first half of the twentieth century."

Simon paid the bill. "Let's go ask Poli if he's seen anything out of the ordinary."

"You had better do the talking."

"Why?"

She hesitated, then burst out, "You seem so comfortable talking to people of any spot or stripe. I feel very self-conscious."

"I don't see why. We're all the same slimy tissue under the skin."

"Under the skin maybe, but people are different in a small community like this. I grew up in a Washington suburb, the only child of two lawyers. Any ethnic groups I encountered belonged to the diplomatic corps."

Her words reminded Simon that she'd only been here for six months. "Well, I grew up here. I've known these people all my life."

"Still, you…you have an easy way with everybody—rich, poor, average, oddball. Remember that old lady, Mrs. Petrov?"

He chuckled. "Poor Maude. Her family were all carnies—carnival workers. When she was fourteen, the snake charmer propositioned her and she ran away." He laughed. "Only one I know who ran away *from* the circus."

"Is that why she had hysterics when she stumbled into a snake nest near her RV?"

"Uh huh."

"You had her in stitches with that story of Arnold Schwarzenegger in a panic over an itty bitty bug in his soup." She smiled at him. "And that time you explained the reason we don't wade in the marsh at night and the whole Cub Scout pack actually paid attention."

Oh my God, how do I respond? Could she…could

she really like me? "I…uh…"

Before he could reply, she said hastily, "Now Thad—he handles the town's elite with such a sure hand. He can sweet-talk the mayor into anything. And"—he knew she was looking at his hooked nose, his thick, bristling eyebrows, and his long spindly legs—"he's awfully handsome, isn't he?"

Unable to come up with a gentlemanly response to this paean, Simon held his hand out. "Shall we?"

When they reached Poli, he was bawling orders at two rail-thin black men who were hauling in nets. A few greasy locks trailed from under his faded John Deere cap. His boots were painted with fish scales, and his jeans barely hung on by clinging to his knees. The only part of him that didn't glisten was his tan chest, covered in rippling muscles and thick pepper-and-salt hair.

"Hello, Sal. What's up?"

The man stopped and wiped a callused palm across his forehead. "Simon! I thought you had a job at the fort? What you doin' here in the slums?" He grinned, revealing a mouth devoid of all but three teeth.

Lost another one, has he? That explains the whistling noise when he talks. "We're checking out the boats in the marina for stowaways."

"Those Girl Scouts get away from you agin?"

"Nah. I've learned to lasso since the last stampede. Say, you guys see anything last Sunday that might help us?"

"Not me. Dunno about t'others. Only 'bout six, seven trawlers go out no more. Most of the trade's out of Jacksonville."

"Shame. I remember when Fernandina was the

main source for shrimp on the east coast."

"You? You is way too young to remember that, Simon. Why, when my daddy set up his business near fifty years ago, he was hauling 'em in so fast, he could kick back and take it easy while his boys did the work." He nodded at the two men working the nets. Their gray hair and leathery hands—fingers gnarled and twisted from too many differences of opinion with a winch— put their age in the late sixties. "Argus an' Frog been workin' fer me since I got my first boat. Frog was headin' shrimp by the time he was thirteen. Captained fer me for ten years afore he threw his back out."

"That's right. Shrimpers were mainly Geechee, weren't they?"

"Crews were, yeah. Most of 'em lived over by Five Points or in Old Town." Salvatore cocked his head. "But you's forgetting us Sicilians. We's the ones who built the trade. Sallecito Salvador—he motorized the boats. And Salvator Versaggi—he had markets all the way up the coast to New York."

Ellie nudged Simon and whispered, "How many Salvators can you fit in a shrimp boat?"

One of the men yelled something unintelligible at Poli, who yelled back.

"What did they say?" Ellie peered at the men.

"He say, 'When we git off fer lunch, Sal?' " The captain snickered. "Thinks I'm gonna spring for a hot dog." He pointed at the Weinermobile parked across the street. "He don' know the Oscar Meyer folks are givin' 'em away free this week."

Simon took Ellie aside. "They're speaking Gullah."

"Gullah?"

"Gullah or Geechee—the descendants of freed

slaves who lived on the Sea Islands. It's a creole—an amalgam of English and several West African languages."

"I've heard of them. I didn't know they still existed."

"Oh, sure. Whole communities thrive on most of the Sea Islands. The women still weave baskets from sweetgrass. The men here on Amelia used to man the shrimp boats. Not many of 'em left."

"How come?"

"The Geechee on Amelia Island assimilated more into the population, while the Gullah of the Georgia islands kept to themselves. There's a commission trying to set up a heritage trail to preserve whatever's left."

Ellie looked at Salvatore. "Too bad they didn't try to preserve the fishery."

Poli scratched his head. "Oh, a few of the Eye-talian families—Polis, Giananos—are left, but we got us some interlopers nowadays. They's even a woman runnin' an operation."

"Shrimping?"

"Yeah." He gestured at a boat a few slips away. Ellie saw a rusting, filthy trawler, listing heavily to port. No one seemed about. "Sank right there after that big storm las' month." He shook his head. "Piece a work, that lady. Run most of the Geechee workers off, brought in her own that didn't speak no Gullah."

"Huh. So what did the Geechee fellows do?"

He shrugged. "Shrimpin's almost all gone. They got welfare now—or work for the Monterey Canning Company down to Jacksonville."

Simon wandered over to the trawler. "Halloo!"

No one answered.

The man named Frog watched him. "She no Gullah, yassir. She Rasta."

Simon swung around. "Rasta?"

For answer, he twirled a lock of invisible hair. "Dre'locks."

"Dreadlocks? You think she's Jamaican?"

Argus joined his mate. "Yup. Tried to sell us weed. I tink she know voodoo. Not nice." He shook his head and turned away. "Not nice."

Ellie turned to go. "This is all very interesting, but don't you think we should head over to the police station? We need to get Amos started on those warrants."

Simon came away grudgingly. "I guess. Still—a Rastafarian, here. Captain of a fishing boat. Crew foreign. Voodoo."

"Oh, for heaven's sake. What are you maundering on about?"

He got in the shotgun seat. "Drop me off at the library, would you?"

"Why? Need another James Patterson?"

"No, I think a Clive Cussler might be more in order. Or…Or, I think I might bone up on Santeria."

Chapter Three
Identity Crisis

Fort Clinch State Park, Wednesday, April 18

"Simon Ribault? Is that you?"

Simon held the phone away from his ear, and still the voice penetrated into the inner ear canal and all the way to his nostrils. "Yes, Mrs. Ironstone?"

"Excuse me? Are you talking to my mother? My name, young man, is Barbara. Barbara Bean. You may call me Beebee. Now, where is my daughter? I thought she had gate duty?"

"Ellie's up at headquarters. Can I help you?"

"I hope so. She hasn't been answering her phone, and I'm dying to hear what's up with the murders. Kenny Mathews is way too tight-lipped for my taste."

Tight-lipped? Nah. It's just that little Kenny can never admit when he doesn't have the answers. "We've only identified one of the males so far—he was an escaped convict."

"Really? From around here?" Simon listened to the clacking of a keyboard. "Closest jail is way out past Yulee."

"He was a prisoner in the Miami Correctional Facility."

"And he got here how?"

"We're working on that."

"Nothing on the woman? I hear she was a black broad. Old. Size of a baby hippo."

Not bad for a newcomer. Beebee Ironstone had only lived on Amelia Island for a year and was already rated among the top ten gossipmongers. Currently, the score was tied between Debbie Daugherty and Beebee, and the village feared it was only a matter of time before they joined forces and no one's affairs would be safe. Simon knew better than to betray any facts that should be kept under wraps a while longer. "Kenny thinks she may be Caribbean. We have some leads, but it might be some time before we have a conclusive identification."

"I see." Mrs. Ironstone paused just long enough to give Simon a false sense of security before barking, "What are you doing about Ellie?"

"Ellie?"

"You know exactly what I'm talking about, young man. I hear Thad Farnsworth is horning in. Ellie's a sucker for a pretty face."

Don't you mean flaccid? "Not my concern...Beebee. Did you have a message for Ellie?"

"It should be. Honestly, young people today...what did you say? Oh, yes. Tell her I left the cookies for her party on her porch."

"Got it." He hung up, locked the entrance gate, and drove up to the station. Hosea's official car and Ellie's pickup were the only ones in the lot.

The superintendent's baritone carried easily outside. "So, what's it like working with Simon Ribault?"

"He's all right, Hosea. A bit quiet. He...sure knows a lot of stuff."

Hosea chuckled. "Yeah, his mother says he was always hungrier for facts than food. I'll bet he's been in more schools than Webster's dictionary."

"Thad is so much livelier."

"Thad?" The park superintendent snorted. "Lively's not the first adjective that comes to mind. I'd say…*hmm*…"

Uh oh. I'd better save poor Hosea before he takes a bite out of that foot. He knocked on the door and sailed in. "Locked up. Any news?"

"There you are." Ellie lifted a relieved face to Simon. "Captain Barnes wants to reconvene at his office tomorrow morning."

"Did he get warrants?"

Hosea answered. "Yes, and his deputies combed the sailboats today."

Ellie pursed her lips. "Should he be using deputies? Why not the forensics folks?"

Hosea rolled his eyes. "Look, I don't tell Amos how to do his job, okay? Next thing you know, he'll start interfering in park service affairs." He checked his watch. "Are all the visitors out?"

"All but the campers."

"Okay. Ellie, could you go by the River campground and make sure the Girl Scouts are behaving properly?"

Ellie coughed delicately. "I…um…have something to do this evening."

"You do? Oh, yeah…" Hosea chuckled. "Nicole's birthday party. Is it a surprise?"

"Yes, although I'm pretty sure she's guessed."

"How?"

"Well, I…um…sort of invited…Thad."

Simon muttered something.

"What did you say?"

I said, there goes yet another chance to talk to you without lover boy salivating in the shadows. "It's not wise to tell secrets to people with big mouths."

Ellie glared at him. "Thad can keep a secret better than you. Why, he was the social director for his eating club at Princeton, and he says you wouldn't believe some of the things that went on he never told anyone about."

"I can imagine. Wait, what secrets have I given away?"

She blushed furiously. "You know...Thad."

Hosea guffawed. "Simon didn't need to tell me— or the entire island—that you have a sweet spot for him. Don't worry." He patted her shoulder. "You'll get over it."

Ellie looked as though she wondered why she would want to, but merely said, "I have to go help set up at Nicole's at six." She picked up her hat.

"That reminds me." Simon almost touched her arm but lost his nerve. "Your mother called to say she left cookies on your porch."

"Oh dear. She probably made meringue kisses again."

Kisses? I would have guessed bourbon balls, heavy on the bourbon. "What's the matter with her kisses?"

She scowled. "Inedible lumps of goo. I wish she'd stick to what she knows."

"What's that?"

"Cocktails."

Ah. "Is Thad taking you?"

"No. He...uh...said he'd meet me there."

Yes. So...I'll get there early and...do what?
****

Nicole's house, Wednesday, April 18

"Carol Ann, can you help me put the cookies out?"

"I'm setting the table, Betty. Katie? Where did Tina go?"

The young woman Carol Ann addressed, attired in a sensible twin set and skirt, shrugged. "No idea."

Ellie checked her watch. "We only have ten minutes. Nicole will be here at seven."

The three women bustling in and out of the kitchen clucked as one. "We're ready."

Simon came through the front door carrying two large paper bags. "Here are the plates and napkins."

"Oh, thanks, Simon. You didn't park out front, did you? She'll know something's up if she sees the Mustang."

"Oh, ye of little faith, Carol Ann. It's around the corner."

"Good. Did Andy get the ice?"

"Fenton has it. Andy isn't coming."

"Not coming to his girlfriend's birthday party? She'll be upset."

"She doesn't know she's having a party, Betty. How can she be upset if he's not here?" Simon paused. "He went to Atlanta for a job interview."

Betty dropped the basket of napkins and put a hand to her face. "Oh dear. Now she'll *really* be upset."

A young man about five feet tall, with a shock of orange hair and a permanent expression of excitement came in. "Ice is in the cooler. What about the champagne?"

Ellie wiped a nonexistent crumb off the table.

"Um…Thad said he'd bring it."

"Thad's coming? You didn't invite *him*, did you, Ellie?" Carol Ann didn't hide her dismay. Behind her, a young girl with dyed green hair and a tattoo on her forehead smirked.

Ellie stood her ground. "Yes, I did."

"Well, keep him away from Betty…" She noticed the tattooed girl. "And while you're at it, from Tina and Katie." She turned away.

Ellie stood alone, her eyes glistening.

Simon took a step toward her but thought better of it. *Nothing I could say would be helpful.*

At two minutes to seven, Thad appeared at the back door. "Well, I'm here." He seemed put out.

Simon couldn't help it. "You remembered the champagne, right?"

He held up a bottle of Lambrusco. "All I could find. When are they going to open a real wine store here? *Some* of us actually have a palate."

Ellie snatched the bottle and stuck it in the refrigerator. "Come on, everybody. Nicole will be home any second." She drew Thad into a closet. He went willingly. Simon started to go in as well but had an inspiration. "Tina, there's room in that closet." He pointed at Ellie and Thad's hiding place.

"Great!" The tattooed girl threw the door open and popped in. "Simon says there's room in here."

Thad squeezed over. "Ellie, can you give us some space?"

"Oh, yeah. Sure." Simon watched, amused, as she scrunched under the overcoats, knocking her head on a hanging umbrella. *Serves her right.* He found a spot behind the kitchen door.

A commotion from the living room drew them out. "Surprise!"

"Surprise!"

"Happy birthday!"

"Oh my God. Ellie?" Ellie's best friend Nicole stood in the middle of the room, tears coursing down her cheeks.

Ellie's eyes widened. "What on earth's the matter?"

Nicole sobbed, "I can't believe you did this. It's…it's not my birthday!"

"What?"

"I was…I was kidding!"

Ellie stared at her. "But when we had tea with Andy at Hoyt House, you said today was your birthday. You made this big deal about how no one ever gave you a party." Her voice rose on the last word. She gave Thad a side glance and colored.

Nicole whispered, "That was for Andy's benefit."

"Andy isn't here," said Fenton abruptly. "He's in Atlanta."

This produced a fresh flood of tears from the spurious birthday girl.

Ellie put an arm around her. "What on earth were you thinking, Nicole?"

"I…I was hoping he'd finally get off his duff and propose, or at least give me a present. I didn't think *you'd* take me seriously!"

Thad jeered. "Aw, Nicole, how obvious can you be?"

Simon said the first thing that came into his head. "You know Andy's totally focused on snagging that opening at the Mercedes dealership in Atlanta, Nicole.

The last thing on his mind is marriage."

Nicole began to wail.

Like an aggrieved family of meerkats, the five women in the room rounded on Simon. Ellie said it for all of them. "*Simon.*"

"Me? What about Thad?"

Carol Ann glared at him. "*You* should know better."

Thoroughly chastened, Simon slunk into the kitchen and retrieved the Lambrusco. He poured it into plastic cups and passed them around, head bowed.

Finally, Carol Ann moved to the table. "Well, no point in wasting all this food, but I *am* taking the toaster back."

Katie, Tina, and Carol Ann gathered around the table, talking and eating, backs stiffly turned to the offending Simon. Thad took the opportunity to crack a series of lame jokes at Simon's expense. As the party began to wind down, Simon went out on the porch to find Ellie consoling her friend. "Oh, Simon."

He patted Nicole's shoulder. "I didn't mean that about Andy, Nicole. I'm sorry. I wasn't thinking."

She blew her nose hard on a tissue. "S'okay, Simon. I don't expect you to be sensitive."

Not having anything sufficiently abject with which to respond, he said, "So…would you like some more Lambrusco?"

Ellie looked through the door into the living room. "I thought Thad had it in there."

Simon checked the fast emptying room. No Thad. *No Tina either.*

"Where's Tina, Katie?"

"She went with Thad out to his car."

"Where's Betty?"

Carol Ann shrugged.

At that moment, Ellie's crush waltzed through the door, Tina draped on one arm and a fawning Betty on the other. "We found some more wine!" He sailed past Ellie and plunked a bottle down on the table. "Oops, gotta go. Come on, ladies." And they left.

Nicole began picking up platters and taking them to the kitchen. Ellie stood rooted to the floor. Thad stuck his head back in. "Aren't you coming, Ellie?"

A dropped jaw wasn't exactly becoming, but she didn't seem to be able to push it back up.

"I promised to take you home, didn't I?"

"Um. Okay." She ignored the raised eyebrows, picked up her purse, and followed him out.

There goes the love of my life. With the love of hers.

****

Park headquarters, Thursday, April 19

"Yes, sir. No, sir. Will do, sir. The police don't think there's any further danger…Terrorists? There's no evidence of terrorist activity. No one's taken credit…But sir, I think terrorists *want* to take credit. That's the whole point." The others could hear a tinny voice raised in anger come through the line. "No, we couldn't, sir—we had a full schedule of campers…" Hosea listened. "Yes, I know the Park Service has jurisdiction, but we don't have the resources…We have a very good working relationship with the police here in Fernandina Beach…No, sir. Just because the chief is my brother doesn't mean we're in competition." He sighed. "All right, sir. I'll keep you informed."

He slammed down the receiver, then immediately

picked it up again and jabbed a finger at the keys. "Hosea Barnes here. Get me Amos...Amos? Any results from the searches? Okay, thanks." He looked up at his crew. "There's no evidence that any of the three victims were aboard any of the sailboats moored in the marina."

"So they didn't come by boat." Thad seemed to think this cleared up the mystery.

"Not necessarily." Simon pulled out his notebook. "During the March to April season, the Southern Coast Cruise Line operates two cruises a week along the coast, visiting the Sea Islands, Savannah, Hilton Head, and Beaufort before arriving in Charleston. On Saturday, April 14, the *Independence* departed Jacksonville for a seven-day cruise up to Charleston. First stop: Amelia Island."

"And are they missing any passengers?" Hosea's voice rose with hope.

"They're checking, but we know at least one of the victims—Alvaredo—wouldn't have been on the manifest."

"And the other two?"

"We haven't identified either one yet. If the line finds a missing person, they'll notify us."

Thad pursed his lips. "I dunno about that. Bad for business, losing people like that. They may not admit to it."

Ellie gasped. "That would be a crime! Accessory to murder or something."

"Could've been an accident."

"I see...so, those two guys accidentally stabbed each other?" Simon's tone was mild, but his eyes sparked with annoyance.

Thad's chest deflated. "The woman wasn't stabbed."

Hosea tapped a pencil on the desk. "No, she wasn't, so there's a possibility she was a tourist who fell overboard. She was dressed in cruise wear after all. Thad, I want you to follow up with the line. If nothing else, get me a signed confirmation that a full complement of passengers arrived at Charleston."

"Yes, boss."

Ellie asked, "Any other news?"

"Nothing much. State police sent fingerprints and DNA to the FBI. We're waiting for identification of the two UFOs." Hosea checked his roster. "Thad, you're scheduled to monitor the Girl Scouts. While you're there, ask if they heard anything the night before our bodies showed up. Ellie, you've got latrines. Simon...why are you here anyway? Today's your day off."

Caught, Simon stammered, "I...uh...just wanted to brief you on the cruise line schedule. And...uh...see how the investigation was going." *It's not like I wanted to find out what happened last night between Thad and Ellie. Nope.*

Ellie picked up a bucket and box of paper towel rolls. "I'll start at the trading post."

Simon helped her put the supplies in the pickup truck. Ellie gave him a curious look. "So why are you here really? Crush on one of the Girl Scouts? They're a pretty mature bunch." She leered at him.

Simon felt his skin heat up and knew he was turning an impressive shade of burgundy. "No. I just...er...wanted to ask about the birthday party. By the way, where did you and Thad go afterwards?"

Ellie dropped a broom on her foot. "Ouch!" As she rubbed the sore spot, she mumbled, "What did Nicole tell you?"

"Nicole? She didn't tell me anything. It's only that you...er...left the party a bit precipitously. I just thought..."

"You just thought." She squared her shoulders. "Let me tell you, Simon Ribault, it's none of your business what Thad did or didn't do." She picked up the broom and jammed it into the truck, then climbed into the cab muttering. Simon caught her wiping a tear away. "For your information, he drove me home. He even...even kissed me."

He watched her roar away. *I bet it was sticky.*

****

Fernandina Beach Police Station, Friday, April 20

"No match for DNA, no match on prints, no police records...we're at a dead end here, Hosea." Amos handed his brother a file.

"Damn. It's like those two are ciphers. How do you live in this world without leaving some kind of trail?"

Simon spoke up. "It's not all that hard. Never buy anything bigger than your head, and don't use the Internet."

No one responded. Finally, Ellie said, "Maybe they were spies?"

Amos nodded. "Interesting idea. Sneaking onto American soil in the dead of night. Makes some sense."

Hosea scoffed. "I'm sorry. Did I miss a declaration of war?"

Simon looked out the window. "I wish we knew how they ended up at the fort."

Hosea faced Amos. "There were no tire tracks at

the sites where the bodies were discovered. Any keel trails?"

The police chief shook his head. "Nothing. Not even a broken twig." He pivoted to Thad. "You found the other two victims. Anything catch your eye before CSI got there? How did the bodies look?"

Thad backed up a step. "Me?" he squeaked. "I...I didn't find them. Rosie did. She was picking up trash along the shore and discovered the woman. That old guy with the dog—Mr. Turley—he stumbled over the man."

"But you checked them out, right?"

"Um, no. When Rosie found it...her...we came straight back to the office."

"Let me get this straight. You left it there unattended?"

Confronted with the others' shocked expressions, Thad went on the defensive. "Well...er...*you*"—he pointed a shaking finger at his boss—"sent me to find Simon and Ellie."

"So..." Hosea's voice held a level of menace Simon had never heard before. "You didn't think to stay at the crime scene? Or secure the area?"

"Look," Thad stammered. "I'm just a ranger—it's not like I'm trained to handle murders."

"You were supposed to take the forensics course last summer."

He had the grace to cringe. "Dad said I didn't have to. He said in my position I didn't need all that technical training. I'd be moving up in the ranks so quickly it was a waste of time." He peeked at Hosea. "Dad said."

There was an ominous silence. Just as everyone in

the room began to sputter, Hosea stood. "Is Mathews here?"

Amos nodded. They walked down the hall to the autopsy room. A cardboard sign had been shoved into a frame next to it. Simon read, *Kenneth Mathews, Medical Examiner, District Four.*

Kenny opened the door to Amos's knock.

"We want to see the victims."

The little man, whom Simon couldn't help but picture dancing at midnight in a fairy ring, gave a high-pitched cackle. "All of them?"

"What?" Disconcerted, Hosea gazed around the room.

Simon grinned. "How many do you have?"

"Lessee. Five right now. Your three, plus two yachtsmen. Got in a yelling match over who had the right of way and both fell overboard. Alcohol was involved. They're out front waiting for the ambulance to take them to Jacksonville."

"You mean the yachtsmen?"

"Yeah, they go first because I've finished processing them and next of kin have been notified."

"How about our murder victims?"

"One's done." He pointed at a shrouded figure on the first of three tables. "The convict. Miami Department of Corrections is sending a van for him."

"What! We haven't finished our investigation yet."

"He's their boy. I can't stop them."

"But what do they want a corpse for?"

"Beats me. Maybe for inventory."

Amos put a hand on his brother's elbow. "Look, we have the knife that killed him. You did a full autopsy, right, Kenny?"

"Yup." He picked up a file from the desk. "Who wants it?"

Amos held out his hand. "Me. And the other two?"

"I haven't completed their examinations."

"Just tell us what you know."

Kenny picked up a clipboard, and they moved to the second man. He read, "Caucasian-Negroid mix, between thirty-five and forty, no distinguishing marks other than a scar on neck. Cause of death: stab wound in chest. Pierced the left ventricle. Died instantly. Clothes wet on admittance. However, few symptoms of long-term immersion—"

"He *was* in the water, though, wasn't he?" Hosea shot a triumphant look at Amos.

"Oh, yes. As I said, his clothes were wet, and there was some slight wrinkling on his palms and feet."

"No obvious relation to the others?"

"Not from the evidence I've got. How far apart were they found?"

Simon answered. "The woman was on the south side of the fort, about half a mile from this man."

Ellie added, "He was northeast of her."

"Maybe he didn't die right away. Maybe he crawled—"

"Or swam."

"Or floated on the tide."

Thad mumbled, "Could it have been suicide?"

Kenny looked at him like he was daft. "Sure, if you can tell me how he inserted a knife into his own chest *before* sticking it into another guy, and then swam to shore."

"I…uh…meant the other way around. The Miami guy—what was his name?"

Amos pulled out a notebook. "Alvaredo. He was stabbed in the back with the same knife. So what could be the scenario?"

"This guy kills Alvaredo, then in an excess of remorse, turns the knife on himself."

The others were quiet, momentarily stunned by the fact that Thad had actually contributed to the debate. Ellie beamed at him.

Simon said slowly, "You're suggesting murder-suicide?"

Thad went up on his toes, his voice rising with him. "See, this guy here's the policeman who sent him to the slammer…or maybe another gang member who Alvaredo fingered to the cops. So when he hears that Alvaredo's escaped, he follows him. They get in a fight, and he kills him. After that he…uh…loses his will to live."

Everyone but Ellie sighed. Simon scratched his chin. "Only one problem"—*besides the sheer lunacy of Thad's theory*—"Alvaredo was found maybe two miles farther south. Why weren't the bodies closer? Assuming they were all on a boat, and he was murdered first, how did the guy who committed suicide end up in the water before he did?"

Rather than pile onto the now simmering Thad, Amos walked to the third gurney and asked Mathews, "How about the woman? Anything useful?"

Kenny glanced at her and flipped a page over the clipboard. "Late fifties. African American or Caribbean. Morbidly obese. Preliminary finding for cause of death: drowning. Ring of broken skin around ankle. Likely from jewelry—maybe a chain that was torn off in a robbery attempt. The only artificial mark a small tattoo of a man's face near her armpit."

"That's a weird place for a tattoo."

"Not if you don't want people to see it."

"Like a jealous husband?"

"Could be."

Simon asked, "Can we take a look?"

Kenny lifted the paunchy arm. Folds of skin rippled in the breeze from the ceiling fan. They peered at a small circle about three inches in diameter. Inside it was a portrait of an older black man with a flat nose and moustache. Simon touched it. "I've seen that face before."

"Movie star?"

"No…it was a long time ago. I think when I was in grad school…"

Hosea prompted, "You mean when you were studying anthropology? Could it be an aborigine?"

"No. I think it was the history degree. I took a course on twentieth-century African-American relations."

Ellie pinched her lips together. "So, two undergraduate majors—"

"Plus the minor in poetry." *Shit, why did I have to remind her?*

Luckily, Ellie had moved on. "And two graduate degrees as well? Isn't that rather overdoing it, Simon?"

He shook his head, distracted. "Not two. Four…no five. I always forget the Masters in Library Science."

"*Five graduate degrees?*" Mathews sneered. "Overcompensating for something, buddy? Or were you one of those whatchacallit—career students? As in, anything to get out of the draft?"

He shrugged. "There isn't a draft anymore, Kenny.

It's just an addiction. I love learning about stuff. The library science was an afterthought—to help me in my research." He looked down at the dead woman. "If you don't mind, I'd like to take a picture of the tattoo."

"Sure, sure."

Simon took out his phone and snapped a shot. "Thanks. Hosea, do you need me?"

"Nope. Ellie, Thad, you're with me."

They parted on the sidewalk, Simon heading to the public library on Fourth Street.

****

Ellie's house, Sunday, April 22

Simon called Ellie Sunday night. She picked it up before the first buzz had faded. "Yes, hello?"

"Ellie? It's me, Simon. Are you busy?"

"Um, no. Um, Thad gave me a ride home."

After a second, he said, "Oh?"

With a rush, she blurted, "Simon, I can't figure him out. He did kiss me after Nicole's party."

"Was it a deep, lingering kiss?"

"N…no."

Yes! Should I? He took two seconds to decide. *Go for it.* "It's possible that Thad is a bit of a flirt. You don't want to take him too seriously."

"I can't help it. He makes my skin tingle. When I'm with him, I find myself hiccupping."

"You might be allergic to him. You know, like contact dermatitis." *Ooh, good one, Simon.*

"That's not funny. So, why did you call?"

"I just wanted to hear your euphonious voice."

"No, really."

"I've found something."

Chapter Four
Jamaica Me Crazy

Cyberspace, Sunday, April 22

"Are you going to tell me what it is?"

"It'll take too long."

"What!"

"I can't help it. You chattered on so long about...*Thad*...you used up the time allotted for this phone call. Are you on duty tomorrow?"

"Yes."

"I'm not. I'll come by the station at four." *Way to play it, Simon. She'll be on pins and needles all day.*

****

Park headquarters, Monday, April 23

As the sun dropped close to the horizon, Simon came up behind Ellie. "Good afternoon."

"Oh. Hi." She left off gazing at the back of Thad's head.

What was that about pins and needles? "Are you working on anything?"

"Sort of." She gave Thad a parting glance soaked in yearning.

"Come on, I'll buy you a beer at the Palace."

"It's only four o'clock."

"I want to beat the rush."

They walked across the tile entrance inlaid with the

words "Palace Saloon" into a dark bar redolent of stale gin and Spanish peanuts. The bartender peered at them through the gloom and called, "Welcome to the Palace Saloon, the last bar to close when Prohibition was declared, and the first bar to open when FDR repealed it. What can I get you?"

"It's us, Mickey."

"Who?"

"Ellie and Simon. Get us two ales, would you? Something from the Cigar City brewery."

"Jackrabbit's good. If you like a Belgian white, try Florida Cracker Barrel. I've only got 'em in cans though."

"One of each then." Simon looked at Ellie. "Is there a reason your mouth is hanging open?"

She shut it with a snap. "You must have very interesting news."

"Why?"

"You ordered something besides Pabst Blue Ribbon."

"Oh that. No big deal. I'm open to different beers. I've been known to eat a hot dog on occasion, sometimes even a whole wheat hamburger bun. I'm not *that* predictable, Ellie." He knew the snarky reply was on the tip of her tongue and was gratified to see her bite it off. *Progress, progress.*

They sat at a rickety table by the jukebox in the empty bar. Mickey brought over two cans and two empty mugs. Ellie picked up the can of Jackrabbit. "Somehow I don't associate neon orange and green with beer." She poured a little out and took a sip. "Not bad."

Simon raised his can. "To my fellow crackers."

She frowned. "I thought 'cracker' was a derogatory term. Doesn't it mean the same as 'redneck'?"

Mickey called out, "Hey, us rednecks are real proud of who we are."

Simon chimed in. "In fact, local Florida folks like to be called crackers. Means their family's been here for generations."

"Where did the term come from?"

Simon put down his beer and prepared to lecture. "Best theory is that it referred to the cracking of the whips the swamp cowboys used to herd the yellowhammers."

"Yellowhammers?"

"Wild cattle—probably descended from the *criollo* breed the Spanish brought. Small, tough, impervious to mosquitoes."

She swatted at a fly. "Were the cowboys Spanish?"

"Uh uh. Soon after Florida became a state in 1845, men from Georgia and the Carolinas came south to seek a better life."

Ellie laughed. "I guess Florida has always been a magnet for fortune hunters."

"Ha ha. Anyway, farming was impossible in the swamps, so they started rounding up the feral cows and driving them to markets. Used to herd them all the way across Florida to the Gulf Coast."

"Do they still do that?"

"Nah. By 1949 or so, free-range cattle were prohibited. Breeds from India and Europe were introduced, and the little yellowhammers almost died out."

"Sad." Ellie finished her beer. Mickey brought her another without asking. "So? Why am I here?"

"I did a little homework."

"I know."

"Want to know what I found out?"

"Nah."

"Ellie." He spoke quietly.

"Okay. Can I get some peanuts?"

"Mickey?" When she was settled with a bowl in front of her, he started in. "That tattoo on the woman's arm? I knew I'd seen it somewhere before. It's a portrait of Marcus Garvey."

"Who?"

"He was a Jamaican who immigrated to America at the turn of the twentieth century, where he founded what you might call the first black pride movement. Eventually, he decided the best course for African Americans was to go back to Africa. He established the Black Star shipping line to open trade routes between the US and Africa."

"Did it work?"

"You mean, was he successful? Well, at one time his organization—the Universal Negro Improvement Association—had four million members. Then J. Edgar Hoover took an interest, and his luck changed."

"Getting on the wrong side of J. Edgar Hoover was never a good thing. Just ask Martin Luther King."

"Right-o. Garvey spent five years in jail on likely trumped-up charges for mail fraud. Later, he worked on a scheme to deport some twelve million African Americans to Liberia. That fizzled too, and he died in London in 1940."

"So…what does any of this have to do with the dead woman?"

"Ah. Remember Kenny pronounced her a mix of

black and native."

"Jamaican?"

Simon nodded. "That's my guess."

"I don't get it. Are you opining she was a supporter of his Back-to-Africa initiative? Or just that she had a tattoo in honor of a fellow Jamaican?"

Simon waved his empty can at the bartender. "I'm not finished. In one of his more bombastic moments, Garvey predicted that a black king would rise in Africa and lead the black race to...I don't know, nirvana I guess. When Ras Tafari Makonnen, prince of Ethiopia, was crowned Emperor Haile Selassie in 1930, Garvey declared him to be the One."

"Haile Selassie? I remember him. He came to America. My grandfather met with him. I think I still have the photo somewhere." She sat, thoughtfully chewing on a peanut. "Go on."

Simon put down the can. "This is the fun part. In an improbable historical turn, Garvey's prophecy that Haile Selassie would be the black Messiah took root in Jamaica, eventually becoming a full-blown religion. Adherents took their name from his pre-throne title..." He waited expectantly.

"Ras...you said Ras something..."

"Ras Tafari. So...?"

She chugged her beer. It must have finally penetrated, because she spit some out and gurgled, "Rastafarians!"

He nodded. "Right. After his trip to America, Haile Selassie decided to go to Jamaica to see what all the fuss was about. They wouldn't let him off the plane."

"Why?"

"Would you really want to come face to face with

God?"

"*Hmm*. I see what you mean."

"Rastafarianism subsequently developed a fairly complex dogma and even denominations. They have a special diet. Some think ganja smoking is required, others don't. They believe in a god named Jah, but not in an afterlife." He scooped up a handful of peanuts. "What I can't figure out is why the victim would have a tattoo. Most Rastas consider scarifying the skin to be a sin."

"Well, she wasn't necessarily a Rasta. She could have idolized Garvey for his Liberian enterprise. Or the black nationalism angle." She put her mug down. "Maybe she *is* Liberian."

Don't scoff at the child. She's doing her best. And she's so cute when she's thinking. "I believe Kenny said she was of Caribbean stock."

"But that included African blood."

"As well as native, maybe even Spanish."

Ellie had stopped listening. "Wait…didn't Frog say that female captain was Rasta?"

"Frog? Female? Captain?"

"The shrimp boat crewman. Remember that sunken trawler in the marina? He said the captain was a woman. He thought she was a Rastafarian."

"As I recall, it was only because of the dreadlocks. Any sap who goes to Jamaica on holiday gets dreadlocks."

"Hello. We've established the dead woman is from the Caribbean. And she has a tattoo of Marcus Garvey."

"But her head was shaved. No dreadlocks." Simon put down his beer. "Still…" He rose. "Has anyone seen this woman since her boat went belly up?" Before she could answer, he loped out the door. "I'll be back."

He found Poli coming out of the marina showers. "You busy, Sal?"

The fisherman buttoned up his ancient plaid shirt. "Whatcha want?"

Simon pointed at the trawler, now up to its gunwales in water. "Didn't you say the captain of that boat was a woman? From Jamaica?"

The man studied it. "Not me. Argus says she's Rasta. Did wear those awful hair braids. I swear I saw a cockroach crawl out of 'em once."

"So, did she just skip town or what? Doesn't she have to deal with the derelict?"

He shrugged. "I heard she'd gone south to find another boat. Tha's all I know."

"Thanks."

Ellie was nursing her third beer when he returned. She put down the glass. "Let me guess. She's disappeared."

"Yup."

"Hasn't been seen since…last Sunday?"

He paused. "Actually, not for a couple of weeks."

"Oh. So she was long gone before our fat lady washed ashore? Well, that sucks."

He brooded. "The question is, what was a wealthy woman of Caribbean descent—in her fifties and, in Kenny's immortal words, 'morbidly obese'—doing on Amelia Island in the middle of the night?"

"Well, we don't know that she set foot on the island…at least alive."

"True. Then where did she come from? Why hasn't she been identified?"

"Not everyone enjoys the kind of vast network of

friends and relations you do, Simon."

Simon wasn't sure if that was meant as a compliment or not. "Well, that's just antisocial of them." He rose. "But you bring up a good point. I'm going to put her photo on Facebook."

"*Ew.*"

"What? Oh."

"Exactly."

"Not a pretty picture."

"No." The corners of Ellie's mouth turned up. "And from the looks of her, that was true even before she drowned."

****

Park headquarters, Tuesday, April 24

The television blared as Simon and Ellie walked into the office the next morning. It appeared the local media were in a tizzy over the news that the former president had signed a secret deal with Castro before leaving office. The anchor turned to an incensed guest. "So what do you think of this latest development, Mr. Noriego?"

"Are you talking about Orloff's promise to abrogate all lawsuits by private citizens against the Castro regime?"

"Yes. He says they're an obstacle to the true friendship that should be revived between the United States and Communist Cuba. Fifty years is a long time to hold a grudge, don't you think?"

Noriego pounded a fist on the table, making the anchor jump. "What about the American citizens who fled the revolution and lost everything? And the Cubans who flew their children to the United States on Operation Pedro Pan to escape Fidel's plans to rip them from the bosom of their families? And the people whose businesses, factories, stores were destroyed or confiscated? Those are the victims who have pending lawsuits."

Attempting to retrieve the moral high ground, the anchor said stiffly, "The president thought we should get over our hate."

"*Ex.* The *ex*-president also said there's no difference between communism and capitalism. Hogwash. Tell that to the fellow tinkering with his '57 Chevy because it's the newest car on the island, or to the maid whose earnings from the *ex*-president's hotel visit are all turned over to the military. Average salary of a Cuban citizen? Twenty dollars a month. Estimated net worth of Fidel Castro? A billion dollars. The left vilifies the one percent of Americans who work hard and succeed, but not the third richest family in the world, whose wealth comes from ransacking the pockets of the poor."

"Third richest family?"

"At one time, yes." The man paused. "You ever notice how in socialist countries wealth is concentrated in a tiny number of hands? In America, there are ten million millionaires. In Cuba, there are two."

After a flustered second, the anchor found his politically correct footing. "Ten million American millionaires? That's awful!" He began to whine. "Why should some guy make all that money while there are people out there who can't afford a big-screen TV?" He straightened his Armani-clad shoulders. "We need to raise their taxes. They should pay their fair share."

"What's a fair share to you?"

The man shuffled some papers. "Look here, it says

the top twenty percent of wage earners pay ninety-five percent of the taxes. That's…er…" The triumphant look disappeared as he realized what the statistic meant. "It's er…not fair…"

"Fair? Are you listening? Is it fair that the people of Venezuela—a socialist *utopia*—suffer over forty thousand percent inflation? There is no food, no toilet paper, no medicine. Crime is at an all-time high. The government has begun forcing citizens to work in the fields—where I come from that's called slavery. Venezuela's population is literally starving to death. Yet when he died, Chavez bequeathed three point four *billion* dollars to his daughter. Where did that money come from? And why is that fair?"

Simon muted it. "What Cuba needs is another José Martí."

"Who's that?"

"I swear, I'm starting a petition to bring actual history back into the public school curriculum. José Martí was a Cuban patriot. Journalist, poet, rabble rouser, he fought for the liberation of Cuba from Spain."

"Oh."

Well, that shut her up. Taking note of the bearish expression on his true love's face, Simon decided to forgo further smug remarks and change the subject. "I've got to check out the southeast area of the park. There was a report of an injured wild turkey by the path. What's on your agenda?"

After a minute, she mumbled, "I've got gate duty all day."

"Okay. See you later."

As he headed toward his car, she called, "Did you

get any response on your Facebook posting?"

"Facebook? Oh, yeah. I got fourteen friend requests from a bunch of people with Indian names and Caucasian faces."

"Those are phishing expeditions. I hope you didn't friend them?"

"Only the pretty ones."

Having trapped the turkey and taken it to the wildlife rescue center, Simon was heading over to the gatehouse to keep Ellie company until closing time when his phone buzzed. He clicked it on. "Hosea? Yeah…Yeah…Yeah. We'll be right there." He rapped on the gatehouse window. "Hosea wants us back at the office."

Ellie came out. "But it's almost five o'clock! I'll miss *Star Trek.*"

"I've memorized every episode. I shall recount tonight's adventure in the car. Come on."

They found Thad sitting on the windowsill muttering angrily while Hosea packed a briefcase. "I've got to go to Tallahassee tomorrow morning. Simon, you're in charge."

"Me?" He threw up his hands in mock terror. "I'm shocked and awed. What shall I do without you, Bwana?"

"Party naked on the parade grounds? Fire the cannon at passing sailboats? Lock hungry raccoons in the latrines?"

"Ha ha."

Ellie asked, "Why the sudden trip?"

"Senate appropriations committee hearing. They're going to go over the budget, and Director Davis wants backup."

"Will they bring up the murders?"

"Dunno. But it's a sure bet he will. After all, what better way to ask for more money than to stem the current crime wave?"

Thad chose the ensuing pause to exercise his spleen. "Why does Simon get the nod? I'm senior here. My father—"

"Number one, you're not senior here. Simon is by eight months and a decade of experience. Number two, your father does not have jurisdiction over my management decisions, Thad." He hesitated. "It's only for two days anyway. Next time, I promise I'll let you be in charge."

Thad continued to pout.

Ellie gave him a sympathetic look. "Hosea says it's only two days, Thad. I'm sure the next time he's away, it will be for much longer."

Thad rounded on her. "You too? Doesn't anybody believe in me?" He put a hand to his chest and squeezed his eyes shut. If Hosea had given him time, he would have let a single tear pulse at the corner of his eye.

Instead, the superintendent clapped his hat on and went to the door. "I'll report in tomorrow afternoon."

Simon saluted. "Any particular instructions?"

"Yes. While we're waiting on identifications, I want you to get in touch with whoever arranged the event Saturday night and interview the guests—see if anyone saw or heard anything."

"You said the organizer was someone named Gregory?"

"Yeah, but start with the event manager. She'll have a list of attendees."

"What's her name?"

71

"Don't remember. It's in the event file. Gotta go." He left.

Ellie checked her watch. "I've…uh…got an appointment. See you tomorrow." She raced out the door.

Simon watched her go. "I don't know why she doesn't just tape the show." He picked his keys off the hook. "Gotta go too. Mother's having her Toastmasters meeting this evening, and I have to eat my supper and get out of there. Coming?"

Thad sniggered. "You still live with your mother?"

"Yes. You still live with your parents?" *Take that, you jerk.* "Look, since you're a *senior* ranger, you have the authority to lock up. I'll leave you to it."

Thad brightened. "Roger that."

Simon left him standing in the middle of the room. He could have sworn he saw him start to twirl.

****

Simon's house, Wednesday, April 25

"Thad, why are you calling so early?" Simon checked his alarm clock. Seven o'clock.

"Um, Simon? Could you come to the fort? Double quick?"

"Sure. What is it?"

"There's been a break-in."

"Did you call the police?"

"Uh, no. Not yet. I thought maybe you…"

"I'll be right there."

Simon barely missed sideswiping Ellie's ancient Toyota as she arrived, squealing her tires and blaring her horn. He jumped out of his car. "You as much as scratch the paint on this beauty, and I'll tear up your autographed photo of Leonard Nimoy."

She looked at his car. "Why so fussy? It must be even older than mine."

"This baby, for your information, is a 1966 Ford Mustang GT, with the original engine and a fully restored interior with vintage vinyl seats." He paused as the fact of her presence struck him. "What are you doing here?"

"Thad called me," she said breathlessly. "He needs me!"

Simon took a gander at her uniform. Shirt tail hanging out, buttons askew, one boot unlaced. "Good thing you didn't have to decide what to wear or you'd still be in your jammies." He squinted at her. "At least you had time to do your makeup." *For Thad.*

She brushed past him into the office and skidded to a stop. "Someone's in the break room. Thad?"

"In here. Just look at this mess!"

Simon remained on the threshold, watching. Ellie zipped around Thad's broad back. The refrigerator door stood open, and food lay scattered all over the floor. He pointed to one corner, where a box of doughnuts had been emptied. "The chocolate one was going to be my breakfast." His lower lip quivered.

Ellie walked to the back door. The remnants of the screen flapped in the breeze. She glared at Simon. "You left this door unlocked?"

"Uh..."

"I'm going to clean this up and then give you a piece of my mind." She got a broom from the closet and started sweeping up Tupperware containers and broken crackers.

Simon cleared his throat.

Thad gave him a frightened look and said,

"Uh…Ellie? I closed up last night."

"You? Why? You know Hosea never lets you…" At the look of resentment that splashed across his face, she backtracked quickly. "Well, you probably don't know the routine then."

Thad made no move to help. After emptying two dust pans, she thrust the broom into his hands. "I've got an idea. Why don't *you* finish? I'm going to survey the grounds for any clues as to the perpetrator's identity. I'm betting it's those Girl Scouts again—a midnight raid on the pantry."

She pushed past Simon and stepped outside. A trail of chocolate wrappers led her to the edge of the fens. "*Hmm*. Perhaps I have misjudged the lasses."

"What's the prognosis?"

"Home invasion."

Simon slammed his fist into his palm. "I knew I shouldn't have trusted Thad. Hosea will have my head. What was taken?"

"The bag of chocolate bars left over from Halloween, all twelve doughnuts, and the tub of Cool Whip."

"A delicious prank perpetrated by either Brownies or raccoons."

"I take Door Number Two."

"Thad didn't lock up."

Ellie sighed. "I'm sure he just forgot."

Simon strode up the steps. "Well, he's going to have to spring for more doughnuts, or I'll rat him out to Hosea."

They found Thad drinking a glass of milk. Simon took a step into the kitchen and stuck to the floor. "You didn't mop?"

Thad gaped at him. "Mc?"

"Oh, for heaven's sake."

Simon left Ellie to explain the finer aspects of swabbing office decks. An hour later, he sat at Hosea's desk sifting through folders. "Do you know where the event file is, Ellie?"

"Didn't Hosea leave it on his desk?"

"It's not here. Maybe he put it in the cabinet." He riffled through all the files. "Nothing." He looked at Ellie, concerned. "Do you suppose the raccoons have learned to read?"

"I wouldn't put it past them. Where's Thad?"

"Out on patrol. I told him to pick up the garbage."

"Call him. See if he put the file somewhere."

Thad had no idea what they were talking about. Simon hung up the phone. "Huh."

Ellie got down on her hands and knees and searched under the furniture. "Nope."

"Was the front door unlocked when we arrived this morning?"

"Of course it was. Thad was here."

"*Hmm*. We can't reach Hosea today. We'll just have to wait. He probably took it with him by mistake."

They spent the rest of the morning registering campers and leading visitors through the fort.

Simon took charge of a group of students from the Citadel. "Welcome to Fort Clinch. Built in 1847, it was part of a series of fortifications to protect Cumberland Sound and the St. Marys River. It was first controlled by Confederate soldiers, but Robert E. Lee ordered them to abandon it and the Union took it over."

"Who was Clinch?"

"General Duncan Lamont Clinch served with

distinction in both the War of 1812 and in the Seminole Wars."

Another young man raised his hand. "I keep hearing about these Seminole Wars. What were they about?"

Maybe I should have taken that job teaching high school. I'd get paid better. He checked the cloudless sky. The sun beat down on his shoulders, taking some of the spring chill out of the air. *On the other hand, I'd be stuck inside on a day like today.* "Between 1817 and 1858, the fledgling American republic and the Seminole tribe fought three wars, mostly the result of misunderstandings. The Indians had been hiding runaway slaves and supplying the British during the War of 1812, and when the war ended, Andrew Jackson was sent to punish them. When Jackson became president in 1829, he tried to force the Indians to move west of the Mississippi, and launched the second Seminole War. Some three thousand were removed, but a third war—really just a series of skirmishes—broke out and continued until 1858. At that point, only about three hundred Seminoles still lived in Florida. They stayed hidden in the swamps for decades."

"So are there any left?"

"Other than Florida State's teams?" As usual this joke fell flat. *Face it, you're going to have to delete it from your repertoire.* "Yes, about two thousand. In fact, they have a compact with the State of Florida to run casinos. They rake in some one and a half billion dollars a year from gringo gamblers. Sweet revenge, I call it."

This also did not elicit the kind of laugh he hoped for.

A tall youth, his crisp polo clinging to rippling abs, walked stiffly over to the edge of the battlement. "How come General Lee ordered the fort abandoned?"

Finally. "Advances in weaponry—specifically, the invention of rifled cannon—made the brick walls vulnerable to attack."

He sent the group off to walk along the allure but not before they had lined up before him and barked in unison, "Thank you, *sir.*"

Ellie appeared at the entrance to the fort and waved at him. "Hosea called."

"Does he have the file?"

"No. But he remembered the name of the contact person—a Judy Holiday. I'm going to see if I can track her down."

Simon checked his watch. "Jack is supposed to relieve me at two."

"Come find me then."

****

Wednesday, April 25

"I am here as ordered. So?"

"Ms. Holiday, of Eight Flags Event Planning, graciously assented to a meeting. Her office is on Centre Street. Ready?"

They found a parking spot in front of the Florida House Inn on South Third, around the corner from the building. A woman of about forty, her brown hair incompetently bobbed, ushered them into her tiny office. "So, Miss Ironstone, what can I do for you?"

Simon gave Ellie the one guest chair and stood, balancing on his toes. "We understand you arranged an event at Fort Clinch on Saturday, April 14."

Her face instantly turned a blotchy blend of mauve

and apricot. She pulled a tissue from her desk drawer and coughed into it before spitting out, "Yes, I did." Simon had the distinct impression she followed those words with an unspoken "the bastards."

He said as casually as possible, "We seem to have misplaced our event file and wondered if you could give us your client's name."

"Carson Gregory. What for?"

"We…uh…need to contact him."

"It's about the dead people, isn't it?" Her eyes closed to slits. "I wouldn't be surprised if they were involved. Dirty weasels."

"My, my. They don't seem to have left a very good impression."

"Except for the deposit, they never paid me. I spent twenty hours arranging for the food, the entertainment, the lighting. Then an hour before it was to start, that…that Babbitt fellow, Gregory, called. He ordered me to remove all the tents and tables, and cancel the food and the band. I'd underwritten two barrel grills, plus a staff of cooks and waiters to handle a hundred people. Even with the refunds, I had to eat a thousand dollars."

"Did he say why he canceled?"

"Yeah. He claimed I misunderstood the contract, that he never wanted all that stuff."

Ellie spoke up. "An event did take place at the fort, though."

She snorted. "The League of the Green Cross turned out to be a grand total of ten people. They required one table and some chairs in that small room under the battlements."

"Do you have a number for this Mr. Gregory?"

"Yes, but he doesn't answer it. I've called twice a day since April 16."

"Surely you have his address?"

"No, we handled everything over the phone or by fax. Nothing had his address on it."

"Can we have the number?"

"Sure." She spun her rolodex. "555-4162."

Ellie put her hat on. "Maybe we'll have better luck."

Judy opened the door for them. "If you find him, he owes me sixteen hundred dollars."

Ellie's mouth dropped open. Simon could only whistle.

Chapter Five
Adventures in Scouting

Fort Clinch, Wednesday, April 25

"Simon, can I ask you a question?"

Simon kept his hands tightly clenched on the steering wheel. He knew from experience that whenever a woman made that request, it involved uncomfortable confessions on one or the other's part. "If you must."

"Do you think I'm pretty?"

Oh my God, you're the most beautiful creature on earth. "Pretty?"

"You don't have to sound so baffled, Simon. It's…hurtful." Her voice dropped on the last word.

"Is this about Thad?"

"No, of course not." When Simon didn't say anything she muttered. "A bit. Simon, do you think he likes me? He blows so hot and cold."

That's because when he's near a bimbo or a beer his brain freezes. "Maybe he doesn't know how you feel." *There's a whopper.*

"Do you think so? Should I be more direct?" Her sapphirine eyes pleaded with him.

Simon knew only too well that the more Ellie threw herself at him, the less Thad would be attracted. "No, Ellie. I think Thad's the type who likes his women hard to get."

"Oh."

Quick. Change the subject. "Good thing the Girl Scouts were the only ones camping the night of the fifteenth."

"Yes. And that they've stayed long enough for us to interview them."

"Indeed. Especially since Thad forgot."

Ellie bristled. "He explained that. What with the stopped-up toilet and the swarm of vultures landing on the cars in the parking lot, he had his hands full."

"Uh huh."

She sighed. "With any luck, the girls heard something that will help us."

"Like a very loud voice yelling about murder?"

"You never know."

He turned into a small graveled lot. The peaks of scattered tents were visible in the surrounding underbrush. "There's the scout mistress. Oh, Miss Churchill!"

A tall, broad-shouldered woman in a military-style khaki uniform turned toward them. She had a bucket in one hand and a roll of toilet paper in the other. "Ranger Ribault, hello! Can I help you?" She nodded at Ellie and gazed adoringly at Simon.

"I hope so. We'd like to ask the girls a few questions." He pointed at the toilet paper. "Did we catch you at a bad time?"

She dropped the roll like a hot mike and ran a hand through her short, tawny hair. "No, not at all! I'll muster the troops." She gave him a shy smile and, making a cone with her hands, called, "Molly! Where are you?" A girl of about thirteen in a uniform splashed with ribbons of mud emerged from the woods and ran up to them. "Oh, it's you, Bernice. Where are the others?"

"We're down by the footbridge, Miss Churchill. Adelaide fell in the creek, and now she says she's stuck."

"She's in the water? She knows she's not supposed to—"

Bernice didn't let her finish. "I *know*, but she was trying to catch a fish with her bare hands and she stumbled over this tree root and landed in the muck. We couldn't reach her, and Doreen is *sure* she saw an alligator lurking in the cattails. She says he's *huge*, an'…an' he looks *real* hungry." Her voice trailed up to a shriek.

"And why did Adelaide want to catch a fish with her bare hands?"

The girl looked suddenly nervous. "I…I bet her."

Her face tight, Miss Churchill turned to Simon. "I'll be right back."

"Do let me, Harriet. I can pull her out in no time."

The woman's drawn cheeks flushed. "Thank you, Simon. You're too kind."

"No problem." He followed Bernice to the edge of the creek. About six feet out, a young girl wallowed in the mud, waving her arms and blubbering. A gaggle of scouts lined the shore, hurling advice and suggestions at her. Simon waded in, retrieved Adelaide, and headed back to camp, clasping the sodden child by her collar. The others ran before him, except for one scout, who trailed behind, piping in a high, thin voice. "I told Adelaide. I *told* her. I saw an alligator. He had his jaws wide open, and he was swimming toward her. I *yelled* and *yelled*, but Adelaide didn't pay any attention to me. I said, I'm telling Miss Churchill. I—"

"Yes, thank you, Doreen." *Why is every other word out of a little girl's mouth in italics?* "Looks like I got there just in time, Miss Churchill. That alligator was awful close." He turned to Doreen, cutting her off before she could start skirling again. "Remember, I told you all when you arrived that they only eat at night, so Adelaide was *probably* safe." He winked at Ellie.

Doreen took this as high praise for her devotion to duty and preened. Harriet waved an imperious hand. "All of you, go wash off, then get started on cleaning the showers. We're heading home at five o'clock, and I want everything spit-spot." She leveled a warning look at Adelaide. "Not like the last time. We're lucky Superintendent Barnes allowed us back."

The girls scattered, and Harriet pulled out a folding chair for Simon. Apparently, she expected Ellie to stand. "So, Simon, what can I do for you?"

"Thanks. You heard about the bodies that washed up on park grounds?"

Her eyebrows lifted. Simon suspected that that passed for astonishment in the rigidly disciplined woman. "Bodies?"

"Oh, I'm sorry, I thought it was common knowledge."

Miss Churchill permitted herself a tiny frown. "You forget, we have been in the park for the last fortnight. As leader of Troop Three-Two-Four, I strive to make our camping trips as close to a wilderness experience as possible. We pride ourselves on limiting contact with the outside world. What happened?"

"We discovered three corpses by the river."

The scout mistress's eyes widened, but she recovered quickly. "On park land?"

"Yes. One off St. Marys River and two along the Amelia River shoreline."

"Do you know who they were? How they got here?"

"We've only been able to identify one of them—a convict who escaped from a Miami prison."

"Oh my! Do you suppose we were in any danger?"

"I don't think so. He appears to have been dead before he washed ashore."

She sat thinking. "When were they discovered?"

"Ten days ago."

"So, the fifteenth. We arrived and set up camp Saturday the fourteenth."

"Correct. Yours was the only group on the grounds that night. We'd like to know if any of you recall anything suspicious—noises, for example—that night or the next morning." He looked hopefully at Harriet.

She stood up. "Let me round up the girls." She gave a long, lilting whistle.

Within thirty seconds, ten little girls had lined up, a few in some disarray, but at attention. A tall girl with tight russet braids stepped forward. "What is it, Miss Churchill?"

"Molly, Ranger Ribault has just informed me that several…er…bits of flotsam and jetsam were found on park land last Sunday morning—the day after we arrived."

One little girl cried, "I couldn't help it. I was sooo hungry, and Doreen ate my last candy bar, and when Adelaide and me went to the office to see if we could find some toilet paper…Well, no one was around, and we saw this box of cookies, but Adelaide grabbed it from me and it fell and…" The rest was lost in a cresting wail.

Simon patted the girl awkwardly while Miss Churchill glowered at her.

When her sobs had subsided, Ellie said gently, "That's all right. No harm done. We're glad you confessed."

Miss Churchill took over. "What Ranger Ribault wants to know is if any of you heard anything unusual the night we arrived. As I recall, we were set up here in time for supper, with lights out at nine after the campfire. Did any of you leave your tents after that?"

A chorus of "No, Miss Churchills" filled the air like a scrum of mockingbirds. Miss Churchill zeroed in on one child whose head remained down. "Charlotte?"

"Yes, Miss Churchill?"

The scout mistress tapped a foot.

"Um, I did leave the tent, Miss Churchill." Her cheeks flaming, she whispered, "I had an accident. It's…you know…that time of the…of the…" She glanced at Simon and burst into tears. Harriet and Ellie rushed to her.

"It's fine, dear, happens to everyone." When Charlotte had calmed down, Harriet asked, "Now, did you hear or see anything out of the ordinary while you were outside?"

Charlotte's eyes swerved to the girl standing beside her. "Letty came with me."

Letty did not immediately reply, apparently mulling over which form of torture she would inflict on her friend. Finally, Harriet said, "Letty?"

"Yes, Miss Churchill. You told us to always have a

buddy when we left our tents, and Charlotte asked me to go to the latrine with her."

"What time was that?"

She frowned. "Dunno. Late. After lights out."

"And?"

"Well"—she glared at her friend—"it took her *forever*. I'm sitting out there in the jungle. Who knows how many alligators…or pigs…or—"

"Or vultures," Charlotte contributed helpfully.

"Yeah. Anyway, I was getting kinda jumpy…and then I heard a *splash*."

"From where?"

"From over by the fort."

"Did you see any lights?"

"Yeah, kind of a flickering…like a torch."

Simon muttered, "Could've been the lights at the event."

But Letty wasn't finished. "And *then* I heard a scream. Well, more like a yelp."

"What did you do?"

"Charlotte finally came out of the latrine, and we ran all the way back to the tent."

Ellie asked, "Did the yelp sound like an animal or more human?"

She shook her head. "Definitely human."

Charlotte spoke up angrily. "Letty's full of it. She—"

"Charlotte!"

"Sorry, Miss Churchill, but she's wrong. It was a raccoon—they squeal like that. I'm pretty sure I saw one run away into the woods as we left. Letty's always making stuff up so people pay attention to her." She made a face at the offending Letty, who returned the favor.

"Okay." Simon got up. "Show me where you were when you heard the sounds."

Letty shyly took his hand. They walked, trailed by Ellie, Harriet, Charlotte, and the rest of the scouts, through the woods and down a dirt path to a small building. Signs with male and female silhouettes were attached to two brown doors. In the distance, they could make out the walls of the fort. Simon surveyed the area. "The only water near here is the river beyond the fort. Seems rather far away."

Ellie had an idea. "How about if I take a brick or something up to the top of the walls and drop it over the side? Let me know if you hear it."

"Okay."

The little group watched her hike to the fort and disappear inside. Soon her figure came into view on the rampart. She lifted her arm and dropped a square object over the side. In the distance, they heard a distinct splash. She hallooed, then loped down the steps and back to Simon. "Well?"

Harriet answered. "We all heard it."

"Thank you, Ellie. Thank you, Harriet." He smiled at the two girls. "And both of you. Well done. We'll take it from here. I believe you all have some cleaning up to do?"

The scouts backed off reluctantly and ran off in whispering clumps. Harriet gave Simon her hand. "We'll be out of here by five tonight. Thanks so much for everything." She squeezed it affectionately.

On the way back to the station, Ellie remarked, "You seem to have a positive effect on women."

Please tell me that's jealousy in her voice. "Only

Girl Scouts."

"That makes sense."

"So the question now is, did the splash and the yell originate inside the fort or outside, and when?"

"An important issue, yes, but before we tackle that one, Hosea wants us to focus on this murky League of the Green Cross."

"Easier said than done. We have one name, a Carson Gregory."

She nodded. "And one phone number. Which he doesn't answer."

"You don't suppose…"

"What?"

"That the disappearance of the event file could be in any way related?"

Ellie wrinkled her nose. "Seems a little over the top just to avoid paying poor Judy."

"Maybe this Green club has something to hide. I've got an idea." He parked and jumped out of the car.

She called, "Don't tell me. You're going to Google them."

Simon skidded to a stop. "Any reason not to?"

"Other than that I already did?"

He took her hand and led her into the office. "Okay, enlighten me."

She sat down and opened her notebook. "I found nothing under League of the Green Cross, so I played around, searching on Green and Amelia Island and Fernandina Beach."

"Good girl." He nodded approvingly. "Boolean logic."

"I thought it was called a keyword search."

"Only by ignorant millennials whose education

consists of oversimplified drivel based on the assumption that they couldn't handle words of more than two syllables."

Ellie stared at him until he began to fidget. "Do you want to know what I found?"

"That in 1817 a Scots mercenary named Gregor MacGregor seized Amelia Island and declared it to be the Republic of the Floridas. That its flag—which he designed all by hisself—was a green cross on a white background. He called it the Green Cross of Florida."

She threw the notebook at him.

He caught it and set it down. "Further, poor MacGregor, unaccustomed as he was to actually running a country, immediately ran his finances into the ground. His luck turned when he made the acquaintance of the French pirate Louis Aury. Said stout fellow graciously took it off his hands and proceeded to give it to Mexico."

"Is that all?"

"Well, there's lots more. Amelia Island has a storied history, full of adventurers and treasure lost and found. Why, there was even a conspiracy in which President Madison was implicated...but I won't bore you."

"I suppose you know all this from your history degree?"

"To be fair, I learned most of it at my mammy's knee. She was a Geechee."

"Like Argus and Frog? They speak that ancient language you were telling me about."

"Ancient, no, but still almost three hundred years old. This researcher named Lorenzo Dow Turner was able to trace vocabulary words and rituals the Gullah use back to specific villages on the African coast. A Gullah woman named Mary Moran actually found one of her distant relatives in Sierra Leone, and they corresponded for years."

"How did she find her?"

"Turner traced a song she had learned from her mother to a song still sung in a Mende village."

Ellie paused. "Wait a minute. Where were we?"

Simon didn't miss a beat. "The Green Cross of Florida."

"Ah. So anyway, I'm thinking maybe this group is some kind of historical society."

"And if we ever find Carson Gregory, we can ask him." He checked his watch. "Four o'clock. Say…it might be nice to tour the old Wienermobile again. I could ask if they'll let me take her for a spin. Can I treat you to a hot dog?"

Ellie wouldn't look at Simon. "I…uh…have a date."

Is that the sound of something ripping out of my chest? "Thad?"

She nodded.

"Did he ask you?" *Uh oh, that was mean.*

A delicate finger traced pictures in the dust on top of the file cabinet. "He…uh…we're all going to Sandy Bottoms."

"Nicole too?"

"Uh huh. And Betty. Betty says it's two-for-one night, and Thad asked if he could join us."

"Well, have fun." *Say you have a date too, idiot.* "Um, well, I'll check with Georgia. She might fancy a weenie."

Ellie's eyes flashed. "Georgia?"

"An old friend. She's in law school in Washington, DC, down on spring break."

"I didn't think they had vacations in law school."

"They take a long recess before they start the big push to study for the bar. She's going to take the exam in July."

"Oh." She played with a pencil. "So she's not here for long then."

Wait a minute. Is she...? Nah. "A week." *How about a little test?* "It will be nice to see her."

"Yes, well." She flung the pencil away. "Gotta go. See you tomorrow." She slouched off toward her car.

Simon watched her leave, then shrugged and bent his steps to his own car. As he drove, he mulled over his feelings. He had loved Ellie for so long it had become a habit, like walking the dog or brushing his teeth. There was no way she would ever think of him romantically, of that he was sure. *I'm too weird.* Not to mention ugly. He looked at his face in the rearview mirror. Eyes the color of swamp cabbage, edged a garish brown that matched his hair. *So what if his mother described them as a brilliant hazel shot through with veins of lustrous copper?* Lashes he considered a little too long for a man, under bushy chocolate brows. *How many times had Georgia complained that she had to do artificially what came naturally to him?* His wavy hair fell over his brow, reminding him that he needed a haircut.

He slowed down for a yellow light, his thin, agile fingers gripping the steering wheel. Behind him, a befinned Oldsmobile the length of a football field screeched to a halt. The driver bellowed, "It's only yellow, jackass!"

Simon stuck his head out the window. "Santa?"

"Is that you, Simon? Pull over."

Simon did as he was told, unraveled his six-foot-three frame from the car, and walked back to the Oldsmobile. "What is it?"

A man of seventy, with a scraggly white beard that lent an air of authenticity when he played Saint Nick at the local hardware store every Christmas, rolled his window down. "Glad I caught you." He set the emergency brake. "Have you seen Georgia?"

"Nope. I heard she's home for spring break."

"Yes. She was supposed to help me clean out the garage. You see her, tell her to get her rump back to the house."

"Sure will."

Simon went back to his car and drove home. The house lay in a curve of road that overlooked Egan's Creek. A sleek black cat greeted him. "Hello, Isis. What'll we do tonight?"

In response, she went to the kitchen and pushed her bowl with a gentle paw. "I get it. 'First eat, then we'll talk.' " After pouring out some dry food, he whistled. A beautiful chestnut-colored dog with delicate pointed ears bounded down the stairs. "Come on, Roan."

He went out the side door and watched the dog racing ahead of him through the woods. As he walked, he laid out the events of the last week in a jumbled heap. *Three bodies. Two related due to mutual encounter with the same weapon. Two unidentified. One convict. The woman could be Jamaican. So how did they get to Amelia Island at the same time? Could they have anything to do with the Green event? Or was their arrival serendipitous?*

He turned back. *That's it. I have to focus on this Green group. They're just too secretive to be irrelevant.*
****

Park headquarters, Thursday, April 26

"So, how was your date?"

Date? What date? Oh...Georgia. He tried to assess Ellie's mood. *Should I play along? Pretend Georgia's my girlfriend?* "She...uh...couldn't come—her dad wanted her to clean out the garage."

"Oh, too bad." Ellie tried unsuccessfully to keep the smugness off her face. "*We* had a lovely time. In fact, I was out much too late."

Am I expected to ask? "Did Thad take you home?"

"He did." Her eyes went dreamy. "He's such a gentleman."

"I'm guessing that means he didn't kiss you."

"If he did, it's none of your business." She flounced to her desk.

Simon poured more coffee into his mug. "I do have one tittle of news."

After a minute, she condescended to ask. "Yes?"

"I think I found an address for Mr. Gregory."

"Aha."

"This morning—*long* before you deigned to arrive—the delightful Judy called to say she'd received a check for six hundred dollars from Carson Gregory. The check had a return address on it."

"Aha."

"You're being redundant."

"Okay, where is it?"

"On Atlantic Avenue. Want to come with me to check it out?"

"Sure."

Nine One Four Atlantic Avenue turned out to be an imposing brick building. "Look, it's got a historic marker." Ellie read it aloud. "Built as Public School #1 in 1886 by architect R. S. Schuyler, it was closed in 1926 and sold for office space. It still contains the original heart pine flooring and grand staircase, original double-hung sash windows, and bronze bell cast in 1880 by the McShane Foundry."

"Let's scout out the directory." The board listed two real estate offices, an accounting firm, and an import business. "I don't see any League."

Ellie pointed at the name of the import company. "Green Cross Partners?"

"*Hmm*. Worth a try."

They climbed the beautiful curving stairs and walked down a carpeted hall. "It's hard to believe this was ever a school," whispered Ellie.

Just then a bell began to peal. Simon pointed above them. "How about now?"

"I like it." She stopped at a door and knocked.

A woman's voice answered. "Come in."

They walked into a waiting room with comfortable chairs and an emerald green carpet. A young brunette, glasses perched on the top of her head, sat behind a desk facing a computer monitor. "Be right with you."

When she turned, the glasses fell off, and her eyes grew wide. "Are you the police?"

"No, ma'am. We're state park rangers…from Fort Clinch?"

"This is about the meeting then. Mr. Gregory isn't here right now." She stood up and began to edge toward a rear door. Simon put his ranger hat back on.

"Yes, but it's not about the payment."

She relaxed. "Mr. Gregory will have the money by next week. He promised. I know Judy Holiday is upset with us, but the other members never paid their dues and he's had to go around dunning them. He's really sorry about it."

"Could you tell us what the event was about?"

"I understand it was an organizational meeting. Green Cross partners are an export-import business. With the revival of relations with Cuba, they are looking into trade opportunities there."

Simon asked gently, "Why not have the meeting here? Why at the Fort?"

"That I don't know. I believe there were some out-of-town investors coming and Carson—Mr. Gregory—wanted to wine and dine them a bit."

"I take it they didn't arrive."

"What do you mean?"

"Mr. Gregory canceled the cooks and staff and had the tables and tents removed at the last minute."

"Really? I didn't know that. Judy didn't mention it."

"Ms. Holiday told us you weren't answering her calls."

"What? I haven't…well, I've been out sick for a few days." Her eyes flicked to the desk phone and back. "The cleaning lady may have erased her messages. If she left any." Her hand swished across the desk, gently closing a day book. "May I give Mr. Gregory a message?"

Ellie tapped a foot impatiently. "We'd like to talk to him directly. Can we make an appointment?"

"Certainly, although he won't be in the office until next week. After that, he's planning a trip to Cuba to start building contacts there."

She took down Simon's number and gave him a card. "My name is Nora Wilson. Call me tomorrow, and I'll have a time and day for you."

They thanked her and walked out.

As they crossed the street, a fire-engine red Miata barely missed them. It skidded to a stop, and a woman who would put Christie Brinkley to shame leapt out of the car. Simon, accustomed to the sight of her waist-length black hair and eyes a remarkable malachite green, didn't notice Ellie's slack jaw. He called, "Hey, Georgia, how's Santa's garage? You didn't unwrap any presents, did you?"

She ran over to them, her short skirt making the long, Tina Turner legs seem even longer. She kissed Simon's cheek and smiled at Ellie. "You must be Simon's new partner. Does he treat you as badly as he treats his other colleagues?"

Ellie made a garbled sound in her throat.

She turned to Simon. "Dollink, I'm only down for a few days, and I need to talk to you. Can you come to dinner tonight?"

Simon started to make a joke about checking his social calendar but caught sight of Ellie's face. She looked pained. *What the—?*

"Well?" Georgia tugged at his arm.

"Oh, um, sure. What do you want me to bring?"

"Some of that fabulous Italian bubbly you brought the last time. It gave me such a buzz." She winked at Ellie, who blinked. "Seven?"

"Okay."

Georgia turned on her heel and ran back to her car, starting up just as the two drivers behind her had stopped admiring her attributes and begun to fret. She roared off.

"Who…who was that?"

Simon turned surprised eyes on her. "I'm sorry. I should have introduced you. Georgia Petrie."

"Oh. Your friend from law school."

"Uh huh." He gazed at the cloud of dust, the only sign of her passing. "We grew up together."

Ellie muttered something.

"Excuse me?"

"Nothing."

"Did you ask if Georgia had seen me naked?"

"Me? That's absurd." Ellie plopped into the driver's seat and waved angrily at Simon. "Get in."

Simon did as he was told. On the drive back to the station, they were both quiet. Simon rubbed a meditative finger over his lips, wondering. *What set Ellie off anyway?* A thought intruded. *No, couldn't be.* He checked her profile. *Nah.* But his mouth formed a hopeful smile, and he leaned back, humming his favorite tune.

Chapter Six
Georgia on My Mind

The Petrie home, Thursday, April 26

"More wine, Pop?"

"Please."

"How was your burger, Simon? Tasteless enough?"

"Yes. Thanks, Georgia."

She pursed her lips. "My dear, you have got to broaden your dietary intake. It's not healthy. When was the last time you had a salad?"

"You know I was a vegetarian for five years, vegan for one. Doc John told me if I kept on like that I'd be dead in six months. Since I went on the meat diet, I've been healthy as a horse."

Santa sat back with a sigh. "Well, I for one fully enjoyed the lamb curry. Nice and spicy, but not so hot my ancient colon rebelled. You're the only one who knows how to make a proper yogurt sauce, Georgia."

"That trip to Epcot Center was worth every penny. How did you like the chutney? I made it from scratch this afternoon."

Simon rose to the bait. "From *my* recipe. *And* you used my secret formula for curry powder. Epcot Center, my eye…" He lapsed into incoherent grumbles.

Georgia batted her eyes at him. "How do you know, Simon? You didn't touch any of it."

"Simple. You left the index card on the counter."

Santa leaned forward. "At least the recipes are being put to use, Simon. God, I miss having Georgia cook for me! Mrs. Daugherty is very kind but easily distractible. The last time she made lasagna she forgot to cook the noodles first."

Georgia rolled her eyes. "She has other qualities, Dad. I saw the way you two look at each other. What's going on?"

The old man blushed. "Nothing. We just enjoy each other's company."

"Florence Smythe told me she saw you two walking on the beach in the moonlight."

"Florence Smythe is scheduled for cataract surgery next week."

"Ah."

Simon was wondering if he should help Santa out when Georgia nailed him with a piercing look. "So what's with Ellie?"

Uh oh. Gotta nip this baby in the bud. "Ellie only has eyes for Thad Farnsworth."

"That twit? She seemed much too intelligent to fall for him."

"How do you know? She didn't say two words to you."

"A woman senses these things about another woman. I think she's torn."

"Torn?"

"Torn between a self-indulgent, cowardly, lazy Adonis and a nerdy history buff with the most beautiful hazel eyes in the world."

"Adonis?"

"Greek demigod. Don't tell me you don't know

your Greek deities?"

"Of course I do." He rattled off twenty names. "Do you want me to name the Roman equivalents?"

Georgia began to shake her head but paused. "Sure."

Santa put down his napkin. "Enough, you two. You've been sparring since kindergarten. I think I'd much rather you were lovers than best friends. Let's go out on the porch. There's a blue moon tonight."

The three settled into rocking chairs, the only light the glowing ember of Santa's pipe. After a few minutes, he said, "All right, Simon."

Simon knew what he meant. "Georgia's wrong. Ellie's not torn. She turns to gruel every time Thad walks by."

"Crush."

"She's twenty-eight. She knows what she wants."

"Really? I'm sixty-eight and just discovering what I want."

Georgia touched her father's hand lightly. "You always were a slow learner."

"It's not that. I think you learn in spits and starts—every few years you reach a certain plateau of understanding. Trouble is, you get to a certain level, you think you've found the answers. Too many people stop at that point. Too many people watch life sail away while they're standing on a desert island."

Georgia said softly, "And regret that they missed the boat?"

"Laugh if you will, but it's true." He took a few puffs. The aromatic smoke drifted toward the creek. "You know I loved your mother very much, Georgia."

"You always say that, but you divorced her. I never

quite grasped why."

"I'd reached one of those levels. I was so sure of my feelings, sure that I had fallen out of love with her. My path was crystal clear. Run away." He closed his eyes. "It wasn't until we were divorced that I realized how wrong I was. See, I'd been treating her like a figure in a picture." He gestured back toward the living room. "Like that one on the mantelpiece of us in Bermuda—our last year together."

"She seemed like a photo to you? As in, two-dimensional?" Georgia's eyes filled with tears. "My mother?"

"No, not at all." He tamped more tobacco into the bowl of his pipe. "It's not that she was a two-dimensional *person*. It was that ours had become a two-dimensional *relationship*. It was good, then it was bad. Simple. Or so I thought."

Simon put down his glass. "I don't understand."

"Let me explain with another story. When I was twenty-one, I fell in love."

Georgia blew her nose. "With Mother?"

"No. Her name was Patience. I met her in Egypt where we were both studying Arabic."

Hoping to lift the mood, Simon joked, "One of your many languages?"

"As Santa Claus, I have to know all the languages of the world."

Wait a minute…Is he…? Simon noted a tiny twinkle in the old man's eye. "Yeah, okay."

"Anyway, I was mad about her, but time went on and after a while I became discontented."

"You moved up another level?"

"No—still on the same one, but this one had high

walls. I couldn't see the horizon. I thought I'd be stuck inside forever. In a fit of claustrophobia, I escaped, leaving her behind. By the time I'd figured out what I'd lost, it was too late."

"And then came Mother."

"And the same thing happened." He blew a smoke ring. "Only years later did I realize that instead of casting her off, I should have held her tight and climbed the rope."

"What the heck are you talking about? What rope?"

"You know, one of those ropes the hero always seems to find hanging down the cliff. He uses it to save himself and the heroine and then, when they reach the top, a Rachmaninoff concerto plays while the sun sets in glorious Technicolor."

Georgia moved restlessly. "So what's your point?"

Santa patted her knee. "I kept focusing on the *me* part of the relationship, not on the *us*. Figured I could tackle that after I fixed myself. Not true. You need to look outward to find true contentment. I'm doing that now…with Mrs. Daugherty."

"Aha, I knew it!"

"She has indeed taken me to another level, and I'm finally able to go willingly." He snuffed out the cigar. "Although I insist on taking a hoard of carry-out menus with me."

Simon finally spoke. "So, what does this have to do with me, if anything?"

Georgia kissed his forehead. "I think Dad means, don't give up. Drag Ellie up to that next level. I'm going to make coffee."

Later, as Georgia drove Simon home, she glanced

at him. "You know, Dad's right. I learned it the hard way."

"You? I can't imagine any man letting you go."

"That's because you're a dweeb."

"True. And your point?"

"I'm not a freak to you. You understand me. So many guys see the long, raven tresses—"

"The hourglass figure, the pert little nose, the jade green eyes—but I'm interrupting you."

She cuffed him. "They think it's great until I open my mouth."

"And then the stream of potty talk puts them off?"

"No, and stop it. I'm trying to be serious here."

"Yes, sir."

"What I'm talking about is my unfortunate inclination to argue."

"Oh, that."

"And worse, to be right."

"That's true. Why, if you had the encyclopedic knowledge I possess, you'd be insufferable."

She turned a corner a little too sharply. When Simon had righted himself, she snipped, "We were talking about me."

"Ah, yes, the usual feminine ploy—distract them, then slosh a bucket of guilt over their heads."

"Anyhoo, I did the same thing—found a man I will love forever and dumped him."

"Really? Anyone I know?"

"No, a guy in college. Or rather, the summer after college. Remember when I had that internship on Capitol Hill? Well, I met this fellow there. He was intelligent, so well educated, handsome, a good listener—"

"I just want to confirm we're not talking about me."

"Shut up. You know you're my best friend. You have to listen to me and be sympathetic. Also, take advantage of my mistakes."

"I do that all the time." He brushed her fist aside. "Okay. But you *will* get to the point soon?"

"Simon, you're a bigger twit than Thad."

"Ouch."

She glanced quickly at him, then back at the road. "I was really smitten, and so was he…I think."

"You don't know?"

"He was one of those reserved types, a man of few words, strong, silent—"

"Good at unclogging drains?"

"How did you know? For some reason, that's the kind of man I'm always drawn to. At least until I can afford a house with modern plumbing…Where was I?"

"Plumbers."

"Oh yes. After a while, his continued reticence stirred a twinge of doubt in me. Did he really care? I wasn't sure."

"You wanted him to grovel?"

"No, I wanted him to fight for me."

"You wanted a Neanderthal—or rather a Cro-Magnon. They were much more aggressive."

"I guess so…" She seemed unsure, but rallied. "I flirted outrageously. I threatened to go off to Chicago. I pouted a lot. Anything to get a rise out of him."

"Oh, I see." Simon snickered.

"Not that way, poor sap. Just 'cause you're not getting any…"

"Hey! I could if I wanted to."

"But you want Ellie—I can see it in your eyes."

"It's dark in here."

"When you were standing next to her. Don't be coy—I know you too well."

"I never should have made you my blood sister."

"Nonetheless, the point is—"

"At last! We've arrived at my humble abode. What did you want to tell me? I need my beauty sleep."

"No use. It won't do you any good."

"Hey!"

Georgia waved him off, but called him back. "I'm giving you one more chance."

Simon stood by the car, keeping his impatience on a slack leash. "Go on."

"So, because Michael wouldn't conform to my picture of the perfect man, I walked away. Or, to use Dad's analogy, I thought he would always be stuck on one level, and I wanted a change. I can still see him looking up at me as I climbed. Simon"—she laid her soft palm on his cheek—"I should have taken him with me. I left him, and I'll always regret it. If you don't haul Ellie up, you'll lose her."

"Enough, Georgy."

"Promise?"

He hesitated, then turned toward the house. "I'll think it over. Thanks for dinner."

****

Park headquarters, Friday, April 27

"I'm edging closer to the idea that Alvaredo—"

Simon looked up at his boss. "Who?"

"Miguel Alvaredo. The convict. That he's at the center of all this."

"Could it be because he's the only one we've

identified?"

Hosea sat heavily. "Maybe. He *was* a hardened criminal. When he tunneled out of the Miami jail, he headed north. Amelia Island could even have been his destination."

"He came here on purpose?" Ellie scratched her ear. "What for?"

"To meet up with his gang. Didn't Amos say they'd nabbed some MS-13 members on A1A?"

"Then what about the other two?" Simon put down his pen.

"Wrong place, wrong time? He killed them—drowned the woman and knifed the man."

Ellie jumped in. "Maybe they were in on it with him. Maybe they helped him escape."

"Possible. And then fought over the loot he'd stashed somewhere. *Hmm.* We'll have a better idea when we've identified them." He crooked a finger at Simon. "Come into my office." Simon followed him to his desk. "I want you to go along with the state police unit that's heading down to Miami. See if we can trace his movements."

"I thought he was last seen near the port."

"The Port of Miami is fifty-two acres. It has eight passenger terminals and thirteen wharves. We have to narrow the possibilities down a little."

Simon stood. "When do I leave?"

"This afternoon." He paused. "I wish I could send someone with you, but I'm short-handed now and the season's gearing up. "

"S'okay. I can bond with the coppers."

Simon turned from Hosea to find Ellie behind him. He thought he heard a catch in her voice when she asked, "You're going to Miami?"

"So it seems." He tried to gauge her expression. "It's only for a couple of days."

"Oh, it's no big deal. We'll manage. Uh…Thad said he could pull a double shift."

Is this the part where I haul her up to my level? "Too bad you can't come. It'll be interesting."

Her eyes glowed. "Yes, it would. But…Thad needs me."

"And Hosea."

"And Hosea."

"Well, I'd better go pack."

"Yes."

"Yes." He backed out of the room.

At the last minute, she whispered something. He thought it sounded like "Call me when you get there," but he couldn't be sure.

****

Port of Miami, Saturday, April 28

Simon waited while the seaport director finished his paperwork. "So, Mr. Brantley, where do we stand? No leads on the container terminals or the cruise line docks. What about commercial fishermen? Where are those wharves?"

Brantley shook his head. "Aren't any. Commercial fishing's banned in Biscayne Bay. Tourism takes precedence here."

"But the waters off South Florida are among the best fishing grounds in the world!"

"Tell me about it. Spend every Sunday out on my boat, but fish for the market are all farmed now or imported from South America. Southern Fisheries is probably the biggest."

The policeman at Simon's side asked, "Do they have ships?"

"Sure, Frasier, but they're flagged in Panama or Costa Rica. The cargo passes through here on its way north. Only fisheries I know are farther up the coast."

Simon said, "Yeah, we still have a few shrimpers out of Amelia Island."

"Amelia Island? That used to be the shrimp capital of Florida—started there as I recall."

"Yup. Turn of the century. Italian immigrants built it up."

"Italians? Never thought of them as fishermen."

"Well, Sicilians. Shrimping couldn't have survived without the Gullah crews, though."

"You mean the black dudes who speak that African language?"

"It's a creole—a blend of languages. Yes. The freed slaves who settled on the Sea Islands. They were the backbone of the industry."

"Huh. All we got down here are Cuban exiles and displaced New Yorkers. Even the crackers are gone." This seemed to depress him. "No small businesses left. It's all big conglomerates and all remote. I don't even deal with ship captains face to face anymore—they just email and Skype."

Simon and Frasier thanked him. As they were heading to the patrol car, Frasier turned to his companion. "Want to grab some dinner?"

Simon checked his watch. "Nah. I think I'll turn in. Heading out tomorrow first thing. We've pretty much hit a dead end here."

"If we come across any trace of Alvaredo, I'll let you guys know."

"Thanks."

Back in his room, Simon dropped his briefcase, filled the ice bucket, and poured himself a drink. Then he went out on the balcony. The azure waters of Miami's famous bay glistened in the evening sun. Two huge cruise ships lay at anchor, armies of tiny creatures bustling over them. *Could Alvaredo have stowed away in the* Queen of the Seas? Unlikely. The security was super tight. *One of the tankers?* It would be even harder to hide in one of those, considering their tiny crew and cramped quarters. No, if he went by boat at all, it would have to be a fishing trawler. *Or maybe he stole a yacht?*

That didn't answer the question of the other two. They had to have met up somewhere or the other guy wouldn't have Alvaredo's knife in his chest. *Knife. How did he get a knife?* Kenny said it was huge, so it wasn't a shiv or a switchblade. More the kind of knife Crocodile Dundee buckled his swash with. He made a mental note to ask the CSI people about it. Pulling out his phone, he dialed a familiar number. "Ellie? Did I get you at a bad time?"

He heard something crash. "Oh, Simon, is that you?" Ellie seemed out of breath.

"I thought I'd update you on my travails."

"Hang on a second."

He listened to voices in the background. *Is that that insipid Exeter accent of Thad's I hear? Damn.* Ellie came back on.

"Hi. Er...what's up? You wanted to talk about your travels?"

"Travails—trials and tribulations." Simon told her about his lack of success. "I'm beginning to think he didn't come by boat. It might be worth checking out the

109

railroads."

"Trains? How would he end up in the water then?"

"I dunno. Maybe he hid in the fort and the Greenies caught him and threw him over the walls."

Ellie sounded dubious. "That's a good long toss. He was found a mile away."

"So…he didn't die right away. He crawled south along the shore and expired at the mouth of the creek."

"Managing to kill the other victim before he died."

"Wait! I've got it. The other guy is one of the Greenies."

"*Hmm*. Okay. I'll consider your theory as a work in progress."

Simon thought of something. "By the way, did Gregory's secretary call?"

"Oh dear, I forgot all about that. No. At least, she didn't call the office."

"Okay, when I get home, let's make an appointment with the elusive Mr. Gregory. I want some more answers."

"When will I see you?"

The words reminded him of Thad's presence. "I guess when you're free. Sounds like you're busy now…with Thad."

"What? Oh no. He just dropped my purse off. I forgot it at the Hammerhead." She paused. "It was awfully sweet of him."

"Yes, indeed." *She didn't hear me gulp, did she?*

"I…uh…so how was your dinner with…Georgia?"

"And her father." He remembered the lectures from father and daughter. "A bit oppressive."

"How so?"

"Never mind. They only want what's best for me."

"Excuse me?"

"Look, I'll see you tomorrow. I'll be home by one."

"Oh, that's nice."

"Nice?" Is that like "eh"? Or more "great"? This one's for you, Georgia. "I can take you to lunch if you like."

"That would be lovely."

"Lovely?" *That's definitely better than nice. Or is it?*

He hung up. It was going to be a long night.

Chapter Seven
Little Shrimp & Big Fish

Seafarers Restaurant, Fernandina Beach, Sunday, April 29

"Your table's ready, Simon."

"Thanks, Hilda." Simon and Ellie edged their way past the clumps of people waiting to be called in the tiny eatery on Centre Street. The Seafarers Restaurant was a tourist attraction, though Simon wasn't sure why. It consisted of about twenty tables crammed into a room fifteen feet square. The noise level resembled the engine room of a Spanish freighter, and the food reminded him of his father's cooking—southern basic. Hilda led them to a two-top by the kitchen.

She bent over them, her large frame eclipsing the fluorescent lights. "The usual, hon?"

"I guess."

"Hamburger, fries. Got it."

In response to Ellie's feigned gasp of surprise, he declared, "Hey, when in Rome…"

"This is a seafood place."

"…Order whatever's the best dish in the house." He ducked to avoid the menu swinging from Hilda's hand. "Joe's burger is a magnificent piece of work, the bun soft and white, the meat gray, devoid of juice, and the ketchup Heinz."

"Just the way you like it." Ellie put down the menu. "I'll have the shrimp gumbo, Hilda. And a glass of Pinot Grigio."

She jotted the order down. "Got it. I suppose Simon wants a PBR."

"Um, you got any porter on draft?"

Shocked into shedding her customary surliness, Hilda stared at Simon. "You sure?"

He gave Ellie a defiant look. "Yes. Oh, and put some lettuce on the burger. Just a leaf. Don't be generous."

When she'd gone, Ellie leaned over. "What's with this new madcap, Katie-bar-the-door attitude?"

"Let's just say I'm slouching toward new horizons." *And a new level.*

Ellie unrolled the knife and fork from her napkin. "So, tell me about the trip. Did you come across any trace of Alvaredo?"

"No. There's no way he could have stowed away in either the liners or the freighters."

"What about fishing boats?"

"There's no commercial fishing in Miami."

"Really? How come?"

"The National Park Service banned it in Biscayne Bay due to overfishing and destruction of corals. They'll allow all other water activities. I guess this is what happens in a one-industry town."

"Let me guess. Tourism?"

"Uh huh. Everything takes a back seat to snorkeling and sun bathing. Even the citrus industry is pretty much gone there."

"What? No Florida oranges in Florida?"

"Not in Miami-Dade anyway. Once they started

building all the high rises, open land disappeared. See, citrus was first cultivated in northern Florida, but it moved south for the warm weather." Simon tapped a tune out on the table with his spoon. "Old Mizz Tuttle certainly changed the face of Florida when she sent that box of oranges to Flagler."

"Wait a minute. What does that have to do with tourism?"

"It doesn't. It has to do with Miami."

"I thought we were talking about oranges. Who is Flagler?"

"Ah, I keep forgetting you're a Yankee. Henry Flagler. One of the millionaires who helped develop Florida. Partnered with Rockefeller in Standard Oil. It's men like him who built America."

"I've been told they were all grasping, greedy, mean people who made millions off the backs of Chinese immigrants."

"I reiterate my statement about the current condition of American public education. Flagler, Plant, Gould, Hill, and Vanderbilt built the railroads that brought goods, services, and settlers to the vast interior. Civilization, if you will. They took huge risks and undertook vast projects, some of which—like the Key West railroad Flagler built at great cost—didn't succeed. Without them, you wouldn't be able to get from here to Oregon except by wagon train. They deserved to be rich."

Ellie obviously didn't think this speech required a reply, preferring to sip her wine. "Well?"

"Well what?"

"What happened when Miss Tuttle sent the oranges to Flagler?"

He gave her a nod of approval. "It was the winter of 1895. A hard freeze hit northern Florida, killing all the citrus groves. The cold temperatures threatened to ruin Flagler's dream of making the state a winter destination for northerners. Meanwhile, Julia Tuttle, a young widow from Cleveland, had been pressing him to extend his railroad to Miami. He demurred, until he saw the ripe oranges and realized that Miami was frost-free. Not only did he build the line to Miami, he took it all the way to Key West."

"There isn't any railway to Key West."

"I know, but there was, and Flagler made the maiden voyage on it at the ripe old age of eighty-two."

Their food came. Simon asked Hilda for another beer. "A Pabst this time, please." He took the top bun off the hamburger and stared. "What's this?"

Ellie leaned toward his plate. "Looks like a very old piece of lettuce."

He prodded it. "Should I leave it on?"

"Yes, Simon. So, what happened to the Key West tracks?"

He sighed. "It's now the Overseas Highway, utilizing many of the bridges and trestles of Flagler's project. His East Coast Railway still runs from Miami to Jacksonville, but I'm pretty sure it only carries freight now."

She paused, fork in midair. "Wait a minute. Railroads. You said last night that Alvaredo might have come by train."

He tapped his can. "A possibility…but he'd have to go to Orlando to catch a passenger train."

"Couldn't he hop a freight train like the old hobos?"

"I think they have more security nowadays, but it's worth looking into. A bus would be too public."

"Hitched?"

"Nah."

"Stole a car?"

"Huh. Yeah, let's check with Amos—see if a hot car has been ditched around here recently." He pulled out his wallet and raised a finger at Hilda.

Ellie finished her wine. "So what did you think of Miami?"

"Unpleasant. It must have been such a paradise before all the development."

"You're really a nature boy, aren't you?"

"I'm interested in all kinds of things. Why, when I was studying the Mesoamerican Indians…"

"Another degree?"

Damn. She's got that glazed look again. Red alert. Downplay! Downplay! "Um, not precisely. As part of my anthropology degree, I spent a summer working in Mexico at Teotihuacan. No one knows who built it."

To his surprise, Ellie perked up. "It wasn't the Mayas?"

"Uh uh. The people of Teotihuacan flourished later, only overlapping the Maya by maybe a hundred years. They disappeared in the eighth century AD." He leaned toward her. "They recently found a tunnel underneath the Pyramid of the Moon. Wouldn't you love to explore it?"

Her eyes sparked with interest, but only for a moment. "I suppose…but Thad was talking about Aruba the other day, and that sounded so cool." She slowed, perhaps noticing Simon's reaction. "To be honest, I'd rather go to the Galapagos."

"Oh, that too!" Simon tried not to bob with excitement. "My ornithology professor—"

"Here's your check, Simon."

"Thanks, Hilda." The hostess swept her eyes over the waiting pack of hungry-eyed patrons and back to rest meaningfully on Simon and Ellie. "Er…Would you like us to vacate the premises?"

She took the cash and stepped aside to let them out.

On the sidewalk, Simon kept rolling the brim of his hat until it sprang out of his hands. He bent over to pick it up and mumbled, "Uh…Are you busy tonight?"

Ellie avoided his eyes. "Sorry—have some things to do." She indicated her car. "I've got to get back to the park now."

Just then, a silver Porsche pulled to the curb. Thad rolled down the window on the passenger side. "Hey, Ellie, see you later!"

She waved and turned back to Simon, only to find him walking rapidly away. "Simon!"

He slowed, his shoulders hunched. "Yeah?"

She was staring at him, an odd expression on her face. "Um…Do you want to go check out the railroad yard tomorrow?"

"Sure."

Her expression did not change. "Great."

Great? He watched her start the engine and ease out into the traffic. *I don't care what Santa says, I have no bloody chance with Ellie. Might as well forget it.* But he knew that wasn't going to happen as long as they worked together. *I could ask for a transfer.* And leave Amelia? *That's not gonna happen either.* He'd spent way too many years away. *The perennial student.* He turned the corner. *I've finally come home—or rather, found a home.* He squared his shoulders. *I'll just have to find a way to get her attention.* A little voice whispered in his head, "You might want to keep a lid on the avalanche of facts you spew out when you're nervous."

****

Jacksonville, Monday, April 30

"I love this drive down A1A. The wetlands, the ocean, the marshes." Ellie pointed out the window. "Oh look, a historic marker."

Simon glanced at it. "American Beach. It was founded by the first black millionaire in the US. One of the few beaches where African Americans could go when Florida was segregated. At one time, people flocked to it to hear entertainers like Duke Ellington, Ray Charles, and Cab Calloway." He shook his head. "Not much there now—except NaNa."

"NaNa?"

"The tallest sand dune in Florida."

"Let me guess: five feet high."

"Close. Sixty."

Ellie sat back. "I'm so glad I moved here."

Me too. "So what made you transfer here?"

"Besides my parents?"

"Maybe I should back up. Why did your parents move here?"

She pointed at the palm trees lining the road. Between them peeked the vivid green of the Atlantic. The cloudless sky above was the deep blue of promise. "Why would anyone *not* move here?"

"Okay, but you said they were lawyers. Is your dad retired?"

"Uh huh. He's a golfer."

" 'Nuf said." Simon always wondered why, with all the fantastic nature surrounding them, people would spend every waking moment batting at a little white ball, but he had given up speculating on the eccentricities of man, at least for Lent.

"Mom, on the other hand, despises golf—even miniature golf."

"What a deprived childhood you must have had."

"Oh, I made do. Anyway, after thirty years as a trial lawyer, she refused to sit on the veranda with a book and a mint julep waiting for Dad to get home. So she looked around for a job that entailed high drama, serial thrills, and a more than ninety-percent chance she'd hear gossip before anyone else did."

"A fact on which Debbie Daugherty is constantly harping."

"Who?"

"Never mind. So did you follow them to keep an eye on your mother?"

"I never intended to come down here, except on vacation. I'd finally wrangled a ranger position in the National Park Service and was packing my bags for Idaho when President Orloff appointed this…this fanatical Luddite as director. She redesignated national parks in Wyoming, Ohio, and Indiana as wildernesses—"

"That's illegal. The Wilderness Act of 1964 mandates that Congress alone can establish a wilderness area." *Shut* up, *Simon.*

"I know. She didn't care. The Feds under the last administration were so arrogant and unaccountable that she just ignored the outrage and ordered the park superintendents to move the ranger stations off the land

and closed it to all but hikers. She even said in a speech to the Natural Resources Defense Council that she would see to it no humans were allowed in at all. They applauded wildly."

"My, my."

"The Senate Energy and Natural Resources Committee scheduled hearings, but with the president's and the director's attitude, it was a safe bet nothing would change until the next election. A friend said Florida State Parks were hiring, so I applied and landed this cushy job." She regarded Simon solemnly. "They promised me: no corpses. Typical government spin."

"Well, Florida is a great state for parks and preserves. Of course it helps that half the land is under water. Did you know Disney World was built on a swamp? Old Walt had to scoop out the Seven Seas Lagoon and use the fill—a layer of dirt four yards high—to build the Magic Kingdom."

Ellie laughed. "Bet he got a good deal on the land though."

"Not really. Story goes that when developers got wind of his interest, the price per acre went from a hundred eighty to eighty thousand dollars."

"Oh." She gazed out the window for a long minute. "So, how far is the Jacksonville station?"

"We're coming up on it."

They parked and walked across a crisscross maze of railroad ties to a line of open cars. A locomotive hissed and moaned at the head as workers linked car after car to it. Simon scrambled over the rough ground to a lanky fellow wiping his streaming forehead with a rag. "You the foreman?"

"Yes, sir. What can I do for you?"

"I'm Simon Ribault, and this is Ellie Ironstone. We're State Park rangers from Amelia Island. We're investigating a murder."

The man didn't react. Simon wondered if he heard this kind of thing all the time.

Ellie explained. "The victim was a convict who escaped from a Miami prison. He washed up on the shore of Fernandina Beach two weeks ago."

"Prolly went by boat then."

"We can't find any evidence of that, so we're exploring the possibility that he came by train."

The man pointed at the coal car. "In that?"

Simon looked. "Well, not in a coal car. We know this line only carries freight, but we were thinking you may have closed cars."

Ellie added, "You know, with those big sliding doors. The ones the hobos rode on."

The man scratched his head. "Yeah, we get some."

"So do the cars move slow enough to allow a fellow to hop on?"

"Depends. Gotta be real good at it. Quick on your feet. And strong arms. Two kids killed a month ago. They were hitchin' on a southbound CSX. Couldn't hold on. Crushed."

"Oh."

A man came around the engine and shouted at the foreman. "Gotta go. Tell you what. See that shed over there?" He pointed at a small building covered in galvanized panels that stood against the chain link fence. A large sign on it said Station Master. "Dunno if Jeff's around today, but you could leave a note asking what trains came through coupla weeks ago."

"Will do. Thanks." Simon stuck out his hand, but

the guy was already halfway across the tracks. They walked to the shed. No one answered his knock.

Ellie found a clipboard hanging by the door. "It's got the schedule for the week ahead." She pulled it off the nail. "If they run the same trains on the same days, this might show what came through on Saturday." She read. "I don't understand this. It has 'intermodal trains,' 'rock trains,' and 'manifest trains.' What the hell are they?"

"Rock trains carry limestone from Miami to cement factories up the East Coast. About as comfortable as the coal cars. I'm not sure what the other two are, but they seem to run on Saturdays." He pulled out his phone and tapped in some letters. "Says here 'intermodal' trains have closed containers that can go from truck to train to ship." He stuck the phone in his pocket. "Methinks we might have found our Miguel's transport."

"What do you mean?"

"He could have sneaked into a container in the back of a truck in Miami, which was then loaded onto a train and then a ship."

"And never see the light of day. Brilliant."

"Right. Come on."

"Where are we going?"

"To the waterfront."

They drove west a few blocks until they hit the St. John's River. Filling slips along the pier were hundreds of boats, big and small—day sailers, sloops, pontoons, and huge yachts. At one end of the marina, houseboats lined the shore, looking as permanent as a mobile home park. Simon stopped a passing man. "Any freighters dock here?"

"Freighters? No. They go from Miami up to Baltimore or the big northern ports."

Ellie touched Simon's arm. "I've been thinking. If he stayed in the container all the way, he couldn't have fallen into the St. Marys River."

"And he couldn't have fetched up at Egan's Creek. Good point. So…"

"Maybe he got out in Jacksonville when the train was waiting to be off-loaded."

"And found a smaller boat to take him up the coast."

Simon turned to the man, who'd been occupying himself by lobbing appreciative glances at Ellie. "Any fishing boats here?"

"Spinnaker Charters has head boats."

"No, I mean commercial trawlers."

The man shook his head. "You might try Mayport. I think that's where they deliver the fresh fish."

Just as they reached the little village, it began to drizzle. They ran inside a seafood market. The fishmonger was happy to talk. "Nope, no fishermen based here. Boats come in from South America, Southeast Asia, North Carolina…lessee, Fernandina Beach—"

"Fernandina Beach? What do they catch?"

"Shrimp mostly, mahi-mahi, grouper, oysters."

"Huh. Well, thanks." They headed back to the car, Simon striding two paces ahead of Ellie.

"Wait!"

He halted to let her catch up. "Oh, sorry. I've got an idea."

She shook the raindrops off her hat. "Tell me about it on the way." They took the auto ferry across the St.

Johns River and headed north. "Okay, the idea. Give."

"I'm thinking I know how Miguel got to Fort Clinch."

"Bus?"

"No. He had an accomplice pick him up in Jacksonville."

"Who proceeded to kill him? Why?"

"Who knows? Criminals aren't particularly easygoing. They tend to take out their grievances in an uncivilized manner." He braked.

"What is it?"

"I have another idea."

"Two in one day? Let me write this down." When he didn't answer and made a sharp turn left onto a single-lane road, she poked him. "Well?"

"Miguel Alvaredo was found on the tiny spit of park land just north of the mouth of Egan's Creek. There's a marina across the creek—Panther Point. He could have been heading there."

"To rent a boat?"

"Uh huh. From there, he could sail down the Amelia River to St. Marys River and straight out to the Atlantic. After that he could go anywhere he wanted to."

"Worth a shot."

They drove past small farms with large vegetable gardens and turned north toward the Egan's Creek marshes. At the end of the road lay a cluster of houses, an ancient gas station and bait shop, and a storefront luncheonette advertising fried grouper cheeks. The rain let up as they got out of the car. Just beyond the gas station lay the wharf. A few outboard motorboats clustered around the dock. Farther out lay a couple of trawlers. In one, two men in high rubber boots sat on the deck separating shrimp from fish. Simon called, "Halloo there, Mr. Bailey. Mr. Garenflo."

Bailey—a grizzled old black man—raised his chin. "Yo, Simon, how ya doin'? Yo maw okay?"

"She's…uh…she's fine, Mr. Bailey. This is Ellie Ironstone. My partner." He beckoned her forward. She gave a shy half curtsy.

"Partner?" He guffawed. "Or yer main squeeze?"

"Leave him be, Linc. Whatcha want, Simon?" called the other fisherman.

"You heard about the dead folks we found up at the fort?"

"Sure. Foreigners."

Garenflo chimed in. "Big black woman. Jamaican man. Criminal."

Ellie's eyes widened, but Simon nodded calmly. "Yup. What makes you think the man is Jamaican?"

Bailey laughed. "His sense o'rhythm, man. Danced between two badasses."

The other man chuckled. "And his baaad sense of timing."

"What about the other two?"

"White guy. Escaped con. Tha's all we know."

"And the woman?"

"Clarence here thinks she must be same lady who waltzed in here mebbe a month ago wavin' dollar bills."

"Here?"

"Yas. Talked to Jo Jo." He nodded at a boat moored at the last floating dock. "He didn' like it. But she had da cash." They both laughed.

"Jo Jo? You mean Diogenes Goodwine? What did she want with him?"

"What does any Jamaican want?"

"Ganja?"

"Clarence here say no. Say she Santeria. She want chickens."

"Hey! I niver said no such thang. You full of it, Linc."

Simon broke up the burgeoning quarrel. "You remember her name?"

"Dint give no name."

Bailey took out a wad of chewing tobacco and stuffed it under his lip. "Fancied herself a pirate, she did. Shaved her head to look scarier."

Simon and Ellie stared at each other. *Shaved her head?* He turned to Clarence. "So where is Jo Jo?"

"Ain't seen him for two weeks. Came back from a trip to Jacksonville, anchored there, and skipped out."

Simon was already moving. Ellie called, "Where are you going?"

"To check out the boat."

He walked down the dock to where the trawler was tied up. "Yoo hoo! Anybody there?" After a silent minute, he climbed aboard. Ellie stayed on shore. "Come on."

"What for?"

"If this boat came back from Jacksonville on Saturday, April 14, and has been here ever since…"

"It may have been involved in our little drama. This woman…Simon, if her head was shaved, like the victim…they could be one and the same."

"Agreed, although we've only got gossip to go on. We should have Amos show Bailey and Garenflo a photo of the dead woman, see if they identify her as the one they saw with Goodwine."

She clambered over the side and started examining the bow. "Nothing here."

"Check the stern. I'm going below."

Ellie systematically searched the stern, lifting up seat cushions soaked from the rain and opening storage lockers. A rope sat in a jumbled heap by the cockpit wall. Under a small fold-out table, she noticed a red stain and bent down. It was dry. She scraped her fingernail in it and brought it to her nose. "Blood. I found blood, Simon!"

"A lot?"

"Puddle about six inches in diameter."

"That's nothing. I found a *lot* of blood. Oh, and a body."

Before Ellie could make it to the gangway, Simon came up, his phone to his ear. "Yes, we're at the Panther Point Marina. Boat named…" He raised an eyebrow at Ellie who dutifully looked over the side.

"*Mercy Louise.*"

"*Mercy Louise.* What? Oh, I'd say quite a while. Yes, we'll wait here."

Ellie tried to peer past him. "Who is it?"

"I'm guessing it's Captain Goodwine."

"How did he die?"

"Can't tell. Don't want to disturb the crime scene. Better wait."

Two hours later, Virgil and Iggy carried a stretcher out to an ambulance. A detective came up from the cabin.

Simon held up a hand. "So? What does the forensics guy say, Zack?"

"He died from loss of blood."

"And how did he lose this blood?"

"When a sharp object, maybe a Bowie knife, passed through his right side. Bled out."

"Any sign of the knife?" When Zack shook his head, he asked, "Did he die right away?"

"Don't think so. From the trail of blood stains, he was probably stabbed up on deck, then stumbled down into the galley."

"But…" Ellie seemed puzzled. "If he was at sea when he died, how did he manage to get back here?"

Zack gave her an odd look. "What makes you think he was at sea?"

Before she could answer, a chubby man in a T-shirt marked Nassau County CSI rounded the wheelhouse, stuffing a small brown envelope into his tote bag.

"Any trace of the murder weapon?"

"Not yet." He yelled down the gangway. "Steve? Find anything below?"

A disembodied voice called, "Blood. Looks like several sets of fingerprints…"

"What about the hold?"

"Opening it now…Wait a minute. Oh, yum." A head topped by fiery red hair and freckles that clashed with his grim expression popped up in the hatch. He lifted a fist, in it a square package wrapped in cloth and tied with string. Simon could make out the words *Cane Sugar, Product of Costa Rica*.

"That the only one?"

"I'll wager we had a bumper crop of sugar cane recently."

Ellie pushed past Simon. "What is it?"

"Cocaine, ma'am. Lots and lots of it."

Chapter Eight
Pirates of the Caribbean

Park headquarters, Tuesday, May 1

Simon and Ellie had just finished telling Hosea about their adventures when the office phone rang.

Hosea picked it up. "Oh? Sure, send him along." He hung up. "Some fellow from the Jamaican police department is here. Wants to see me."

"Jamaica? *Hmm.*"

Ellie looked at Simon. "Our lady victim?"

"We could be in for a break in the case."

A few minutes later a slight, very dark man came through the door, shaking out an umbrella. From his grave demeanor, Simon put him in his thirties, although his smooth skin and crew cut made him look younger.

"Is it the rainy season here? I have yet to see the sun, and I've been in Florida for a week."

"It usually starts next month, but yes, we've had quite a bit of rain in the last couple of days." Hosea took the man's raincoat and offered him a chair. "I'm the park superintendent, Hosea Barnes. What can I do for you?"

The man flashed his badge. "Detective Patrice Labadie from the Montego Bay police department. I am searching for a colleague, a Detective Sergeant Winston Virtue. He was last seen in Jacksonville."

Hosea started to say something, but Simon interrupted. "Was he on the trail of someone?"

"Yes. For several years now, he's been working undercover to infiltrate a gang that has been smuggling marijuana and cocaine through Jamaica and up the East Coast. According to Virtue, their MO is to transfer the drugs from ship to ship over short distances between small marinas and fishing ports. That way they could skip the larger ports, the ones with tight security."

Ellie and Simon exchanged looks. *Alvaredo?* "Miami has probably the tightest security in the US."

"Yes, but a little farther north is Fort Pierce. It's quite small, mainly pleasure yachts and some commercial fishing."

Ellie stood up. "Would you like some coffee, Detective Labadie?"

His face lit up in a smile, his strong, white teeth flashing. "I would love some."

"Cream? Sugar?"

"Yes, please."

As Ellie pulled a chipped white mug from the cabinet, Hosea leaned forward. "So, why are you in Fernandina Beach?"

"As I say, Winston had been ingratiating himself with the gang leader, trying to get on one of their runs. He finally got a call from her about a month ago. A sailor had fallen sick, and they needed a substitute. He flew to Miami to check it out."

Ellie handed the Jamaican a steaming cup and glanced inquiringly at Simon.

Simon, tapping his fingers on the desk impatiently, shook his head. Facing Labadie, he barked, "And?"

"He managed to wangle a berth. They sailed from

Fort Pierce up the coast, but we lost touch with him after Jacksonville. Fernandina being the next small port, I came up here. I had no luck at the port authority or the marina, but the marina dockmaster told me about the recent discoveries at this park, and I thought I'd inquire if you had any information."

Ellie, who had been staring out the window, started and looked at the detective. "Wait a minute. The gang leader. Did I hear you say 'her'?"

"Yes. She is a woman who goes by the name of Odessa Bonney. According to reports, as big as she is strong. And very, very mean."

Simon muttered something.

"What was that?"

"Is your drug smuggler by any chance Rasta?"

The man curled his lip. "No. At least, not a true Rastafarian."

Simon looked meaningfully at Ellie. "Why not?"

"According to Virtue, she asserts she is, but doesn't practice any of the tenets of the religion. What she's really pursuing is a new Back to Africa movement. With the proceeds from the drug trafficking as seed money, she plans to establish a country in Africa for American blacks."

"Like Marcus Garvey." Simon was thoughtful. "Does she have a tattoo of him?"

He seemed surprised by the question. "Not in any of the photos I've seen of her."

Ellie stated, "Not dispositive. It wouldn't show in any picture."

Hosea poured more coffee into his cup. "Wait a minute. Didn't they already do that? Go back to Africa? Wasn't Liberia established as a new home for the descendants of freed slaves?"

"Yes, but Bonney claims it doesn't count because white people helped found it. She says it was just a cover for getting rid of undesirables—crooks and thugs."

Ellie murmured, "I believe all the land in Africa is currently taken. Does she plan to conquer Togo or something?"

Labadie almost laughed. "I'm not sure she's thought it through that far."

Simon said heavily, "I don't think it's going to happen."

"Well, I know that, but why do you?"

"Because I'm pretty sure she's the woman whose remains we found on the shore two weeks ago."

Labadie pulled a photo from his briefcase. "Is this her?"

The three rangers studied it. "She's younger here, but the grimace looks familiar."

Simon looked up. "This one has dreadlocks. The woman we found had her head shaved."

Ellie plucked his sleeve. "Didn't Frog say the Fernandina shrimper captain wore dreadlocks?"

"That's right, but Garenflo—"

"Who?"

Simon answered Labadie. "A man who works at a marina near where the last victim was found." He directed his next words at Hosea. "He told us the woman who hired Jo Jo was bald."

"To look more frightening," Ellie added.

"What does one have to do with the other?" Hosea seemed confused.

"There's a sunken boat at the marina. Salvatore

Poli said it belonged to a female shrimper. He says she abandoned it a few weeks ago and went off to look for another."

"We think to Panther Point Marina and Captain Goodwine."

Labadie sat up. "Where is the first boat?"

"At the Fernandina Beach marina, but last time we saw it, it was up to the gunnels in water."

"And it may have nothing to do with our victim."

"*Hmm.*" He looked thoughtful. "Still, it's worth a look. Perhaps someone there would recognize Bonney's photo." He dropped the picture of Bonney on the desk and slid it over to the superintendent.

Hosea looked at Simon. "Where's it moored?"

"Dock B. Someone should also take both photos of Bonney to the fellows at Panther Point."

"I'll get Maurice from Nassau County CSI to do it." When Hosea got off the phone, Labadie said, "I understand there were three victims. Have you identified them yet?"

"Actually, there are four. The captain of the shrimper Bonney may have hired was found dead on his boat. Of the three that washed up, the only one whose identity we've confirmed is Miguel Alvaredo, a man who escaped a Miami prison."

"And now Bonney." Labadie pursed his lips. "This Alvaredo may have signed on to Bonney's crew. I have no knowledge of him." He pulled another photo out. "How about this person? Do you recognize him?"

Hosea tapped the picture. "The third man. Is this your detective sergeant?"

"Yes. Winston Virtue." He sighed. "This is most unfortunate." He put the photo back in his briefcase.

Ellie whispered to Simon, "So Bailey and Garenflo were right about him."

"Caught between two badasses? Yes, I guess so." Simon turned to Hosea. "All right. Now we know who victims number two and three are. Since they're Jamaican, that might explain why the FBI had no records on them."

Labadie looked up. "What have you done with the bodies?"

"Bonney and Virtue are still at the morgue. Now that we have identities, we can dispose of them."

"I'd like to take Virtue home. His family will want a memorial service. And closure."

"Don't see why not." Hosea picked up the phone again. "Fred? Can you put Kenny on? Thanks...Kenny? I have a Detective Patrice Labadie from Jamaica here. He's identified our other two victims. Can we come down to Jacksonville? Good. Right now. Okay." He got his hat. "Let's go."

"Who's going to mind the store?"

"Rosie and Thad. Jack's coming in too. And that new volunteer—what's her name? Martha?"

Simon pulled out his phone. "I'll let them know, then we'll follow you."

Labadie jiggled his keys. "Why don't we take my rental car, Superintendent? You can direct me."

"Good idea...Wait, are you coming back here?"

"Oh dear, I forgot. I have some other things to do this afternoon."

Hosea pointed a chin at Ellie. "That's okay. I'll ride back with them."

They parked near the coroner's office on Jefferson Street and followed the receptionist to the morgue. The

Jamaican policeman confirmed the identities and studied the reports. "Odessa drowned? That's surprising."

"Why?"

"She was a pirate, a sailor. Fancied herself the descendant of Anne Bonney, a female buccaneer and scourge of Jamaica."

Ellie and Simon shared a glance. "Argus thought she was a pirate. Or was it Clarence?"

Labadie said, "According to Winston, she had a knife the size of a saber."

"Could it be the one that killed Virtue and Alvaredo?"

"I have no idea. I never saw it." The detective frowned. "I wonder what happened."

"Maybe we'll never know. All four people are dead."

"Four? Oh, yes, the boat's captain. Do we know for sure they were on his boat?"

"CSI found fingerprints on the deck and cocaine in the hold. They've matched the fingerprints to three of the victims so far. Plus we have the testimony of Mr. Bailey and Mr. Garenflo that a female Jamaican contracted with Jo Jo. If they confirm the photos, we'll have definite proof."

Ellie nodded at the detective. "Together with Virtue's report that he signed on with her, we should have enough evidence."

"Yes." He pointed at the body of Captain Goodwine. "How did he die?"

"Stabbed, like the other two."

"With the same knife?"

"We don't know."

135

"So…" Labadie rubbed his chin. "How did the boat get back to port if they were all dead?"

Simon looked at Hosea, who looked at Ellie, who looked at the ground. "Um."

"Um."

"Um."

"Maybe…" Simon rubbed his chin. "Maybe Goodwine was in the marina when he died."

"But what about Alvaredo then? He and Virtue were killed with the same knife and both washed up on the shore."

"Yeah, Alvaredo about a mile from the little marina where the boat was moored. Tide could've carried him out."

Hosea harrumphed. "First, we have to confirm that the knife we found in Alvaredo's back killed the captain."

"And that the knife belonged to Bonney."

"Then we have to figure out how Alvaredo is related to the other two, and when and where Virtue was killed."

The detective blinked. "Why?"

"Because they were found over a two-mile range."

"Okay, but I'd still like to take Virtue's body with me."

"Can you hold off for a few days?"

"I suppose. I'll go back to my hotel and let headquarters know. And break the news to his family."

"Where are you staying?"

"The Ritz-Carlton."

Simon's lips formed an *O* but before he could whistle, Hosea laid a warning hand on his arm. "That's a very nice hotel."

The man shook his head. "I'm afraid it's a bit rich for my policeman's salary even with the per diem, but it was the only hotel with space at the last minute." He checked his watch. "Speaking of, could you recommend a reasonable restaurant in Fernandina Beach? I have another appointment."

Ellie said, "There's a Mexican place on Centre Street."

Both Simon and Hosea stared at her. "We...um...don't eat there."

"How come?"

"You might want to check the inspection reports. Just sayin'."

"Okay, what do you recommend?"

Simon immediately said, "El Toro. It's on South Fourth Street, just off Centre. Best Spanish food in northeast Florida."

"Sounds good. Thanks."

They all left the morgue, trailed by Hosea. Labadie drove off.

Hosea fanned his red face. "What now?"

Simon took the driver's seat. "I'll drop you two off at the park. I want to see if I can hook up with our Mr. Gregory."

Ellie spoke from the back seat. "I'm going with you."

"I thought you were on duty with Thad this afternoon?"

"Oh...er...yes." Flustered, she muttered, "I'd forgotten."

Simon goggled at her. "How is that possible?"

She seemed genuinely perplexed. "I don't know."

Simon called Ellie later that night. "How was your

day?"

"Nothing very eventful." She paused. "Not like when I'm working with you."

He laughed. "Well, you'll be looking forward to tomorrow then. I failed in my quest today, so I'm going to attempt a rendezvous with the slippery Mr. Gregory at two."

"I'm coming."

"I thought you might."

****

Gregory's office, Wednesday, May 2

They pulled into the parking lot of the old school house and climbed the stairs. Nora was at the reception desk. "Hello…Miss Wilson, isn't it?"

She gave them a less than welcoming look. "Yes. Can I help you?"

Simon dredged up a hearty air of bonhomie. "We're back! Rangers Ribault and Ironstone at your service. You said Mr. Gregory would be in this week before his trip to Cuba. We'd like a few minutes with him."

She pretended to check her day book. "I'm afraid he's not in today. I can ask him when he calls."

"You don't have his schedule?"

"No. He calls in regularly, and I relay any requests at that time."

"And what time is that?"

On the brink of falling into what he hoped was a clever trap, she stepped back. With a gleam in her eye, she smiled. "He's already called in today. You'll have to come back tomorrow."

"I see. So he never comes into the office?"

"Sometimes."

"And when does he go to Cuba?"

"Um…next week. I don't have the exact day." She dropped her gaze.

"Well, thank you."

As they walked down the corridor, a man pushed past them, head down and swinging his arms like a pugilist. Simon swerved, catching the man's sleeve. "Why, Mr. Gregory, I'm so glad we didn't miss you." When the man shook him off, he loped after him and nicked inside just before the man could slam the door. Ellie stuck her foot between the jamb and door and forced it open.

Gregory faced them. Of middle height, he sported a salt and pepper goatee and a military buzz cut. His small eyes blazed black with anger. "Who are you and what do you want?"

Simon tipped his hat. "We're from Fort Clinch State Park, and we'd like to talk to you. Shall we go into your office?"

"We can talk here."

Simon gestured at Nora. "You would prefer to discuss the murders in front of Miss Wilson?"

His eyes closed to slits. "Murders?"

"After you."

Gregory hesitated only an instant, then led the way into an inner office and closed the door. "What's this all about?"

"I'm Simon Ribault, and this is my partner, Ellie Ironstone. We're park rangers at the fort. Your League of the Green Cross held an event there on Saturday, April 14. On Sunday the fifteenth, three bodies were discovered on park property—one of them directly under the walls of the fort. We'd like to know if you heard or saw anything unusual that night."

His face relaxed a little. "I'm afraid we didn't hear anything outside of the fort. It was a large event. We had a band, and there were barbecue grills going."

Ellie started to say something, but Simon put a hand on her arm. "You might want to tell the truth. We *are* talking about murder."

The man rose from his chair, his cheeks blazing. "How dare you!"

"We know you canceled the band and the food. We also know you failed to reimburse Judy Holiday for the total cost. You did, however, hold an event in the room under the *pas de souris* stairs. So if anyone, say, screamed, you likely would have heard it."

Gregory sat down again. In a steady voice, he said, "I heard nothing."

"How long were you there?"

"I arrived early. Most of the guests came about eight."

"And left?"

"Maybe eleven, eleven thirty."

"Could we have the guest list? We'd like to interview them."

"Absolutely not. I do not disclose members' names."

"I see." Simon's mouth turned down in an almost believable display of regret. "I hate to have to take this to Judge Farnsworth. His son works with us at the fort, and he is a big promoter of our park. I know he would frown upon any…questionable activities going on there."

Gregory jumped up again and pounded his fist on the table. When Simon continued to stand quietly, he snapped, "I'll see what I can do. But if you go snooping in the League's affairs, I won't hesitate to press charges."

"For what?"

"Harassment. Infringement of civil rights. Abuse of power."

Ellie's eyes grew wide. "Oh my. How exciting. I've never been accused of police brutality before."

This speech had an unexpected effect on Gregory. He burst out laughing. "All right, all right. I'll get back to you." He escorted them out past the uneffusive Nora. They could hear raised voices as they strolled down the hall.

"Wait a minute." Simon swung around and pushed back through the office door. Ellie held it open.

"Mr. Gregory?"

The man turned from the cowering Nora and snarled, "What *now*?"

"Did you happen to take a file from Fort Clinch park headquarters?"

His face closed down. In a low growl, he said, "Get out."

They left. "I guess we have our answer."

As they got in the car, Simon chuckled. "Volatile kinda feller, isn't he?"

"I guess it keeps his heating bills low." Ellie rolled the window down and let the breeze cool her face. "What do you think made him suddenly acquiesce?"

"Your incredible beauty?"

"Which he only noticed after twenty minutes?"

"Your quirky sense of humor?"

"I wasn't joking."

"Your exquisite timing?"

"Doubt it. Know what I think? I think our Mr. Gregory is hiding something, but that underneath he's a pretty good guy."

"Huh. What is this, some sort of fey feminine intuition?"

"Maybe."

Simon decided not to pursue an obviously losing hand. "All right, tomorrow I shall petition Miss Wilson for the guest list. Here's hoping somebody on it squeals."

"Aren't we only concerned with them as witnesses?"

"Yes, but I also think you're right. Our Mr. Gregory *is* hiding something. I'd like to take a crack at what it is."

"Thank you for taking me seriously." Ellie kissed his cheek.

His foot went down on the accelerator, and they burst through a red light, narrowly missing a little red sports car.

"Hey!" Georgia raised a middle finger at her best friend.

In response, Simon turned on his flashing light and roared down the street. *With any luck, she'll think we're answering a distress call.*

"What on earth are you doing, Simon?"

"Um…acting important?"

"Well, for heaven's sake, slow down. I saw Bobby in the squad car at that last intersection. You want a ticket?"

"He can't give me a ticket. I'm a park ranger."

Just then, a siren started up behind them.

Chapter Nine
Little Green Men

Fernandina Beach Police Station, Wednesday, May 2

"Thanks for lending me the money, Ellie. I find myself a little short of cash this time every month."

"Really?"

Simon pretended not to notice Ellie's pointed glance at the calendar and handed the bills to the desk sergeant. "We square, Tommy?"

"For now. Don't let me catch you playing around with your emergency equipment again, Simon. They're not toys, you know."

"Yes, Tommy. I'll be good, Tommy." He rifled through his wallet and pulled out a five-dollar bill. "Here. Get yourself a new coffeemaker."

Ellie grabbed Simon and pulled him through the revolving door. He headed to his car. She got there first. "I'll drive you home."

"What? How will I get to work in the morning?"

"I'll pick you up."

When they pulled up in front of Simon's bungalow on Wolff Street, a familiar red Miata sat in the driveway. Steam poured out of its hood, mixed with the steam rising from Georgia's head.

Ellie gently shoved Simon out of the car and roared

off. He stumbled over to Georgia. She stood, arms crossed tightly across her pert breasts. "Why aren't you in jail?"

"Because my *real* friend Ellie bailed me out."

"What!"

He said smugly, "I only had to pay a fine for the moving violation."

"But I specifically told Bobby to arrest you."

"Apparently, Bobby is more afraid of Ellie than he is of you. Go figure."

"Wait'll I pass the bar. You'll be sorry." Georgia pushed Simon aside and went straight to the kitchen. "You got anything besides Pabst?"

"Damn, I keep forgetting to pick up that peach-flavored wine spritzer." He fluttered his lashes. "I know it's your favorite."

She opened the tab on a can of beer. "So, how are you progressing with the delicate damsel in khaki?"

"Don't start on me, Georgia. I'm trying to focus on the murder case."

"Okay. What's going on with that?"

He told her about Gregory and about the Jamaican detective.

"So you're really moving on this case. You've identified all four victims and the murder weapon. You know what this woman was doing and why."

"Yes, but what *happened?* What went wrong? Why did they all end up dead?"

"How did the pirate—Odessa—die? Who killed her?"

"She's our one ringer. She might not have been murdered at all."

"Huh?"

144

"According to Kenny, she drowned."

The telephone rang. "Hi, Santa. Yes, she is. I'll tell her." He tapped the phone. "Your Dad says you promised to take him to the grocery store."

"Oops! I forgot all about it."

"This is what happens when you allow your obsessive lust for revenge to distract you."

"Yeah, yeah." She picked up her purse.

Simon's phone buzzed again. "Ellie?"

Georgia threw a smooch at the phone.

"Really? Great. We'll get started first thing. I'll be ready at eight…nine it is." At Georgia's raised eyebrows, he said, "Miss Wilson sent over the guest list for the Green event."

"You're going to interview them."

"Yes. Ellie says there are some *very* interesting names on the list."

****

Park headquarters, Thursday, May 3

"Okay, let's see it." Simon whistled. "The mayor?"

"Uh huh. And Nathan Hearst, the *Register* publisher."

"And Judge Lester Farnsworth. No wonder Gregory seemed unimpressed when I dropped his name." He peered over her shoulder. "Looks like all the city fathers are involved. Do you suppose the Green League is in and the Freemasons are out?"

"No idea." Ellie kept reading. "Lisabet de Angeles. Who's she?"

"Lizzy? She owns El Toro in Old Town. Used to be on the town council. Still pretty influential."

"El Toro. Didn't you tell Detective Labadie to go there?"

"Best Spanish restaurant between here and Miami. I can just taste her *vaca frita*."

"*Vaca*…whatta?"

"Fried cow. It's shredded flank steak topped with onions."

"I thought you only ate hamburgers."

"I said beef. Hamburgers are just the most efficient delivery system. Besides, *vaca frita* is really just another form of chopped beef."

"That impressive ability to spin should have landed you a PR job. So…Ms. de Angeles is a business woman. A city mother, as it were."

"Who else?"

Ellie consulted the list. "There's just one more name."

"Go on."

"You're not going to like it—or rather, Hosea won't. It's Sylvia Barnes."

"Amos's wife? Not so strange. She does pull some weight around here, if not in an official capacity. She fundraises for several causes—Friends of the Pupfish and Monkeys National Monument, Crusade for Protein, Cuban American National Foundation, that sort of thing."

"Well, we still don't know what the Green group's mission is—maybe it's a charity."

He touched the paper. "That's five. Judy said there were ten at the meeting. Who else?"

"Number six must be Gregory himself."

"That still leaves four. We'll have to pry the others out of him. I think it's time we paid another visit to our import/export entrepreneur."

"Ahead of the interviews?"

"Yes." He picked up his hat.

To their surprise, Mr. Gregory was in. "You got the list?"

"Yes, thanks. There seem to be some names missing."

He didn't equivocate. "Mine, of course. The others are charter members and organizing partners. They prefer to remain anonymous."

"I see. Before we talk to your guests, it might help if we know what your mission is."

"Certainly." His tone was as smooth as a baby's bottom.

It occurred to Simon that the man was being remarkably cooperative this morning. *I wonder what's changed?*

Gregory pulled out a glossy brochure. "You've heard of Sister Cities International, right?"

Ellie ventured, "Isn't that the group that sets up cultural exchanges between cities in different countries?"

"Right. Not just cultural, but educational, municipal, and business connections as well. For example, Miami is a sister city to Lima, Peru, and Tallahassee to St. Maarten."

"And the Green League is involved in this?"

"We hope so. With the recent rapprochement between the US and Cuba, thanks to our former...president..."

Did his eyes just flicker?

"...my company has been exploring opportunities for importing Cuban goods. The possibility of partnering with Havana as a sister city is under consideration—as a goodwill gesture."

Ellie's eyes bugged out. "You're kidding."

His eyes definitely flickered that time.

"My colleagues and I think it will help bring economic and social prosperity to both our nations." He handed Ellie the brochure. "Here, this explains the concept. We are still working on our own prospectus but should have it within the week. Our meetings have been very productive." He smiled. "Does that help?"

"But—"

Simon interrupted, his hand squeezing Ellie's arm. "Yes, thanks so much. We'll be in touch. We'd appreciate it if you told your colleagues we have your approval to contact them."

"Not a problem." He ushered them out.

When they reached the parking lot, Ellie puffed, "Okay, who's on first?"

"Who's on third."

"You win. Should we start at the top?"

"Mayor Crowley? All right."

They drove to City Hall. Simon marched into the mayor's reception area and announced curtly, "Miss Teresa, I want to see Randall. Park business."

The diminutive brown-skinned woman, her dove gray hair pulled back in a severe bun, pursed her lips. "Simon, you haven't changed since the fifth grade. You were a martinet as the school monitor, and you're a martinet now. Ordering people around like that…you want me to tell your mama how you've been acting?"

Simon's shoulders sagged. "I'm sorry, Miss Teresa. I was rude. Please don't tell Ma. She's on my case as it is."

Ellie tugged on his sleeve. "Introduce me," she whispered.

"May I present Ellie Ironstone? She's a park ranger. Like me."

The old lady turned gracious eyes on Ellie. "Oh, yes, you're the young lady from Virginia. Welcome to Geechee land."

Simon laughed. "Miss Teresa comes from one of the most prominent Geechee families on the island. They've been here since 1752. She taught me fourth grade."

"And manners, mister."

"And manners." He bowed. "Miss Teresa? We would very much like to talk to Mayor Crowley. It's about the murders."

"Oh my, yes. I heard one body was found near the fort the day after the mayor attended an event there. It was most upsetting. His wife is still nervous about it. She's positive it was a case of mistaken identity—that the killer meant to assassinate her husband. Some kind of an anarchist." She sniffed. "Hardly likely."

"Why do you say that?"

"What good would that do? Assassinating the mayor of a beach town in the middle of nowhere would hardly create the kind of chaos anarchists seek. No, sir. You go after icons like George Clooney or Carrot Top. That would shake people up."

Simon dragged a staring Ellie toward an inner door. At that moment, it opened. "Miss Teresa? What…oh hi, Simon."

"Randall. We only need a minute of your time."

The man, more belly than legs, although his head could have been used as a whiffle ball, gave Teresa a meek glance. "Is it okay?"

"Yes, sir. You go on and have a nice chat with

Simon, but remember, you have a meeting with Mr. Hearst and Judge Farnsworth at three."

The man led the way into his office and pointed at two visitor's chairs. "This is what happens when you hire your elementary school teacher as secretary." He donned a broad smile. "And who, may I inquire, is this lovely lady?"

"This is Ellie Ironstone. We're partners, and we're investigating the murder of four people found on Fort Clinch property."

"I heard that only three of the four were within the park limits."

For the first time, Ellie saw Simon hesitate. She spoke up. "True, but the deaths are related. We're helping the police where we can by interviewing everyone who was at the park Saturday, April 14, and Sunday, April 15."

Crowley fiddled with a pen. "I, uh…let me see."

Simon interrupted him. "You were at an event sponsored by the League of the Green Cross, Randall. We have the guest list."

"Oh, in that case. It's just…we're in the very beginning stages, and we don't want it to be public knowledge yet."

"I see. Beginning stage of what?"

His voice dropped. "We want to become a sister city to Havana. See, we're not yet sure how people will react. I mean, here in Florida, there's a lot of anti-Castro feeling, but Lester and I think it could really boost our tourist income. Nate isn't entirely on board, but I'm sure he'll come around."

"I see." Simon's face was blank. "Was the Saturday meeting your first?"

The mayor clearly didn't want to look like he was playing catchup. "Well, some of us have been discussing the idea since President Orloff dropped the travel restrictions to Cuba at the end of his term. We—"

Simon interrupted. "I thought his move was rather controversial—that it's not clear he had the authority to do what he did."

He puffed his chest out. "Let's leave that to Congress, shall we? After all, they haven't repealed or repudiated any of his orders so far, and he, shall we say, bent the limits of his authority for his entire tenure."

Simon pressed his lips together. Ellie said, "Perhaps we should get to the reason for our visit. The meeting started at seven and ended about eleven, correct?"

"Actually, no. We were supposed to have a barbecue and some entertainment, but at the last minute Gregory called it off. I think he couldn't get the crowd he'd hoped for."

"So just a small group met—when?"

"After dark, around eight o'clock. Gregory had a private room set up for us. He gave a presentation and introduced the man he hired as translator."

"Translator?"

"Fellow by the name of Martí. Gregory said we'll likely need his help in the negotiations."

"He's not a partner?"

"No, I don't think so."

Still, it gives us seven attendees. Only three to go. "Mr. Gregory told us there were ten guests. Who else came?"

Crowley moved restlessly. "Carson didn't want to publicize the other names yet."

Simon persisted. "But you know who they are."

The mayor frowned. "Now, Simon…"

I'd better back off a bit. "I see. During the event, did you see or hear anything unusual in or around the fort?"

"No. We just had our meeting and went home."

"Did everybody arrive at the same time?"

"Pretty much. Gregory and Marti were there when I arrived."

"Were the silent partners there?"

Crowley had grown increasingly agitated. "Look, I can't tell you any more, okay?"

Damn.

Ellie resumed. "Did everyone leave at the same time?"

"I think so. I came with Nate. The rest came in separate cars."

Simon rose. "Well, thanks, Randall."

The mayor eyed Simon. "You won't tell anyone about our little scheme, will you?"

"No. I'll leave that to Miss Teresa."

His eyes bugged out. "Oh, dear." They left him pulling out his phone.

"Okay, I think Lester's at the Historic Courthouse today. Let's try him next." They drove to Centre Street and parked in the spot marked Police Cars Only. Inside, the young woman started to remonstrate but, when she saw their uniforms, asked how she could help. "Is Judge Farnsworth in his office?"

"Yes. He presides on Thursdays, but today he's working on the docket."

"May we see him? It's part of an investigation."

"Go on upstairs. Olive can take you in."

A middle-aged woman in a finely tailored scarlet suit sat at a small desk in the antechamber. "Hi, Simon."

"Hi, Olive. Can we see Lester for a minute?"

"I'll check." She looked at Ellie. "And you are?"

"This is Ellie Ironstone. She's new on the force—"

Olive rolled her eyes. "What is this, NYPD Blue?"

"Okay, okay. She's the new ranger. We're investigating the recent deaths."

"Oh my! Go right in, then."

When they entered, the judge was just setting his phone down. He rose and stretched out a hand. Ellie gasped. Simon knew it was because he looked like a much older, more pompous—*as if that were possible*—version of Thad. The buttons of his silk waistcoat strained against the product of many a beef-heavy meal, while his suspiciously blond hair rolled in waves over the wide beach of his forehead. When he spoke, his stentorian tones rang in the room. "I'm just off the phone with Randall. I understand you're asking about our little affair."

"Actually, we're only interested in your meeting of April 14 at Fort Clinch."

He shook his massive head sadly. "Terrible business. I understand they found a fourth victim. Does Amos think we're looking at a serial killer?"

Ellie opened her mouth, but Simon jumped in. "We're leaving the criminal investigation to the police, but since three of the bodies were discovered on park property, we're pursuing that angle. Now, you were at the fort from what time?"

"About eight."

"Did you come alone?"

"Yes."

"And when did you leave?"

"We all left at the same time—around eleven thirty, I believe."

"All? Who was there?"

"I thought you had the list?"

"We're missing a couple of names."

He pushed his lower lip out. "I don't know if I'm supposed to tell you."

Sigh. "We have Randall, you, Nathan, Lisabet de Angeles, and Sylvia Barnes."

"And Gregory."

"Anyone else?"

"Um…Oh yes, that translator. Gregory hired him to help. Spanish fellow. Can't remember his name."

"Anyone else?"

The big man turned his back to them and faced the window. "That's my recollection."

Ellie jostled Simon's elbow. He knew she was telling him to give it a rest. *I suppose we'll find out who they are soon enough.* "Did you hear or see anything that caught your attention? Anything outside?"

"No. I thought about it after Randall called. It was very quiet."

"Okay. Thanks." Simon rose. "If you think of anything, let us know, would you?"

"Sure." He emitted an artificial laugh. "So, how's my boy doing?"

Simon cracked a smile. "He's holding the fort."

As they hit the sidewalk, Ellie's stomach growled. "Lunch time."

"Why don't we walk down to the Florida House Inn? Libby's is having a special lunch buffet—ten dollars gets you her prize-winning fried chicken and all the trimmings."

"Wait a minute. First *vaca...vaca...*"

"*Vaca frita.*"

"And now this? What has the world come to?"

Maybe I have *been in a rut. She probably thinks I'm dull as dishwater in everything, including...well...* "I mean, the chicken would be for you. I'm quite content with my standard fare."

She eyed him. "I'm beginning to wonder if your, shall we say, *singular* palate is just an act. Admit it, you're a closet gourmet."

"I used to be."

"The Nero Wolfe days?"

"Uh huh. I would try anything. Ask Georgia." He closed his eyes. "I can still taste that goldfish—like a rather gamey oyster."

"Let me guess, after that you turned to ground beef."

"No, I went through several fads, or rather, phases. Let's see. There was the paleo diet. That's when I was working on the cave paintings at Lascaux. During my Kurt Vonnegut period, I subsisted on the two-martini breakfast. For one awful month, I gave the all-carrot diet a try."

"Why awful?"

"I turned bright orange. That's when I decided to stick with beef. I've been clean and sober ever since."

She looked him over, her eyes twinkling. "That explains the yellowish cast to your tan." When he started to huff, she grinned. "It becomes you."

They walked down to Third Street and entered the side door next to the venerable nineteenth-century inn.

"This place always reminds me of a land-locked sternwheeler."

"You mean the wide porch and upper gallery? The inn was originally a boarding house for the workers David Yulee imported to construct his Florida Railroad."

"Another railroad? Gosh, it seems that's all anybody built in Florida."

"It was the only way for the Flaglers and Plants, Ringlings, and Chipleys to ferry their northern customers to the grand hotels they were building. Yulee is known as the Father of Florida Railroads, although I'm not sure why. This one only lasted a few years."

"Where did it go? I mean run?"

"Across the state, from Fernandina to Cedar Key. Yulee completed it in 1861, but within a couple of years, successive assaults of Union and Confederate soldiers destroyed most of the rolling stock and equipment. It went through several restructurings."

Ellie whistled. "As you say, building railroads is a tricky business."

The hostess approached.

"Hey, Zoe, any chance of a table?"

"Hi, Simon." She looked around. "It'll be a ten-minute wait, if that's okay."

"Sure. We'll be out on the porch."

Ellie plucked one of the paper fans out of a large Chinese bowl, and they headed toward the rocking chairs. As they sat down, three men came out of the inn's front door. Simon nudged Ellie. "Gregory."

Ellie whispered, "And Kenny Mathews."

"What would the medical examiner be doing with an import/export businessman?"

"Maybe they're friends—or neighbors. Who's the other guy?"

"No idea. I've never seen him before." They examined a gaunt, thin-faced man with a drooping black moustache and oily black hair. His nostrils flared with irritation at something Gregory said. When Gregory continued to speak, he raised his voice. In a thick, Spanish accent he cried, "Enough! We're wasting time. We must move more quickly, before—"

At this point, he noticed the two rangers, and his mouth snapped shut. Gregory followed his gaze. Before he turned away, a twist of emotion crossed his features. *Apprehension? Anger?*

Zoe touched Simon's elbow. "Your table's ready."

They followed her into the cool dining room. Darkly varnished floors stood in contrast to the bright white walls and vases of flowers. "Hi, Bill."

"Hi, Simon." The waiter didn't bother to ask Simon what he wanted. Ellie ordered the special.

Bill nodded in approval. "Good choice. Best fried chicken in Florida."

She pointed at the menu. "Who is 'What's Her Name'?"

"As in 'What's Her Name's Coleslaw'?" Simon grinned. "My friend Tony always called his wife Elsie 'What's Her Name.' Elsie ran the kitchen here for three decades. Tony was the happiest man I've ever met—especially after a meal."

"And?"

"She made the best coleslaw in the world, but she wouldn't let anyone have the recipe. She kept it in a safe in their barn. When she died, he and I cracked the safe open and took it."

"That's robbery!"

Zoe, passing their table, cried, "No, it was actually in her will!"

"You're kidding."

"Not at all. Elsie loved explosions. After her funeral, we took the safe out into the backyard and blew it up. Then we gave the recipe to Libby."

Ellie shook her head in disbelief. "The strangest things happen in small towns."

"They are indeed microcosms. In Agatha Christie's *The Companion*, Miss Marple said, 'Human nature is much the same in a village as anywhere else, only one has opportunities and leisure for seeing it at closer quarters.' "

Later, gorged on chicken, biscuits, and coleslaw—which she pronounced superb—she let Simon drag her outside. "What's next?"

"We see Nathan Hearst."

"What about Gregory and his friends?"

"Let's just do the interviews, then we'll have an excuse to see Gregory again. The black-haired fellow he walked out with may be the translator Mayor Crowley talked about."

"Somehow I doubt he'll tell us."

"Why do you say that?"

"I got the feeling they didn't like us eavesdropping."

"You too?" He scrunched up his nose. "Do you smell something fishy?"

She sniffed. "No."

"Ellie, jeez. I mean there's something fishy about Gregory's activities. We need to find out more about him."

"Wait—you're not suggesting he had something to do with the murders?"

"It sure seems awfully coincidental." A thought blossomed. "You know, if Judy was right and there were ten people at the meeting…"

Ellie picked up the thought and ran with it. "And we're missing three names…"

"And we have three victims…Let's go."

They crossed the street and passed the courthouse before stopping at the offices of the *Fernandina Beach Register*. A young woman sat at the lone desk typing on her laptop. The name plate said Katie Daugherty. She looked up. "Oh, hi, Ellie. Hey, Simon, I heard Georgia's home. How is she?"

Simon felt Ellie stiffen beside him. "She's fine, Katie—down for the week to take care of her father."

"I know. My mom says she's loving the break from babysitting the old fart." She winked. "What can I do for you?"

"We'd like to see Mr. Hearst."

She frowned. "He's really busy. The deadline for this week's issue is five o'clock. Can I make an appointment for you?"

Just then a handsome man in shirtsleeves and khakis burst through a door behind Katie. With his ruddy face and side whiskers, he always reminded Simon of an English beadle. As Georgia was fond of saying, the three city fathers—Crowley, Farnsworth, and Hearst—could easily sit for a Hogarth etching of gentlemen at a London club. "You know, the hale-fellow-well-met types who play whist."

"Katie, I need those statistics *now*." The publisher skidded to a halt in front of the rangers. "Simon? What are you doing here?"

"Hello, Nathan, this is my partner, Ellie Ironstone. We're investigating the murders."

He stopped. "Good, good. Come on in." He ushered them into a glass-walled cubicle. "What can you tell me? I'll have Fenton write it up for this issue." He shouted, "Fenton! Get in here!"

A familiar pint-sized figure topped by bright pumpkin hair bustled in. "Hey, Ellie. That was some party."

The publisher looked from one to the other. "Party?"

"Only the lamest of the century." He guffawed. "Ellie threw a surprise birthday party for Nicole, but the only surprise was that it wasn't her birthday."

Before Ellie could respond, Nathan hissed, "Fenton, you are aware we're under a deadline?"

"Yes, boss." He pulled out a tablet, finger poised.

Simon took the floor. "We've identified all four bodies now." He stared hard at Nathan, but the man's face remained blank. He described them and where they'd been found.

"So, the woman was just south of the fort? How did she die?"

"We think she drowned. Mathews hasn't provided a full report yet."

"I heard she had a white line around her ankle. Hogtied?"

Simon shrugged. "Still working on it." Before Hearst could say another word, he said quickly, "We know you attended a meeting at the fort the night she died. Did you hear or see anything that would help us solve the case?"

The man rose from his chair. "What are you talking about?" He glared at Simon.

Simon said mildly, "Mr. Gregory of Green Cross Partners gave us the guest list. We've already spoken to Judge Farnsworth and the mayor. We know you stayed from about eight to eleven thirty on Saturday, April 14."

He sat down again. "So, what did they tell you?"

Ellie said, her face showing only mild curiosity, "We'd like to hear your impressions."

She kept smiling until he laid his pen down. "Look, with the shrimping industry practically moribund, and the economy in the crapper, we need to find new sources of income. Tourism is our best chance, but being an island—and not as famous as St. Simon's or Hilton Head—it's hard to figure ways to draw people here. So Gregory—"

"How do you know Mr. Gregory?"

"He incorporated his business here about six months ago. He advertises with us."

"Let me rephrase the question. How well do you know him?"

He hesitated. "He's not a local." He didn't look at Ellie. "You know how that is—no family, no reputation, no strings. He seems a great fellow, and very gung ho about improving the fortunes of Amelia Island. He came up with this idea of sister cities." Hearst shook his head. "I must say I wasn't all that keen on it being Havana, but he says with the sanctions lifted and now cruise ships going to Cuba, we can cash in. We have to act fast, he says, before some other town gets the idea. So we started meeting in secret, hashing out the details. Gregory will do the legwork and make the contacts. I think he's heading to Cuba this week."

"Next week."

"Oh. So, we'd appreciate it if our little undertaking wasn't publicized until we have our ducks in a row. *Capisce*?"

"I think that can be arranged." Simon took out the list. "I understand ten people attended the event. We have Crowley, Farnsworth, you, Gregory, Sylvia Barnes, and Lisabet de Angeles. That's six. Can you tell us who the other four were?"

"One's probably the translator. He works for Gregory."

"And the other three?"

Nathan pushed around the papers on his desk without looking at them. "Sorry."

"Why not?"

"Um. They asked to remain anonymous."

Ellie and Simon eyed each other. *So far no one's cracking.* "Any idea why?"

"Not a clue." He closed his mouth with a snap.

Moving on. "So back to the night. Did you hear or see anything that struck you as out of the ordinary?"

"Nope. Thought it over when I heard about your 'flotsam.' " He grinned. "But no."

"Did you come alone to the event?"

"Uh uh. I came with Randall."

"Okay, thanks for your time."

"Wait, don't you have anything else for me? Plan any arrests soon?"

"Sorry. If you think of anything, let us know."

Simon muttered as they swung along the sidewalk. "This is frustrating. Why won't they just tell us who the three are?"

Ellie said tentatively, "If you're right, and the other three attendees were our victims…"

"Or they know something about them and are covering it up…I don't know…" He lifted his hat and scratched his head. "Maybe we should see what Hosea thinks before we waste time on idle speculation."

"Makes sense." Ellie seemed relieved. "If not our threesome, who else would be likely participants?"

"There are several community leaders in the League. How about Kenny?"

"You mean because Kenny was with Gregory?"

"Could be."

Ellie stopped suddenly and planted her feet, exasperation plastered on her face. "Simon, what are we doing?"

"Huh?" Simon, trapped in an expanding whirlpool of plot twists, blinked.

"I mean, isn't our first priority solving the murders? Who cares if the eighth person is Kenny? Do the activities—secret or otherwise—of these guys even matter?"

"It does if the three missing names belong to the three victims or—more likely—the greenies know something."

Ellie threw up her hands. "All right, I give up. We'll pursue this…this cabal for now, at least until Hosea tells us to stop. Agreed?"

Simon, engrossed in watching a crow peck at a wedge of pizza in the middle of the street, hadn't been listening. "I'm sorry. What?"

"Sigh. So who's next?"

He looked at his watch. "It's getting late. I think we'll save the ladies for tomorrow. We'll have to try to catch Lisabet de Angeles during the slow part of the day, about two thirty. Then hopefully, Sylvia."

"Fine. I'm ready to go home."

To wait for a phone call from Thad, I'll bet. They passed an open restaurant. Two television screens showed alternately hockey and basketball. A radio blared over them in Spanish. *Miller time. This should buy me at least an hour more with her.* "You fancy a beer?"

She checked the sign and frowned. "In Pancho's? Isn't this the Mexican place you warned the detective about?"

"That's why we'd only have a beer."

They ordered two lagers and sat at the bar. The radio announcer continued to shout. Simon cocked an ear.

Ellie watched him. "How much Spanish do you know, Simon?"

"Some. Studied it in college. It's not really one of my languages."

"Oh? What *are* your languages?"

He said, "Lessee. French, Arabic, Farsi, German, and…wait a sec." He held up a hand. "Hey, Roberto, what's that station?"

"Radio Martí. It broadcasts to Cuba. Supposed to brighten their poor, oppressed lives with news of our booming economy and freewheeling political system." He snorted. "Hasn't worked so far. Maybe with Papa Fidel dead, things will improve even without the broadcasts—which he blocked anyway."

"Who's the announcer?"

"Dunno." The bartender stopped to listen. "Oh yeah, that's Julian Martí."

"Martí, huh?" Ellie took a sip from her mug. "Does he own the station?"

"No. It's named after José Martí." Simon stopped. "Wait a minute…"

The bartender leaned on the bar. "You guessed it. This guy claims to be a direct descendant of José Martí."

Ellie put her small hand on Simon's. "José Martí? You mentioned him before."

Please make the tingling stop before she notices me trembling. Simon closed his eyes. "Uh, yes, I did. He helped organize the rebellion against Spain and was considered the father of Cuban independence, although he failed militarily. Expatriate most of his life." He opened them again. "If I remember my history, he planned his attack right here in Fernandina Beach."

Chapter Ten
Open Secrets

Pancho's, Thursday, May 3

"For a little island way off the beaten path, this place sure has a remarkable history." Ellie checked her watch. "I…uh…"

Damn. "Right. You said you had to go home." He paid the bill and followed her out to the street. When they reached the Mustang, he let her in the shotgun side and sat in the driver's seat. He took a deep breath. "You…uh…have a date?"

"Thad called."

"I see."

She said quickly, "I think he wants to talk about his father. Or the investigation. I think."

"I see."

"What do you mean by that?" She gazed at him, her eyes liquid.

He found himself leaning toward her, lost in the shadows of her eyes. "I mean, er, okay. I guess."

Her lashes dropped down, freeing him. "If it's not okay, it's…er…okay to say so."

Oh my God. Could Georgia and Santa be right? Should I go for it?

He reached a tentative finger out. She looked down at it, then up at him. "Simon…"

The magic word. He walked the finger up her arm, circled her neck, and brought her lips to his. The kiss lingered, but not enough to satisfy him. He had adored this little creature for so long—since she arrived at the fort in fact, in a crisp new uniform, her campaign hat still unfaded, her expression a mix of terror and determination. He had fallen like a shooting star and could still feel the burn marks. But he had never in his wildest dreams thought she might feel the same way. He sat back, letting his hand fall.

She pulled him toward her and kissed him again. As the kiss wound down, they heard a tapping on the window. Georgia stood on the sidewalk grinning. "There's a hotel around the corner, you know."

Ellie bent over, pretending to look for something on the car seat. Her scalp shone crimson underneath the blonde curls. Simon rolled the window down. He looked at his best friend, but no words came to mind. His mouth opened, then shut. Georgia laughed, saluted, and walked away.

Simon swiveled to look at Ellie and found himself the butt of a furious, hissing face. "*You.*"

"Me? What are you talking about?"

"Two-faced, two-timing, two-dollar bill. Or should I say multiple timing. How many other women do you have hidden in island nooks and crannies—this island which you know so well?"

"Huh?" *This isn't going as swimmingly as I thought.* "I...uh."

"Take me home. Now."

"Ellie..."

"*Now.*"

When they rolled up in front of Ellie's house, a

cheery yellow bungalow on Fletcher Avenue with a wide porch and hanging geraniums, a silver sports car sat at the curb. *Oh great, the mighty Thad.*

Simon's nemesis disentangled himself from the wheel. Slowly, as if for maximum effect, he unfurled his powerful body, planting his size fourteen shoes solidly on the ground. A beefy hand languidly brushed the sandy hair from his forehead. Strapping shoulders squared, he loped over. "Hey, Simon. Thanks for giving Ellie a lift home." He opened her door. "I didn't want to have to schlep all the way back to the park to get her."

The stinging words died in Simon's throat when he saw Ellie's face crumple. "Sure. Yeah. What are you guys doing tonight? They're screening old Peter Sellers movies at the Carmike."

"Movie? No time for that. I've only got two weeks before the exam. Come on, Ellie." He headed toward the house. After a second, she followed him.

Simon watched them go. *So...she's helping Thad study for the protective service test.* He suddenly felt much perkier. Then he remembered her anger. *What the hell was that all about?*

Georgia called that night. "Did I catch you at a bad time?" She giggled.

"No."

"Oh, right. Having a mother in the house can be so hobbling."

"I hear from Santa that having a nosy daughter in the house can be even more hobbling."

"Yes, well. Both problems are temporary. Speaking of, when is your mom due in Minnesota?"

Simon stifled the sigh. *She's not going to let me wallow in willful ignorance.* "I don't know. Soon."

"It'll be fine, mark my words."

"Sure." *And I'm going to win the lottery without even buying a ticket.*

As though she knew he was teetering on the brink of melancholy, Georgia raised her voice. "So, I see you're making progress. That was a well-executed kiss. I think you've got Ellie on the hook."

"Then why did she call me a two-timing, two-faced twerp?"

"She did?" He listened to the gears in her brain click over. "Aha. This is better than I thought. She's jealous."

This was a new idea. "Jealous? Of what?"

"This may come as a shock, but I've grown out of the gangly, pimply, ratty-haired tomboy you grew up with. In fact, many men find me attractive. Also, many women's eyes turn green at the sight of me, even without the benefit of tinted contact lenses."

Simon took a minute to take this in. "You think she's jealous of *you*?"

"You are a monumental idiot, Simon, my love. How do you even dress yourself in the morning?" She huffed. "It would not be inconceivable that she considers me a threat…say, there's a way to confirm it."

"I will not be a party to one of your practical jokes. They always get me in trouble."

"That's because I always leave you holding the bag with the bees."

"And the pig poop. Don't forget the pig poop."

"That was a funny one. I can still see the mayor's face."

"Luckily, the eminent Mr. Hanes is long gone. I

don't think he'd be as easy to work with as Randall on this investigation."

"Yes, tell me what's up with that."

"Not yet. We weren't finished talking about Ellie and her true feelings."

"She adores you. Now, have you fingered the culprit?"

"You're just saying that."

"Well, I know it's slang, but I thought it would add a colorful touch to our conversation."

"I mean about Ellie."

"No, I'm not. Simon, you dolt, don't you see the way she looks at you?"

Simon conjured up the glittering eyes and snarling mouth he'd been subjected to only recently. "It's not exactly affectionate."

"Let me put it this way. Why would she be jealous if she didn't like you?"

"I suppose it's just…I don't know…but she is definitely enamored of the inimitable Thad."

"Old news. I was having a beer at Sliders yesterday. Gretchen told me about the night he took Ellie, Betty, and Tina out to Sandy Bottoms. They stopped in at Sliders, and Ellie tried to slip away. Thad went after her, and she gave him a piece of her mind. Gretchen says Ellie made it damn clear she didn't think he was worth a pile of dung."

"You only get that angry when you care."

"I'm getting to that. But then Gretchen says Ellie fastened him with a malignant brown eye—"

"Blue. She has blue eyes. Dark, with little silver flecks in them."

"Into which I saw you gazing deeply. Blue it is.

Where was I?"

"Ellie glaring at Thad." The words felt good.

"Yes, she said—and I quote—'You couldn't hold a candle to Simon Ribault. Don't even try.' And she marched out."

"Oh."

"She wasn't angry at Thad. She was disgusted. She was angry at you."

Simon couldn't respond because his jaw had separated from his head, plus his brain was making hops, skips, and jumps around the inside of his skull.

"I take it from your silence that we have concluded the Ellie portion of the agenda and can proceed with your report?"

He took a deep breath. "Later."

Thad's Porsche was leaving as he arrived. He knocked on the screen door. "Ellie!"

She came out with a tumbler in one hand and a liter bottle of Jack Daniels in the other. "Simon!"

"Is that for me?"

"No. It's for me. I've taken to drink since I agreed to help Hollow Head study for the exam. Come in."

Okay, no more pussy-footing around. He took the bottle and glass from her and set them down. She stood staring at him. "Ellie, that kiss was not enough."

She continued to stare.

"Ellie, I'm not a two-timer, nor am I two-faced. I only have one heart too, and I gave it to you oh, about six months ago. I'm hoping you want to hang onto it." He waited.

Her lower lip trembled. "Oh, Simon."

That was enough. A very satisfying kiss was followed by an even more satisfying one, which led to the couch. A very satisfying interlude ensued. Finally, Simon came up for air.

Ellie stood up and took his hand. "Come."

Later, they discovered just how much more satisfying a kiss can be in a bedroom.

At one point, Ellie tittered. "I feel like I'm undressing myself."

"Huh?"

"We're in identical clothes."

He unbuttoned her shirt and kissed the top of her breasts. "There are vast differences in the uniforms. For one thing, you have darts." He pulled the shirt off and undid her bra. "And lacy underthings." She straightened, her nipples standing at attention. He rolled her trousers down and she stepped out of them. When he had peeled off the rest of his clothes, he sat on the bed and pulled her onto his lap. She settled down on him, and they moved into a hazy world of rocking, swaying, and heaving. Finally, with a great shudder, she collapsed on him. Simon, his arms wrapped around her, felt her shiver. "Are you cold?"

"No." She purred. "It's just the aftershocks. Simon?"

"Yes?"

"Do me again."

"Okay."

It wasn't until after midnight that Simon went back to his car and drove home whistling.

He was met at the door by a desperate dog, an angry cat, and a eupeptic mother. He let the dog out, fed the cat, and tried unsuccessfully to avoid his mother, who took his hand and led him into the kitchen. Her brilliant white hair shone under the fluorescent light, and the elegant fingers he'd inherited touched his cheek. "I didn't mean to wait up for you, Simon. I didn't even know you had gone back out. I felt a bit peckish and heard your car when I came down for a snack." She patted her stomach.

"I…uh…"

"Would you like some water?" He could only nod. She poured him a glass and set it before him. "You want to tell me about it?"

"I…uh…"

She took a bottle out of the refrigerator and poured a glass of wine. "I saw Debbie Daugherty in the Publix this morning—or rather, yesterday morning." She waited.

"I…uh…"

She finished the wine and stifled a yawn. "Since my time is limited, I'll skip the preliminaries. When do I meet Ellie?" She left him gawking after her and tripped up the steps.

****

Park headquarters, Saturday, May 5

Simon and Ellie both arrived at the ranger station late. Hosea surveyed their radiant faces. "Well, finally."

Simon wasn't sure which of them blushed the deeper. *No point in denying it. Just change the subject.* "Want to hear what we've found out so far?"

"Besides that you're made for each other?"

Ellie began to cough and ran out the door. Simon glared at Hosea. "You've got to remember that Ellie comes from the big city. She's not used to a small town's instant lines of communication."

"It's not rocket science, Simon. You might want to check the mirror. Don't think I've seen such a fat, contented grin on a man's face since my wedding day—or rather, wedding night." He closed his eyes. "Cornelia made me a very happy man. Miss her every day."

When he couldn't come up with anything to match this observation, Simon said, "Why don't I fill you in on our progress." He told him about the interviews with the mayor, the judge, and the publisher.

Ellie sidled in during the recitation, slid over to her desk without looking at either man, and began fumbling with something in her drawer.

Hosea cast an arch look in her direction but evidently decided not to tease. "Okay. So they all gave the same reason for their meeting, and no one saw or heard anything. And you still don't know who the last three are?"

"No." *Time to run my idea up the flagpole.* "Our interest was piqued by the fact that there are three corpses and three missing names."

"*Hmm.*" Hosea scratched his chin. "I can't see our city fathers involved in murder." He shook his head. "Anyway, the three victims seem hardly the types to be invited to participate in a civic project."

"No, no. We were thinking the event attendees may have witnessed the murders, and clammed up to protect themselves."

Hosea leveled an incredulous look at Simon. "Really? You're talking about the mayor and the district judge. There's no way they could keep quiet about a crime."

Simon slumped. "I guess it *is* a bit far-fetched."

"Don't worry, we'll find the answers soon enough. Just keep plugging away." The park superintendent sat down at his desk. "All right. What's next?"

"We'll try to see Lisabet de Angeles and Sylvia Barnes this afternoon."

"Sylvia...I wonder what she was doing there? Does Amos know she's involved?"

"No idea. Why don't you ask him?"

"Will do. Oh, by the way, I heard from that Jamaican policeman, the one with the exotic name— kinda, you know, swishy." He swayed his hips.

"Patrice Labadie? I thought he'd gone back to Jamaica."

"He said he's staying on for a few days, that he had two possible leads on the murders. His colleagues in Montego Bay faxed a photo of Bonney's knife. I asked him to send it to the lab."

"And the second lead?"

"He found a phone number. He thinks it may be her contact here. He's going to follow it up."

Simon pursed his lips. "Not much to go on. Did he say anything else? Were there any other clues in her stuff?"

Hosea shrugged. "They have yet to search the house in Montego Bay. He'll get back to me when and if he has something new."

"Okay." Simon rose. "I'm going to see if the docents at the fort need anything." He started to walk out, then paused. "Say, do you know anything about Radio Martí?"

"Radio Martí? Isn't that the station that broadcasts Cuban propaganda?"

"No, it broadcasts news in Spanish to Cuba. Supposed to give the Cuban people a link to something *besides* propaganda."

"Right, now I remember. I thought it fizzled years ago."

"No. It's still broadcasting. Heard it last night. Announcer's named Martí."

"Martí? Didn't you tell me Gregory has a translator name of Martí? Any relation?"

"So he claims."

Hosea shrugged again and turned back to his work.

After a morning struggling with a newly trained volunteer afflicted with a fear of heights—"Tell you what, Martha, you stay in the officer's mess, and I'll send Jack up to the battlements"—he retrieved Ellie from the campground, and they headed into town. "I suggest we have a delicious meal prepared by the chef of the renowned El Toro restaurant."

"The place owned by one of our greenies?"

"The very one."

Ellie played a tattoo on the hat in her lap. "The plan being, I suppose, that when we've softened the owner up with our effusive compliments, we hit her with searing questions."

"Exactly. That reminds me—they say Cecil's seared steak chimichurri is fantastic. You should order it."

"Why don't you?"

He saw no reason to answer. They pulled into a parking lot. "Here we are."

A thin young man with a ring in his nose, his Mohawk tinted purple, took them to their seats. "Thanks. Would you ask Miss de Angeles if she could see us when we've finished?"

"Sure thing. And you are?"

"Simon Ribault."

Ellie watched him leave, then turned to her companion. "I do believe that's the only person on Amelia Island who doesn't know you."

Simon picked up a menu. "Newbie. The Beer and Marching Society hasn't vetted him yet. Debbie says they have a backlog from spring break."

"Excuse me?"

"That's right, you haven't met the ladies yet, have you?" He grinned.

Despite aggressive cajoling and heartfelt pleas, he refused to say more. "Don't worry, they'll find you." At her look of distress, he relented enough to say, "Katie Daugherty is Debbie's daughter."

"That's not much help." She opened the menu. "Okay. Fine. What should I order?"

"You're asking me?"

"Yes. I've noticed that while you may not eat anything but beef chum, you know what's good."

He had to admit it was true. He'd always been fascinated by cooking and culinary traditions. "In that case, I would recommend the *boliche*."

She read the description. "That's a curious combination. Pot roast stuffed with olives and chorizo?"

"Trust me, according to all the gourmet magazines and TripAdvisor, it's great."

"I don't know...I'm more in the mood for fish." She continued to read.

The waitress, a buxom woman sporting a cascade of chemically enhanced black tresses, came over. "Ready?"

Ellie didn't answer, so Simon quickly scanned the menu. "Yes, Inez. We'll have a pitcher of the white sangria, and the lady will have the *enchilado de mariscos*."

"The seafood stew. Excellent choice." She jotted it down. "And for you, Simon?"

"How about the *picadillo*, but could you hold the raisins, capers, and olives?"

"So…you want plain ground beef. You want that over rice?"

"How about maybe a bun?"

She suppressed a smile. "Got it."

As they finished their meal, Inez came out to say that Ms. de Angeles would be happy to see them. They followed her to an office tucked away next to the kitchen entrance.

A tiny woman, her glistening sable hair drawn into an elaborate twist, sat behind a mahogany desk smoking a cigar. She wore a plain black silk dress. A black silk scarf was knotted skillfully at her shoulder. "Hello, Simon…and?"

"This is Ellie Ironstone, Lisabet. She's new at Fort Clinch. We've been assigned to investigate the murders."

"Ah, yes. Terrible business. And not good for *my* business." Her smile contained more cunning than distress. Simon wondered if in fact Lisabet hoped the notoriety would bring in customers. "I do hope you find the murderer quickly. Do you have any idea of motive?"

"Not really. There are a lot of loose ends. The victims turned up at locations rather distant from each other. They may not be related." Ellie gave Simon a look. He knew she was wondering why he was lying to the woman. *Time to start probing.*

"Really?" The woman looked a bit alarmed.

"We're talking to everyone who was at the meeting at Fort Clinch on April 14. I understand you were there."

She paused, her eyes guarded. "How do you know that?"

"Mr. Gregory gave us the guest list. Can you tell us what the meeting was about? He just said it was a meet and greet."

She let out a breath. "Yes, it was. Of course most of us already knew each other."

"Who was there?"

"You just told me you had the guest list."

Damn. He mentally kicked himself. "A partial list." He cited the seven they knew.

"Yes, the first six make up the committee. The Spaniard—Martí—is merely staff." Her nose rose an inch in the air.

My my, is that a whiff of Old World snobbery I detect? "Is Martí by any chance also a radio announcer?"

She paused. Simon got the distinct impression she was weighing her words carefully. "I think so. I'm not sure."

"Okay. We're still missing three attendees. We'd like to interview them as well." He looked expectantly at her. "Strictly routine."

"We've been asked not to publicize their names."

And we're back to square one. "We understand the topic was a proposal to make Fernandina Beach and Havana, Cuba, sister cities."

"Sister cities, yes." She shifted to Ellie. "So, how do you like Amelia Island, my dear? Where are you from originally?"

"Virginia. And yes"—her eyes slid to Simon—"I like it a lot here. So many things…to do." She bit her lip.

Simon coughed. "You're from Cuba, aren't you, Lisabet?"

The woman froze, her eyes wary. "Why do you ask?"

"I just wondered how you felt about the recent warming in the relationship between our two countries."

"I'm a businesswoman. I stay out of politics. My mother and I fled Castro when I was eighteen. She died in Miami." Her eyes clouded. "My father stayed in Cuba."

"How come?"

"He believed in Fidel's revolution." Her lips twisted. "He was wrong."

"He let his family escape?"

"He couldn't stop us." She shrugged, her tone light. "Cuba holds little interest for me now." She rose, stubbing the cigar out in an ashtray. "At least, until I can make some money there. Now, if you'll forgive me, I have to supervise the prep for dinner."

Simon held a hand up. "Just one moment. We haven't gotten to the reason we're here. We think the victims were killed Saturday night, while you were at your meeting in the fort. Did you hear any noises outside the fort that evening? A scream? A splash?"

Before he'd stopped speaking, she was shaking her head. "Nothing. Although you might want to talk to Sylvia Barnes. She stepped outside for a few minutes."

"She did? What for?"

Lisabet allowed herself a sly smile. "It was a long meeting. I think she had quite a bit of wine."

"I see. Well, thank you, Lisabet. Once again, El Toro has produced a memorable meal. Next time, I'll have Ellie try your Moors and Christians."

She stared at him blankly for a moment before breaking into a laugh. "*Moros e cristianos.* Very humorous."

Simon answered Ellie's quizzical look. "Black beans and rice. Black beans are the Moors and white rice are the Christians."

This seemed to bewilder her, but she consented to being led out of the restaurant. Once out of earshot, she asked, "Why did you tell Ms. de Angeles that the bodies were unrelated? The two men were killed by the same knife. They had to have been in close proximity at one point or another."

"Or in close proximity to the murderer. He could have run across them at different times and killed them separately."

"You're positing that someone *else* killed them both? That they didn't kill each other? Could Judge Farnsworth be right—there's a serial killer running around loose?" She halted. "I just thought of something."

"We should ask the lab what fingerprints they found on the knife."

"Right."

After a few minutes, Simon muttered, "I wonder why she lied about Sylvia."

"Sylvia Barnes? What do you mean?"

"She implied that Mrs. Barnes went outside to pee, but she wouldn't have gone to relieve herself—"

"Women only do that in emergencies anyway."

"Yes, but more to the point, we had portable latrines set up inside the fort."

Ellie got in the car. "The Barnes homestead?"

"To Gardenia Street and step on it. I happen to know she has a yoga class at five."

"Is there *no* privacy in this town?"

They drove down Citrona Street and took a right on Park Avenue into a new development. Full-grown Christmas and royal palms had recently been planted along the narrow lanes. Bentleys, BMWs, and Infinitis parked nose to rear in front of spanking new stucco condominiums. On their left lay a marshy park graced with huge live oaks and sprinkled with roseate spoonbills and white ibis.

Ellie regarded her surroundings. "So, the other half."

"I prefer the old town. Much more interesting."

"Me too."

They pulled into the driveway of a large house almost hidden behind oleanders and bougainvilleas. No one answered the doorbell, so Simon called around the back. "Sylvia! Are you there?"

"Is that Simon? I'll be right around." A handsome woman in her fifties, her still-dark hair sculpted in what had to be a very expensive cut, came around the corner, a book in one hand and her glasses in another. "Well, look at you! You've grown."

"Sylvia, I'm only fifteen years younger than you."

"I know, but I still think of you as that skinny young man going off to Princeton. We were all so proud of you. Although"—she leveled an admonitory look at him—"we still think you should have married

Georgia."

Ellie took a quick step back, and Simon said hastily, "You know that would never have worked out. She's much too grumpy. May I present Ellie Ironstone?"

"Oh, is she the new ranger? Are you two partners? I'm not sure I approve of a male and a female team. Could cause tension." She shook the glasses at him. "You know what I mean. Of an *emotional* kind."

Simon's lip twitched. "Not in our case."

"And what about Georgia? She's in town. I saw her at Publix with her father." She smiled fondly. "She's so beautiful—and intelligent."

Ellie was becoming restive. *Quick—redirect.* "Yes, well, that's why she's my best friend. Did we catch you at a bad time?"

"Not at all, dear boy. I was immersed in this delectable murder mystery—it's set on Longboat Key over on the Gulf Coast. Did you know John Ringling, the circus king, tried to build a Ritz-Carlton there? He never finished it, and it sat derelict for decades. The locals called it the Ghost Hotel. Awash in apparitions." She closed the book. "I really should be working on the Gullah-Geechee Corridor Commission stuff instead. Amelia Island has been selected as the southern terminus of the historic trail. We're having a presentation and reception here next week. It's going to be a grand affair. People are coming from as far away as Hilton Head."

Simon waited impatiently for her to wind down. "I understand you're also involved in another civic project—with Randall and Nathan…and Carson Gregory?"

The glasses clattered to the ground. "What do you know about that?"

"Only the bare details. We're investigating the deaths that occurred the night of April 14, when you had an event at the fort. We're asking all the attendees if you saw or heard anything that might be of interest."

She relaxed slightly. "Oh, okay. Did Carson tell you we want to make Havana our sister city? It's really his baby, but when Randall told me about it, I opted in. With my experience, I had to make sure if it's done, it's done properly."

"What do you mean?"

"Cuba is still a communist dictatorship. Fidel's death won't change anything." Her eyes glittered with what to Simon seemed awfully close to hate. "I don't want us to be used as a propaganda tool by the regime."

Keep it casual now. "So…who's on your planning committee?"

Sylvia named the six they already knew. "And Mr. Martí. He's going to help Carson in his dealings with the Cubans."

"We understand there were ten at the meeting."

She picked up her glasses and studied them. "Ten?"

"Sylvia," he asked gently, "you named seven. Who are the other three?"

"I'm sorry, Simon. I'm not supposed to."

"But—"

Ellie apparently decided to move the conversation along. "At any rate, did you hear anything strange? Loud noises? Yelling?"

She raised her eyes to the sky, pretending to think. "No, nothing of that sort. We met about eight and were gone by eleven or so. Little was accomplished." This seemed to annoy her.

Simon said tentatively, "Even when you went outside?"

"Outside? Me?" She fingered her glasses. "Why would I do that?"

"That's what we'd like to find out."

Suddenly, she tossed the book away. It landed upside down in a patch of pansies. "All right, but if you dare breathe a word…"

Simon had a flash of intuition. "You went out for a smoke, didn't you?"

"Damn it, yes. I know I was supposed to quit three months ago, but every now and then I sneak one. I can't help it. Please don't tell Amos. He'll kill me."

Simon patted her shoulder. "No, of course not. Are you sure you didn't hear any sounds down by the shore?"

She shook her head. "Positive. It was dead calm."

As they were leaving, she called, "How did you know I left the fort?"

"Lisabet told us. Don't worry. She covered for you. Said you'd gone to find a latrine."

"Oh. Well, say hi to Georgia for me."

Ellie was very quiet as they threaded the streets of the old town. Simon hoped it had nothing to do with Georgia, that she was simply contemplating the mystery, but didn't have high hopes. "Ellie?"

"*Hmm*?"

"There was never anything but friendship between Georgia and me."

"I know."

"Does that…does it still bother you?"

She twisted to look at him. "Of *course* it bothers me, you silly git. A lot of people have trouble with the idea that a man and a woman can be merely friends. I can't believe you never…never…" She turned away.

He pulled over to the curb. "Ellie, I never, never. Until I met you. I fell in love with you the day you walked into the station. I've wanted you for six months. Georgia's the only one who knew how I felt." *At least the only one I told.* "She nagged me about it—she was sure you cared for me, even though that prat…er…Thad, seemed to suck up all your affection. I didn't think I had a chance—I didn't think you could like a kook like me."

"Kook?"

"You know—chock full of minutiae, boring, unadventurous, living in the town I was born in…with my mother. I mean—" He didn't get the rest out.

After a breathless kiss, Ellie murmured, "I have a feeling everyone knows about us now."

"Why do you say that?"

"Because they're all staring at us." She nodded at the crowd on the sidewalk, pointing and smiling.

"Oh my God, that's the marching society. See, there goes Debbie Daugherty pulling her cell phone out. It's all over."

"Ah, the notorious Mrs. Daugherty." She tapped the steering wheel. "Let's leave them to their task. We have better things to do."

"Oh?"

She gave him a knowing smile. "Oh, yes."

Chapter Eleven
Hatfields and McCoys

Ellie's house, Monday, May 7

"Did you call your mother?"

"Mother? Why?"

"You've been gone all weekend. She'll worry."

Simon rolled over and propped himself on a pillow. "I don't have to check in with my mother. I thought I made it pretty clear last night that I'm a grown man."

"Yes, you did." Ellie giggled. "You grew at least two inches last night alone."

He kissed her shoulder. "Just so you know, Mother has been off visiting her cousin since Friday."

"What about Roan and Isis?"

"Taken care of." He rubbed her nose. "I must say I like this new arrangement. Beats the heck out of mooning over you."

"You did that last night too."

"Mooning? Oh, you mean…" He patted her rear. "Much as I'd like to revisit all the positions we explored, we have a job to do."

Ellie pulled him closer. "Give me ten minutes." She began to nuzzle his neck and stroke his back. Things grew heated rather quickly. "Hurry, hurry," she breathed.

"There's time."

"No! Now, Simon, now!" She thrashed, trying to draw him in, but he moved deliberately and slowly, bringing her to a fever pitch. "Simon, I can't wait!"

"Good." And with that, he began driving in over and over until they hit the point of no return. Slowly, they fell back to earth. Just as Ellie's eyelids drifted closed, Simon whistled. "Damn."

"What?"

"That took fifteen minutes. I can imagine the snide remarks and innuendos Hosea will indulge in this time." He leapt out of bed. "I've got to let Roan out. I'll run over to my house and meet you at the park."

"Don't you mean your mother's house?"

His voice harsh, he growled, "Yes. Of course. See you later."

Half an hour later, they met in the ranger station parking lot. Ellie regarded him timidly. "Simon? Are you mad at me?"

"Mad at you? For what?" He pecked her cheek.

"You seemed so abrupt when you left." Her lower lip trembled. "I was only making a joke."

He stared at her. "A joke?"

"About you living with your mother."

"Oh. Well, never mind." He dropped his eyes. "Let's go in."

Thad sat at his desk. "There you are. I've been working my tail off while you're out harassing my father."

Ellie started to respond, but Simon said mildly, "Hosea asked us to question all the people who were at the fort the Saturday before we found the bodies. It's just routine." *I'm beginning to sound like Sergeant Friday.*

"He said you cornered him in his office and forced him to confess about the sister-cities project."

"Did he really? Interesting…" Simon moved to his own desk. A tiny smile flitted across his lips as he picked up his phone. "Maybe I should call and apologize."

Thad's eyes grew round. "Wait! Er…I may have exaggerated a bit. He…uh…didn't actually use the word 'harass.' "

"Perhaps he said 'interviewed'?"

"Yeah, I think so. Now that I recall. Anyway"—he wrinkled his nose—"while you guys have been out, I've had to do the latrines twice. Some dumb camper's dog got loose on Saturday, and then this kid tried to jump off the fort walls while his dimwit mother talked on her cell phone. Caught him in the nick of time. Did the hag thank me? Nooo. Haven't had a moment's peace." He continued to grumble. "I actually had to eat lunch at my desk yesterday."

Ellie's mouth fell open. "You saved a child? Why, Thad, you're a hero. Does Hosea know?"

Hosea walked through the open door. "Yes, in fact it's indelibly etched into my memory—that's what unrelenting repetition will do. Thad, I've recommended you for a citation."

Simon glanced at Ellie, whose expression mirrored his thoughts. *He'll be unbearable for at least a month.*

Hosea turned to Simon. "What's on the agenda today? Are you getting any closer to answers?"

"Not really." He smirked at Thad. "We've *chatted* with Judge Farnsworth, the mayor, and Nathan."

"Yes, you already told me. That's it?"

"Then Friday we talked to Lisabet de

189

Angeles…and Sylvia Barnes."

"Ah. That woman gives me the heebie-jeebies."

"Your sister-in-law?"

"No, of course not…oh." Hosea glared at him. "The de Angeles woman. She's so, I dunno, foreign."

Ellie couldn't resist. "Is it that, or the fact that she's a successful businesswoman?"

He ignored the question. "You know what I mean, Simon. Those flat black eyes and that tight bun. Sylvia's sure she dyes it. She must be over sixty."

"Sheath those claws, Miss Hosea. She's a fine woman and a fabulous cook. We had lunch there, and the *picadillo* was superb. Ellie declared her seafood stew also memorable."

"Okay, okay. Did you learn anything new?"

Ellie gave Simon a warning glance. *She thinks I'm going to blab about the smoking, but this town didn't raise no dummy.* "Nope."

"Huh." Hosea tapped a pencil on the desk. "So we still don't know who the three anonymous members are."

"Gregory said they were charter members but wished to keep their identities private."

Ellie chimed in. "The rest of the guests were equally noncommittal. No one would name them."

"You said the project is to link up with Havana? Could they be philanthropists or something—maybe worried about political repercussions?"

"Or," Thad piped up, "there's a lot of money to be made, and they want first dibs."

The others turned toward him. "There might be something in that," Hosea said in a wondering voice. "Thad, I've got a job for you."

The young man held up his carefully manicured hands. "I refuse to clean any more latrines."

Hosea eyed him. "Good. I'm tired of fielding complaints about dirty sinks and no toilet paper. Thank God Rosie's back from vacation. No, Thad, I want you to compile a list of Chamber of Commerce members who might be interested in an investment like this."

"I'll get right on it."

"And talk to any prospects."

"Yes, sir!" He leapt toward his computer.

Hosea pointed at Simon. "What's your next move?"

Caught off guard, Simon racked his brain. Ellie said tentatively, "We could try to catch up with the translator. He may not be sworn to secrecy like the others."

"You said his name was Martí?"

"That's right. Gregory was with a Spanish fellow at the Florida House Inn. Could be him."

"Okay—"

"Kenny Matthews was there too."

"Mathews, huh. Think he might be involved?" Hosea reeled around. "If you can't find this Martí, go talk to him. I believe he's at the district office today. If he knows Gregory, maybe you can weasel the names of the partners out of him."

"I'd better call first. Don't want to schlep to Jacksonville if he can't see us." Simon got off the phone a minute later. "Fred's at reception today. He says Kenny's not busy right now, but Virgil and Iggy are finishing up at a crime scene at the Ritz-Carlton. If we get to the morgue before they do, he should have a free minute."

"The Ritz-Carlton!" Hosea put down his mug. "What happened there?"

"Some fellow murdered. Fred didn't give details."

"This is turning into a circus. Do me a favor, make sure this one has nothing to do with ours."

"Will do."

Ellie and Simon drove down A1A toward Jacksonville. As they came up on the entrance to the fanciest hotel in town, an ambulance roared out of the driveway, followed by a squad car, its sirens blaring. "Damn. We're too late. Kenny will be tied up for a while. Might as well check out the scene." Simon spun the steering wheel left and pulled up in front of the hotel. Police swarmed the building. He stopped one. "Hey, Bobby."

"Oh, hi, Simon. What are you doing here?"

"We're investigating the Fort Clinch murders. Thought we'd see if this one was connected. What happened?"

Bobby wiped his forehead. "A guest was found dead in the restaurant kitchen."

"In the kitchen? That's weird. Aren't there always people around?"

"Likely happened about three in the morning. Lock jimmied. Zack thinks maybe the guest was looking for room service and ran into a burglar."

"So he was shot?"

"Nope. Killer used a cleaver. Cut his head off."

Ellie turned away. The others heard a gagging sound. Simon spoke a little louder. "Have they identified him?"

"No ID on him. Haven't found the head yet, but hotel did a room check and found one guest missing."

"Who was it?"

Before he could answer, a man in a jacket marked "CSI" yelled at Bobby. "Got it!"

He turned. "The head?"

"Yup. In the dumpster. It was the missing guest all right. ID confirmed. Steve's taking it to the morgue."

Bobby started to go, but Simon stopped him. "Who is it?"

"Lessee…" He opened his notebook. "Labadie. Patrice Labadie." He grinned. "You suppose his friends called him Patty?"

Simon took a deep breath. "Shit."

Bobby stared at Simon. "You know anything about him?"

"Yeah, but we gotta run. Have to chase the ambulance."

"You a trial lawyer now?"

"Not anymore." He tapped his ranger hat.

Bobby laughed. "Well, you'll have Georgia to do your legal work soon enough."

Ellie took hold of Simon's belt and dragged him to the car.

They rolled into the morgue parking lot as Iggy and Virgil bent over a shrouded shape on a gurney. Virgil yelled, "Get him inside."

Simon and Ellie followed them. Simon put a finger to his lips. "Keep quiet. If they don't notice us, they won't throw us out."

The two men rolled the gurney into a well-lit room and locked the wheels. Vicious-looking instruments were laid out on a steel-topped table. Iggy wiped a damp brow. "Thank God he bled out before we got there."

Virgil blew his nose on a grimy handkerchief. "I don't envy the kitchen staff."

A uniformed officer came in carrying a large tote bag. "Where do I put the head?"

"Over in that basin. Here, Iggy, help me get the clothes off."

"CSI already checked him?"

"Yeah."

The medical examiner skipped in, pulling on latex gloves. "Ooh, what a fun way to start the day! We have any paperwork on the guy?"

"Hey, Kenny." Virgil handed him a clipboard. "Jamaican, name of Patrice Labadie. Gave the hotel an address in Montego Bay—construction company. Here on business."

"Staying at the Ritz?"

"Uh huh."

"Firm must be doing pretty well. I had dinner at the Salt once—fabulous food and service. And super pricey. Good thing rich Uncle Herb offered to foot the bill for me and Donna."

"Um, Kenny?"

He twisted around. "Simon? What are you doing here?"

It couldn't hurt to do him a favor before we begin the interrogation. "I think I can help you. I know the victim."

"You do? Have you told Amos? He's here."

"Not yet. We…uh…were passing by the Ritz and heard what happened."

"Well?"

"Labadie came to see us about a week ago. He's not a businessman. He's a detective. From the Jamaican police."

Amos stuck his head in the door. "What did you just say, Simon?"

Ellie and Simon followed him out to the corridor. "The dead man is Patrice Labadie, a detective from Jamaica. He was tracking—"

"Let me guess. Alvaredo, the escaped convict."

"No. He was looking for a colleague, who turned out to be the first body we found in our little crime spree."

"A colleague. Another Jamaican detective? So, *he* was on Alvaredo's trail?"

"No." When Amos rolled his eyes, Simon hurried on. "According to Labadie, Winston Virtue—"

"*Really*?"

Simon shrugged. "What can I say?"

Ellie picked up the narrative. "Virtue was on the trail of a cocaine-smuggling gang. The ringleader was a woman named Odessa Bonney. Labadie told us Virtue had managed to sign on the last trip."

"I take it she's also Jamaican?"

"Yup."

"Is she by any chance the female victim you found?"

Both nodded.

"I see." Amos tapped his chin. "The fishing boat in Egan's Creek where we found cocaine…hers?"

"No, that one belonged to Diogenes Goodwine. We're pretty sure her own boat sank in the Fernandina Beach marina."

"How would you know that?"

"We…uh…Hosea asked Maurice to go over it. He also asked him to take photos of her to both marinas and see if anyone recognized her."

"Oh, he did. Let me get this straight. Hosea—without mentioning it to me—gave my forensics man an order?"

Oops. "I'm…um…sure he assumed Maurice would inform you."

Amos made a visible effort to quell his anger. "Well, if the smuggler's boat was out of commission, how'd they all end up in the Amelia River?"

Ellie gulped. "Our theory is Bonney made a deal with Goodwine to use his boat."

"But you've no proof."

"We have gobs of circumstantial evidence."

He took off his hat and scratched the top of his head. "And you fellows didn't see fit to share any of this information with the police?"

"We assumed you and Hosea were in constant communication." *Hell, it's worth a shot.*

Amos squinted at him. "You know better than that, Simon. He'd better not be trying to do a number on me again. I warned him last week."

"Of course not. He's…had a lot on his mind." Simon and Ellie exchanged glances. *Is he keeping Amos in the dark on purpose? Could it be because of Sylvia's involvement?*

The police chief pursed his lips. "So, the Jamaican detective—Virtue—is dead. Bonney is dead. Goodwine is dead. Alvaredo is dead. Who's left to kill Labadie?"

Simon shrugged. "Who knows? Another member of the gang?"

"I think I'd better get in touch with Labadie's colleagues in Montego Bay." He tipped his hat. "Thanks, Simon. Your input has been invaluable. Be sure to thank my *brother* for making you available." He left.

Simon stared at the closed door. "Damn, I forgot to tell him about the phone number."

"Phone number?"

"Yes. The one Labadie told Hosea he'd found."

"Right. He thought it could be Bonney's contact."

"Let's see." He pulled out his phone. "Hosea? Heads up—Amos is on the warpath. He didn't know about Labadie or that we had identified Bonney...I told him, that's how...Why not? Oh...That's ridiculous. But...all right. By the way, what did the lab say about the knife?... *Hmm*. And did Labadie get back to you with that number? Damn...What? Oh really? Well, I guess that clinches it." He pocketed the phone.

"Why is Hosea keeping all his toys from his twin?"

"The director of State Parks got on his case. Said not to fraternize—and stop that giggling; it's not that funny. Davis ordered him to keep our findings close to the vest until we have more to go on."

"So much for interagency cooperation." She put a hand on his arm. "The knife? The number?"

"The knife is indeed Bonney's, a scimitar worthy of Blackbeard. Hosea never got the number from Labadie."

"Okay...so what's clinched?"

"The crime lab found the fingerprints of all four victims on the murder weapon. Bonney's matches the one faxed by the Jamaican police. Also, Clarence Garenflo at Panther Point and Salvatore at the marina both identified Bonney from the photos. To top it off, when they examined the sunken trawler, they found traces of cocaine in the hold."

Ellie said slowly, "So Salvatore's shrimp boat captain and Miss Bonney are definitely one and the same, and it was her knife that killed all three men."

"Looks that way. But…"

"But what?"

"Since Jo Jo made it all the way to the marina, he must have been the last one killed. So how did the knife end up in Alvaredo's back and not in his?"

Iggy came out pulling his lab coat off.

"Hi, Iggy. Got a minute?"

"Sure. Let's go to the break room." He washed his hands and poured a mug of coffee. "What's up? I hear you know who the guy is."

"Yes, but we'd like to ask you about something else." *Let's see if my hunch is correct.* "Kenny was at the event at Fort Clinch Saturday the fourteenth, right?"

His eyes grew shifty. "How did you know? Did you see us there?"

Us? Hmm. "We have the guest list. Some pretty prominent names on there. So"—*play it cool, Simon*—"how come you were invited?"

He looked left and right. "Kenny made us come."

"You and Virgil?"

"Uh huh."

Simon glanced at Ellie. *Iggy and Virgil. Eight and nine. And Kenny Mathews makes ten. So much for our theory about the murder victims. But why the secrecy about these three?* "Okay, so Kenny invited you two. Did he say why?"

"No." Iggy writhed nervously. "Virgil got the impression we were there as backup."

"Backup for what?"

"You know, muscle."

Muscle? Backup? "What was this do anyway, a Mafia summit?"

Ellie asked, "Muscle for what?"

"Not sure. We came late. This guy Gregory was in the midst of a presentation about sister cities and how Havana would soon be opened up to commerce and how we should get in on the ground floor. The mayor and judge were all gung ho. The others were kind of skeptical, but seemed open."

"Iggy, do you have any idea why Crowley and the others wouldn't give us your names?"

He shrugged. "No idea." His lip curled in disdain. "Maybe they thought we'd spoil their image."

Ellie added, "Or maybe they thought bringing in 'muscle' looked a little heavy-handed."

"Or suspicious." Simon lowered his gaze to Iggy. "I hate to agree with you, but you don't exactly run in the same circles as the city bigwigs. They must have worried that your presence would strike the wrong tone as it were, maybe draw our attention."

Iggy nodded. "Yeah, like in, 'Who brought the scum to the party?'"

Ellie clearly thought the pettiness had gone far enough. "How long did the meeting last?"

"Maybe forty, forty-five minutes or so after we got there."

"Everybody left at the same time?"

"Pretty much. Oh, wait. Kenny sent Virgil and me outside while he and a coupla others went off to confer."

"Who were they?"

"Gregory—he's in some kind of import/export racket. Just set up shop in Fernandina. Don't know much about him."

"And the other one?"

Iggy rolled his eyes. "Slick Latino dude. Never said a word during the pitch."

"Gregory didn't introduce him?"

"Not while we were there."

The mysterious Martí. "Why didn't they leave the fort with you?"

"Started to, but when one of the women came around the corner they went back into that room under the cannons."

Virgil entered and headed to the coffee urn. "What's going on?"

"Simon here's asking about that meeting at the fort."

"Oh, you mean the night before those people were murdered? I hear you've been asking whether anyone saw or heard anything."

"And did you?"

Virgil cast an inquiring look at Iggy, who said, "They know we were there, Virg."

"Oh. Okay. What was the question?"

"Did you hear any noise outside the walls?"

"Nah. Meeting was pretty dull. Then we went down to the truck to wait for Kenny."

"Any idea why you were invited?"

Virgil glanced at Iggy. "Kenny wanted us there."

The subject of their discussion took that moment to come through the door. He leveled a hard stare at Iggy and Virgil. "Yo, Simon. You have business with my guys?"

Iggy said quickly, "He asked about the meeting. About the sister-cities thing."

Ellie turned to the medical examiner. "Virgil and Iggy say you were there."

"Oh, yeah. Yeah, I was there."

"Why weren't you on the guest list?"

He didn't look at Ellie. "I asked to be a silent partner. Don't like to seem too political. Not in my position."

"Is that why everyone was told not to mention Iggy and Virgil as well?"

Kenny glanced at his technicians. "I figured if people knew they'd been invited, they'd assume it was because of me."

"I see." Simon avoided Iggy's eyes. "I understand ten people attended, including Lester Farnsworth, Nathan Hearst, Randall Crowley, Sylvia Barnes, and Lisabet de Angeles. Along with Gregory, there's you, Iggy, and Virgil. The tenth is...?"

"Must be Martí. He's the translator Gregory hired."

"Julian Martí?"

"That's the guy."

Simon remembered the Spaniard's brusque manner, the manner of one used to being in charge. *Just a translator?* "Translator? Or silent partner?"

Mathews started down the hall. He said over his shoulder, "Sorry, can't help you."

Simon turned beet red and yelled, "Kenny, you can't just walk away. This is a murder investigation."

The medical examiner skidded to a stop and turned around. "Not of me, it isn't. You can't come waltzing in demanding information like you were some kind of a policeman. You're nothing but a glorified Boy Scout."

I should have flattened him in the fifth grade when I had the chance. "Perhaps you are unaware, but on

State Park property, I have police authority. I can even arrest you."

His adversary's eyes closed to slits. "You piece of shit. You think because you're a Ribault, you can throw your weight around. Well, your family may have been here longer than the Mathewses, but don't forget, we once *owned* Amelia Island."

Simon snorted. "Yeah, for a single day. Big effing deal. You gave it up without a fight. We at least defended the island from the Spanish."

Mathews shouldered past Virgil and Iggy. "Not very well, did you? Aviles routed your pathetic little Frenchies with one arm tied behind his back." He stalked down the hall but only went a few steps before veering back. "And you know full well that giving up the island was part of the plan. They stripped it from the fucking Spics so they could give it to the Americans. President Madison himself praised my ancestor."

"Then how come he made him lower his flag? As I recall, it was a really cool one, with that blue soldier's silhouette. Did Governor Mathews pose for it? Lemme see…what did they call themselves? The Patriots of Amelia Island? Everybody knows about the secret plot. Not everybody knows Mathews wanted to run the island himself. Didn't get away with it, did he? Madison fired him. What a buffoon."

The punch came out of nowhere and connected with Simon's nose, accompanied by a loud crack. "Don't you *dare* call my ancestors buffoons. They were patriots—all of them!"

Iggy got hold of Kenny's arms and pulled him back. Ellie took a tissue from her pocket and held it against Simon's nose. She snarled, "What the hell do you think you're doing?"

When Simon realized she was addressing him and not the detestable Kenny, he pushed her hand away. "I cad hep it—Kenny's always goink on about his stupid fably history."

Kenny shook Iggy off. "Just because half your ancestors were renegades and the other half native, you can't appreciate real red-blooded Americans."

"Dat's ludicrous. You dow I cad trace by fably to da French settlers."

"Yeah, those were some lily-livered frogs. Skedaddled at the first sign of trouble when the Spanish arrived."

"Dey didn't skedaddle. Dey were bassacred, and you dow it. Dey would have beaten Aviles if dey hadn't lost deir fleet in da hurricane." He stopped to catch his breath.

"You have no proof of that. The *Trinité* disappeared in 1565 and was never heard from again. It obviously turned tail and ran."

Simon dabbed at his nose and tossed the tissue on the floor. Frowning, Iggy picked it up with a pair of tweezers and threw it in a wastebasket. "Aha! Wrongo. If you read anything besides that rag the *New York Times*, you'd know they just discovered it off the coast of Cape Canaveral."

Kenny took a step back, eyebrows raised. "Really?"

Virgil spoke up. "It's true—I saw an article about it online. That treasure hunter—what's his name?" This last was directed at Iggy.

"Um. It's on the tip of my tongue. He's famous for finding sunken ships…"

Simon waited a minute before giving up. "Robert Pritchett."

Virgil went on enthusiastically. "Yeah, that's the guy. He found it with his whaddyacallit, magnetometer. They're pretty sure it's the *Trinité*, Ribault's galleon."

"Huh." Kenny looked almost ready to concede defeat, but rallied. "How do we know they were going to fight Aviles? More likely they'd abandoned the settlement."

"Oh, yeah? Well, old George Mathews was a known pervert. In his own wife's diary—"

Ellie spoke in a low, rumbling voice that made everyone pause and listen. "Enough with the insults. I can see you two have a long history of ill will between you. We're grownups now and we have a job to do. Whatever your distant ancestors did or didn't do is irrelevant. Mathews, tell us what you know about Labadie's death."

The question took the medical examiner by surprise, and he made a visible effort to calm down. "The latest victim? Doubtful that it was premeditated. He was likely killed where he was found, probably by an intruder in the kitchen. The murderer seized the nearest weapon, which happened to be a Chinese cleaver. Forensics is still inspecting the scene, but I heard Thompson say they found steel shards in the big butcher-block chopping board. I'm guessing he held Labadie's head over it and chopped it off."

Virgil said brightly, "Like a haunch of beef."

Ellie said hesitantly, "In one blow?"

"No. Marks on the neck indicate it took several tries. You'd have to be exceptionally strong to do it in one whack."

Simon took another tissue from Ellie and blew his nose carefully. "So, they're interviewing kitchen personnel?"

"I imagine. Look, Simon, I'm…um…sorry I hit you." Kenny held out a limp hand.

Simon mumbled, "Shouldn't have baited you. Ellie's right, we've got to get over those old grudges. It's not"—he avoided Ellie's face—"mature. Truce?"

They shook hands. As they left, Simon called, "I'll keep you posted from our end if you do the same from yours."

"Yeah. Okay."

Once outside, Simon gently probed his nose. "Boy, he may be a pantywaist, but Kenny packs a helluva right cross."

"Yes, I think I'll drive."

"Why?"

"The loss of blood from your brain renders you unfit to take the wheel."

When they arrived at the ranger station, Thad put down the phone and pointed at Simon's face. "What happened to you?"

"Never mind."

"Well, anyway, I'm glad you're here."

"Really? I'm honored."

Ellie gave Simon a noogie.

"Ouch! Piling on a bit, aren't we?" He limped to his desk.

Thad looked hurt. "Don't you want to hear my news?"

"Sure." *Then I'll tell you mine.*

"You know Hosea gave me the job of checking through Chamber of Commerce potential donors. Olive,

Dad's secretary, helped me out."

Sigh. "Great."

Ellie asked, "Did you find anyone?"

"As a matter of fact." He looked like he would have burnished his medals if he had any. "Two Hollywood types have been snooping around talking to people. I think they might be interested in making a movie here."

"About what?"

"Duh—about our history of course, but especially the MacGregor affair. You know, the Republic of the Floridas. Good swashbuckling stuff. Say…maybe Russell Crowe would be interested. Or Tom Cruise…" He pulled open his desk drawer. Simon caught the glint of a mirror inside.

"What does this have to do with investing in sister cities?"

"I don't know, but it's pretty cool."

Simon threw his hat down. "Oh, for God's sake. I'm going home. Mother needs me."

Ellie said something inaudible. Simon touched his ear. "What was that?"

"Er…nothing."

They started to walk out, but Thad jumped up. "Wait! I almost forgot. Kenny called here after you left Jacksonville. That woman? She didn't drown."

"Woman? You mean the victim, Odessa Bonney? She didn't drown?"

"Nope. She was strangled."

Chapter Twelve
Patriot Games

Park headquarters, Monday, May 7

Simon did a double take. "You want to run that by us again?"

"Report came in from the lab right after you left. They had assumed drowning because there were no obvious marks on the body."

Ellie said drily, "Not to mention that she was waterlogged."

"That's right." He turned back to Thad. "Didn't she have water in her lungs?"

His eyes bugged out. "How would I know?"

Ellie tapped Simon's shoulder. "We can check with Kenny."

He continued to concentrate on Thad. "So, do you at least know *how* they figured out she was strangled?"

This only produced an indifferent shrug. "Beats me. I just took the message."

"Damn. We'll have to talk to Kenny."

Ellie looked at him. "I just said that."

"Oh, right." Simon stood tapping a foot, his eyes distant.

"Simon?" She shook his arm. "Kenny?"

"Yeah, yeah…Damn."

She peered into his face. "Are you sure you two are

copacetic?"

"Copa—? What a wonderful word to use, Ellie." He kissed her. "I knew I had a good reason to fall for you."

They were halfway out the door when a gasping sound made them pause. Thad's eyes shot from one to the other with first wide, then narrowed eyes. "What the hell's going on?"

Simon put an arm around Ellie's waist and remarked innocently, "You didn't know?"

In response, Ellie's former crush reached them in one stride and tried to pry them apart, but she clung to Simon. "Thad, I told you last week I didn't want to see you anymore. Remember?"

"No." He tossed his blond hair back, a gesture surely practiced several times a day. "You've always been sweet on me, Ellie. I mean, look at me." He pointed at Simon. "And look at him."

Ellie kissed Simon's cheek. "Precisely." She smiled at Thad and walked out.

At the car, Simon dialed the medical examiner's number. "Kenny? Simon. Yeah, we just heard about Bonney. How did you figure it out? Oh? Okay. See you in a bit." He hung up. "He says it's easier to explain in person."

"Another trip to Jacksonville?"

"Nah. He'll be up at the Fernandina police station in fifteen minutes. He's got the report with him. He can tell us and Amos at the same time."

They parked in the police lot on Lime Street and went straight to the chief's office. Kenny was already there, along with Iggy. He had a bound report in his hand. Amos, forehead creased with annoyance, was asking, "How come it took you this long to ascertain cause of death?"

"You know we were inundated with victims after that fifty-car pileup on 295. Plus, I couldn't finish processing your guys until you had confirmed their identities. Protocol. So I deferred action on them while we worked on the backlog."

"But—"

Simon interrupted. "I think Amos is asking why it took so long to determine she was strangled instead of drowned. Shouldn't that have been obvious from the start?"

Kenny slapped the report on Amos's desk. "Hey, it's not always that cut and dried. External signs of strangulation are absent in maybe half of all victims—sometimes there are no marks at all on the body. In this case, the very thin red welt on her neck was almost impossible to make out given the rolls of fat in the area. Iggy here saw it"—he patted his assistant on the shoulder—"just as we were sending her out for cremation." He paused, considering. "Actually she could have been both."

"Both drowned and strangled?"

Amos choked on the pencil he was chewing. "So, which came first?"

"Ah, that's an interesting question. She could still have been breathing when she went in the water."

"As in, not dead?"

Simon ground his teeth. "That's absurd. You're postulating she was strangled *after* she drowned?"

Kenny held up a hand. "Let me explain. We found a small amount of seawater in the victim's lungs. She could have aspirated it—in other words, drowned. On the other hand, according to some research it's possible to ingest a certain amount of liquid even after death. I'm not in a position to confirm what the sequence of events was, but I can say they came in pretty quick order. The floridity—"

"Let me get this straight. Bonney may have died twice?" Simon, trying to make sense of Mathews' statement, ran his fingers through his hair. "Shades of Rasputin."

Ellie perked up. "Rasputin? Wasn't he that horrible Russian monk?"

"What does that have to do with the price of bread?" Amos's irritation had increased exponentially with the conversation.

Ellie, undeterred, prompted, "What about Rasputin?"

"You're correct. He was the confidant of the Tsarina Alexandra and fervently hated by many in the aristocracy, who conspired against him. The assassins tried to kill him *eight times* in one night—poisoning, shooting, beating, and finally drowning. Despite that, it was never definitively determined how he died."

"Not by drowning?"

"The autopsy only showed a small amount of water in his lungs—"

"Like Bonney." Ellie was fascinated.

Amos interrupted the flow. "*Again,* can we focus please? What difference does it make *how* Bonney died? It had to have been murder with all these other corpses lying around."

Simon muttered, "Not necessarily."

"What?"

"Well, if she was throttled, it's definitely murder. If

she drowned, it could have been an accident."

Ellie objected. "Even if asphyxiation wasn't the ultimate cause of death, someone *did* try to kill her."

Amos asked, "Do we know for certain she was on Goodwine's boat?"

They all looked at Kenny. "There were traces of fish guts on her clothes."

"And Labadie told us Virtue had landed a berth on the boat."

"*A* boat. It could have been the one that sank."

"The one in the marina?" Simon screwed his face up. "Damn, I wish Labadie weren't dead. There are still lots of questions he might have had answers to."

Ellie said slowly, "Still, we have evidence that only makes sense if the boat was Goodwine's."

"Like what?"

She ticked off her fingers. "One, the captain of the shrimp boat in Fernandina Beach was a Jamaican woman. That's unusual right there. When her boat sank, she went off to get another one. No one has seen her since."

"No one in Fernandina Beach, that is."

"Two, Labadie identified the dead woman as Odessa Bonney, a Jamaican drug smuggler. Three, your friends at Panther Point said Goodwine had contracted with a Jamaican woman and was none too happy about it."

Simon chimed in. "And they recognized Bonney from the photograph."

She nodded. "Right. And four, we found cocaine on both boats."

Everyone was silent for a minute, digesting Ellie's words. Finally, Amos said heavily, "Well, that's at least one mystery solved. Now for the other two thousand."

"Yes, like who killed her?" Simon looked around at the doubtful faces.

Ellie ventured, "She could have tumbled off by accident and made it to shore, where she was killed."

"By whom?"

"Alvaredo?'

"You're suggesting he got off the boat, killed Bonney, then got back on the boat, and proceeded to Panther Point?"

Amos intervened. "No need to be snotty, Simon."

Iggy offered, "Um…what about Goodwine? He was the last one standing. He could have killed her."

Ellie said, "Hold on. We don't know for sure in which order they died."

Amos turned to the medical examiner. "Kenny?"

"Time of death was so close for all four that it would be impossible to tell who died first. Or second. Or—"

"Okay. But she still had red marks on her neck."

"True." Everybody sat quietly, mulling this over. Finally Amos rose. "Let's leave the problematic demise of Miss Odessa Bonney aside for now and deal with the other four."

Ellie had one last suggestion. "Maybe she killed them all, then committed suicide."

"Now you're beginning to sound like Thad." Amos sniffcd.

"Let me get this straight. She came back from the dead long enough to kill Labadie? I suppose that's when the guilt finally caught up with her?"

"Don't take that tone with me, Simon."

He headed to the door. "It's getting late. We'd

better get back to the park before it closes."

They drove down the winding lane past hardwood hammocks and extruding sand dunes to the ranger station. Simon was quiet.

Ellie nudged him. "Penny for your thoughts?'

"See, there's another reason to keep pennies around."

"Yes."

"I've been thinking. It seems strange that Gregory feels the need for an interpreter for the green league."

"So…you've given up on the knotty question of the demise of Bonney and friends?"

"What? Oh. Sorry. Yes. For now." He paused a second before returning to his ruminations. "Most Cubans speak English. All the business will be conducted in English. And why use a radio announcer? Why not a professional translator?"

"Martí is a well-known figure—maybe he's a figurehead."

"Then why keep his name out of it? No, he's got to be a silent partner." He rolled the window down and stuck his head out.

"What are you doing?"

"I need fresh air to think properly." He pulled his head back in. "Something else to consider. Radio Martí is anathema to the Castro regime. They regularly block the broadcasts and anyone caught listening to them is arrested. He'd hardly be considered a goodwill ambassador."

"*Hmm.*" Ellie pressed her lips together. "Unless…Didn't the bartender at Pancho's say this Julian Martí is a descendant of José Martí?"

"Yes." He bounced on the seat with renewed

excitement. "And José Martí is a hero not just to Cuban exiles but to the Castros—revered as the liberator of Cuba."

"Really? That's odd."

"Odder still is that Martí was vigorously opposed to socialism."

"Why would Castro honor him, then?"

"Good question." Simon slapped a hand on the dashboard. "You know what, I think I'm going to do a little background check on Martí."

"Why?"

"I have a bad feeling about this whole enterprise. Too many secrets. Too many shifty eyes looking anywhere but at me."

"You still believe it might have something to do with the murders?"

"I don't know, but at the very least, isn't it kind of implausible to rent the entire Fort Clinch for a few hours, sans food or entertainment, just for a meeting with only ten people?"

"I suppose that's a rhetorical question."

He got out of the car. "I'm off to do some Googling. See you tomorrow?"

Ellie leaned out of the window. "Don't I get a kiss?"

He started. "Oh my God, I'm taking you for granted already." He kissed her tenderly. "And I should be punished."

The kiss softened her mood. "What did you have in mind?"

"I think…yes…I should be stripped naked. You will be allowed to have your way with me. Over and over. Oh, the agony."

"A full night of such activity should turn you into a seething mound of lusty flesh."

"With any luck."

****

Park headquarters, Tuesday, May 8

"Well, this is interesting."

"What?" Ellie got up from her desk and looked over Simon's shoulder at his computer.

"Last night, I searched on José Martí. He spent most of his life outside of Cuba, writing poetry and political screeds. He's best known for leading the Cuban rebellion against their Spanish overlords. He died in 1895 on the battlefield."

"Cuba wasn't liberated until the Spanish American war of 1898, though, was it?"

"Right. And Martí was as opposed to American interference as he was to the relatively new Marxist ideology of communism."

"So why is he a hero to both Cuban Americans and the Castros?"

"Fidel didn't take power until 1959, by which time Martí's actual writings were less well known and Castro could spin his exploits into his revolutionary narrative. It was a simple matter to claim Martí fought for independence, not from Spain, but from capitalism. Without access to a free press, Cubans had no way to know the truth. Enter Radio Martí."

"All right. So what did you find that's so interesting?"

Simon pointed at the screen. "Here's an article on the program. Disseminating fact-based news to the masses was the original concept, but it's not been very influential, mainly because the Castro government stifles any access to it." He chuckled. "More effective was the scrolling electronic billboard the Americans installed on top of our interest section in the Swiss Embassy. When they broadcast that Fidel Castro is the third richest man *in the world*, Cubans started to ask questions. Fidel's response? He erected tall poles with big black flags that screened the billboard."

"Lucky for him Havana is a windy city." She read a little further. "I suppose it must be frustrating for the staff at Radio Martí to know they're not getting through."

"Yup." He clicked on a link. "So…I checked Julian Martí out. He broadcasts Monday, Wednesday, and Friday for four hours. Here's a picture of him."

"That's the guy who was with Kenny and Gregory."

"Right. Says here he's a writer and journalist whose parents fled Cuba a year after the revolution. Virulently anti-Castro."

"So there's as much chance he would see the attraction in a sister-city idea as sharing a meal with Alferd Packer."

"Alferd Packer? There's hope for you yet. You know about the prospector trapped in the Colorado mountains who saved himself by eating his fellow travelers?"

She grinned. "I only know because the students at the University of Colorado named their cafeteria after him."

"Sheesh." Simon rolled his eyes. "Can we get back to Martí? I think there's more going on here. We have to find out what his role is in the obscurely named League of the Green Cross. We know from both

Randall Crowley and Iggy that he was there on Saturday night." He rubbed his jaw. "I've been thinking about Kenny too."

"I'm glad to see you two are fast friends now."

"That'll never happen, but we can at least work together. You remember our…er…discussion yesterday?"

"I remember the sucker punch."

"No, before. The tension goes back a long way. His grandfather and mine had several altercations. Didn't speak to one another for the last fifty years of their lives."

"How come?"

"The Mathewses and Ribaults consider themselves rivals to the claim of First Family of Amelia Island. My ancestor, Jean Ribault, was a French Huguenot explorer and the first European settler on the island. He, along with a small French community, lived for three years in harmony with the Timucuan Indians, until Pedro Menendez de Aviles rousted them in 1565."

"So you should share an aversion to the Spanish."

"Unlike Kenny, I'm above such petty spite." He raised his voice to drown out her bleat of laughter. "The Mathews family has always claimed to be the real heroes of Amelia Island. They insinuate that the French were sniveling cowards who gave up without a fight and that if it weren't for their brilliant maneuver, Spain would still control eastern Florida."

"But that's rubbish."

"I know, because they lost the island to Spain in even less time than it took the French to lose it."

"I don't understand."

"Let me back up a little. The Mathews family

originally came from Georgia. George Mathews had been governor of Georgia until 1795, but had fallen into disfavor after a scandal. In an effort to revive his political career, he and President Madison conceived this cockeyed notion that they would annex the eastern part of Florida and claim it for the US. This is how it was told to every schoolchild in Emma Love Hardee Elementary School at least once a year."

He put a hand on his heart. "Under cover of darkness on March 16, 1812, a band under Mathews' command calling themselves the Patriots of Amelia Island attacked Fernandina. They were supported by nine American gunboats, which trained their guns on the fort. A Colonel Lodowick Ashley carried the Patriot flag to the fort and demanded the Spanish governor surrender, which he did. The Patriots held the island for one day before turning it over to the American forces." He dropped his hand. "Unfortunately, Congress was not amused by their little escapade and made them give it back to Spain. It was returned to the Spanish in May of 1813, who controlled it, with a few interesting exceptions, until 1821."

Ellie sat down hard. "All I can say is, yikes!"

"To get back to my original point. Since then the Mathewses have always entertained a particular hostility toward all things Spanish. I just can't see him being in favor of cozying up to Castro."

"So, you're postulating that he and this green party have an ulterior motive?" She rolled her eyes. "Like what? Annexing Cuba?"

"Don't laugh. Americans have done all kinds of nutty things over the centuries. Remember Aaron Burr and the Republic of Texas? Why, even here on Amelia we had a repub—wait a minute!" He started clicking some keys and read the screen. Then he got up, reached for his hat, and ran out the door.

"Simon!"

"I'll be back!"

He raced down to the Green Cross Partners offices, only just missing Georgia's sports car and his mother's minivan. He tried the office door, but it was locked. He ran back down the stairs to the lobby, snagged a brochure for the import business, drove back to the park, and pitched the trifold on the desk, announcing, "Ta-dah."

Ellie opened the brochure. At the bottom was a logo for the company. Shaped like a flag, it sported a green cross on a white background. Underneath it said: "Green Cross Partners, Import/Export."

"What's this all about?"

"Now I'm sure these guys have something up their sleeve, and it doesn't include making nice with Cuba."

"Go on."

"I mentioned Aaron Burr. You know about his adventures?"

"Remind me."

Simon was pretty sure Ellie was pretending to knowledge she didn't have, but didn't mind. He loved rattling off stories like this. "After he killed Alexander Hamilton, he fled New Jersey and eventually made his way to the Louisiana territory. There he schemed to help Mexico throw off Spanish rule in exchange for some Mexican territory in which to set himself up as emperor."

"Emperor, huh. Delusions of grandeur?"

"Many who knew him believed he often teetered

on the edge of sanity."

"And this has to do with the League how?"

"Well, the same thing happened here."

"Aaron Burr crowned himself king of Fernandina Beach?"

"Ha ha. No. Mathews has a competitor in the category of failed attempts at control of this island. Remember the Scots mercenary named Gregor MacGregor?"

"Wait. You told me about him. I…uh…"

He took pity. "Let me refresh your memory. A few years after George Mathews surrendered Amelia to the Spanish, a Scotsman took a crew of a hundred or so men and stormed the Spanish fort."

"Fort Clinch?"

"No. An earlier one close by—Fort San Carlos."

"What happened?"

"They drove the Spaniards out and settled in, declaring the Republic of the Floridas. Don't ask me what they hoped to get out of it."

"Maybe pry ransom for it out of the US or Spain?"

"Possibly. Anyway, that was June of 1817. By September, MacGregor had run out of money and the Spanish were threatening, so he sold the island to a French pirate for the princely sum of fifty thousand dollars."

"Aha, I was right."

"I think by then he just wanted to move on."

"With his 50K."

"Okay, okay. You know you malign my Scots ancestors with all this cynicism."

"I thought they were French?"

"I'm a mutt as it were, like many Americans—

French, English, Scots, a touch of Timucuan, or so my father always claimed. I've always been rather proud of the fiery Scots blood in me."

"I've been to Culloden. Have you ever read about that debacle? It set the standard for how not to run a battle. So I know what bunglers the Scots can be"—after a look at Simon's face she added hastily—"although also adorable. What happened next?"

The door opened, and Rosie peeked in. "You guys see Thad anywhere?"

"No. I thought this was his day off."

"He wanted to trade with me. Said he had a big date tomorrow."

Ellie cocked an eyebrow. "Didn't take him long, did it?"

"Thad is adept at finding consolation in record time." Simon ducked to avoid the blow. "I think there's even a plaque honoring him in the high school. Or was that for his brother Wesley? *Hmm*."

Rosie took her phone out. "Well, if Thaddy boy doesn't show up in five minutes, he's going to have to cancel this entry in the competition." She left.

Ellie turned to Simon. "So? You were saying?"

"The French pirate? Louis Aury raised the Mexican flag over what by now was a totally confused populace for a grand total of two months, when the American Navy rousted him—"

"So it became American territory."

"Let me finish… and immediately turned around and gave it back to Spain."

Ellie let out a belly laugh. When she'd caught her breath, she gasped, "What goes around comes around, eh?"

"So it would seem. Now, what I propose—"

"Excuse me?"

"What? Oh, never mind that now." He brushed aside her bemused expression. "I propose to do a little digging on our Mr. Gregory. He's at the center of this."

"How do you know?"

Simon pointed at the brochure. "See the logo? It's identical to the flag of the Republic of the Floridas—Gregor MacGregor's flag."

Chapter Thirteen
The M Word

Park headquarters, Tuesday, May 8

The wall clock dinged. "It's five o'clock. Can't we do it tomorrow?"

"*Urp*. I hadn't noticed the time. Shall I come over and fix you something for supper? Then I'm afraid I have to get back to Mother."

"That would be nice if I knew you could cook anything besides well-done hamburgers."

"You wound me. I happen to be an accomplished cook…book reader. Food was one of my best categories on *Jeopardy*. Ask me what a 'mirepoix' is. Go on."

"It's a mix of diced vegetables, sometimes with ham or bacon added, cooked until mushy, to enhance the flavor of slow-cooked pot roast."

A bit put out, he muttered, "Could be. Sometimes."

"How about if I cook for *you*?"

"Depends."

She threw her hands up. "All right. We'll stop somewhere to pick up a burger, and I'll make something for myself."

"Okay."

They locked up the office and the visitor center and, while Simon stopped at the drive-through, Ellie went on to her house. She had set a pot of tomato soup on the stove to heat and retrieved bread, peanut butter, and apricot preserves when Simon came in carrying a white paper bag. She held out a can and a carton. "Do you want milk or beer?"

"I'm not a child. Milk."

"Got it. I'll be ready in a jiffy. Go ahead and check out which action figure they gave you."

"For your information, I gave Darth Vader to little Gary Slocum." *Heck, I don't need three after all.* He watched her lithe figure at the counter, her graceful fingers spreading peanut butter on the toast in slow swirls, then moving to stir the soup gently but firmly. *Gulp. It wouldn't kill you to eat a chicken leg now and then, ya know. Or a salad.* "Could I…could I have a little soup too?"

Without a word, she poured soup into two bowls and brought them to the table. He silently blessed her. *Yes, indeed. It could be worth it.*

After a comfortable meal, Simon took the dishes to the kitchen. "Nothing like home cooking. Thanks, Ellie. I have to run."

"Oh."

He noted the crestfallen look before she wiped it off. He took her in his arms. "I promised Mother I'd be home this evening."

He knew she longed to make a snarky comment but bit her tongue. *I'm going to have to tell her sometime.* He only wanted to be sure the relationship was on solid ground before he did. He kissed her lingeringly. "I'll be back if I can."

When he arrived at his house, his mother stood facing an upright piano, its walnut panels polished to a

224

high gloss. "Do you want it, Simon? Velma says she'll buy it from me for her granddaughter."

"Oh, Mother, I know I was never very good, but I still love to tap out 'Taps' or 'When Johnny Comes Marching Home' on it."

"As I recall, the only two tunes you ever mastered."

He ran a hand over the carved frontispiece. "Besides, Dad found it for me, remember?"

"Yes, it was on its way to the dump. Painted a dirty white, keys broken, out of tune. If it weren't for Bartholomew…"

"Nothing like a fine cabinetmaker with perfect pitch. It is a beautiful piece."

"Okay. I was only kidding about Velma." She pointed toward the garage. "I've been going through boxes. It's a good thing I never unpacked most of this stuff."

Simon fought back the gulp. "Yeah. You labeled them, didn't you? So they'll be easy to place when you get back."

She gazed at him gravely. "Tilting at windmills again, Simon?" At his stricken face, she said lightly, "I'll want my own place when that happens anyway."

****

Ellie's house, Tuesday, May 8

"*Psst*, you awake, Ellie?"

"I am now. My God, you made enough of a racket to wake the entire cemetery."

"Why didn't you meet me at the door with a shotgun then?"

"I'm saving it for the wedding."

"No, really, why didn't you call the police?"

"Because I saw your car pull up and you get out. I saw you jiggle the front door, then go around to the back. I can't believe how long it took you to find the side door I left open. I was almost forced to give you a hint."

"I had located a handy vine, which I was inclined to use until I recognized it as poison ivy. With *my* voice, serenading seemed out of the question, so I opted for breaking and entering."

"Well, you're here."

"I am indeed."

"Say, I have an idea."

"Must be telepathy. Move over."

****

Ellie's house, Wednesday, May 9

"Good morning, Snookums."

"Don't bug me. I'm exhausted." Ellie pulled a pillow over her head. "And don't call me Snookums."

"It's your own fault, pussy cat. You were insatiable last night."

"Me! Every time I nodded off you'd prod some sensitive part of me until I had to respond—willingly or not."

"Well, you're not on duty till this afternoon, so you have the morning to recuperate." He cast a critical eye over the mound on the bed. "And maybe change the sheets. Who's been eating crackers in bed?"

"You." She peeked at him from under the pillow. "Are you off to work?"

"No. I've got to get home. Mother needs help with some boxes. And I need my laptop."

"Boxes? Are you finally moving out?"

His face tightened. "No."

Ellie had apparently learned the warning signs that she was treading into forbidden territory. "Just joking. See you later."

He tried not to think about Ellie on the way home. *I do have to tell her about Mother soon. It's not fair to her.* He knew it wasn't so much that he didn't want her to know; it was the saying out loud he wasn't sure he could manage.

When he reached the house, his mother stood in the door. "Where have you been?"

He smelled something burning. *Oh yeah, my ears.* "I…uh…"

"It's about time." He caught the hint of a grin. "I mean, about time you two got together. Waiting six months…you should be embarrassed at your age."

"How did you know?"

"Besides your doodling Ellie's name all over the phone book? Debbie, of course. She and Phyllis and Glenda and I were at our usual happy hour yesterday. She said she passed Thad Farnsworth talking to Betty Lawrence on the street. He seemed very upset. Debbie says he was practically in tears, moaning about you stealing Ellie from him. Betty was doing her best to soothe him."

"Naturally."

"Naturally. He seemed to respond to her ministrations."

"Well, that's a relief."

"So…when will I meet the enchanting Miss Ironstone?"

He suddenly realized that he wasn't ready for any of this. Worshipping Ellie all those months had become a nice comfortable place to be. A change in the circumstances was rather scary. He hadn't really thought about the implications of their recent encounters—beyond the pure pleasure of it. *Can't we just keep it the way it is?* "Soon. Soon. Why don't I start by getting your books out?"

His mother surveyed the living room. Three walls were covered with floor to ceiling bookcases. Books were stacked in corners, on chairs, on every table. She pointed at one volume teetering on top of a lamp shade. "Perhaps we should begin with my pots and pans instead."

By six o'clock, Simon lay in a bedraggled heap on the sofa. His mother bustled about in the kitchen. "Mother, aren't you even the least bit tired?"

"You did most of the heavy lifting, dear. I'm fine. In fact, I'm going with Debbie to Santa's for dinner. We have things to discuss." She came out, wiping her hands. "Now you, don't stand on ceremony. Get thee back to thy honey. No buts."

He didn't argue.

****

Ellie's house, Thursday, May 10

"You're leaving me again, aren't you?"

"Only for a little while, my dear. And only because you're on duty at the front gate this morning."

"I am? Oh my God, I forgot to check the schedule."

"That's what you have me for."

"I knew there was a reason. When did you see it?"

"On Monday. When it comes out. Having an eidetic memory helps. Thad is on latrine duty again. Rosie's still out sick."

"And you're off today?"

"I have a date with the alphabet."

"Huh?"

"Google. See you for lunch?"

"Where?"

"You pick. Any place except Salt—I hear their kitchen is closed for spring cleaning."

"I save that for my sugar daddy anyway."

"See you later."

Four hours later, Simon and Ellie sat on the outdoor deck of the Salty Pelican watching Bert direct yacht traffic. "I'll have the grouper sandwich please."

"And for you, Simon?"

He pretended to look over the menu. "I guess…"

Ellie said, "He'll have the hamburger, Laura."

"Side?"

"Fries."

"Not yet ready to take the plunge, eh?" Laura grinned. "Pabst or something wild and crazy? We have this new red ale from the Florida Beer Company—it's called Alligator Drool."

"Ha ha. Bring me a PBR. And iced tea for the lady."

Elle leaned her elbows on the table. "How did your date go?"

"With the attractive and accomplished Google? It was almost too easy. Our Mr. Gregory is in fact Carson MacGregor, descended from the noted highland warrior and profligate-cum-mercenary—"

"You can't be both."

"In this case, you can. As I was saying, Carson MacGregor is the descendant of Sir Gregor MacGregor, of the Clan MacGregor of Glen Orchy, Glenstrae, Glengyle, Glen Lochay, and Glenlyon."

"Whew. They didn't stray far from the bonny glen, did they?"

"Unfortunately, they had no choice. They were banished for a hundred and seventy years after murdering the king's forester in retaliation for his hanging one of their own."

"What was the MacGregor executed for?"

"Poaching. Considered by most Scots as a minor offense—more of a prank really."

"But apparently not by the king."

"No. During the diaspora, the MacGregors scattered to the four winds, and came to be called the 'Children of the Mist.' "

"How romantic." She took a sip of her iced tea and made a face. "Damn, this is sweetened. I guess I'll have to get a beer instead." She signaled to Laura and pointed at Simon's glass. "I gather one of those winds brought a scion of the family to the shores of La Florida?"

"You are clever, aren't you?"

Laura approached and placed a grouper sandwich and bottle of beer in front of Ellie. "Simon, here's your happy meal. I brought the relish tray in case you…well, never mind."

Ellie spread tartar sauce over her grouper and took a bite. "How did you find out that Gregory is MacGregor?"

"Simple. He incorporated his business under his legal name."

"And this gets us where?"

"Remember I told you about the Republic of the Floridas?"

"Yes."

Simon drained his mug and waved it at Laura. "And about Mathews and the Patriots of Amelia Island?"

"Uh huh. I'd like another beer too, you know. I'm off this afternoon."

"You sure? All those calories?" He pinched her waist.

"*And* lots of nutrients. Hydrating too."

Simon noticed Laura watching and removed his fingers, brushing Ellie's hip lightly. "Anyway, it seemed a bit odd to have the descendants of two such illustrious residents of this sainted isle in cahoots as it were. I thought to myself, Simon, I thought, there has to be a connection."

"They both want to clear their names of the stain on their illustrious reputations?"

"No, it's more. Both Mathews and MacGregor have an ax to grind with Spain."

"Spain! But that's just silly!"

"Silly? Remember our convict, Miguel Alvaredo? Maybe we've been looking at this all wrong."

"So in an act of mindless revenge, MacGregor and Mathews murder a fellow because he has a Hispanic name?"

"According to his file, Alvaredo was convicted of murder, but also of racketeering. Picture this scenario. He has bamboozled the two and sneered at the inept Americans. They learn of his escape and that he's linked up with a Jamaican cocaine smuggler and vow revenge. Together they—"

"Wait a minute—how did they propose to catch him?"

"They arrange the event at the fort, and when the

231

boat passes, Mathews or MacGregor runs out and shoots him."

"They didn't leave the fort. Virgil and Iggy would have seen them."

"Um." He paused. "Sylvia. That's it. When Sylvia came out for a smoke, she distracted the boys and MacGregor slipped out."

"Alvaredo wasn't shot."

"Picky, picky. *Hmm*." He bit into his burger. "How's this? They use a trebuchet to hurl the knife, striking their target right in the old bull's eye they managed to paint on his back earlier."

A commotion at the front drew their attention. Georgia saw them and rushed toward their table. "Simon, hurry!"

He got up. "What is it?"

"It's Santa." She whirled and ran out the door. He tossed some bills on the table and followed her, Ellie behind him. The Miata roared off.

"Where is she going?"

"Looks like her house." They jumped in the car and started after her, turning on Ash, then down South Eighth and left on Jasmine. At the end of a small development stood a white house, its front yard a riot of lantana and blue daze. Rising from the flowers grew a wiry old tree covered in lemons.

An ambulance sat in the driveway, its engine running. Virgil pushed a gurney out the door while Iggy attached an IV to the man on the cot. Georgia stumbled over to the gurney and gazed, anguished, down at Santa. "Daddy!" She grabbed Iggy's arm. "Is he…is he…?"

"He'll be okay, Georgia. You can come along in

the ambulance if you like."

She hopped in.

Virgil caught sight of Ellie. "Hey, Ellie, your mother wants you to call her."

Simon drove while Ellie dialed.

Beebee answered immediately. "9-1-1. Ellie?"

"Yes, Mother. What did you want?"

"I wanted to confirm the ambulance got to the Petrie place in time. They had a flat tire on the way."

"Yes. It was here when we arrived. It just left." She watched the spinning lights out of sight. "Where will they take him?"

"To Luther Memorial. It's the only hospital on the island. Keep me informed, will you, dear?"

"Sure, but why—"

"I promised Debbie."

"Debbie?"

"Debbie Daugherty. She…Oops, incoming call. Talk later." Her mother hung up.

Ellie was quiet for a while, then, "Simon? In the restaurant, Georgia called her father Santa. Why?"

"Switched at birth." *That should keep her occupied for a while.*

"Excuse me?"

Not long enough. "He's played Santa Claus at the local hardware store every year for twenty years. We all call him Santa."

"What's his real name?"

"Um…lessee…" When she began to hiss, he answered, "Felix. His mother named him that because as an infant he fell off the changing table five times— without breaking anything." *Let's just see how much Latin she knows.*

"*Felix, felicis, felici, felicem, felici*. Latin for 'fortunate.' "

"I—" He braked suddenly as a Volvo station wagon roared out of the hospital entrance. At the wheel, he saw a familiar face, her features locked in grim terror. *Debbie…I hope that doesn't mean…*

When they reached the Emergency Room lobby, a tall man in scrubs was speaking to Georgia. "…keep him overnight for observation, but I think he'll be fine."

She saw Simon and Ellie. "Oh, Simon!" He enveloped her in a tight embrace. "Doctor Hanrahan says he'll need a splint or stitches or something."

Simon gave the doctor an inquiring glance.

The other man asked, "Are you her husband?"

Simon jerked, and Ellie sat down hard. "No, no. I'm her best friend. What's going on?"

The doctor caught sight of Ellie. "Oh…sorry. Miss Petrie's father has had a mild heart attack. We're keeping him here until tomorrow to be on the safe side, but I've ordered a referral to Dr. Swain at St. Charles Hospital in Jacksonville. He'll evaluate the patient and likely recommend a stent."

"Oh, a *stent.*" He patted Georgia, her face hidden behind a wad of tissues. "It's a very common procedure."

She sniffled. "I'm sorry—I was too upset to really listen."

Ellie stood up. "Let me get you a cup of coffee."

"Okay."

The doctor turned back toward the ER. "If you can wait, I'll give you a full report when we're sure he's stable."

"Yes, Doctor. Thank you, Doctor."

Ellie came back with a cardboard tray and three steaming cups. "By the way, who was that rushing out of the parking lot?"

"Debbie Daugherty." Simon turned to Georgia. "She didn't look happy. What happened? Why did she leave?"

"She had an appointment she couldn't break. Something about a traffic ticket. She was terribly upset to have to go before we had seen the doctor."

"The way she was driving, she'll be lucky if she doesn't get another ticket."

"I'll call her with an update as soon as Dr. Hanrahan comes back."

Ellie said timidly, "My mother wants to be updated as well."

Simon raised his eyebrows. "Do I sense a bit of one-upmanship in the gossip world?"

"Competition is always healthy," Georgia muttered absently.

"She *said*," responded Ellie stiffly, "that she was doing it for Debbie."

The three of them sat in the waiting room, Simon twiddling his thumbs, Georgia sipping coffee, and Ellie staring at them both. She whispered to Simon, "I wish I knew her better. I don't know how to comfort her."

"Distraction may work. We could talk about our theories."

Ellie seemed uncertain, but before she could respond, Georgia put down her coffee. "I almost forgot. Simon, your mother phoned just before this happened. I think she needed you."

"I'll go outside and call her." He went through the revolving glass door. As he dialed, he watched the two women. *I told Ellie to keep Georgia occupied. I hope she doesn't start asking leading questions. Better make this short.* "Mother, are you okay?"

"Oh, yes, hon. I just wanted you to pick up some wine on your way home."

"I don't think you're supposed to drink while you're on that new medication."

"And *I* think we're beyond worrying about that, aren't we?"

She's right. I have to keep reminding myself that…that…"All right. Any word from—?"

"I'll tell you when you get home. Where are you?"

"At the hospital."

"*What?*"

"At Luther Memorial. Santa had a heart attack. He'll probably need a stent."

"Oh, dear. I hope he isn't too miffed about it. He's such a curmudgeon when it comes to his health. And with Georgia going back to study for the bar exam…"

"He's got Debbie Daugherty."

"Yes, that is a blessing. I'm surprised she wasn't at the hospital before Santa got there."

"She was."

His mother laughed. "I should probably turn on the radio—it's sure to be on the four o'clock news." She paused. "So…I want to meet your Ellie."

"Mother!"

"Now that you're finally going with her, I think it's time she met your alter ego."

"But—"

"Now, Simon, just because I'm on my last legs doesn't mean I can't play the intimidating parent."

"I've got to go."

"Bring her to dinner tonight. And don't forget the wine."

He came through the door to hear Ellie mumbling, her eyes shy, "Um, Georgia, do you know why Simon still lives with his mother?"

"He doesn't."

"What do you mean? He hasn't been…has he been…lying to me?"

Shit. Shit. Shit. But…wait a minute. If Georgia tells her, I won't have to. He paused in the doorway.

"What?" Georgia put down the cup. "No. That's the lawyer in me, I suppose. No, she lives with him. It's his house."

"I see."

Georgia peered at her. "He hasn't told you?"

"Told me what?"

"His mother's house burned down six months ago. They retrieved some items, but not much. It doesn't really matter since—"

That's it. Simon slammed a fist into his palm, making the two women jump. "Georgia." His voice trembled with anger.

"How do you do that with your voice, Simon? It's very dramatic."

He let his breath out in a whoosh. "Georgia, one of these days…"

"Tell her."

"No, not now."

"Then when?"

"Mother wants her to come for dinner."

Ellie watched this exchange with wide eyes.

Simon yanked her up. "Come on, Ellie."

She rose obediently but pulled at his hand. "How is

Georgia supposed to get home?"

He halted. His best friend waited long enough for him to start squirming and said cheerily, "Virgil's taking me home. Thanks anyway, *Ellie.*"

He dropped Ellie off at her house. "I've got to go back and tell Hosea what's been going on and buy some groceries. I'll pick you up at seven?"

"I can drive if you give me the directions. Your mother may need your help."

"Oh. Okay. It's 2750 North Wolff Street. Go left on Atlantic, right on Wolff. It's on the right just before the road turns into Highland—the blue cracker house."

"Cracker house?"

"Old Florida. Two-story, raised off the ground, tin roof, big porch. Looks out on the creek. Alligators bask on my deck."

"Oh, dear."

"No worries—I'll shoo them off before you come."

She wrote the address down, then looked up, smiling nervously. "Simon? Is your mother like you?"

"God, no. She's normal." His eyes misted. "The best mother a man could have." He left her on the curb and drove away.

****

Simon's house, Thursday, May 10

Simon came out when he saw Ellie's car pull up. She handed him a bottle of wine. "Oh, you didn't have to."

"It's my pleasure."

Simon's mother stood in the doorway. An apron tied around her waist sported a large chili pepper in a sombrero and the words, "Taste buds? We don't need no stinkin' taste buds!" "Welcome, Miss Ironstone."

"Please call me Ellie, Mrs. Ribault. It's wonderful to meet you."

Simon noticed Ellie's voice cracked a bit.

"And you must call me Madeleine. Do come in."

As Ellie stepped into the hallway, his mother held back and whispered, "She's lovely, and so sweet."

Simon grinned. "You haven't seen her pissed."

Madeleine said she needed to finish the sauce and left the other two in the living room. The cat and dog apparently decided to make Ellie feel welcome, for Roan settled on her feet and Isis on her shoulder. Suddenly anxious, Simon asked, "Er…drink?"

"I think a glass of wine?"

Her discomfort gave him strength. "Go ahead, make a decision. It's one small step for mankind."

"A glass of white wine then."

"Muscadet?"

"Perfect." Ellie looked around the book-filled room. An overstuffed couch kept two leather chairs company. On the fourth wall stood a piano. She pointed through an open door. "Is that your study in there?"

"Yes. It looks out on the back deck and the creek."

"How wonderful to have a water view."

"You do too."

"True, but there's more variety on the river—the marshes, the birds, the boats—"

"The alligators, the snapping turtles."

"Right. It *teems*. The ocean only has waves and the occasional alien-looking jellyfish."

"You just haven't been here long enough. We should go horseback riding on the beach some morning. You'll see more then."

"I'd love to."

Madeleine came in. "Dinner's ready. Simon, will you light the candles?" She set two bowls of mussels steamed in garlic and olive oil on the table and a basket of rolls by Simon's side.

Ellie stared at the plates.

"What is it, dear?"

Her mouth opened and closed. "For some reason, I expected…hamburgers."

Madeleine laughed. "Not at my table. Simon will have to make do."

The mussels were followed by veal rolls filled with spinach and cheese. Simon thought it just as well Ellie didn't notice that his loving mother had left the spinach and cheese out of his veal roll. *Take it slow. Don't want to shock my taste buds unnecessarily.* Something gurgled under his belt. *Or my digestion.*

"I'm glad to see you enjoy good food, Ellie." Madeleine did not look at her son.

Ellie, busy scarfing up the last of the fresh tomato sauce, could only nod.

The older woman rose. "Let's take our wine out to the front porch so we can watch the sunset." She whistled for Roan to follow her.

As the purples, oranges, and yellows flickered above the trees, Madeleine sighed. "I shall miss this place." She turned to Ellie. "You know, my home burned down in December. Faulty wiring. Thank God for the alarm. Simon got me out, but we lost a lot of family heirlooms. I was so lucky he'd moved back to Amelia Island and could put me up."

"Georgia told me about the fire. Will you look for another place or will you stay here with Simon?"

"Oh, dear, no." She laughed. "I couldn't deal with

him underfoot all the time. Not to mention tripping over his books everywhere. There isn't enough room for both me and his collections. Besides, I have to register at the clinic next week."

"Clinic?"

Simon held up a hand. "Mother." His voice was low but full of heavy meaning.

His mother ignored him. "The Zimmerman Clinic. Since I've been given a month or two to live, I volunteered for an experimental drug trial there. It's only been tested on rats so far. I get to be one of the first human guinea pigs." She chuckled. "I guess they're moving up the chain of rodent evolution. I asked to be in the control group, but the old duffers said if I knew I was taking the placebo, it wouldn't be a real experiment."

Simon's hands were rolled into fists so tight the fingers turned white. "Mother."

"What, honey?" She gazed innocently at him. "Shouldn't I have told Ellie? If you're going to marry her, she needs to know there may be some hurdles to leap first. Or would you like to tie the knot right away?"

"*Mother.*"

Ellie put a hand on his arm. "Thank you for telling me, Madeleine. I am so sorry you're ill. Perhaps the drug will work, and I'll have a chance to get to know you. That would be marvelous." She smiled, but Simon saw tears glistening in her eyes.

He took a deep breath. "Okay, it's out. Now, it's getting late...we have to be at the park by eight tomorrow." His tone was firm. "I'm sure you want an early night."

"I'd like to help with the dishes first."

Madeleine filled her glass. "Don't you dare. I'm going to sit here a while and enjoy the evening. I suspect Simon wants to talk to you alone."

He walked her to her car, his lips set in a tight line.

Ellie waited until they were on the sidewalk. "Why are you so angry?"

He kicked at a stone. "I don't want her to die, okay?"

"Well, of course you don't."

"She's all I have left of my family. My father was lost at sea ten years ago. My sister died in a car crash when she was fifteen. My brother…my brother went to Alaska and hasn't been heard from since. He always was an odd duck." He stopped at the slight snuffle coming from her vicinity. "What's that?"

"Takes one to know one."

He almost laughed. "I guess I've just been telling myself all will be well, that Mom will recover. I couldn't bear to talk about it."

"Women need to, though. If you don't allow us to vent, we shatter."

He kissed her forehead. "You're right. Men are perfectly happy to overlook life's unpleasantnesses. Except of course, when we're sick. Then you can't get us to shut up. I read that more men than women believe they have the flu when they only have a cold. In fact—"

"Simon."

"Yes?"

"You're talking too much. Kiss me."

He obliged. When they came up for air, he started to say something.

She held a hand over his mouth. "*Shh*. I've got to go." She nodded at the figure on the porch. "Your mother's dying to find out what we talked about. Tell her we didn't get around to discussing it."

"But we did. We—"

"It."

"It?"

"Marriage." She got in the car and roared off.

Chapter Fourteen
The Plot Thickens

Simon's house, Thursday, May 10

When Simon came inside, his mother called from the study. "I've been checking my emails. I have good news and bad news."

Damn. "Good news first."

"If you're sure…The clinic wants me in Rochester and prepped by Monday, so I won't be in your hair much longer."

"That's the good news?"

"The bad news is we have to pack my stuff quickly. I have to be on a plane tomorrow."

"That's the bad news?"

"This is not a productive line of questioning, son of mine. Now help me get my stuff together. I've made a reservation for a two o'clock flight from Jacksonville, so we've got some time."

"But I thought we were going to drive to Minnesota together?" He could hear his voice spiraling up from tenor to falsetto, but he couldn't help it. "It was supposed to be a last—I mean, a special—trip."

"Can't be helped. The progress of science must not be slowed. What if they tossed me off the trial?"

Sigh. "Okay, what do you want me to do?"

"How about you gather some reading material for

me." She patted his cheek. "You're so good at that."

The next afternoon, as he drove back to Fernandina Beach from the airport, Simon mulled over his new life. *It's so unfair. I'm finally back home and Mother goes, and here I am alone again.* He thought of the years of solitude, just him and his books. Women came and went—attracted to the coppery flecks in his hazel eyes and his craggy cheekbones. One woman—*Sarah, wasn't it?*—claimed they reminded her of Jack Palance. The cheekbones, not the eyes. They loved his chocolate-colored hair, usually tousled, and thin but muscled frame. Before long, though, they'd withdraw, driven off by his inability to communicate. *It's not that I couldn't, I just didn't want to. Too busy learning too many things. Let's face it, I was more titillated by exotic mating rituals than by flesh-and-blood sex.* Ellie's image rose before him. *Yes, but she's different. She gets me. She doesn't press me to open up. And...* The activities of previous nights returned in all their glory. *Wow.* His mother's casual reference to marriage tickled. Am *I ready to settle down?*

He found a note on his door from Georgia.

Dad home. Please come over. G.

The sun was setting when he reached the house on Jasmine Street. As was his wont, he knocked twice and walked in without waiting for an answer. He found Santa on the couch, a blanket tucked around his knees, Georgia at his side. When he saw who their companion was, he jerked back. "Oh, hi, Ellie. What are you doing here?"

Georgia answered. "I asked her to come. I needed some help, and since you had disappeared, she was kind enough to drop everything and pop over." She smiled at

Ellie.

"Debbie's not here?"

Santa growled, "She was driving me crazy. The woman has a fetish for herbal suppositories."

"Don't you mean supplements?"

The old man stared at him. "Supplements? Oh...um...yeah. I guess so. I wondered why she seemed so baffled when I threw her out."

Georgia goggled at him. "You thought they were *suppositories*?" She chortled. "That explains a lot. Too cute."

Ellie glanced at Simon. "So where have you been?"

"I had to take Mother to the airport."

Georgia was surprised. "You did? Why?"

"The Zimmerman people got expedited permission to start the experiment. They needed her by Monday. There wasn't time to drive her to Minnesota."

Ellie knit her brow. "So she's alone?"

"No, no. They'll assign her a full-time health aide and put her in the dormitory there. She'll call when she's settled."

Georgia picked up her glass. "I hope she remembered to sneak in alcohol. Those places are so dreary."

"Actually, it's quite nice. We visited there when they first approached Mother. She can't have alcohol during the test phase anyway."

"Hasn't stopped her yet."

"I doubt if the aide will put up with what we put up with."

"When I figure that sentence out, I'll be suitably offended."

Simon sat across from the old man. "How are you

feeling?"

"Pampered." He grinned. "I should scare my daughter like this every day."

Georgia sniffed. "He's still tingling from the jolt they gave him. Hopefully, it'll drop a few synapses back into place."

Ellie got up and poured lemonade into a glass for Simon and refilled the other three. "Georgia was telling me about your friendship when you came in."

"Where did she start? Kindergarten?" He closed his eyes, humming "Ring Around the Rosie." "It was our first day. The teacher had sent us outside for recess. I was happily swinging..." He opened them and glared at Georgia. "When she pushed me off and grabbed the rope out of my hands—"

"And you slugged me. You slugged a *girl*. Miss Chloe was aghast."

"Yeah, and your father shook my hand and said you deserved it."

Santa chuckled. "That I did."

"So the relationship went downhill from there?" Ellie's voice brimmed with mirth.

"Pretty much. It helped that all the kids were jealous of my black eye. Then in fourth grade—"

"Are we going to describe every brawl we got into?"

"How about just the one where we teamed up to run down that bully Wesley. That was a great night."

Ellie said, "I'm beginning to see a pattern. So you two never tried to...er..."

"Let the relationship ripen into romance?" Georgia smirked at Simon. "Once. You'd better tell it, Simon."

"Not me."

Georgia emitted a theatrical sigh. "It was in high school, our senior year. We decided that if there was anything there, we'd better find out before we both left for college. We went to a concert—"

"A movie."

"That's right. You wanted to see *The Gangs of New York* so we settled on *Almost Famous*."

"Then we drove to the local lovers' lane."

"Actually, to Egan's Creek playground. Looks out over the swamp."

"Marsh." Simon beetled his brows at Georgia. "Anyway, we sat there discussing tort reform and sustainable fisheries until Georgia decided the time of reckoning was upon us."

"Go on." Ellie's lips were pressed tightly together, but Simon noticed her eyes danced.

Georgia took over. "So…the great Lothario makes his move. He yawns, then slowly raises an arm, the idea apparently being to let it fall with studied insouciance across my shoulders. Unfortunately, his sleeve catches on the gear shift. Feigning calm—his hands are shaking so much the whole car rocks—he extricates himself. Then, ignoring my helpless titter, he leans toward me. I attempt to reciprocate, but my foot gets stuck on this disgusting piece of chewing gum." She directed a pointed look at Simon. "I don't know why you kept that car in such gross condition."

"I didn't. That car was as pristine then as it is today."

Ellie looked at Santa. "The Mustang?"

Simon let just a wee bit of pride seep out. "The very one. I bought it from the pharmacist—"

"Mr. Eckart."

"Yes, and stop interrupting. I bought it with money I made working at the ER diner summers."

"ER diner? I don't know that one."

Santa leaned in. "ER for Emergency Room. It's a block from the hospital, so most of its regular customers are doctors and recovering patients." He chuckled. "They'll eat anything. Its real name is Duffy's."

Simon waited a minute in the vain hope of bullying them into silence before resuming in a slightly louder voice. "As I have explained to Ellie—and regret to see I am forced to reiterate—my car is a vintage 1966 convertible Mustang GT, fully restored. The model recently sold on EBay for…er…a *lot* of money."

Georgia, undaunted, disagreed. "He kept the *outside* pristine; the inside was packed floor to ceiling with books and magazines. I had to sit on top of a pile of old *Popular Mechanics* issues."

"Journals in mint condition, mind you—I don't dog ear my books, let alone my journals, like *some* people do. And I would remind you that the gum was yours." He turned to Ellie. "At the last minute, it occurred to her that having a gob of Doublemint stuffed in her cheek while making out might dampen the mood. She lobbed it onto the floor when she thought I wasn't looking."

"I dropped it on a piece of tissue you'd left there. At any rate, I couldn't get close enough to Simon's lips, and we eventually gave up."

"Suffice it to say, it was a fiasco."

"And we both realized it was not to be. It came as such a relief."

Simon put down his glass. "Satisfied?"

"I guess." Ellie rose. "I've got to get home. Do you need anything else, Georgia?"

"No, no. Thanks so much."

Simon watched her go. "You two have become fast friends. I'm not sure I like it."

Georgia kissed his cheek. "I find it refreshing to have a female friend. We have so much in common." Simon opened his mouth, but no clever reply rose to mind. She took up the slack. "Well, wouldn't you like to have a bosom buddy, a guy friend?"

"I…uh…have a vast assortment of friends."

"Name one. Thad?" She couldn't keep the disbelief out of her voice. "Hosea?"

He rose. "I don't need this abuse. Besides, you have to get into that short nurse's uniform you entertain your boyfriends with. I think Santa deserves a little show."

"That's shocking."

"Good. I haven't lost my touch."

****

Park headquarters, Saturday, May 12

Rosie put the doughnut down. "Oh, Simon, a Mr. Gregory called. He'd like to see you."

MacGregor? Does he want to confess? "Did he say why?"

"Nope."

"Okay." He drove down to the Green Cross office.

Nora dropped her pen. "You."

"Mr. Mac—I mean Mr. Gregory—wants to see me."

"Really?"

"I have the hall pass right here."

"Oh, okay. Go right in."

Gregory sat at his desk thumbing through a newspaper. He didn't look up. "I understand you've been snooping around about me."

"Snooping? In my dictionary, it's called research. I've been assigned to investigate several murders. You are a possible witness to them. You have not been very forthcoming, Mr. MacGregor."

He started. "So you know."

"Yes, but what I don't know is why you're using an alias."

He put the paper down. "It's business. I've got other interests besides this one. I like to keep them separate."

"I see." Simon pretended to consider. "You know, around here, the name MacGregor carries some weight. I presume you know your family history."

"I don't know what you're talking about."

"I think you do. You're a descendant of Sir Gregor MacGregor, who declared the Republic of the Floridas right on this spot. And he raised a flag over the fort—a green cross on a white field. Sound familiar?" He pointed at the logo on Gregory's desk.

"All right. So what? When I set up shop here, I didn't know about the island's history. I came across the story of my ancestor, and figured if I had any trouble getting the Fernandina moguls to go along with the sister-city idea I could use my background as leverage."

"Is that why you planned such a big event at Fort Clinch? What happened? Why did you call it off?"

Gregory drummed his fingers on the table. "We weren't quite ready to go public, okay? We're waiting on an associate to come up with more backers. That's all I'm going to tell you. It has nothing to do with those murders. Nobody saw or heard anything." He rose. "I'll see you out."

Simon left. His phone buzzed. "Simon? It's Amos. Where are you?"

"On Atlantic Avenue."

"Can you come back to the police station?"

"How come?"

"Iggy's here. He says he has a story to tell."

When Simon arrived, Amos and Hosea were in Amos's office. "So, you two have decided to cooperate despite orders?"

Hosea hitched up his pants. "No need to make a state case out of it. We can handle this ourselves."

Amos chimed in. "Yeah. We'll…uh…call them in when we've solved it. Next time, they won't be so quick to interfere." He prodded the slight figure of Iggy Freeman, who sat hunched on a chair, his scrubs stained and wrinkled. "Okay, Freeman, Simon's here now. What did you want to tell us?"

The poor man looked extremely ill at ease. "I just thought I'd better come forward. Virgil thinks so too."

"And where is Virgil?"

"He's at the morgue. We thought it would look suspicious if we both left."

"Go on."

"Well…" He looked at Simon. "Remember when you were asking about that event at the fort? The night before the murders?"

"Yes."

He suddenly pushed back the chair and stood, laying a hand across his heart. "I swear this has nothing to do with them. Nothing. I'm pretty sure. But it's…it's…" The last sentence came out in a rush. "We just get the feeling there's something iffy going on."

"I see." Simon waved him back down.

"I told you Kenny asked me and Virgil to meet him there that night."

"Uh huh."

"He said there were going to be lots of people—mebbe a hundred or so, and that there'd be beer and a country band. You ever hear of the Wailing Cowboys? My cousin Jeremy plays bass for them. They're real good. Well, when we got there the place was deserted—no barbecue, no lights, nothing."

"What time was that?"

"Maybe ten, ten thirty."

"Why so late?"

He shrugged. "That's when the boss told us to come. We were about to turn around when we heard Kenny's voice. We followed it to that little room under the walls. The place was lit up with all these candles, and there were several people inside besides Kenny."

Hosea leaned forward. "Who?"

"Crowley, Hearst, Farnsworth. Mrs. Barnes." He shot a quick glance at Amos. "The lady who owns El Toro. And the Hispanic guy—remember? The one who never opened his mouth."

"Okay, so then what happened?"

Iggy fidgeted. "Like I told you, Mr. Gregory was finishing up his pitch about sister cities. Then Kenny told us to go wait by the car."

"That's it?"

"No, no. See…" His eyes darted around. "There's more. After we left, the mayor, the judge, and Hearst came out and got in their cars. A coupla minutes later, this commotion starts up. Virgil walks back through the entrance to see what's up. Mr. Gregory is in the silent dude's face, screaming something about not coming through with his end of the bargain."

"Bargain?"

"That he had promised a hundred men."

Simon leaned forward. "*Men? He said 'men'?*"

"Not contributors or supporters?" Hosea was puzzled.

Iggy shook his head. "He said a hundred men. Virgil was positive."

"Did you stay by the truck?"

"No, after that I joined Virgil. We stayed in the shadows, but we could see and hear."

The other three were quiet a minute, digesting this information. Finally, Simon asked, "How well do you know Mr. Gregory?"

"Not very well. Kenny had us help him move some big boxes a couple weeks ago. Told us then that they were teaming up on some project."

"The guy Gregory was yelling at. What did he look like?"

"Like I said—Latino. Tall, moustache, shiny black hair."

I was right—Martí's not a translator. He's the other silent partner. "Hearst, Farnsworth, and Crowley were gone. Where were the rest?"

"Lessee, I didn't see Kenny." He frowned. "Missus El Toro was sitting in a big easy chair. She was listening to the argument between Gregory and the grease monkey. Had this little smile on her face."

"Anyone else?"

He looked carefully at Amos. "Well, as we headed

back to the pickup, we…uh…saw…"

"Who?" Hosea prompted gently.

Iggy hunched his shoulders a little more and spoke to the floor. "It was after eleven. Mrs. Barnes came out and walked around the corner of the fort. She…uh…had a cigarette."

"Oh, she did." Amos uttered a low growl.

Hoo boy, I'm glad I'm not the one who blabbed. "How did you know she had a cigarette? Wasn't it dark?"

"There's a lamp near the fort entrance. It was easy to make out that it was a woman. Plus we could see the lit end. Then the restaurant lady came out and joined her—"

"Lisabet de Angeles."

"Uh huh."

"How long were they outside?"

"Just a minute or so. Mrs. Barnes came down the path and got into her car and drove off. Then Kenny came out and told us to go on home."

"What about the others?"

"They were coming to the parking lot as we left."

"And that's it? That's all you have?" Amos shrugged and turned away.

Iggy stared at his back. "But what about the hundred men? What does a sister city need a hundred men for?"

Amos didn't answer. Hosea's face was blank. "Staff?"

Time to share my information.

Simon opened his mouth, but Iggy spoke first. "Me and Virgil saw the dark guy again."

Hosea began to pace. "Get on with it, man."

"He and Kenny and Mr. Gregory—"

Simon interrupted. "His name is MacGregor. Carson MacGregor."

The others stared at him. Amos spoke first. "As in Gregor MacGregor?"

"Correct. His descendant."

Amos, who seemed to have recovered from his wrath, or else had worked out a plan of retribution for his straying wife, asked, "Why the alias?"

"He says he has different projects and uses different names."

Amos rolled his eyes. "Yeah, right."

"I wonder why he didn't use the MacGregor name here then," mused Hosea. "He could have parlayed it into all sorts of lucrative deals."

"He says he planned to use it as a backup plan if he needed it."

"*Hmmph.*" Amos tapped a pencil on the desk. "All right, so you saw MacGregor, Kenny, and the other man—"

Simon had to interrupt again. "Martí. His name is Julian Martí."

Hosea rolled his eyes. "Let me guess, descended from José Martí, liberator of Cuba."

"Yup. I've been trying to figure out what the offspring of three such notable personages are doing working together. They all have a history with Amelia Island..."

"Martí too? How?"

"Didn't you know? It was right here in Fernandina Beach that he set his revolution in motion."

"Huh."

"Huh."

Iggy chimed in. "Huh."

I'd better clarify. "I mean the Cuban war of independence from Spain. He lived in the Florida House Inn."

"And what does this have to do with the Green Cross people?"

Iggy interrupted impatiently. "If you'll let me finish, maybe I can help with that."

"With what the three are doing?"

"Yeah. See, last week Virgil and I went to the inn to pick up a case of soda for the station. Martí, Kenny, and MacGregor were all in that private room. I guess the door was open a crack, and we could hear them talking. Kenny mentioned the two ladies. He said they hadn't come up with the cash yet."

"Cash? Did he say how much they needed? What it was for?"

Simon could see Amos was struggling with the news. He said soothingly, "I'm sure it's all perfectly legitimate, Amos. Sylvia wouldn't be involved in anything shady."

"Who knows?" His tone was worried. "You know she was born in Cuba—her parents sent her to the States when Castro took over. Most of the family is still stuck there. It's always haunted her. She feels guilty that she's, in her words, living the high life and they're suffering under that filthy dictator."

"Which one?"

"Fidel."

"You do remember he's dead."

"What difference does that make? Raoul is just as bad."

Iggy's voice startled everyone. "At any rate, it

sounded like they're planning a big event. We heard Kenny ask about the progress of recruitment, and Martí said he'd been successful in Miami."

"The hundred men?"

"I guess so. But then—and this is where it got interesting—he asked MacGregor if he'd procured the guns and the boats."

"*What?*"

"Did you say guns and…?"

"Boats."

Finally Simon asked, "What was MacGregor's answer?"

"Don't know. Zoe came out with the soda, and we had to leave."

A collective sigh wafted around the room. After a minute, Hosea said, "We can probably find out if MacGregor's purchased any guns recently. I wonder what kind of boats they were talking about?"

"And what did they plan to use them for?"

"You don't suppose they want to conquer Amelia Island again?"

An awkward pause followed this suggestion. The phone rang. Amos picked it up. "Uh huh. Uh huh. What was his name?" He wrote something down on his blotter. "Oh, really? Thanks for the information."

He hung up. "That was the Nassau County sheriff's office. They had a call from a Detective Brown who's taken over the case from Labadie. He's found evidence that Bonney, the drug smuggler, had a contact here on Amelia Island."

Simon slapped his forehead. "The phone number! I keep forgetting about that."

Amos blinked. "Not that. He found some notes

from Virtue that mention a correspondence he'd come across."

"Correspondence? Between Bonney and a partner?"

"Captain Goodwine?"

"Nope. See, funny thing is, it was in Spanish."

Chapter Fifteen
Rope Tricks

Ellie's house, Saturday, May 12

"Another slice?"

"Yes, please. Key lime's my favorite. Did you make it yourself?"

"Of course. Mother always said that a good wife has to know how to make a perfect soufflé and a perfect pie crust."

Simon stared at her. Ellie hadn't mentioned the marriage thing again. As she busied herself cutting a large wedge of pie, his mind shut down, desperately seeking an escape route. At last a bit of trivia rolled onto the stage, and he latched onto it like a shipwreck survivor to a floating plank. "In the Middle East, a woman's suitability for marriage is judged by her Turkish coffee. See, you put the fine ground coffee in the bottom of the *jezve* and—"

"Speaking of mothers, have you heard from yours?"

Phew. Or...wait. "Yes. They start the trials Wednesday. Right now, they're plying her with hormones. Apparently, she needs elevated levels of estrogen to handle the experiment. She says she's been having wet dreams."

"I thought only men had those."

"Well, the equivalent. She's fantasizing about a fling with Sean Connery."

"Isn't he a little old?"

"Not for her."

She sat down. "Okay, so you told me what Iggy and Virgil overheard. Before we get into that, did the Jamaican detective offer any more information about Bonney's Spanish partner?"

"No. They never found the phone number Labadie told Hosea about. They did find a cryptic note in Virtue's file. Something about following her, meaning Bonney, to the source."

"*Hmm*. What about the captain of the boat?"

"Messieurs Garenflo and Bailey didn't get the impression he was entirely on board with our lady pirate's ambitions."

"But he took her money."

"Uh huh." He looked at her. "You thinking what I'm thinking?"

"A visit to the Panther Point marina tomorrow?"

"Saddle up."

Ellie covered the pie with plastic wrap and put it in the refrigerator. "Okay, that's one down. Now, this affair of the three *caballeros* and their boats and guns and money. You assert that at one time the ancestors of these guys all tried to take over Amelia Island?"

"Only two of them. And not just tried. Did. Not particularly successfully, but nonetheless. MacGregor managed to hold on to it for about three weeks longer than Mathews did. José Martí only plotted—from the comfort of the local hostelry. And that wasn't to free Fernandina Beach, but to free Cuba from Spain."

"Perhaps that's what his descendant wants to do

now."

"Last I looked, Cuba has been independent for more than a hundred years."

"Okay…Spanish…Could Martí be Bonney's correspondent?"

He shook his head. "Makes no sense. For one thing, he speaks English."

"Bonney was Jamaican. What do they speak?"

"English. And a creole language called Patois. Although I'm sure with all the Spanish-speaking islands around them, most Jamaicans have a smattering."

"Maybe they used Spanish to keep their negotiations secret?"

"From whom?" Simon shrugged. "And anyway, what would he want with a drug smuggler? Wait a minute…the guns and boats."

Ellie shook her head. "What really doesn't make sense is why Bonney would take up with *him*. She had a lucrative trade going. She wouldn't give it up for a cause."

"Cause?"

"The sister cities."

"I forgot about that."

"So, I repeat. How would it profit a drug smuggler?"

"Ease of access?"

"Possibly. But—"

Simon interrupted. "Wait. Remember, I speculated a while ago that two members of the Green club, MacGregor and Mathews, have an anti-Spain bias. And now we learn that Martí and Sylvia have reason to hate the communist government. Why on earth would they want to *improve* relations with Cuba? What's in it for them?"

"Follow the money?"

"The drug money? *Hmm*. Perhaps we should take a different tack. Why couldn't Bonney have been the ringleader?"

"And MacGregor et al. were her flunkies?" Ellie shook her head. "I can't see Sylvia Barnes involved in anything more illicit than cigarette smuggling."

He frowned. "What about the mayor and the judge? Could it be election related? Could they be laundering funny money through Cuba?"

Ellie took his plate and put it in the sink. "Well…"

Simon rubbed his temples. "This is getting too complicated. So far we have no evidence of a link between the murders and the Greenies. On the other hand, the timing is awfully pat."

"Okay, after we visit the marina, we check on Julian, see if we can dig up any ties to the seamy Cuban underworld. Radio Martí could be the perfect cover." She rinsed out her wine glass. "The night is still young. What now? Want to go over to my house and watch a DVD?"

"No. Now we make love."

"Here?" She looked around. "I don't even know where your bedroom is."

"Upstairs. Oh, watch those books…I'll move them." He toppled the pile of books off the stairs and held out his hand. "Come on." *If I can keep her occupied she'll maybe, hopefully, with any luck, not bring up this marriage thing. At least not until I've sorted it all out.*

****

Simon's house, Sunday, May 13

"Yes, Hosea. We'll let you know what we find out."

Ellie rolled over and wiped the sleep from her eyes. A loud crash made her sit up. "What was that?"

Simon bent down and gathered up a heap of magazines and notebooks. "Sorry."

She watched him drop the pile onto an armchair already overflowing with papers. "I didn't notice last night what a dump this room is."

"That's because you were too busy winding yourself around me like a warm pretzel right out of the oven."

She picked up a heavy tome from the bedside table. "*Larousse Gastronomique*? What the hell?"

"I told you, I'm a foodie."

"But you don't cook."

"And get my hands dirty?"

Ellie sighed and got out of bed. "I need a bathrobe or something if I'm going to stay overnight here."

Oh shit. "Um, here. Put this shirt on. I'll take you home and you can change before we hit the marina."

Ellie shot him a wary glance. "Okay. Don't I get breakfast? It's the least you can do after all my efforts last night."

"No time. I've got to walk the dog. We'll pick up a doughnut on the way."

"And coffee."

He jingled the coins in his pocket. "You got a buck?"

"Oh, for heaven's sake, just take me home." She didn't speak until they got to her door. "Don't get out."

"What?"

"I said, go on. I'll call you when I'm ready to go."

She leaned in the window. "And by the way, I'm not interested in marriage, especially with *you.*"

Simon was absolutely positively certain that he shouldn't let the relief show, so he reversed the car and left, tossing her a cheery wave. On the way back to the house, an unexpected depression settled on him. *Why* not *me anyway? Why doesn't she want to marry me?* He thought of those long, shapely legs, those eyes the color of a gale-tossed sea, her key lime pie. *She must think—with some justification...well, a lot—that she can do better than me.*

****

Panther Point Marina, Sunday, May 13

Two hours later, they pulled into the little harbor town. Goodwine's fishing boat was still moored in the marina. No one was around. "I'm going into the bait shop. You wait here."

"Why?"

"It's just the way it's done."

Simon opened the screen door and stepped into the gloom. A man wearing thigh-high fishing waders and a straw hat stood by the vending machine holding a candy bar and a bag of chips. "Is Harvey here?"

A voice came from the back. "At the fish tanks. Who wants to know?"

"It's Simon. Simon Ribault."

A heavy-set man in overalls came through the back door wiping his hands on an oily rag. All the hair from his crown had migrated to a thick, gray ponytail, leaving behind a shiny red pate and bristling black eyebrows. "Why, little Simon. Ain't seen you since you was in high school. Lemme look at you." He scrutinized the uniform and hat. "You in the poleece force now?"

"No, sir. I'm a park ranger up at Fort Clinch."

"Wall, tha's better. Coke?"

"Sure, thanks."

They settled on stools next to a counter littered with match boxes, used lottery tickets, and flyers for gun shows. "You here about Jo Jo?"

"Diogenes Goodwine? Yes."

"Too bad about him. Got hisself mixed up wit' some bad comp'ny. Should'a stuck to shrimpin'."

"How involved was he in the drug smuggling? Did he provide more than just the trawler?"

"Nah. He took his cut though." Harvey spat. "Dirty money. No Geechee fella should touch drugs. It's like a new slavery."

"How'd he get suckered in?"

"This whale of a black woman shows up one day. Nasty piece of work. Bailey says she handed Jo Jo a wad of cash."

"When was this?"

"Mebbe a month ago."

"That would be, say, mid-April?" *Okay, so the time is right.* "Then what happened?"

"Nothing for a coupla days. Then he gets this call."

"How do you know?"

"Diogenes didn' have a phone, so he used the one here now and then. Person left a message for him."

"What was the message?"

"Just a time and day." He scratched his beard. "But the caller had an accent. Hard to understand."

"Gullah?"

He laughed. "No'um, little Simon. Everyone around here in Old Town is Geechee but me. I know what it sounds like."

"Jamaican'?"

"Uh uh."

"Then what?"

He screwed up his eyes. "If I had to say, I'd say Spanish."

Martí. Simon nodded. "So after the call, Diogenes left?"

"Yup."

"Did he say where he was going?"

Harvey screwed up his eyes. "Pretty sure it was Jacksonville. I dint pay much attention."

"Did you see the boat return on April 14?"

"Saturday? Nope. Heard a ruckus though."

"What kind of ruckus?"

"Shoutin'. Yellin'."

"No shots?"

"Nope."

"Any idea how many people were on the boat?"

Harvey shrugged. "It didn' have no running lights when it came in. Got no street lights here neither. It's really just me and the Baileys now. Although…"

"What?"

"I did see some headlights around midnight. Car pulled up to the dock. Big sedan, maybe a Lexus or Mercedes. Sat there a while."

"Did anyone get out of the car?"

Harvey screwed up his eyes. "Mebbe. Heard a slam after the splash. After a bit, heard another slam."

"Splash?"

"Me an' Bailey, we figure it was the convict, the one they found on the shore with a knife in his back. Must've fought with Jo Jo. Either he fell or was pushed off the boat."

"Then what happened?"

"Car turned around and left. Really burnin' rubber."

Simon finished his soda and stood up. "My partner, Ellie Ironstone, is outside. Mind if we take a look at the *Mercy Louise* while we're here?"

"Be my guest. Police took the yellow tape off last week."

"What's going to happen to it?"

"I hear there's a cousin up on Sapelo Island coming down to take it off my hands."

Simon walked out into the blazing sun. Ellie sat on the dock, feet dangling close to the water. "You know a catfish can jump that high. Bite a toe off."

"Good thing I have my boots on, then, huh?" She looked down at the muddy water. "Catfish are carnivorous?"

"If they're hungry enough. Come on, I want to look at the boat again."

The old trawler listed even more than it had two weeks earlier. The last thunderstorm had left piles of leaves on the deck. Simon climbed over the gunwale. "You searched the deck last time, right?"

"Yes. So did forensics."

He tripped over the rope. "Look at this, what a mess. No sailor worth his salt would leave a rope all fouled up like this...Wait a minute." He bent down. "Where did you find the blood?"

"Over there, on the port side."

"Did we get a report on whose blood it was?"

"I'll give the lab a call." Ellie wandered to the bow. When she came back, she said, "Blood was

Goodwine's."

"Okay." He pointed to the other side of the boat. "The rope's been hurled willy-nilly to starboard. I'm betting the captain didn't have time to coil it before the fight broke out."

Ellie sat on a cushion. "Go on."

He paced the deck, his legs spread wide to compensate for the angle. "Remember when Kenny first examined the three victims? Virtue had been stabbed in the chest. Alvaredo had been stabbed in the back. In that preliminary survey, he saw no visible wounds on Bonney—"

"Which is why he assumed she drowned."

"Except. Except for a red cut around her ankle." He picked up one end of the rope. "Help me straighten this out." They slowly unknotted the rope and laid it in long loops on the deck. Starting at one end, he examined it minutely. About halfway down he yelped. "Found it!"

"Found what?"

"Blood. I'm guessing this isn't Alvaredo's blood, nor is it Captain Goodwine's."

"Odessa Bonney's?"

"Uh huh. If it is, I can guess what happened. Somehow, she got the rope wrapped around her ankle. It tripped her up, and she went overboard."

"That would explain why she ended up on the shore halfway between the two men." She looked into the water. "You know, if we could find her other shoe we'd know for sure."

"It could have fallen off anywhere between the fort and the marina." He noted the mulish expression on her face. "All right, all right. I'll see if I can persuade Amos to dredge the marina." He pulled his phone out.

When he returned, Ellie was fingering the rope. "Kenny says she was strangled. Could Alvaredo have killed her with this and then dumped her body in the water?"

"I don't know." He jumped off the boat and ran to the car, coming back with a large gunny sack. "Let's get the rope in the bag and take it to the station."

Mathews was at the district office in Jacksonville, but Iggy took the bag. "I'll take it over to the lab. They can test the blood and see if there's a match."

"Thanks. You…um…haven't suffered any repercussions from your…er…confession?"

Iggy grinned. "What Kenny doesn't know would fill the Ark."

"Should we come back or wait?"

"Give me a couple of hours."

Simon looked at Ellie. "How about if we get a spot of lunch?"

"Fine by me."

"Want to hit El Toro again?"

"Sure. I have a yen for solid food. Since I didn't get any *breakfast*."

They had waited at the desk for ten minutes before Inez noticed them. "Sorry, Simon. We're between managers. I'll seat you." She found them a table in the corner.

Ellie read the menu carefully. "What's this pickled fish? Sounds different." She looked up at the waitress.

"Escabeche? Yes. It's mackerel that's first fried, then marinated in vinegar, and served with thinly sliced onions. Delicious."

"I'll have that."

Simon ordered the *ropa vieja*. "But could you hold

the vegetables?"

Inez sniffed. "So…plain stewed beef?"

"If you wouldn't mind."

Simon was ignoring Ellie's disparaging comments when he spotted a waitress taking a tray to the small curtained alcove set aside for special guests of the owner. "Wonder who Lisabet's wining and dining today?"

"She's a pretty powerful businesswoman here in Fernandina, isn't she?"

"Not just here. Besides El Toro, she owns a chain of taco stands across the northern part of the state."

"Is she married?"

"You know, I'm not sure." The waitress passed them. "Hey, Inez, is Lisabet married?"

Inez glanced quickly at the curtain and back. "She was."

"Divorced?"

"Uh huh. Three times I think. The last one was a real skunk."

"What about the first two?"

"Mark—the second one—now, he was a sweetheart. I remember him bringing flowers to her every day." Inez sighed. "Lisabet said she couldn't live with anyone that nice."

"And the first?"

"She doesn't talk about him much. I gather she left him in Cuba."

Ellie buttered a roll. "Maybe he worked with her father. She told us he stayed behind when she and her mother escaped."

"That must have been hard on her." Simon gazed thoughtfully at the alcove.

Ellie whispered, "Remember, she said she couldn't care less about her Cuban heritage. But…to lose both a father and a husband? If it were me, it would break my heart."

Did she say "husband"? Urk. "*Shh.*" He raised his voice and said boisterously, "So who's she entertaining today? A new beau?"

"Nah." Inez knit her brows. "We haven't seen her with a man—on a date, that is—in years. Sylvia Barnes is lunching with her."

A busboy brought their plates. Simon kept a watchful eye on the curtain. After fifteen minutes, it opened and Lisabet and Sylvia walked out. They stood talking in low voices by the cash register. Simon dropped his napkin. "Be right back."

He strolled past the women, bumping Lisabet's elbow. "Oh, I'm so sorry, Ms. de Angeles! Guess I was blown away by the fantastic food and wasn't paying attention." He acted surprised. "Hi there, Sylvia. You two cooking something up?"

Both froze. Lisabet said in a tight voice, "Is that a joke, Simon?"

Sylvia started to brush past him, but he stepped in front of her. "I just wondered how the fundraising was going for the sister-cities project. How much do you need? Do you take donations?" He kept his expression bland.

Sylvia's mouth opened and shut without speaking. Lisabet said, "I believe it's going well. We're not actively involved in the financial side."

"Oh? That's not what I heard. I heard you two were given the lead on the money end."

Sylvia continued to stare, her lashes fluttering.

Again it was Lisabet who responded. "We're just part of the committee. If you have questions, feel free to ask Mr. Gregory."

"Gregory? Oh, you mean, Carson MacGregor."

Sylvia found her voice. "MacGregor? I…uh…"

Lisabet put a hand on her arm but spoke to Simon. "Yes, we know. He told me the other day that he uses different names for different enterprises. Very common." She squeezed Sylvia's arm. "Now, didn't you have a hair appointment, dear?" When Sylvia didn't move, Lisabet gave her a little shove.

"Oh…er…yes. Well, goodbye, and thanks for lunch." Her eyes grazed Simon. "Goodbye."

He shuffled back to the table.

Ellie watched him pick up his water glass and sip from it. "How do you manage to make your face look so vapid?"

"Vapid? I was going for expressionless. So the suspects don't know what the detective knows and doesn't know."

"I see. And do you know anything?"

"I think," he said carefully, "that Sylvia is frightened about something."

"Amos finding out that she's been sneaking cigarettes?"

"Maybe."

"What about Lisabet?"

"I think her job is to keep Sylvia from going wobbly."

****

Fernandina Beach police station, Sunday, May 13

"Well?"

Iggy handed Simon a sheet of paper. "Lab found a

273

match. Blood on the rope belongs to the female victim, the Jamaican woman."

"Could the rope have been used to strangle her?"

"You'll have to ask Kenny. He's on his way up from Jacksonville."

"Ask me what?" Kenny came through the door. Iggy told him what they'd found. "Let me see it." He came back a minute later. "It wasn't used to kill her. Something much finer and thinner was used."

Ellie hefted the rope. "Could she have gotten tangled up and lost her footing?"

"Makes sense. And it must have happened before the other two, Alvaredo and the captain, killed each other."

"So, an accident."

"Looks that way."

Ellie mused, "Well, if she fell off the boat, but didn't drown, she must have made it to shore alive."

"Where someone killed her."

Kenny looked at them both. "But who?"

Chapter Sixteen
Walk Softly and Carry a Big Stick

Police station, Sunday, May 13

"Who killed her? *Hmm*. She was well dressed but wore no jewelry. Perhaps the motive was simple robbery."

"A passerby? A homeless person?" Kenny seemed unconvinced.

Ellie said, "We did have a problem with that vet with PTSD. He was camping in the woods a few weeks ago."

Simon shook his head. "I took him to the VA hospital in St. Marys beginning of April. They got him off the meds, and he's working down at the sub shop on Sadler Road now."

Kenny started to leave. "Well, I've got work to do."

"Yeah, thanks for your help." Simon screwed up his mouth. "Say, Kenny, I hear your fundraising for the League of the Green Cross isn't going well."

The man stopped. "I don't see that that is any of your business, *Ribault.* Shouldn't you be out riding the Park range?"

"Boy, would I like to be doing that. Instead, I'm investigating the murder of five people, one of whom washed up right under your nose, *Mathews*. Until we're

275

satisfied they're not related to your little project, it's my only business."

Mathews shut his mouth and, turning his back, stomped down the corridor. They heard a door slam.

"Come on, I want to go someplace and think about this."

As Simon and Ellie drove down Centre Street, Nathan Hearst hailed them. Simon pulled over. The publisher, a newspaper under his arm, stuck his head in Ellie's side. "You have any news for me on the murders?"

"What don't you know?"

"Now there's a question a good journalist should keep in his portfolio. Let's see. I know about the fifth murder—of the Jamaican detective. I know about Captain Goodwine. And I know the woman was strangled, if not drowned. Anything else?"

"Do you know if MacGregor has procured the guns and the boats yet?"

Nathan dropped his paper and his jaw. "What? What are you talking about? Who's MacGregor?"

Simon shot a glance at Ellie. "Never mind. It's another case we're working on. I think you're up to speed on the murders." They left the publisher standing in the street. Simon pulled around the corner and parked.

Ellie tried to keep up as Simon strode purposefully toward the courthouse. "What's the plan?"

He paused. "Oh, you out of breath? Let's sit a minute." When she was settled, he spoke. "That was indeed interesting."

"How much Nathan knows about the murders, or that he didn't know about MacGregor?"

"The latter. He seemed genuinely surprised—as opposed to the ladies. I'm wondering if perhaps some of our committee members have not been fully briefed on the program. I want to talk to Judge Farnsworth and the mayor. Quickly, before Nathan calls them."

"Sweetie, it's Sunday. We'll have to wait until tomorrow."

"Damn." He smacked his knee.

"I guess there's nothing more we can do today." She yawned. "Oh, will you look at the time."

"Time?" He looked at his watch. "It's only…Oh, but…oh."

****

Fort Clinch, Monday, May 14

"Hosea, we have to go into town."

"Not yet. I have plans for you." The superintendent handed them the duty roster. Simon was dispatched to the fort to clean up the mess left by local juvenile delinquents disporting themselves in the barracks over the weekend. A day dealing with competing Cub Scout packs and a family reunion from Ohio left Ellie limp and thirsty. She lolled at her desk, mumbling to Hosea about feuding in-laws and pugnacious terriers.

At four, Simon strolled in. "Let's go."

"Already? At least let me grab a bottle of water."

As they walked into the courthouse, two men in overcoats with uninformative eyes and pale lips passed them. Ellie shivered. "G-men if I ever saw one."

"When I figure out how to say that in proper English, I'll give you a dressing down worthy of my tenth-grade composition teacher."

They took the elevator to the second floor. Olive sat at her desk, blowing her nose into a yellow handkerchief. She looked up with bleary eyes ringed in smeared eyeliner. "What do *you* guys want?"

"We want to see Judge Farnsworth." *Duh.*

"He's busy."

Just then the judge opened his door. "Olive, get me that file on…Oh, hi, Simon."

"Can we come in? We have a couple of questions."

"I'm very busy."

"This will only take a minute."

Grudgingly, he ushered them inside. Behind him hovered Thad. Farnsworth didn't invite them to sit. "Well?"

"Do you know anything about—"

Olive knocked. "The FBI agent just called. He said you're to get those papers together by close of business." She bit her lip. "He said the IRS is insisting they conduct a preliminary inquiry."

The judge dropped into his chair and wiped a sweaty forehead. "Son, take these good people outside please."

Thad, his face a mask of terror, led Simon and Ellie out. Simon asked, "What's going on? Inquiry about what?"

Thad tried to retrieve his customary swagger with only limited success. "It's bullshit. Typical IRS bullying. They claim Dad took illegal campaign money. All a buncha hooey."

Simon glanced at Ellie and raised his brows.

"So what did you want to ask him? I'm sure I can answer any questions—me and Dad are tight." They watched, amused, as the notion that this might not be something to brag about made its painful way through the mush of his brain. "Um…"

"That's okay. We just wanted to wrap up a few loose threads." *Before this gets any more convoluted.* "We'll wait till your father has time."

Back on the sidewalk again, Simon turned toward City Hall.

"Um, Simon?"

"What?"

"You planning to catch the mayor?"

"Of course."

Ellie showed him her watch. "It's ten of five. I'm pretty sure the town offices close at five."

He slowed. "Blast. We'll have to hit both Crowley and Farnsworth first thing tomorrow. It'll probably be too late though."

"You mean Hearst will have given them a heads-up?"

Simon pinched his lips together. "Or, presuming he didn't know about MacGregor, he might have done even more damage. He might have called the man directly."

"I'm hungry."

"My God, woman, you're always hungry. Let's go get Georgia. I want us to put our heads together."

"Good idea. We need some brains in this outfit."

"Ha ha."

Georgia was free. "They let me postpone my finals so I can stay with Dad, but I could sure use a break. I called Debbie Daugherty. She's coming over. Where do you want to go?"

"David's? We need somewhere quiet to talk."

The elegant restaurant was empty on a Monday night. A young man greeted them. "Hi, Georgia."

"Hi, Yuri. Can we have a table?"

279

"No problem. Season hasn't really started yet. Pick one."

They found a booth in the far corner and ordered drinks. Georgia opened the voluminous leather-bound menu. "I know this 'earth, wind, and fire' stuff always confuses you, Simon. Shall I order?" She said the last in a bright chirp.

Simon just looked at her. Ellie replied, "Sure."

A young man in black appeared and handed glasses of wine to the two women. "Your Pabst, Simon."

"Thank you, Henry." Georgia turned a page of the menu. "I'd like your crab bisque—it is sooo good. And the lady will have the beet salad." At Ellie's skeptical expression, she said kindly, "Trust me. Then…how about the Dover sole *meunière* for Ellie and the truffle scallops for me?"

Henry wrote it down. "The usual special plate for Simon?"

"Yes, and this time make sure the burger is well done. We don't want a repeat of the last time." She patted Simon's arm.

When the waiter had gone, Simon related all their activities and conclusions to Georgia.

She whistled. "Okay, this calls for a list."

Simon laughed. "Georgia is famous for her lists."

His friend stuck her tongue out at him and dropped a notepad on the table. Henry appeared with their appetizers. Simon ordered another beer.

When Georgia had scraped the last spoonful of bisque from her plate, she finished off Ellie's salad and a second basket of rolls.

Simon knew Ellie was wondering if Georgia would have any room left for her entrée. "Don't worry, El.

Georgia never met a meal she couldn't swallow whole."

"Someone has to make up for the one-dish wonder here." Georgia pushed her plate aside and drew the notepad toward her. "Okay, first the victims." She clicked open her pen and began to write. "Bonney, Virtue, Alvaredo, Goodwine."

"Don't forget Labadie. He was tracing Virtue's activities—he may have uncovered something incriminating about one of the others."

"You don't think he was beheaded by an irate line cook for messing with his mise en place?" Georgia didn't wait for an answer. "All right, all right, five victims. Moving on to the League of the Green Cross."

Henry appeared with the entrees. He set Simon's unadorned hamburger down with a snicker. Georgia and Ellie traded tastes of their meals, oohing and aahing. Georgia graciously accepted the last half of Ellie's fish.

Once the table was cleared, they studied the second list. Georgia sighed. "No crossovers. No relation between the two groups. I say it's just serendipity that they all ended up at the same spot."

Ellie said, "The Green group are trying to raise funds. Could it be by smuggling drugs?"

Georgia shook her head. "Can you see Sylvia Barnes, green visor on her head, sitting at a grimy desk in a warehouse, counting drug packets and thousand-dollar bills?"

"No."

Georgia stopped, glass halfway to her mouth. "How about the judge? He's under investigation by the IRS. Last time I checked, they were all about money."

Simon nodded reluctantly. "I still need to ask him

and Crowley about MacGregor—check their responses. And I want to do a little more research on Martí."

Ellie had been quiet for a while. "You know, I think Georgia's right. I can't see any common thread between these two groups. Perhaps we've gone off on a wild goose chase. We should be concentrating on the murders."

"But—"

Georgia interrupted. "No buts. I'm going to have dessert before I descend on Debbie and my father, hopefully *in flagrante delicto*."

The other two had coffee while Georgia polished off a slice of salted caramel cheesecake the size of Delaware. As they left the restaurant, Simon noticed Mayor Crowley ducking into the Palace Saloon. "I think I'll share a mug with our esteemed mayor. See you ladies later."

****

Ellie's house, Tuesday, May 15

"Did you have a good time with the mayor?"

"So-so. Beer was flat. His conversation was even less effervescent."

"Did you ask him about MacGregor?"

"Yes. He just looked blank. If there is indeed something illicit going on, I think at least he and Nathan aren't privy to it." He pursed his lips. "I wish I could get hold of Farnsworth."

"Er…Simon? Can we get back to our real task?"

"Oh, my God, you're insatiable."

"Not that. Although you are improving rapidly in your approach."

"I am a fast learner, after all." He waved a hand at the piles of books before flicking one of Ellie's nipples.

"Ouch."

"Oh, sorry. I think I know how to make it better." He bent over her and began to massage her breast.

"Not bad...um...ah...have you been reading the manual again?"

"Boning up for the test, yes."

"Ha ha. I grade on the curve, you know."

He ran a palm over her thigh and cupped her mound. "This one?"

She lay back. "Well, it's not Laffer's curve."

An hour later, she came down the stairs to the smell of hot coffee. "What's on for today?"

"It's a nude day. You don't have to wear clothes."

"I don't think that's regulation."

"As you wish. I want to talk to Amos—see if he knows what this investigation of Farnsworth is all about. And try to get in to ask Lester about MacGregor."

"I'm on gate duty again till closing."

He finished his coffee and kissed her. "See you later."

He stopped for another coffee at the corner store. An ancient pickup pulled in, its cargo bed filled with crab traps and fishing gear. Harvey got out. "Oh, hey, Simon."

"Hey, Harvey."

"I'm glad I caught you. T'other day you was asking about the night Jo Jo Goodwine was kilt?"

"Yeah."

"Well, I remembered something after you left. Might be important, might not."

"Yes?"

"I tole you a car sat idling for a while, right?"

"Yes."

"Big car. White."

"Yes?"

"Well, when the car backed up and roared off, I noticed the left rear light was out. I'm a'sittin' thinkin' that a big fancy car like that should be taken better care of, you know? Effen I had such a car, I'd make dam' sure it was kept in tip-top condition. Have her washed reg'lar. Don't leave no crap in it." He gestured at his truck. "Like mine. Old Nellie's lasted thirty years. Tha's 'cause I *maintains* her."

Simon didn't laugh. "One rear light out, huh?" *Bonney's contact?* "Worth checking into."

"Might want to ask at Moses' garage or that service station out on 200. See if it's been brought in."

"Excellent. Thanks, Harvey. Buy you a soda?"

"Don't mind ef I do."

Simon left the old man nursing a bottle and went to find Amos.

The police chief was on the phone. His secretary whispered, "He's talking to his wife. Just be a minute."

"Thanks, Flo." Simon sidled over to the door, hoping to hear something useful.

"No, Sylvia, I'm not angry with you, but you've got to keep using the patch...How did I find out? Sylvia, I'm the chief of police. I know everything that goes on in this town." Simon made the mistake of looking at Flo. A slight giggle escaped her. Barnes looked up. "Gotta go. See you tonight." He hung up. "Hello, Simon. Did you get my message?"

"No."

"We found the shoe."

"Shoe...oh right, Bonney's shoe. Was it in the

marina?"

"It was on the north bank where Egan's Creek enters the river. Stuck in the mud."

"Well, that confirms our theory of what happened on the boat. The railing probably ripped it off when she went overboard."

"In that case, it would have turned up on the shore closer to the fort. No, I think it got caught in the rope. Alvaredo found it after Bonney was swept overboard and threw it over the side to hide the evidence." Amos picked up a file, dismissing Simon with a wave.

"Actually, Amos. Um. I'm here for a different reason."

He sighed. "What can I do for you?"

"I have a lead I thought your boys could use."

"Lead on what?"

"The murders, of course." He told him about the car at the dock. "If you put out an APB on a white luxury sedan with a rear light out, we may find Bonney's contact."

"Assuming the light hasn't been fixed yet."

"So visit repair places as well."

He picked up the phone. "I'll get right on it."

"Wait a minute, there's one more thing. Lester Farnsworth is being investigated by the FBI at the request of the IRS."

He put the phone down. "How do you know about that?"

"We saw two Federal agents coming out of his office. I overheard them say there was going to be a preliminary hearing. Call you tell me what it's about?"

"And this is your business how?"

"Until I have positive evidence there's no

connection between this enigmatic cabal—who met on park property—and the murders—three of which occurred on park property—yes, it *is* my business."

The policeman rubbed his forehead. "Lester's been accused of accepting contributions from foreign nationals during his last campaign."

"Foreign? Could they by any chance have been Cuban?"

"Yes. How did you know?"

"I just guessed. Cuba figures in all this—I can't yet put my finger on how."

"Of course it does. They're trying to make Havana our sister city."

"No, it's more than that. Look, will you do something for me?"

"What?"

"Will you ask Sylvia if she knew that Carson Gregory is in fact Carson MacGregor before I mentioned it?"

"Odd question."

"Indulge me."

Amos picked up the phone, but Simon laid a hand over his. "No, I'd like you to do it in person—see what her reaction is."

"All right, but I won't be able to get back to you until tonight."

"No hurry." Simon headed over to the courthouse. The receptionist regretted, but the judge was unavailable. "Is he at the Foster Center today?"

"Nope. He called to say he's taking the week off. He…uh…has some paperwork to do." She wouldn't look at Simon.

"Thanks." *I'll just have to keep trying. I think I*

know the answer to my question anyway. If neither Randall nor Nathan knew Gregory's real name, chances were good Lester was unaware of his identity as well. Simon started back to the park. As he passed the Louder Brothers hardware, he noticed Santa's glossy two-tone Oldsmobile in the parking lot. *I'm surprised Georgia let him out. Ooh, wait. I'll bet he's playing hooky.* He found the old man in the tool aisle hefting a crowbar. "Is that for offense or defense?"

"Hey, Simon. Both, I guess. Georgia needs something up in the attic, and the trapdoor cable broke. I thought I could pry it open with this."

Simon eyed the tool critically. "Don't you need something longer? Attic door is eight feet up."

"Oh, you noticed that too? I guess that's why I got the ladder out."

Simon chose to deflect the jab. "Does Georgia know you're driving?"

Santa snapped his mouth shut and began to closely examine a box of nails. "I'm fine. Just a little short of breath. Can't sit on the couch all day like some old fogey. Women like me spry."

Simon laughed. "I suppose your love life is a little hampered with a nosy daughter in the house."

"You betcha. And Katie's back living with her mother, so we're reduced to sneaking around back alleys for a quick pucker."

"It's more fun that way."

Santa peered at Simon. "Speaking of…I hear you and Ellie have finally found each other."

Simon felt the blush start behind his ears and move across his face. A bead of sweat trickled down the back of his neck. "Er."

"Have you set a date yet?"

"Huh?"

"My God, man, are you a-scared of commitment? As my daughter would say, 'Grab her while she's hot.' And then she'd add several derogatory terms relating to your mental capacity. Befuddled being the first. Then maybe brainless. Or addlepated. Boneheaded? *Hmm…*" His brow furrowed in concentration.

Simon mustered what little dignity he had left and loomed over his friend. "I will treat your counsel with the respect it deserves." He sailed out.

The rest of the day was spent in the company of a family of campers from Missouri who seemed to have difficulty reading the regulations. "Yes, sir, here where it says, 'Keep your dog on a leash at all times,' it does in fact mean your dog must be leashed at all times."

"What about on the beach?"

"On the beach as well."

"How about here, where it says, 'No loud radios'?" The man gestured at another campsite. "Those guys are way out of range. And anyway, I'm sure they don't mind a little country western in the evening."

Sigh. "The regulation is not only for humans. The noise disturbs the wildlife. You *are* here to see wildlife, correct?"

And so it went. At five o'clock, Simon hung up his ranger hat in the station mud room. "I need a drink."

Thad looked up. "You want company?"

A nightcap with Thad? That would sure round out a perfect day. "No, thanks, I want to stew in my own beer, I think."

Ellie walked in, tossing her own hat on her desk. "What an afternoon! Two hikers stuck in the mud, one lost boy, eight swimmers stung by jellyfish. I guess they were blinded by the shiny No Swimming sign."

"Serves them right, I say."

"I'm not finished. And an Airstream that broke down right at the gate. Cars backed up out to Atlantic Avenue."

"Why didn't the other people go through the exit side?"

"By right at the gate, I mean under it. The bar caught on their kayak rack. Both gates automatically locked."

"Ah."

"I could use a stiff one." She looked at Simon invitingly. "Want to join me?"

Before he could answer, Thad jumped in. "He says he wants to be alone...*but*..." He took his hat off the peg. "I'm available. I'll even buy."

Ellie stood between the two men, blinking rapidly. "Uh, sure, Thad. Let me freshen up, and I'll be right with you."

"I'll meet you by my *Porsche*." Thad walked jauntily out the door. At the threshold, he turned and saluted Simon. "And that's how it's done."

Santa's words rang in Simon's head: "Grab her while she's hot." *Shit.*

He found his way to the Dog Star Tavern. "Gimme a PBR, Junior."

"Comin' right up."

He sat alone until the sun had finished its last goodbye with mostly a whimper. When he'd drained his fourth beer, Junior came over and swiped the bar with a grimy cloth. "Woman troubles?"

"I don't want to talk about it."

"That's not in the script. Georgia says your cold feet are icing up. Soon, frostbite will set in. After that comes gangrene. Not to mention long lonely nights before the remains of a fire."

"You been reading poetry again, Junior?" *Shoot, did I just slur that last word?*

"Still on that one book you gave me last year. *A Bad Girl's Book of Animals*. Bit of a slog, but gives me nice word pictures to use on my customers. Still, you shoulda told me it wasn't porn. I expected the girl to…you know…with the animals." He snickered.

Simon slapped a bill on the bar. "I'm off."

As he walked at a slight tilt down the alley to Second Street, he mulled over Junior's words. *They're actually pretty good. Oh yeah, Georgia said them.* Gloom settled on his head. *Why are these people pushing me so hard? Even my own mother. I'm only thirty-five—plenty of time to settle down. I've got a Mack truck of wild oats to sow yet.* He slowed, thinking of Ellie. *It'd be awful nice to have eggs and bacon with her every morning though.*

Busy with his thoughts, he didn't hear the rustle behind him. "Ribault? Is that you?"

He swung around. Three men stood in the dark, taking up most of the space between the narrow walls. "Who's there?"

One said to the other, "It's him. The ranger who's been badgering us."

A voice with a thick Spanish accent said, "Perhaps a broken nose would make him think twice about his meddling."

The third man spoke. "Come on, Julian. That's not necessary."

Simon recognized Kenny's brittle voice. "Kenny? What are you doing back there?"

"I'm outta here." The figure swirled and ran down the alley. The other two advanced on Simon. A light came on in an upstairs apartment, and he got a glimpse of their faces. *MacGregor and Martí. Uh oh.*

MacGregor spoke, his voice low and whiny. "Why are you dogging us, Ribault? You're just a lame old park ranger. Go back to trapping raccoons and ticketing RVs."

Martí's tone was a little more threatening. "Our affairs are none of your business. We know nothing of these murders you're investigating. Stop this persecution, and leave us alone." He took a step closer.

Simon stood his ground. He looked up, but the light had gone out. *Is the window open? If I call, will someone hear me?*

MacGregor raised a fist. "Are you gonna back off or not, punk?"

Simon took another step back and stumbled over a brick. "I…uh…"

A rich mezzo-soprano rang out behind him. "As a matter of fact, if *you* don't back off, he might press charges. This looks like assault to me. What do you think, Dad?"

"Georgia? Santa?" His friends came around either side of him. Santa carried a crowbar. Georgia carried a take-out pizza. Simon squared his shoulders. "MacGregor. Martí. I'd like you to meet my lawyer. And my bodyguard."

The two men wheeled around and tore after Kenny.

The three left stared after them. Finally, Santa remarked, "Interesting."

Georgia said, "Want some pizza?"

Why not? Simon said, "Sure. Just this once."

As they left, Santa looked back. "Yes. Interesting. I think it's time you brought in the big guns."

"Who?"

"Debbie Daugherty and the Ladies' Beer and Marching Society."

"Oh God."

Chapter Seventeen
You Ain't Nothing But a Hound Dog

Santa's house, Tuesday, May 15

"So it's come to that."

Santa slid another slice of pizza onto his plate. "Not enough anchovies. Dana never puts enough anchovies on."

Simon picked up the small pile on his plate and plopped it on Santa's slice. "There."

"You're a saint. Now, where was I?"

"Little Debbie and her intrepid band of gossipeers."

Georgia raised her eyebrows. "Gossipeers?"

Simon put down his pizza. "Poetic license."

"Poetic license doesn't give you license to make up words."

"It does too. Did you know that several of Lewis Carroll's invented words in 'Jabberwocky' made their way into mainstream English?"

"Name one."

"Chortle. We can chortle freely now, thanks to the intrepid vorpal sword swinger. Also galumph."

Santa broke into the staring contest. "I propose we ask the ladies to do a bit of snooping. See what they can find out about the Greenies' activities." He pointed at Simon. "You are officially on the lam from the goons and have to lie low. Return to your fort. Or better still, go to the mattresses."

"Sorry, Godfather. Have to work."

Georgia folded her hands primly in her lap. "Dad's right. I can't chaperone you twenty-four-seven. Besides, you need some time off to figure out how you're going to propose to Ellie. I'm thinking jumbo screen."

Santa shook his head. "Not his style. How about a jug of wine and a loaf of bread under the spreading...what are they under anyhow? What kind of trees do they have in Persia anyway?"

Georgia picked up her phone. "Pistachio trees? Tulip trees? Hang on..."

Simon couldn't resist, even though he knew full well they were baiting him. " 'A book of verses underneath the bough, / a jug of wine, a loaf of bread— and Thou, / beside me singing in the wilderness, / O, wilderness were paradise enow.' " He popped the last piece of pizza into his mouth. "Because you two rescued me from a possible thrashing, I'll forgive your impudent intrusion into my personal affairs. I am not contemplating marriage at this time. Nor is Ellie."

"How do you know?"

"She told me." He walked out quickly, followed by loud guffaws.

****

Simon's house, Wednesday, May 16

Simon hadn't wanted to give Santa the satisfaction of knowing Wednesday was in fact his day off. Thinking he'd relax and read all day on his porch, he discovered to his chagrin that he couldn't sit still. By Wednesday afternoon, he'd fished, kayaked, biked, napped, watched the talk shows, and downed two beers. He sat leafing through the menus he kept by the phone. "White Castle? Wendy's? T-Ray's Burger Station?" He threw them all back down. *Think I'll just have another beer and leave it at that.*

He refused to even consider the subject he knew everybody assumed he was dwelling on. Not that he was scared. Oh, no. But he had to admit doting on Ellie from afar had felt nice and safe. Now that the relationship had evolved, he found himself harried and unsure. *And scared.*

Marriage? Marriage had never been in the picture, mainly because he was positive no one would have him. *Who wants a fellow with knobs on his nose from constantly rubbing it inside books?* He'd had a few short-lived girlfriends, but after college, he'd been too obsessed with mastering every subject that came his way to waste time on amatory pursuits. His mother always said he should have been a librarian. He had obliged her by collecting yet another master's degree, this time in Library Science. *Yes, that's where I belong. Snug inside four wood-paneled walls lined with shelves filled with other people's stories.*

What does she see in me?

His mother phoning should have been a bright spot. "Hello, dear, I just wanted to remind you I go under the knife today."

"Knife!"

"Figuratively speaking. I'm starting the drug this afternoon. Not a minute too soon either—they've had me fasting since last night."

"You hate that."

"You betcha. However, I am allowed clear liquids.

Luckily, my sweet, oblivious nurse neglected to list unacceptable beverages, and I neglected to ask directly about vodka, so I'm in a fairly mellow mood."

"Oh, Mother."

"Now, Simon…Yes?…Wait a minute, dear." Her voice faded. He heard her say, "Yes, I'm ready, Frieda," before coming back on the line. "Gotta go. I'll have my people contact your people about the results. Love you, honey." And she hung up before he could protest.

Things went downhill after that, and by Thursday morning, he was thoroughly depressed. When he walked into the ranger station, Hosea gave him what's commonly called the "fish eye." "I hear you've been drinking too much."

Sigh. "Let me guess. Georgia."

"No. Santa." He patted Simon's shoulder awkwardly. "I didn't tell Amos—don't want him dumping you in the tank until we figure this thing out."

"Agreed. I did ask him to feel Sylvia out."

"Hasn't done that in months."

"About the Green project."

"Oh."

"And the judge."

"The judge?"

"Lester's being investigated by the FBI for illegal campaign contributions. Could the money be going to the Green league?"

"What makes you think that?"

"Because they're donations from Cuban citizens."

"Is that legal?"

"I don't know. I have Georgia working on it, but I sense there's more to it. We may be dealing with a national security issue."

Thad poked his head in. "Boss? Can I leave early today?"

"What for?"

"Have to take Dad to a lawyer."

Hosea crooked a finger, beckoning him in. "Thad, do you know why they're interested in your father?"

The chiseled features solidified into a mask. "No idea. He's got nothing to hide. Probably just routine. Bye." He backed hurriedly out.

Hosea looked at Simon. "Do you think he knows anything?"

"Nah. He's a moron. Even Lester knows that."

"Now wait a minute. He's not a bad ranger."

What Hosea doesn't know about the doughnuts won't hurt him. "Yeah, he tries. Look, I need to bug out for a bit for some research. Are you staffed?"

"Yes. Rosie and the new girl are here. And Ellie's coming in." He paused. "You want me to give her a message?"

"No!" He slammed out the door and fumed all the way home. "God damned small town. I'm tired of this. I'll do what I want. When I want to." A car passed him. *Ellie.* His mood darkened. *She said she didn't want to marry me. So why don't they pick on* her? *Why don't they explain to* her *how she feels about* me? *Huh?* A little voice that sounded a lot like Georgia whispered in his ear. "She's waiting for you, you jackass."

After that, it was hard to concentrate.

Three hours later, he set down his pen. "I give up." Someone knocked. He went to the screen door. "Ellie!"

She came in, a rather dazed expression on her face. "Hosea told me to come find you."

"What for?"

"He didn't say. He just said to find you. And here you are."

"Here I am."

They stood a few feet apart, gazing into each other's eyes. Ellie shrugged. Simon took that as an invitation, leapt the short distance, and took her in his arms. A fairly long, wet kiss ensued, involving a lot of tasting and cooing with a little moaning thrown in.

She broke away first. "Simon?"

"Ellie?"

"I…uh…heard about the alley."

"Oh." *She's going to laugh at me. Saved by an old man and a slip of a girl. So what if that girl has a black belt in karate?*

"You were so brave. Standing up to the mob like that. I"—her eyes dropped—"I didn't think you…well, you're so bookish…that you could…well, I'm so proud of you."

"But I…I…Santa…"

"*Shh.* Come with me." She took his hand and led him upstairs, neatly avoiding the piles of papers as well as the half-empty water glass.

The rest of the evening played out just as Georgia had planned.

****

Simon's house, Friday, May 18

Simon woke to the feather light touch of Isis's tail. He shot up. "Ellie?"

"Downstairs. Making breakfast."

He stifled the feeling of comfort the words gave him and dressed. He stumbled down to the kitchen to find her, two plates of scrambled eggs and toast, and a purring cat eating his last can of tuna. Roan lay, head on paws, under the table. Ellie poured juice. "Someday, I'll have to learn how to make grits. Everyone says—"

"A good southern wife should know how to make grits, right?"

"Everyone says they're delicious."

Damn. Now I'm *doing it.* He took a big bite of egg. When he'd gulped it down, he looked up into Ellie's grinning face.

She said, "Are they getting to you?"

"Who?"

"They are, aren't they? Well, don't pay them any mind. I've got your back."

"That's easy for you to say. They're not hounding you."

Pain darkened her eyes to the blue of a starless midnight. "Oh, sorry. Well, perhaps we should keep our distance from each other after this. They'll back off when they see they're wrong about us." She left the dishes in the sink and untied her apron. "I've got to get to work."

Before he could stop her, she picked up her satchel and walked out the door.

Now you've done it. Again.

The office was empty when he reached it. He found a note on his desk. "Big to-do at fort. Child hanging from wall. Wait at gate for fire department." *Great. What's that Milton line? They also serve who only stand and wait. Not.* He drove back down the canopy road to the entrance.

A few minutes later, a pulsating siren rent the air and a fire engine roared up to the gate. "Hey, Simon, trouble at the fort?"

"So I hear, Paulie. Kid jumped off the battlements. I'll raise the bar for you."

"Thanks."

Simon spent the rest of the day directing traffic and watching ambulances and emergency vehicles pass in and out. Paulie told him they'd had to rescue two kids and a dog. "Dumb mutt was chasing a ball and jumped over the parapet. Kids went after him."

"Are they okay?"

"Aside from the whacking the boys got from their mother, yeah. Dog didn't make it."

"Too bad."

Paulie wiped a tear away. "Looked just like Charlie—remember my old blue tip?"

"A good dog."

"They were getting ready to bury him when I left."

"Shouldn't they take him to the vet?"

"Well, the kids were so broken up, Hosea said they could find a place near Egan's Creek."

"Alligators'll get him."

"Yeah."

About five, he got a call from the superintendent. "You can lock the gate now. Head on home. No reason to stay."

But…Ellie.

"Ellie's finishing up some paperwork, and Thad's taking her out to supper." He paused. "She seemed enthusiastic. Maybe she regrets jilting him."

****

Simon's house, Saturday, May 19

"I did it. I asked Sylvia about MacGregor."

"Good for you, Amos. How did she react?"

"Well, she reached for her purse. I happen to know

she keeps a cigarette pack in a secret pocket. I took her brazen action—right in front of me—as clear evidence that she's rattled."

Simon moved the phone to his other ear. "Remember Iggy told us she and Lisabet de Angeles are charged with fundraising for the sister cities, but they denied it. Did you ask her directly?"

"I did. She admitted she's working on it, but says they're just in the planning stage. They'll have fundraisers over the summer."

"This thing with the FBI and Lester Farnsworth. I know it's illegal to accept contributions from foreign nationals for a campaign—but what about for a civic project?"

"I should think Lester would know the answer to that. If it's legal, why not just tell the Feds?"

"I don't know. Maybe the Green Cross project isn't exactly what they're making it out to be."

"What makes you say that?"

Should I tell him about Martí and MacGregor threatening me? No, he'll bring them in before we know enough. "They…uh…just seem so furtive. Like they have stuff to hide. MacGregor was downright…hostile the last time I spoke to him."

"And Sylvia is definitely spooked."

"Amos, she's your wife. Can't you make her confide in you?"

A snort came through the telephone. "You're not married, are you?" He paused. "Speaking of, when are you going to pop the question?"

Something blocked Simon's windpipe. He finally gurgled, "Is there anyone in this town who doesn't have an opinion on me and Ellie?"

"I think Gus over at the Marathon station is waffling. Other than that, no."

"Okay, listen. Keep working on Sylvia. And maybe Lester as well. They're both low-hanging fruit. I have some other hooks in the water."

"Oh?"

"Let's just say, there are experts in this field with untapped potential."

"Oh my God, you've reeled in Debbie Daugherty and her crew."

"Let's see if they catch the worm."

Everyone seemed to be out on patrol again at the park, so Simon sat down at the computer to see if he could find any more on Julian Martí.

By lunchtime, he had enough to give him pause. Martí had grown up in the Cuban section of Miami. His father, a journalist, was known to be virulently anti-Castro, as were most in the community. Julian went to the Columbia School of Journalism, where, according to articles he'd written for the school paper, he became enamored with communism. Simon found nothing further until ten years later. The *Miami Herald* ran an obituary on Carlos Martí. Julian gave the eulogy for his father, in which he dwelt on Carlos's love for his native country and desire to be buried in Cuba. He went on to give an impassioned rant against Castro. *Maybe he figured out that communism's not the contented, prosperous utopia portrayed in the halls of academia.*

Simon stood and stretched his legs. *Might as well head over to the ER diner for a bite.* A car pulled up outside. He looked out the window. Ellie and Thad sat in the car, making no move to get out. *Are they laughing? She looks awfully happy.* Finally, Thad came

302

through the door, went to Ellie's desk, and picked up her purse. Nodding at Simon, he walked back out. The car roared off. *What the hell?*

He found he'd lost his appetite. *Maybe I'll do a little more research, see if they come back.* He knew they wouldn't, though. He knew they'd gone to lunch. *Together.*

He typed in "Radio Martí." Julian was listed on the staff page. He had joined the radio as a producer in 2014 and was promoted to host a year later. The station broadcast network news in Spanish around the clock. *Let's see if he has a bibliography.*

Sure enough, Martí had written some freelance articles for local publications, mainly on economics. Simon was about to sign out when a letter to the editor caught his eye.

Fidel and Raul Castro are among the wealthiest people in the world, wealth gained by raping the Cuban people and their economy over five decades. They must be stopped by any means possible and the country returned to its people. In 1898, the United States invaded Cuba to liberate it from Spain. In the twenty-first century, we must do the same. I call on the exiles of Miami to rise with me and rid Cuba of this vermin.

It was signed "José Martí." A note from the editor below the letter identified the writer as Julian Martí, a direct descendant of the great liberator.

"He's a real piece of work, isn't he?"

"Who are you talking to?"

"Oh, hi, Hosea." Simon pointed at the screen. "I've been reading about Julian Martí. He went from a wild-eyed communist who participated in Occupy Brickell and lived on a commune with three women to a radical capitalist who wants to rid the world of the scourge of Marxism."

"Well, you know what Winston Churchill said."

" 'Show me a young Conservative, and I'll show you someone with no heart. Show me an old Liberal, and I'll show you someone with no brains.' "

Hosea chuckled. "You know what I think? I think it's that first paycheck. I remember my daughter coming in waving it at me and yelling. When I asked what the problem was, she pointed at the payroll tax figure. Here she was, just starting in her first job and—these are her words—the frigging government took half of her hard-earned money. Right there, she decided to go to business school."

"Be glad she didn't opt for a life of crime."

Hosea got up. "Well, I've got to get up to the fort. Jack needs a hand with the Elder Hostel crowd."

"Have you…have you seen Ellie anywhere?"

"She and Thad went to lunch, then I think they were going to check out the east beach access. There was a report of a giant alligator in the mangroves."

"Oh."

Hosea gave him a hard look but didn't say anything. An hour later, Ellie and Thad had not returned. He spoke to the empty room. "I'm off then."

When he got home, the answering machine blinked red. Five new messages. *Ellie?* He pressed the button.

"Simon, it's Santa. Call me right away."

It went to the second one. "Simon, this is Georgia. Call me ASAP."

The third was from an air conditioning company, the fourth from a real estate firm offering a free cruise in exchange for a "short" presentation. *Ha.* He deleted those. The fifth message gave him pause.

"Simon Ribault, this is Debbie Daugherty. We know what the Green bunch is planning. Come over to 1010 Cedar Street tomorrow morning at nine."

Chapter Eighteen
Gunboat Diplomacy

Debbie Daugherty's house, Sunday, May 20

When Simon arrived at the Daugherty house, there were several cars parked out front. Santa and Ellie met him at the door and walked in with him. Simon gave Ellie a perfunctory nod, and she pretended not to see it. Debbie led the way into her comfortable living room.

Seated on chairs and the sofa were five women, all in their fifties. "You know everyone, don't you, Simon?"

He surveyed the people whose offspring he'd played with as a child—Debbie's best friend, Glenda Slocum; Phyllis Farnsworth, Lester's wife; Alison Parker, the public librarian; and Velma Royce, principal of Emma Love Hardee Elementary School. He was surprised to see Beebee Ironstone ensconced in the middle of the sofa. She grinned at him and shouted, "Hey, Simon! Welcome to the Amelia Island chapter of Busybodies Anonymous."

Debbie patted his arm. "Beebee is our newest member. She's already made several significant contributions to the cause." She gave her former rival a dazzling smile. "She kept me informed about Felix's condition and, thanks to her, we're up to speed on the bumpy road to romance." She turned the still dazzling smile on the hapless couple. Both Ellie and Simon jerked and glared at an unrepentant Beebee.

Santa had focused on another issue. "Cause? You finally came up with a slogan?"

Glenda piped up. "Sure did. 'In pursuit of the general health and welfare of the community, we dedicate ourselves to the collection, verification, and dissemination of current news and events.' "

Velma said comfortably, "Nathan won't admit it, but we're his greatest asset."

Beebee preened. "The ladies tell me they are thrilled to have a new compatriot. In my position—"

"Yes, well, we'd best get to the purpose of this meeting," Debbie interrupted hastily. Simon wondered if she worried that he'd disapprove—or worse, tell the mayor—of their rather unorthodox use of county personnel.

Just then, Georgia pushed open the kitchen door. She gave the tray in her hands to Ellie and took her place against the wall. Ellie passed the glasses around. "Lemonade, Mr. Ribault?"

It's going to be like that, is it? "Thank you, Miss Ironstone."

When Simon and the others had been supplied with drinks, Debbie took the floor. "All right, let's get started. As you know, Felix asked our little circle to look into the activities of the shadowy group calling itself the League of the Green Cross." Here she nodded at Santa, who blushed. "We learned quickly that the man known as Gregory was in fact Carson MacGregor, a descendant of Gregor MacGregor, the Scots mercenary. Alison uncovered the fact that two other members were also descended from men associated with Amelia Island's history. It seems they are the principal players in the plot."

"The plot?"

"To invade Cuba and oust the Castro regime."

Simon whistled. "You ladies are awesome."

Georgia cheered.

"Mr. MacGregor's secretary, Nora, was very helpful. In fact, she was our most valuable informant. She and Sylvia."

"Sylvia Barnes?"

"Piece of cake to break her down," said Velma cheerfully. "Took Glenda less than five minutes."

"What did she tell you?"

Debbie responded. "Well, we all know Sylvia was born a Sanchez. Her parents put her on one of those flights—"

Simon perked up. "Peter Pan flights?"

"Yes. She told Glenda that in the first years of Castro's regime, he systematically separated children from their families, shutting down all private schools and sending the children to school in the Soviet Union. Frightened parents put some fourteen thousand children on planes to the US to keep them out of Castro's clutches. Sylvia was sent to an aunt over in Yulee. Well, she's always felt guilty about being free while her family remained in Cuba, and when Castro slapped her cousin Yesenia—"

Beebee interrupted. "A journalist and dissenter."

"—with house arrest, she felt she had to do something. She'd been talking to Lisabet de Angeles about her feelings—"

"Lisabet's family also comes from Cuba."

Debbie paused a moment to fix her new ally with a

look noteworthy for its lack of warmth. "Yes…When Lisabet mentioned the Green League, Sylvia got in touch with MacGregor and was invited to join them."

Simon swiveled to a mousy woman in a flowered dress sitting quietly in the corner. "We know the women were in charge of fundraising. Was Lester involved as well, Phyllis?"

"Not in the fundraising, but if you're referring to the IRS investigation, Simon, Lester is completely innocent of any improprieties. And before you ask, my husband would never be a party to a foolish idea like invading a sovereign country. He hasn't mentioned a MacGregor. As far as he knew—or Nathan or Randall—Mr. Gregory was trying to establish a sister-city affiliation between Havana and Fernandina Beach. Lester is a big supporter of lifting the sanctions on Cuba. He always believed—"

"Yes, thank you, Phyllis." Debbie put down her glass. "She's right that those three were ignorant of the true purpose of the group. What did you call them, Felix? Useful idiots?"

"Uh huh. Lenin's phrase for the western liberals who bought into communist propaganda."

Before Phyllis could rise in defense of her husband, Simon interjected, "What about Iggy and Virgil?"

"They were supposed to help Kenny recruit locals as foot soldiers."

"Did he tell them what it was for?"

Alison answered. "Not exactly. Anyway, Iggy and Virgil are not the type to ask questions, especially if they're getting paid under the table."

"Who's left?" Santa looked at Debbie.

"Martí. His job was to garner support from the

Cuban community in Miami."

"And MacGregor took on the task of procuring guns and boats." Simon rose. "We'd better bring this to Amos."

As they left, Debbie ran out. "We'd be happy to investigate the murders too. We have an inside man to draw on."

A chorus of voices yelped, "No!"

****

Police station, Monday, May 21

Debbie insisted on accompanying Simon, Ellie, Santa, and Georgia to the police station. Amos heard them out. "So, these bozos thought they could cobble together a motley crew of hicks and Latinos to attack Cuba. Sort of a reverse Mariel boat lift."

"And just as successful." Georgia nodded sagely.

Santa added, "Cuba would naturally consider it a provocation, and we'd have an international incident on our hands."

"If it got that far." Amos tapped his lip. "I'm guessing the event at the fort was a flop because they couldn't drum up any donors."

Debbie piped up. "So, can we go with you to arrest them?"

"Arrest them? What for? Rampant ineptitude? Extreme stupidity?"

The room went quiet. Finally Debbie muttered, "But…"

Georgia spoke up. "What about the guns? Maybe he bought them illegally."

"Do we know whether he actually bought any guns?"

Suddenly, all five detected something fascinating

under their fingernails.

"All right, I'll pursue that angle. Debbie, your ladies have done enough for now. I'll be sure to call on you again if I need you." The group filed out. Amos stopped Simon at the door. "Why don't you ride along with me?"

"Where are we going?"

"Out to Bulletproof Guns and Ammo."

"You think MacGregor bought guns locally?"

"It's a place to start."

Buddy had no record of either a Gregory or a MacGregor buying guns from him. "You might try Alpine over in Callahan. If he bought any, he most likely acquired them in Florida. It's illegal to bring them across state lines without a carry permit."

"True." The two men left. As Amos parked his squad car in front of the station, he said, "I'm going to get the sheriff's office on this. They can check gun permit applications."

"Okay." Simon got out of the car. "Keep me informed."

"Will do. What are you going to do now?"

At that moment, a silver roadster whizzed by them. Simon caught a glimpse of a wind-blown Ellie talking animatedly to Thad. "I don't know, but I'd better do something and fast."

Amos looked after the sports car. "I could give him a speeding ticket."

Ooh, Thad in a perp walk. That'd be a pick-me-up.
"Go for it."

Amos zoomed off, his siren blaring.

A few hours later, ensconced in his favorite chair, Simon put down his beer to answer the door. Ellie stood on the other side of the screen door. "You did that on purpose."

Why quibble? "Yes. So I take it you saw me with Amos?"

"Are you going to let me in?"

"Depends. Do you plan to hit me?"

"I haven't decided."

"In that case, I'm going back to the kitchen."

He got another beer from the refrigerator and peeked out. Ellie still stood outside. He took a deep breath. "Won't you come in?"

"Why, thank you. Most kind."

He held out the can. "Would you like a beer?"

"No, thanks, I had one with Thad. At lunch."

"Oh."

She gazed at the ceiling. "Thad's not as dumb as he looks, you know."

Really?

"He does like me. A lot."

Before he could stop himself, he asked, "How about you?"

"Me? I'm warming up to him. After all, he's promised to renounce all other girlfriends. He wants to date me exclusively."

"Why?" *Oh shit, I can't believe I said that. She's not going to understand. She's—*

"You really are bad at this, aren't you?"

"Bad at what?"

"Making up." She sat down next to him. "Your mother's right. You need guidance." She picked up his arm and placed it across her shoulders. "Now, move a little closer...Okay...now kiss me."

He did as he was told. When they broke apart, he

panted. "Now what?"

She leveled a pitying look at him. "You're pathetic, you know that?"

Something snapped at the words. "Pathetic? I don't think so." He stood up and putting one arm under her legs and the other under her arms, he lifted her from the chair.

Alarmed, she stuttered, "Are you going to throw me out?"

"No, my dear, I'm going to take your breath away."

And he did.

****

Hammerhead Beach Bar, Tuesday, May 22

"No guns purchased by Gregory anywhere?"

"There's no record at any of the dealers. Acquiring them illegally seems a bit too daring for these folks." Amos put down his tablet. "You know what I think?"

"That Lester, Nathan, and Randall aren't the only patsies?"

Both Amos and Hosea nodded. As always, it was hard not to laugh at the twins' identical mannerisms, and Simon avoided Ellie's face. They were sitting in a bar popular with bikers, each holding a mug of beer. She said, "What about the boats?"

"What boats?"

"Iggy said MacGregor was responsible for obtaining both guns and boats. You say he didn't buy guns. Did he buy any boats?"

"Hang on." Amos got up and walked away, pulling his cell phone out.

Simon watched him go. "Presuming they are seriously intending to invade Cuba, why would he need boats if he didn't have any guns?"

Before Ellie could answer, Amos came back. "Redmond Boat Sales sold a 1998 Crown 4100 fishing cruiser and a forty-four-foot Sea-Girt motor yacht two weeks ago. Purchaser answers the description of MacGregor."

"So, I repeat. What would he want with boats if he didn't have guns?"

The brothers spoke in unison. "Drugs."

Ellie leaned forward. "You think he was working with Bonney?"

Amos's nose wrinkled. "The fort event could have been a ruse. He could have been going to meet her."

Simon cleared his throat. "Remember, Virgil and Iggy said no one left the fort except Lisabet and Sylvia. Wouldn't they have noticed MacGregor sneaking out? After all, he was running the show."

"Maybe he didn't plan to meet her at the fort. The white car Harvey saw could have been his. Maybe he intended to use the lights at the event to guide the boat past the fort and later rendezvous at the marina."

Simon shook his head. "Diogenes Goodwine knew these waters like the back of his hand. He wouldn't need extra light. Besides, there's a buoy right there at Tiger Island."

Ellie chimed in. "Or...MacGregor was waiting for a signal from Goodwine?"

"Or..." Hosea was thoughtful. "The event may have been real. Lisabet and Sylvia handed over cash, with which MacGregor purchased the boats."

"That would make sense, except that the women haven't raised any money so far."

"So they say." Hosea avoided his brother's gaze.

Ellie scoffed. "Sylvia would have to be a lot better liar than she is."

The police chief made a face. "I guess I should be grateful for that."

She blew him a kiss.

"All I'm saying is this whole thing may be a snow job." Hosea rose. "I think it's time we paid a visit to Mr. MacGregor."

Simon put a hand on his arm. "Let's check the boats first. If there's contraband or drugs in them, we'll have the goods on him."

Hosea asked, "Where are they moored, Amos?"

"In the Olde Town marina. I'm going to get a warrant and call in the drug unit. We should be able to check them out tomorrow."

Hosea snickered. "You might want to ask Judge Rackham for that warrant. Not sure Lester would be amenable."

"Can we come?"

Amos surveyed their eager faces and shook his head. "MacGregor may not have bought any guns himself, but I wouldn't be surprised if there were armed guards at the boats."

"So what do we do?"

"Sit tight."

It was a long night. And a long morning.

****

Park headquarters, Wednesday, May 23

Simon got to the phone first. "So?" He listened. "Okay, we'll be there in ten." He hung up. "They found drugs. Come on, he wants to meet us at MacGregor's office."

"I thought MacGregor was supposed to go to

Cuba."

"Debbie says Nora told her he postponed the trip. He's coming in for a meeting at two."

Ellie checked her watch. "It's one thirty now. We'd better hurry."

They reached the parking lot as Amos arrived in an unmarked car and sat, waiting. After fifteen minutes, a sleek white Lexus turned into the lot and MacGregor got out. Amos raised a hand, signaling not to move. They waited until he had entered the building, then Amos and his deputy headed toward the entrance. "Come on. I think if we confront him he'll have to confess."

"Are you going to arrest him?"

"Not yet. I need proof that he's involved in the smuggling."

When they got to the office door, it stood open. Amos entered first. Nora looked up. "He's in there."

The police chief went through, and the others wedged in behind him. MacGregor's eyes widened at the array of uniforms. "Hello. What can I do for you?"

"Mr. MacGregor, I'm Amos Barnes, Chief of Police of Fernandina Beach. You recently purchased two fishing boats. This morning we searched those boats and found cocaine. Can you explain how it got there?"

The man sprang up, knocking his chair over. "*Cocaine?* That's preposterous."

"Approximately fifty pounds, in one-pound bricks, were hidden in a false dry well."

"Oh my God, I know nothing about that!"

Simon stepped forward. "What did you buy the boats for, MacGregor?"

He dropped his eyes. "Um…it was for the sister-cities program. We…um…were going to use them as sightseeing boats." He picked up the chair.

Amos said, "I have Forensics examining the boats for fingerprints and evidence. If they find anything linking you to the drugs, I'll have you arrested."

"I swear I had nothing to do with it." He stopped. "Those boats have been sitting unoccupied at the marina for two weeks. Redmond said they'd been for sale for months. I was in no hurry to check them out, so I told the dockmaster I'd get back to him. We wouldn't need them anyway until we had the money to buy…um…" He faltered.

"Guns?"

"Shotguns. Our next…er…event was to be a skeet-shooting party. On the water. The ladies are working on raising cash, but we're temporarily short."

That's why we haven't found any record of his buying weapons.

"So, see…" He couldn't quite keep the triumph out of his voice. "Anyone could have used them as a convenient storage locker."

Ellie began to laugh. "Really? That's the best you can do?"

Amos cast a glance at Simon. "Ask him."

He snapped, "Who exactly are your confederates in the scheme to liberate Cuba?"

MacGregor fell back onto his chair. "What? What in hell are you talking about?"

"We know that you're planning to invade Cuba. That's really why you need the guns and boats."

"Where on earth did you come up with such a bizarre notion?" He picked up a pen and tapped it on the blotter.

His cheek is twitching. "Are Hearst, Crowley, and Farnsworth in it with you, or are they mere stooges?"

"Stooges? You're nuts. The sister-cities project is legit. Those three believe in it." He surreptitiously slid a folder into his drawer and closed it gently, then laid his hand casually on the desk. "I haven't taken any money from the city fathers, if that's what you're accusing me of. They're involved to lend gravitas to the affair." He coughed. "Both Crowley and Farnsworth immediately recognized the advantages—they didn't take much persuasion. Hearst was doubtful at first, but he came on board soon enough."

Ellie stepped forward. "What about the others? Why are Mathews and Martí silent partners?"

MacGregor got up and paced. "That's their business."

Simon spoke softly. "Martí is virulently anti-Castro. He couldn't possibly be in favor of any rapprochement between us and them."

MacGregor stopped pacing. "How did you know that?"

"It's not hard. He has a paper trail a mile long."

His expression altered, tightened. "He's right. Those…city fathers…all they care about is a new revenue stream. That, and sounding like enlightened progressives." He sneered. "They have no idea what a brutal regime it is. They believe all the crap the ex-president and the media fed them about it being a paradise that's only suffering because of the mean-spirited American embargo." His eyes grew hard. "Kenny and Julian and I, we know better. Julian showed us what those bastards did to what had been one of the most prosperous countries in all of Latin America."

"So he talked you into mounting an invasion to free Cuba?"

"What? Don't be ridiculous. Sounds like a grade B movie."

"But…" *This man hops from one lie to another like he's on a pogo stick.*

The room fell silent. Simon assumed his companions were as perplexed as he was.

Ellie finally spoke. "If you feel that strongly about Castro, why would you want to make Havana a sister city?"

Gregory was quick with his answer. "It would make it easier to get a foothold in the country. Open it up to a free exchange of ideas. Julian thinks Radio Martí has outlived its usefulness. We need to take a more aggressive approach if we want to help the Cuban people. Farnsworth and the other bigwigs were happy to pony up."

"I thought you said you didn't need money from them?"

"Only a bit of seed money. That's all. To get the ball rolling."

Aha. So it's only that he hasn't taken a lot of money from them…yet. I wonder…"Why don't you come clean, MacGregor. What's the scam?"

"Scam? There's no scam. I resent your insinuation, Ribault." He pointed an accusatory finger at Simon. It shook slightly.

Inspiration hit. "Admit it. The whole invasion thing is bogus. So is the sister-city idea. You planned to bilk your partners out of any funds raised. You never intended to use them for either."

"My God, man, where do you come up with this stuff?"

Amos was getting impatient. "All right, then. What's your *real* plan?"

MacGregor rose and went to the window, facing away from his inquisitors. Simon was sure he was running out the clock while he thought of a new lie. The phone rang. He sprang to pick it up and said quickly, "I have to take this. It's an overseas call." He pointed at the door.

Simon was ready to wait him out, but Amos lifted his chin. "Come on." They filed out.

When they reached the cars, the police chief said, "I don't think we'll know anything until tomorrow. I suggest we regroup in my office after I hear from the lab."

Ellie halted. "We can't just let him get away with avoiding our questions."

"You heard the man. Whatever you hit him with, he comes up with another whopper. He's a world-class liar."

Simon agreed. "We have to be able to nail him with undeniable proof, or he'll wiggle out of it before you can say Br'er Rabbit."

"But—"

Simon grasped Ellie by the hand. "Come on."

"Where are we going?"

"Wait a minute." When they were out of earshot, he stopped. "Home. I didn't get enough last night."

"Direct, aren't you?"

He looked down at her. "It's about time I was more direct with you. Ellie, I—" His cell phone burbled.

"Ribault. My mother? How is she?" He listened to a long speech. "I see. When? Okay. Thank you." He flipped it closed, hiding the emotions roiling his chest. When he turned to Ellie, dread etched her face. He kissed her forehead. "Mother's okay. The drug seems to be working. They have found no trace of the cancer in their last two examinations. They've declared her in remission."

Ellie let the long-held breath go. "Oh, thank God, how wonderful. And amazing. Can she come home?"

"They're going to keep her there for a few more days, to make sure the tumor doesn't start to grow again. She'll have to take the drug regularly for the rest of her life."

"But that at least will be a long one! Oh, Simon."

He clasped her in his arms and kissed her. "That means you only have a little while to make me into something you can love."

She whispered something.

"What's that?"

"You already are."

A few hours later, Ellie sat up in bed and threw her arms out, knocking Simon over the side. "Hey!"

"Oops! Sorry." She helped him back up.

He took the opportunity to fondle a breast while rubbing the bruise on his elbow. "What was that all about?"

"I've been thinking."

"You're not supposed to be thinking. You're supposed to be pondering the pleasures of the flesh— my flesh. Barring that, sleeping."

"*Shh*. MacGregor said he didn't bilk the city fathers for the money to buy the boats—"

"Yet."

"Yes, and that for now he was only using them for publicity and prestige."

"According to Iggy, Sylvia and Lisabet have had no luck fundraising so far."

"So…"

"So?"

"So, where'd he get the money for the boats?"

Chapter Nineteen
The Fast and the Furious

Simon's house, Thursday, May 24

"Is breakfast ready yet?"

"No, boss."

Simon ambled into the kitchen. Ellie was at the stove with a large frying pan. "I guess I'll make coffee then."

"Good."

Simon busied himself filling the carafe and thinking. "About the money for the boats. Maybe the women did raise it after all. They hedged about it when we asked them. Plus MacGregor used the word 'temporarily' when he said they were short on cash."

"How do you propose to find out?"

"Simple. Call Debbie."

"Ah, the go-to gal. She's one talented lady, isn't she?"

"Yes. Santa is lucky to have her. She's also a superb baker."

Ellie broke eggs into a bowl and added milk. "So when did he and Debbie become an item?"

"Their spouses—that is, Debbie's husband and Santa's ex-wife—died in the same month five years ago." Simon moved aside the pile of cookbooks on the counter and set Ellie's cup down. "They met at a grief-counseling session and have been inseparable ever since."

"They do make a cute couple." She thought for a minute. "I don't suppose she bakes cookies around Christmas. It would be nice to eat an edible one for once."

Oh yeah, Beebee's "kisses." "Dozens."

"I begin to think there is a God."

"Of course there is. And on the eighth day, He invented cookies."

While Ellie made french toast, Simon called Debbie. "She says not a problem. She'll see Sylvia for coffee after their aerobics class and winnow it out of her. After we eat, want to hit the beach?"

"Sure. Let's swing by my place and go from there." By the time they reached Ellie's house, however, a thick, dark cloud hung low on the horizon like a heavy winter blanket. "Damn, our timing's off."

Simon squinted up at it. "Shelf cloud. Don't worry. It'll pass."

Sure enough, half an hour later the sky was again clear and blue. They strolled down the splintery boardwalk to an empty beach. "Everyone else must've made other plans."

Ellie threw her arms wide. "We have it all to ourselves!" They began to walk north up the wide brown beach. In the distance, she spied a line of horses picking their way over the shells. "Will you look at that—those people are riding on the beach!"

"I told you."

She stopped before a round gelatinous blob in the sand. "I saw one of these the other day. What is it?"

Simon came up. "A cannonball jellyfish. Don't

touch it."

"But it's dead."

"It can still sting you. They eat them in Japan."

"Why am I not surprised?"

They walked for another hour, then went back to Ellie's cottage. "Oh, that's where I left my cell phone. Let's see if Debbie called back." He checked his messages. "Nothing yet, but here's one from Amos." He read. "They've located a car that might match the one Harvey saw the night of the murders. Want to go see?"

"You have to ask?"

They changed and drove to the address Amos had given. It turned out to be a Mercedes dealership on Route 200. Two police cars were pulled up on either side of a white sedan. One policeman was examining a dent in the front bumper. Another sat at the wheel. He turned the headlights on and off, blew the horn, then turned the rear lights on. The left one stayed dark. They saw Amos talking to a man in a shirt with the words "Andy Kelly" and "Manager" embroidered on it and walked up to them.

"Hey, Simon. Hi, Ellie. Have you met Andy Kelly?"

Ellie looked at Andy through narrowed eyes. "Yes, I have. Nicole says hi. She...*missed* you at the party."

The man blinked. "Uh...er..."

Simon intervened. "Come on, Ellie, you know Andy was in Atlanta. And besides, it wasn't Nicole's birthday after all."

The manager turned to him, mouth open. "It wasn't? She didn't say...she didn't tell me...why'd she accept the roses then?"

Before Simon could find a rock to crawl under, Amos broke in. "Kelly says a guy brought the car in for repairs about three weeks ago."

"What was his name?"

Kelly looked at a clipboard. "Nothing here. Let's go check the computer." He clicked a few keys. "Oscar Neely. Left it here April 30. Says the service department called the number he'd given with the estimate and got a busy signal. Tried four more times—never got in touch with the fellow."

"So you didn't do the repairs?"

"We wouldn't do anything until we had his consent."

Ellie waved back toward the lot. "What happens when someone abandons a car like this?"

"We keep it for up to two months, then have it towed."

Amos looked at the rangers. "What do you think?"

"Let's get Harvey Denton over here, see if he can make a positive identification."

"Okay. While you do that, I'm going to see if I can get a bead on this Oscar Neely."

"Rendezvous back here?"

"Yeah. Buzz me when you have Denton in hand."

They found Harvey on his porch, rocking in an old rattan chair, its wrappings coming off in tattered curls. "Sure, I'll come, but remember it was dark. I only got a general impression of the car."

When Amos returned, Simon sat in the Mercedes while Harvey circled, eyeballing it. "Pretty sure it's the same one. I remember that boxy shape. Shoulda known it was a Mercedes." He looked up. "Rear light out?"

"Yes."

"Left rear?"

"Yes."

"It's the car all right."

Amos stuck his head in the passenger side window and scanned the interior. "You didn't see who was driving it, right, Harvey?"

"Right. I mean, no, I didn't."

"Not even whether it was a man or a woman?"

He shook his head.

Ellie said, "I don't understand. We know Oscar Neely dropped the car off. Last I checked, Oscar is a man's name."

Simon added, "Ergo, the driver must have been a man."

"Not necessarily." Amos was grim. "Oscar Neely is the manager of El Toro. He works for Lisabet de Angeles. The car is registered in her name."

****

El Toro restaurant, Thursday, May 24

"She can? Good. We'll be there at two thirty." Amos put down the phone. "Lisabet can see us after the lunch rush is over."

Simon, Ellie, and Amos arrived at the restaurant at the same time and stood waiting at the reception desk until Lisabet was available. Acting as though the thought had just struck him, Simon barred the hostess's way. "Say, Clarice. What happened to your manager—the one with the tattoos?" He ignored the leery look Ellie directed at him. "Ellie here had the most exquisite mojo pork at a place in Jacksonville and wants to ask him if Cecil can duplicate it. He's been missing in action the last two times we've been here."

"Oh sorry! Ms. de Angeles let Oscar go a few

weeks ago and hasn't hired anyone new yet. That's why she's so busy."

Simon glanced at Amos inquiringly. The latter said, "I only went by the website. Guess it hasn't been updated."

Lisabet came out of her office and ushered them in. Ellie and Simon stood by the door, while Amos kicked off the proceedings. "Ms. de Angeles, can you tell us what you were doing on the night of April 14?"

She seemed surprised. "Didn't Simon tell you? I was at the Green League event at the fort."

"And when did that break up?"

"I don't remember—late."

"And did you drive to the event?"

"Yes, of course."

"What kind of car do you drive, Ms. de Angeles?"

She gave a delighted cackle. "Chief Barnes, I have eight cars. I choose one as the fancy takes me. How could I possibly remember which car I drove six weeks ago?"

Ellie interrupted. "We understand you recently fired your manager."

"Oscar Neely." She pressed her lips together. "Dishonest. Lazy. I should have known not to hire him. He had a juvenile record, but I wanted to give him a chance. Why, he even took one of my cars joyriding one afternoon! That was the last straw."

"And when was that?"

For the first time, she looked a bit uncertain. "A few weeks ago. I don't remember."

"Which car did he take?"

"A Mercedes." She sighed. "I loved that car. My second husband gave me that car."

"Did he bring it back?"

"What?"

Simon tried to be patient. "Did Neely bring the Mercedes back?"

"No, as a matter of fact. Let me think." She raised her eyes to the ceiling. "Now I remember. He confessed he'd run over something and punctured a tire, so he ditched it."

Amos asked, "Why didn't you report it?"

"I told him to go find it, but he'd been so drunk he couldn't locate the spot. That's when I fired him."

"Why didn't you report it after that?"

She shrugged. "From what he told me, it was deep in the swamp—wrecked. Why go to any more trouble?" An arch look passed over her dark features. "No need for the insurance people to know, right?"

Simon said slowly, "He did find it, you know."

She stared at him, her eyes hooded. "He did? Where?"

"That we don't know. He took it to the dealership to be repaired, but he never went back to retrieve it. Do you have any idea why?"

"No." She seemed rather put out. "No idea at all."

Amos picked up his hat. "Well, thank you for your time, Ms. de Angeles."

"Certainly."

As Simon left, he looked back. She stood there, her expression mystified.

When they reached the sidewalk, Amos stood, keys in hand. "Now what?"

"We need to find Neely."

"I'll get Zack on it."

Simon's phone rang. "Hi, Debbie. Any word?" He

listened. "Thanks." He hung up.

"What?"

"Sylvia claims she hasn't raised any money yet. Debbie believes her because she used the thumbscrews." He grinned. "Hell of a woman."

Amos gaped at them. "Are you alleging Debbie Daugherty tortured my wife?"

Ellie said mildly, "Simon is being facetious."

"Sure I am. Debbie only asked her if she had raised any money for the Green League, specifically for the boats. Sylvia says she's been unsuccessful shaking down her friends…" After a side look at the police chief, he amended the sentence. "…er…soliciting money, but that Lisabet had unearthed an anonymous donor."

"*Hmm.* I wonder who it is…and if he or she knows the true purpose of the Green League, whatever it may be?"

"Another mystery to solve."

"I think we need sustenance. Let's go to Sliders."

Amos said, his round face grim, "I'm going home."

"Okay, Ellie and I will somehow carry on."

Once in the car, Ellie said, "Poor Sylvia."

"Poor Sylvia? She brought it on herself."

Sliders was very crowded. As they passed through the bar on the way outside, Ellie halted. "Nicole!"

The young woman turned, a sheepish grin on her face. Simon wondered at her reaction until he recognized the man sitting next to her, still in his uniform shirt. *Andy Kelly.* "Why, Andy. I see you and Nicole are back on speaking terms." He tossed a waggish look at Ellie and gave Andy's shoulder a spirited pat that propelled the poor fellow off his stool.

As he brushed off the seat of his pants, Andy mumbled, "Yeah, hi." He wouldn't look at Ellie, which was just as well. "Hi, Ellie."

Nicole cast a pleading look at her best friend. Ellie took pity. "We're heading outside for a bite. See you later."

Gretchen brought a single menu and gave it to Ellie. "Plain hamburger, well done, fries, and a PBR, Simon?"

"Tell you what," he said expansively, "I'll try the crab cakes."

Everyone stared at him. The couple at the next table snapped a picture. Gretchen said smoothly, "And for you, Ellie?"

"The same."

When she'd gone, Ellie leaned toward Simon, and, after a glance at their neighbors, whispered loudly, "You'd better clean your plate, young man."

Simon didn't think that required a response.

Gretchen brought their beers. After a sip, Ellie said, "So where are we?"

"We've uncovered Gregory's alias, all ten names on the guest list, the extent of their financing, and two—no, three—possible motives for the League's establishment."

"And also that we can't prove anything they've done is illegal."

"Damn. Too true. Let's assume the sister-cities proposition is on the skids—due, I'm sure Mr. MacGregor will say, to our meddling. I propose we set the League aside and concentrate on the murders."

"Okay. The dead are Bonney the drug smuggler; Virtue and Labadie, Jamaican detectives; Alvaredo, the escaped convict; and Captain Goodwine."

"The only logical motive we have is for the Virtue killing—that Bonney murdered him when he got too close. But how did Alvaredo end up on the boat? Was he part of her gang?"

"He'd been in jail for years."

"There's always a grapevine in prison. He could have been in contact with her."

"What about Goodwine? Was he in on the smuggling?"

"According to Bailey, he provided the boat in return for a cut. So, either he killed Alvaredo, or Alvaredo killed him."

"Then who killed Bonney?"

"And Labadie?"

Their meals came. Simon picked at his crab. "Do I put ketchup on it or what?"

"Tabasco sauce. Lots of it."

He shuddered. "You must hate me."

"Nobody forced you to order it."

"I'm trying to be more adventurous." He put a hand on hers. "For your sake."

She laughed. "You may be sorry. I think tonight we try…bouillabaisse."

"Seafood stew from Marseille. Flavored with Pernod, it features clams, langoustes, assorted fish, vegetables…and the kitchen sink."

"So you know what it is. Have you ever eaten it?"

He just stared at her. She munched calmly on her sandwich.

Simon was quiet for a while, nibbling on a french fry and avoiding the crab. When they'd paid the check, he said, "I propose we visit the *Mercy Louise* again tomorrow. I have an idea."

****

Panther Point Marina, Friday, May 25

The boat seemed a little more desolate this time, like an abandoned cocker spaniel. No one was about. Simon jumped onto the deck and held a hand out to Ellie. She took a hesitant step aboard, slipping slightly on the railing before he caught her. He observed tartly, "If you're going to live here, you'll have to learn to be more comfortable with boats."

"I suppose. Do you own one?"

"Of course. You can't live in Florida without having a boat. It's statutory."

She surveyed the slimy, leaf-strewn deck. "I think I'll start with a kayak."

"Great. I'll take you out some evening. We can go through Egan's Creek."

"So what are we doing here?"

He stepped to the starboard side. "Remember what a mess we found the rope in?"

"Uh huh."

"And we figured that's how Bonney ended up in the water."

"Right. We now have the shoe to prove it."

"Okay." He paced from stern to bow, examining the deck. "Bonney had already killed Virtue and thrown him overboard. That's why we found him the farthest northeast. Then, something happened with Alvaredo."

"Maybe he witnessed her murdering Virtue?"

"Good. So, she tries to kill him with the same knife—"

Ellie objected. "But then we would have found his body next."

"She didn't succeed. He got the knife away from her and threatened her with it. She backed away, hands up to fend him off. Her foot gets caught in the rope."

"It winds around her ankle. She can't move."

"He pushes her into the water, one shoe coming off in the process."

Ellie put a restraining hand on Simon's flailing arm. "Why didn't she drown then?"

"Because by the time she'd hit the water, she'd freed herself from the rope. Otherwise, we wouldn't have found it on the deck."

"I see. So she swims to shore, where she...wait! Could she have strangled herself?"

"What do you mean?"

"You know—she's hurt, she's exhausted. She crawls out of the river and flings herself on the sand. Her necklace gets twisted so tight around her neck it kills her."

He shook his head. "The chain would have been embedded in her neck then. Kenny didn't find any jewelry on her."

"It could have been a scarf."

"A bellicose, shaven-headed brigand wraps a gauzy floral scarf around her gazelle-like neck?" When Ellie began to pout, he said quickly, "How about we leave aside how she died for now. So who's left on the boat?"

"Alvaredo and the captain."

"Who do we find next on the shore?"

"Alvaredo."

"Ergo, he died before the captain. Goodwine was able to steer the *Mercy Louise* all the way to the marina."

"They both died of knife wounds."

"Goodwine in the side and Alvaredo in the back. Hang on." He dialed a number. "Iggy, is Kenny there? Oh, he doesn't? No, no—I don't want to talk about the Cuba thing. I want to ask a question about the murders….Oh really? Well, tell him I don't have time for this now. I want to know how long it would have taken for Captain Goodwine to bleed out from his wound….Maybe an hour? Okay, and Alvaredo was stabbed in the back. Same question…it punctured the left lung, huh. So? Ten, twenty minutes? Great, thanks…What? Tell Kenny I'll deal with him later." He hung up. "Got it."

"Spill."

"As I said, Alvaredo wrestles Bonney for the knife and snatches it away. Bonney topples off the boat. Goodwine comes up from below to see what all the fuss is about, and Alvaredo attacks him. When he's not looking, Goodwine stabs him in the back."

" 'When he's not looking?' Why wouldn't he be looking? And how did the captain get the knife?"

"Uh…" Simon tapped his chin. "Wait—Amos had it right."

"Had what right?"

"The shoe. See, Alvaredo figures Goodwine is down for the count. He turns around to check if Bonney is really gone and sees the shoe tangled in the rope. He pulls it out and tosses it into the drink. That's why they found it closer to the marina than to the fort."

"What does that have to do with the knife?"

"He had to put it down in order to extricate Bonney's shoe."

"I see. And the captain grabbed it and killed Alvaredo." Ellie thought about it. "That fits the evidence, but we still don't know who did Bonney in."

"No, but we do know that little Letty did not hear a human scream."

"Who?"

"Letty—the Girl Scout. If she heard a noise, it couldn't have come from any of the victims. They were all too far away."

"A raccoon then, as surmised by Charlotte. So much for Letty's fifteen minutes of fame."

The sun dipped behind the pines. Simon peered at the sky. "It's getting late. Time to go home." When they reached his house, Ellie remained in the car. He put a hand on the window. "Didn't you promise to cook bouillabaisse for me?"

"And see it wasted on you like those poor crab cakes? No, sir." When he didn't dispute the charge, she kissed him. "I forgot—I have some things to do. I'll see you tomorrow. You might consider writing all your theories down for Amos and Hosea."

I have to ask. "By the way, what happened with Thad?"

"Thad? I…uh…I'm going to see him later."

"Hey!" But she had driven off.

What the hell? She can't date us both. It isn't ladylike.

He watched the news, picked up a book, put it down, walked the dog, scratched his nose. When the moon rose, he took a bag of peanuts and his beer out on the deck and counted stars. By eight o'clock, he was driving toward Old Town. The Palace Saloon was busy. Music from the jukebox spilled into the street along with a mob of college kids. *Oh yeah, spring break. Think I'll head to Fourteenth Street.* He parked on

Sadler Road and walked down the nearly empty avenue, peering into darkened shops. The only place open was the Pink Quartz, a glass-fronted fast food restaurant. The garish pink neon sign complemented the garish pink vinyl banquettes. *Amazing that a place that serves hamburgers even I won't touch has stayed in business for so long.* He started to enter anyway but stopped on the threshold. Ellie and Thad sat in a corner booth, their heads together. Simon backed out and went home.

The phone was ringing when he arrived. "Simon? It's Georgia."

Oh, thank God, someone to talk to. "Georgia, I'm so glad you called. I—"

"I'm running out the door. I wanted to let you know they rescheduled my bar prep class. I have to get back up to school right away. I'm leaving in five minutes."

"But I need—"

"I heard about your mother. Great news. I'll be in touch." The phone went dead.

The cat chose that moment to take a claw to his favorite leather chair.

Chapter Twenty
Riding in Cars with Boys

Park headquarters, Saturday, May 26

Simon had planned not to speak to Ellie at all the next day, but when she breezed in, she landed him a wet, smacking kiss on his mouth. "Top of the morning!"

Over her shoulder, he saw Thad getting out of his Porsche. "How was your date? Nice?" *Did I put sufficient venom into that last word?*

Apparently not, since she grinned at him and patted his head. "Fine, fine. Can't talk about it now, with you-know-who here."

"I see." *My displeasure doesn't seem to be getting through to her.* "No need. Your private business is your business." He sniffed and rattled his paper.

Thad came in. "Hi, all." He gave Ellie a meaningful look. "I did what you asked. We'll see what comes of it."

"Keep me posted," she responded gaily.

Simon spent the next half an hour stewing over what to say to Ellie that would really put her in her place. Nothing came to mind. Finally, he stood. "I think I'll go check the fort. We've a new docent."

Thad looked up. "I hear she's a real looker."

Aha. "She is indeed. I intend to guide her through

her paces."

Ellie said sweetly, "She's not a horse, you know."

"I *know.*" *Damn her, why does she always get the last word?*

He found the young lady in the barracks. To his eyes, she was barely out of grammar school, undernourished if not anorexic, with short-cropped black hair and a tattoo of a dragon running down her arm. "Wendy Adams? I'm Ranger Ribault. How's everything going?"

"Oh fine, Mr. Ribault. I've only had two groups so far, and I could answer all their questions. The handbook Superintendent Barnes gave me is very thorough."

Natch. "Good to hear. You can call me Simon."

She blushed furiously. "Er…okay."

How old does she think I am? Eighty? He said quickly, "So how long is your shift?"

She relaxed. "Only three hours today. Superintendent Barnes says he wants me to get my feet wet. Tomorrow, my shift will be longer—from noon to closing time." She hesitated. "I…heard about the murder victims." She shivered a little. "Where exactly were they found?" She gazed fearfully around the large courtyard.

"Not to worry, they were on park land but outside the fort. Quite far away." *She doesn't need to know just how close Bonney's body was.*

She hunched her shoulders. "I sure don't want to be here at night."

"We do occasionally have evening events here. Most of the time, it doesn't require a docent, but for the historic reenactments, we may need reinforcements."

"Oh dear." She was quiet, then spoke softly. "My friends Hillary and Jeb were out in a boat the…the night…that night."

"Really?" *Witnesses?* "Did they see anything?"

She nodded.

"Why didn't they report it?"

Wendy looked uncomfortable. "I think it…uh…slipped their minds. Hillary remembered it yesterday when she read the article in the *Register*."

Patience. "So…what did they see?"

"Well, they had come up from Egan's Creek and were floating along by the park. They cut their motor because they were…well…you know." She focused on the buttons of her uniform.

Simon thought he knew. He said encouragingly, "And?"

"They saw these lights on the shore near the fort walls."

"Lights? Tiki torches?"

"Not that big. One was a tiny little light."

Sylvia. "Like a lit cigarette?"

"I guess it could have been a cigarette. But then this second one flashed on."

"Another cigarette?"

"A little bigger—maybe a penlight? After a minute, the small light disappeared. The other one moved along the shore and then stopped and flicked out. Hillary says they were going to move on, but it came back on and started to bob up and down." She closed her eyes tight. "Hillary says it kept bobbing and bobbing and bobbing and—"

Got it. "So it was bobbing? Any idea why?"

"Uh uh. Hillary said they were so mesmerized by

340

it, they ran aground. They dragged the boat off the sandbank and hightailed it home. They didn't even realize it was the same night until Hillary saw the bit in the paper. See, Jeb had…well…he'd borrowed his dad's boat without permission, so he was too scared to say anything."

That's at least confirmation of Sylvia's story. Could the second light have been Bonney's? No, she was in the water. "Well, carry on." He went back to the station. Ellie stood by the water cooler in close conversation with Thad. They jumped apart when he came in. "Don't mind me."

"Oh, we're not. There was a spider on Ellie's cup."

He looked at her. "Did you eat it?"

"No, of course not. I never eat between meals. Thad got rid of it. Thanks for your concern."

Since the conversation didn't look to be getting any better any time soon, Simon changed the subject. "Wendy Adams seems a bright girl. A little spooked by the murders."

"I'll be glad to go cheer her up." Thad put on his hat.

"You do that."

When he'd gone, Simon got himself a cup of water, checking the cup carefully. "Wendy told me an interesting story."

"Oh?"

"Two friends of hers were on the river the night of April 14. They saw a glowing light outside the walls on the shore."

"Sylvia's cigarette."

"Right. But they also saw another light."

"Simultaneously?"

"For only a minute, but yes. The second one was larger. According to Wendy, it bobbed."

"Must have been Bonney using a flashlight. That means she was alive and conscious."

"My conclusion as well, but then it hit me. How would she have a working flashlight? She'd been in the water for who knows how long."

"True." Ellie pursed her lips. "And anyway, CSI didn't find it on her, so she must have dropped it."

"Then they would have found it on the ground. *Hmm*." Simon tapped his chin. "Gimme a sec." He dialed a number. "Maurice? Can you check the evidence box for the Fort Clinch murders?...Oh, you have it open? Great. Is there a flashlight in there? No? Oh, there is?...Does it work?" He waited. "Aha. Thanks...No, no, that's all I needed." He hung up. "No flashlight."

"Then why are you smiling?"

"CSI did pick up a lighter, and it works. One of those fancy survival ones that are sealed."

"Of course! Any pirate worth her salt would have one of those. Where did he find it?"

"Under Bonney's body."

"Okay, so Bonney's walking along the shore using her lighter to show the way...Why didn't Sylvia tell us she saw her?"

"Maybe the other light wasn't visible from where she stood."

"You should ask Wendy how far apart the lights were."

He looked out the door. "It'll have to wait. There goes Thad." Wendy sat next to him.

Ellie followed his gaze. "I'm going to take an early

lunch. Care to join me?"

"Oh, so you're free today?" He couldn't keep the resentment out of his voice.

She leveled a stern look at him. "You're in a foul mood."

"Shouldn't I be?" He nodded at the wisps of exhaust left by Thad's car.

"I don't know what you're talking about."

"I'm talking about you and the BMOC, that…Brando, that…that Fabian, Thad Farnsworth," he bellowed.

Her response was unexpected. She started to giggle. When she caught her breath, she gasped, "Oh, Simon, you're jealous. How funny."

"*Funny?*" He whirled and headed toward the door, intending to break something or at least chop down a large tree.

Ellie called him. "Simon, do come here."

He permitted her to take his arm and draw him back inside. He allowed her to take his hat off and brush his hair back from his forehead. He consented to being kissed. Things were looking up.

"I'd better tell you what's been going on between me and Thad."

"That would help."

"You know Judge Farnsworth is under investigation for accepting illegal campaign contributions."

"Yes. From Cubans. An angle we have yet to explore."

"Well, I happen to know a lawyer in the District of Columbia who specializes in these cases. I put Thad in touch with him."

"That's it?"

"Yes. Mr. Hickey says there's a widespread racket that uses political campaigns to get cash out of Cuba. Cuba has severe restrictions on legal tender leaving the country, and he believes someone may have hacked into Farnsworth's account. He thinks he can get him off."

"Oh."

"So?"

"So what?"

"So how about an apology?"

"For what?"

"For impugning my motives. For jumping to conclusions. For being jealous." She waited.

"I'm sorry I jumped to a conclusion. I'm not sorry I was jealous. I mean, look at the fellow. How can I compete with Hercules?"

"Brains trump brawn." She kissed him again. "I prefer my men to have a few operative neurons. While we're at it, you should apologize to Thad. He's been a perfect gentleman."

Accepting defeat, he nodded. "I'll use one-syllable words though."

"That will help. Now, about this bobbing light—"

Hosea rushed in. "News!" He stopped to catch his breath.

"What?"

"They…" *Pant pant*. "…they think they found Lisabet's manager—Neely."

"Oscar Neely, the fellow who left her Mercedes at the dealership?"

"The very one." Hosea held up a hand. "Give me a minute." They waited impatiently. "He's in the pinewoods over by Five Points."

"Camping out?"

"No." He shook his head. "He was stuffed under a fallen oak. Body's at the morgue." He looked up at Simon. "Examiner on call thinks he was strangled."

Simon's eyebrows rose. "Another one? What possible relation to Bonney could Neely have?"

Ellie piped up. "Drugs. With that purple hair and nose ring, he sure looked like a user. And Lisabet said he'd been in jail."

"Possible. At any rate, it's the same MO."

Hosea muttered, "MO? Dunno about that. There are only so many ways to kill a person. Stabbing, shooting, strangulation…"

Ellie took up the refrain. "Smothering, poisoning…walling alive behind a brick wall…" The two men stared at her. "What?"

"Anyway…" Hosea sat down at his desk. "…Starr's doing the autopsy now."

"Not Kenny?"

"Kenny's off today. Starr thinks the guy's been dead several weeks."

"As in, two weeks? Or six?"

Hosea shrugged. "Don't know yet."

"In that case, we can't assume it's Neely."

"Right. Amos sent Bobby back to the Mercedes dealership to see if Kelly can identify the crime scene photo. If he recognizes him, someone should take it to Lisabet."

Simon and Ellie said together, "We'll go."

Hosea eyed them. "You wouldn't by chance be putting lunches at El Toro on the expense account?"

Simon grinned. "Hadn't thought of that. Good

345

thing I kept my receipts."

As they drove downtown, Ellie said, "I've been thinking. Perhaps we should wait for the formal identification before we disturb Lisabet?"

"Let's swing by and check with the deputy."

They found Bobby sitting in his car on the phone. "Yes, sir, Wilbur was sure. Yes, I know it's weird, but Kelly never actually saw the person who brought the car in…Okay."

He hung up. Simon leaned in through the window. "Kelly identified the photo?"

"Oh, hey, Simon. Like I was telling the captain, he wasn't there when the car came in. So I talked to Wilbur Stevens, the service coordinator on duty. He says it wasn't a man at all. It was a woman."

"In the photo? Neely was a transvestite?"

"No." He looked about to make a crack but thought better of it. "The person who brought the car in was a woman."

"Then why was Neely's name on the ticket?"

"Wilbur says she told him the car belonged to Neely, but he was out of town and she was doing him a favor."

"Could he describe her?"

"Didn't remember much. Dark hair, dark eyes. Short. That's it."

Ellie said, "Could be Lisabet."

"That makes no sense. Why would she use his name? The car belonged to her. No, that description could fit half the women in Fernandina Beach." He gave her an appreciative look. "It lets you off the hook though." He put a hand on the car's window. "Can we have the photo, Bobby? We'll take it to El Toro and see what the staff has to say."

"Sure, but you might want to cover up the yucky part."

While they walked, Ellie mumbled to herself.

"Speak up."

"What? Oh. Lisabet may not have taken the car in, but she might have an idea. Oscar might have had a girlfriend."

"A girlfriend…who hated him."

"Why do you say that?"

"Well, whoever brought the car to the service station must have killed Neely."

"*Hmm*."

The restaurant was very crowded, but Clarice found them a small table after only a short wait. When Simon showed her the photograph, she nodded. "Yes, that's Oscar. What happened to him?"

"I'm afraid we have bad news. Could you ask Ms. de Angeles to stop by when she has a minute?"

A busboy appeared. "Miss Bucket? Chef needs you in the kitchen. Right away." He beetled his brows.

"Oh, sorry, I have to go. Cecil's in one of his moods." Clarice left, but not without casting a fearful eye at Simon and Ellie. The waitress appeared, order book in her hands.

"What's the special, Inez?"

"*Rabo encendido*. You've had it before, Simon."

Ellie opened a menu. "So how come you won't eat anything exotic anywhere else, but here you'll order *rabo encendido*?"

"Inez told me it was braised beef."

"That's right, Spanish is not one of your languages. *Rabo* means 'tail.' As in 'oxtail.' "

Simon closed the menu. "I don't think I'm in the mood for the special after all." Inez held her pencil poised. "I'll have the hamburger."

"Fries?"

"Yes, please."

Ellie ordered the *boliche*. They were finishing up when Lisabet came to their table. "Clarice says you have something to tell me?"

"Yes. Your former manager, Oscar Neely, has been found dead."

She put a hand to her mouth. "Oh, dear. Where?"

"In the woods by Five Points."

"Do they know how long he's been dead?"

"Not sure yet. Could be anywhere from two to six weeks."

She frowned. "I'll have to check my records to see when I fired him. I'm pretty sure it's been less than a month. Didn't you say he dropped the car off for repairs? He must have gone back to look for it after I fired him. I'll bet he thought he could get his job back if he did. No chance of that." She didn't seem too broken up at the thought.

"Except he didn't take the car for service after all. A woman did." Simon watched her carefully.

Her lips stretched across her teeth, leaving a smudge of crimson. "The swine," she snarled. "It was that floozy."

"Floozy?"

"His girlfriend."

"You seem angry."

She wasn't listening. "Liar. Thief. He stole my money. For her."

Ellie asked in a soft voice. "What did she look

like?"

"Only saw her from a distance. Dirty blonde. Tall. He never brought her to meet me. *Hijo de puta*. And after everything I did for him." She shook off the anger. "So…I bet he found the car and…no, wait. He caught her stealing the car, and she bumped him off. Yes…that's it." She looked up. "White trash like that will steal the polish off your fingernails. My beautiful Mercedes…" They left her muttering to herself.

On the sidewalk, Ellie said, "Tall and blonde. Whatever Ms. de Angeles's fevered imagination conjures up, that lets the girlfriend out."

"Why?"

"Remember? Wilbur said the woman was short and dark."

"Oh yeah." He opened the car door but closed it abruptly. "I think we need to ask Lisabet a couple more questions."

They returned to the restaurant. They found the owner in the kitchen screaming at a cowering line cook, a butcher knife in her hand. "This is how you cut up onions. See?" She held half an onion on the huge maple chopping board with two fingers, and with her other hand, sliced the onion at lightning speed. Then she expertly flipped the onion and chopped it lengthwise. "Every time, Marco. Every time."

She turned as Ellie and Simon entered, the knife raised over her head. Simon had the distinct impression she would have happily sliced and diced them, but she lowered it. "What are you doing in my kitchen?"

"We have another couple of questions. Can you spare a minute?"

She gestured toward her chef. "Get to your station,

Marco." When he'd moved off, she said, "Make it quick."

Ellie began carefully. "The car Oscar crashed was brought to the dealership for repair by a woman matching your description. It was registered in your name. Tell us, please, were you with Neely at the time of his death?"

"Certainly not." Under their scrutiny, she calmed down. "The last time I saw him he was, as I said, intoxicated. We had a…an argument."

"And then what did you do?"

"We were in the rear parking lot. I'd just come back from the bank. He told me he was leaving me. I called him on it—said I knew he was taking off with that buxom bleached bimbo he'd picked up in the restaurant—*my* restaurant! I begged him to take me back. He was drunk. Flat on his ass, he was. He grabbed my keys. I told him that he'd better sober up before he drove anywhere, but he jumped in my car and careened out of the lot."

"And you didn't see where he went?"

She pulled another onion out of the basket and chopped it in half. "No, I went back inside." She held up the knife. "I do have a restaurant to run after all."

"And you never saw him after that?"

"No…no…wait, yes. I saw him the next day. He told me about the car. That's when I fired him."

"Did you get a chance to check on the date?"

"Don't need to. It was four weeks ago. First week of May."

****

Simon's house, Sunday, May 27

"Great, Mother. I'll pick you up at the airport

Tuesday. See you in a few days."

"She's coming home."

"She is indeed." Isis jumped into Simon's lap and started to knead. He scratched the top of her head to make her stop. "It will be a good time to tell her."

"Tell her what?"

"About us."

Ellie finished her beer. "She knows about us."

"Well, not…not."

"Not what?"

"That we're…" *Oh God, am I going to have to put it into words?* "You know…together."

Ellie stared at him. "What are you talking about?"

How do I wiggle out of this? "I mean…she'll be in the house. She'll know when I'm…I'm…not." *Soooo lame.*

"Didn't you tell me she wanted her own place?"

"Well, that might take a while and—"

"And what's wrong with my place, anyhow? I thought you liked being so close to the beach. It's cozy and clean and has a great view and it's convenient…"

Simon put a gentle hand over her mouth. "You're not going to stop on your own, are you?"

She shook her head. He slowly removed his hand only to slap it back on when she started muttering angrily. Suddenly, she paused. "Simon? What were we arguing about?"

He picked up his keys. "I'm sure not going to remind you." He zipped out the door. *Why does the word marriage keep streaming through my head? I have to either accept it or step away. Before she does.*

****

Amelia Island, Tuesday, May 29

"So, you're in complete remission."

"That's what Doctor Goombah says."

Simon left the strip malls behind and crossed Kingsley Creek to Amelia Island. The little bridge curled up and over the expanse of rushes and rivulets that separated the island from the mainland. White egrets dotted the water while a pair of ospreys sailed overhead. A great blue heron landed in the middle of the road. Just before the car reached him, he rose in a shower of rattling feathers. *How do they know exactly when to get out of the way?* "Goombah?"

Simon's mother rolled the window down and looked out over the marshes. "The man's got one of those eighteen-syllable Indian names. We settled on Goombah." She paused reflectively. "I do hope it's not some sort of insult in his language. Every time I use it, he sniggers."

Simon chuckled. "I believe it's Italian-American slang for a close friend."

"Really? I wonder which part he finds humorous, the friend or the Italian?"

He gave her a fond side glance. "So…as they say in Paris, what are your plans for the evening, madame?"

Madeleine moved restlessly. "I know you want to get rid of me as soon as possible, but I need a few days to get organized." She patted her purse. "Plus I've got a load of prescriptions to fill."

The car pulled up in front of Simon's house. "Don't be ridiculous. You're staying here with me."

Madeleine heaved herself out of the car and marched up the steps. "Not on your life. Unless you've gone and done something stupid."

"Stupid? Me? When have I ever done anything

stupid?"

She turned to face him, the corner of her mouth twitching. "You'd better sit down for this."

He opened the door for her and rolled her suitcase in over the threshold. "No, you sit. You want some lemonade? Water?"

She settled herself on the sofa. "Water, please...with a dash of bourbon, there's a dear. It's been a long flight." When he'd delivered the drink, she indicated the chair opposite. "I mean Ellie, of course."

"Ellie?"

"Don't tell me you've let her get away."

Why am I suddenly sorry she's home? "We're...uh...ironing out a few rough edges."

"That metaphor is not up to your usual standards." The phone rang. He picked it up. "Hello? Oh, hi, Debbie. Yes, she's here."

Madeleine took the phone and listened. "That sounds ideal! How did you find it so quickly? He did? She did? When? Where?" She waved her hand in the air, two fingers touching to indicate a pencil. Simon handed her a pad and pen. She wrote something down. "Thanks, Deb. You're a peach."

Two minutes later, when she still hadn't explained, Simon took her glass away from her. "What was that all about?"

"Hey! I hadn't finished that. But since you're up, could you put a tad more bourbon in it? Thanks."

"Mother."

"Debbie Daugherty found me a place to rent. It's right in town on Beech Street. You know that old Victorian on the corner? Well, Justin Whittaker converted it into apartments. He eventually wants to make them condos, but for now he's willing to let me rent to own. Debbie's going to take me to see it tomorrow morning." Simon didn't respond, too busy with mixed emotions to decide which one had priority. "I'm off to bed. Would you mind picking up these prescriptions for me? And maybe a bottle of that Green Treefrog Pinot Grigio I like?"

****

Simon's house, Wednesday, May 30

They were at breakfast when Simon's cell went off. "Ellie? What is it? I see." He went for his hat. "Ellie says Lisabet's photo didn't match the person Wilbur remembered, so we're back to square one. Amos sent out a notice on social media with an artist's rendition of the woman and a description of the car. I've got to get to the park."

"You go on. I'll be fine. Debbie will be here any minute."

"You're sure, Mother?"

"Git."

"Okay."

She called after him. "If you stay for dinner, bring me back a piece of Ellie's key lime pie. Debbie says it's divine."

Ulp. "Sure thing."

As he drove through the park entrance, his phone buzzed. "Simon? Can you come down to the police station? I think we may have made a breakthrough."

"I'm supposed to meet Ellie at the park."

"She's here."

He made a U-turn, barely missing a wild turkey pecking at the roadside. Pulling into the Lime Street lot, he dashed into the building. He skidded to a stop by the front desk. "Hey, Tommy, what's going on?"

The sergeant waved him to a glass-walled office and followed him in. A young woman sat on a straight chair, Amos, Hosea, and Ellie huddled around her. Her dark hair was pulled back in a ponytail, and her tanned skin hinted at too many days in the sun without a hat. A backpack of indeterminate age sat on the floor dribbling mud onto the industrial carpet.

"Oh, there you are, Simon. Tommy, take notes. This is Stephanie Edwards. She answered our ad."

She gave him a perky smile. "I'm here for the puppy?"

Ellie laughed. "Stephanie is a junior at Bob Jones University in Greenville. She's been backpacking through Gullah country for her spring semester. Anthropology major." She looked expectantly at Simon.

"Oh? Is old Professor Hempstead still teaching Mesoamerican archaeology there?"

"Yes, he is. Did you go to Bob Jones?"

"No, but I had a bit of correspondence with him when I was digging in Teotihuacan. Nice old bird."

"I'm in cultural anthropology. I'm hoping to do field work with the Gullah people. They are so fascinating—a distinct creole culture quietly humming along in the middle of our southern coast. I found an article that says they've even located some of their ancestors in Sierra Leone and Senegal!"

"Yes, I know. I did a couple of papers on them for my bachelor's degree. Tried to find a relationship between Marcus Garvey's Back to Africa movement and the Gullah ancestral lore."

"Really? I'd love to read your papers. Do you—"

Amos interrupted. "Could we get back to the issue at hand?"

"The puppy?"

"The Mercedes. Stephanie, why don't you tell us your story."

"Sure. It was about a month ago. It had been raining a lot, and most of my gear was soaked through. See, I'd borrowed my grandfather's World War I pup tent for the trip. Do you know that if you touch the walls, it lets the rain come right through? It turned out to be more uncomfortable staying *in* the tent than out of it."

"I had one of those," observed Tommy reminiscently. "Dad and I would go duck hunting down at Merritt Island. He slept in the VW van, and I got to camp out. Never failed to rain." He smiled.

Amos gave his deputy a long-suffering glance and cleared his throat. "Please continue, Stephanie."

"Sure thing. I was walking along the road about midnight when it began to pour again. I figured there would be more shelter in the woods, so I turned down a little dirt track that led under the pines. About half a mile in, something white glimmered in the dark. When I got closer I saw it was a car—a top-of-the-line Mercedes. Very expensive. It had a dent in its front bumper and a smashed rear light, but otherwise seemed okay."

"Can you lead us to the exact spot?"

"I can try."

"Okay, we'll get to that later. Go on. Was anyone in the car?"

"No, but the keys were. Someone left in a hurry. I got in—I figured they wouldn't mind if I snatched a little shut-eye. But then it occurred to me that it might be hot—you know, stolen. I wasn't sure what I'm supposed to do in a situation like that." She gave Amos a questioning glance. When he didn't respond, she went on. "I decided I'd better report it. I don't know the area very well, but I'd seen a motel about a mile back so I thought maybe I'd drive it there and have them call the police. It wasn't 'til I put the car in gear that I realized why it'd been abandoned."

"What was the problem?"

"It was stuck in the mud. I got some branches and stuff and laid them under the rear tires and got the thing out easy peasy. Not sure why the driver didn't do that."

Maybe because he was dead?

"Then what did you do?"

"I checked into the Motel 8. The night clerk said it was too late to call, and anyway he was going to charge me five dollars to use the phone, so I took a nice hot shower and got a good night's sleep. The next day I looked for a service station. If it was stolen, they'd deal with it." She fidgeted in her seat. "See, I was afraid I'd get stuck here, and I still had a few places to visit before the new semester starts."

At her guilty look, Amos harrumphed. "Go on."

"The first place I came to was the Mercedes dealership, so I left it there."

"Why did you give the name of Oscar Neely?"

"I found a business card with his name on the floor of the passenger side. I assumed even if he didn't own it, he'd know who did. I...uh...didn't tell them where I found the car...but I *did* go into town to see if there were any lost cars advertised—you know, like posters stapled to telephone poles with the smiling grill of a

2013 Mercedes-Benz S-Class sedan and the words 'Our Beloved Muffy' underneath."

"And?"

"Nada." She sighed. "If I'd been able to stay, I could've claimed it if this Neely guy didn't show up. I could sure use a car. My brother got the family station wagon when he went to college and all I got was a lousy bus pass." She lapsed into a rancorous silence.

Amos stood. "Are you willing to show us where you found it?"

"Sure. Mind if I…uh…freshen up a bit first?"

Simon, hearkening back to his days as a student, recognized the desire to take advantage of any opportunity to use free facilities.

They waited in the street for the girl, and a caravan of two squad cars and a park truck drove out of town. Stephanie leaned out the window of the first car. Amos drove rather erratically, and Simon guessed she was having some trouble remembering her way. Finally, she pointed to the left where a fire road led off into the woods. Everyone deplaned and walked down the path a few hundred yards until they fetched up in front of a length of yellow police tape strung between two trees.

Stephanie fingered it. "Why did you need me if you already knew where the car was?"

"We didn't. The tape is for something else."

She pointed to the side of the road. "That's where it was stuck." She pulled up a mat of dead branches. "I used these for traction. See, you can still see some tire tracks."

Amos let out a deep sigh. "You've been most helpful, Miss Edwards."

She gave him a puzzled look. "So, why the police

tape?"

"It's to mark the spot where we found the body of Oscar Neely."

Chapter Twenty-One
Tall Tales

Fire road, Amelia Island, Wednesday May 30

Stephanie backed away. "I didn't do it. There wasn't anybody here. I swear!"

"He was found about ten yards away." Amos gestured. "Over there. CSI thinks he was dragged to that log and jammed under it after he was killed. You didn't see anything? Blood in the car? Broken branches?"

She shook her head. "No. The car was clean. I remember, it had white leather seats." She took a moment to sigh dreamily. "A really nice ride."

Simon pointed at the rutted road. "We'd had a lot of rain. If whoever stashed the body came back to the car, he would have left mud on the floor."

Ellie added, "As to blood, Neely was strangled, wasn't he? So there wouldn't have been any."

"Unless he struggled with the murderer." Hosea turned to Stephanie. "No signs of that?"

"I didn't see anything except the card on the floor."

Simon scratched his head. "That points to him knowing his attacker."

"Who could have been the girlfriend. She can't be ruled out now."

Amos patted Tommy on the shoulder. "Go see if

you can find this elusive girlfriend. Miss Edwards, are you staying in town?"

"I wasn't planning to. I'd stopped for coffee at a McDonald's near the highway when I saw the notice in the local paper about the car. I…uh…I'm…"

Amos gave her an appraising glance which gradually softened. He finally said, "Why don't you stay with my wife and me? I'll give her a call. You can get a hot shower and a solid meal. Maybe call your folks."

The young woman's shoulders sagged. "Golly, that would be swell. My parents are in Asheville. My cell phone's dead, and I haven't talked to Mom in two days. She worries."

Simon took Amos aside. "Are you sure you want her in your house? She's still a suspect."

"We'll keep an eye on her. Sylvia has a great nose for people. She'll be able to tell if she's hiding anything."

Sylvia certainly knows how to keep secrets. "Well, she's hardly going to murder the police chief in his own home."

Amos recoiled, then chuckled. "Yup."

****

Police station, Friday, June 1

It took two days for Tommy to interview all the restaurant staff and Neely's roommates. "No girlfriend, Captain. Cecil—he's the chef, said he would have known if Oscar had one. Especially if she was stacked." He turned a page. "Coupla the waitresses were sure Ms. de Angeles had a sweet spot for him, though."

"Reciprocated?"

He wrinkled his nose. "You kidding?"

Amos huffed. "No call for snide remarks, Sarge." He turned to Simon. "Any chance he could have killed himself?"

"Accidental asphyxiation? Unlikely. And don't forget someone dragged him under that log."

"Then why didn't they take the car?" Ellie's question drew no response.

Simon shrugged, frustrated. "What are you going to do with it, Amos?"

"The car? I guess we'd better tow it to the police impound lot. I want the crime lab to go over it one more time. Not much else we can do."

They were in the parking lot when Simon muttered, "So that leaves us with Stephanie." He started the car and suddenly braked. "Oh, God."

"What?"

"Something Lisabet suggested…that the girlfriend stole the car…" He turned to Ellie, his eyes troubled. "Stephanie sure loves that Mercedes."

Ellie rubbed her forehead. "That child? I don't see it."

"She did harp on needing a car."

"Yes, but she also turned the car in and answered our flyer."

"Still, we'd better make sure she stays in town."

When Simon returned to the park, Hosea was hanging up the phone. "That was Judy Holiday, Eight Flags Event Planning. She wants to schedule an event for Saturday night. I'm assigning you and Ellie to work with her."

"Isn't it Thad's turn?"

"He…uh…he'll be out of town. Family business."

"He's going to Washington to see a lawyer."

362

"How did you know?"

"Never mind. Does Judy want us to go to her office?"

"No, she's coming here. With her clients." He checked his watch. "They'll meet you at the fort entrance at two thirty."

"Okay, I'll grab some lunch then."

When he returned to the fort, there were three cars already parked. He saw Ellie's official pickup, a Mini Cooper, and a battered Alfa Romeo. Standing in a tight circle in front of the drawbridge were Kenny, Martí, and the middle-aged woman he recognized as the event planner. Ellie got out of the truck and joined him. Together they approached the group. Simon singled Kenny out. "Don't tell me you want to have another event here?"

"Why not? We're entitled to use it same as anyone else."

Judy shrugged. "Business is business."

Martí leveled a gaze rife with antipathy at Simon. "And it's none of *your* business."

Kenny swaggered in place. "Yeah. That's right. What do you care?"

"Number one, I thought the last one was a washout, and number two, I know all about the invasion plans. When were you going to explain to Nathan, Lester, and Randall what you really intend to do?"

Martí recovered first. "What are you talking about?"

"Didn't MacGregor tell you? We know all about the real purpose of your *club.*"

Kenny raised a fist in Simon's face. "It's a lie! Who told you?"

"It's not important. But you might want to ask MacGregor what happened to the money he was supposed to buy the guns with."

Dead silence greeted this remark. Judy, who had been withdrawing inch by casual inch from the group, made a break for it, jumped in her Mini Cooper, and roared off.

Simon continued, a slight smile on his lips. "Attempting to overthrow foreign governments is frowned upon by the authorities, you know. The Navy will certainly object, not to mention the Coast Guard. They feel—and I believe the Constitution bears them out—that such enterprises are their bailiwick. But of course, like your ancestors, I guess you prefer to take matters into your own hands." He turned to Martí. "Your ancestors as well."

They all began to talk at once. A voice behind Simon rose above the hubbub. "So the clever park ranger has found us out."

MacGregor stepped around Simon. Kenny and Martí glowered at him. Martí growled, his teeth clenched, "Where are the guns, MacGregor?"

It occurred to Simon that this was a rather ill-advised thing to say, since it constituted an admission of guilt. He didn't reckon with MacGregor's resourcefulness, however. The man's confident tone grated like knuckles on concrete. "The *replicas* are in locker D-35 at the Compass Self Storage on Bailey Road." He gave Martí a piercing look, then pivoted to Simon. "I couldn't explain the other day because I didn't have permission from the others to divulge our little contribution to the festivities on Eight Flags Day. The guns are nonworking copies of the muskets used by

364

the Patriots and Gregor MacGregor's men in the early nineteenth century. We have been planning a reenactment of the battle of 1812." He kept the smug smile under wraps with difficulty. "It was supposed to be a surprise."

Kenny nodded vigorously, sweat dripping down his temples in great globules. Martí glanced sharply at MacGregor but merely said, "Our secret is out."

MacGregor resumed before Simon could speak. "The boats were to be decked out just like the nine American gunboats that forced the Spanish to capitulate on March 16, 1812. Unfortunately"—he turned to his colleagues—"they have been confiscated by the police. Apparently, some drug smugglers thought they'd make a convenient spot to stow their merchandise."

Dumbfounded—that's the word I'm looking for. I haven't seen people quite so nonplussed since Georgia replaced Principal Royce's morning announcements script with a word jumble.

Ellie searched the faces of the three men. After a minute, she said simply, "I am sorry you cannot tell the truth." She went back to the truck.

Simon followed her. "Not that I disagree, but what makes *you* think they're lying?"

"Did you see the shock in their eyes when MacGregor told those whoppers? And what about Sylvia? Why would she confess to the invasion plans if this were simply an historic reenactment?"

"What should we do?"

She opened the car door. "Let's try to catch Sylvia out—repeat MacGregor's new story and gauge her reaction."

"I know that. I meant, what about the event?"

"Let them hold it."

He stopped short. "Why?"

"So we can eavesdrop, silly."

"Isn't that illegal?"

She shot him a look that all but shrieked, "Try to keep up," reminding him unpleasantly of Georgia. "Not if it's on our property. I'll see about Sylvia. You get over to the hardware store or wherever one goes to buy bugs."

"A bait shop?"

"Ha ha. You know what I mean."

Simon did but had no clue where one obtained listening devices. "I'll ask Amos."

Ellie looked him up and down. "I'd better go with you. Wait for me at the police station."

"Yes, ma'am."

****

Lime Street, Friday, June 1

Ellie found Simon standing on the sidewalk. "Amos is out of the office all day today."

"Really? Sylvia's unavailable as well." Her brow furrowed. "I wonder where they are?"

Debbie Daugherty saw them and pulled to the curb. She rolled her window down. "Who are you looking for?"

"Sylvia and Amos."

"They went sailing for the day. Trying to smooth things over. Bit of tension after Iggy blabbed about her smoking."

"Not to mention the revelations over the nefarious invasion plot."

"There's that too."

"So, Debbie…" Simon felt funny asking the

question. "Mother's been so busy, I haven't had a chance to talk to her about the apartment. Did she like it?"

"She adores it. Justin said she could move in in a couple of weeks. All he has to do is paint the living room." She gave him a sly look. "I don't think it's Madeleine who's been busy though."

"You probably already know about the hitchhiker and the car." He stopped. "Oh, you mean..." He decided checking the sidewalk for cracks was the safest thing to do.

Debbie gave him a minute to stew, then turned to Ellie. "Have you heard from Thad about the meeting with the lawyer?" She laughed at Ellie's shocked expression. "The ladies believe Lester's too decent a fellow to be a part of any money-laundering scheme, and not just because his Phyllis is one of us."

"Do you think he may have been used as a straw man?"

"Likely. I'd look to the three amigos for answers. The fact that the donors were Cubans should ring alarm bells. Too neat."

"Did you know they now claim it's to be a reenactment for Eight Flags Day and not an invasion at all?"

She raised her eyebrows. "Well, Sylvia will be surprised to hear that. This MacGregor fellow is a piece of work." She peered at Simon. "What are you going to do about their little gala Saturday?"

"We'll let them have it."

"Who's going to spy on it?"

"Spy?" Simon doubted his innocent act would fly.

He was right. Debbie looked him up and down. "If

you're not up to it, I'll get the oversight committee on it. Just say the word."

Ellie took a deep breath. "Thanks, Mrs. Daugherty, but—"

"Call me Debbie."

"Oh…er…Debbie. We should have it covered."

"Try Baby and Me. It's down Eighth. They have monitors."

Why am I not surprised she knows where to go? Simon decided to change the subject. "How is Santa doing with Georgia gone?"

Her eyes went dreamy. "We…I mean he…is doing just fine. Not that I don't adore Georgia," she added hastily. "It's just that…"

Ellie smiled. "It's nice to have some alone time with your fella. I know."

The two women exchanged looks. Simon desperately hoped they weren't thinking what he knew they were thinking. After a minute, Debbie shook herself. "Gotta run. I said I'd return this library book for Felix."

Ellie said, "I'd better go with Simon—he won't know what to look for."

They parted ways. Ellie, after helping Simon pick out three baby monitors—"they'll work just fine"—took him home and demonstrated to him just how delightful playing hooky on an afternoon can be.

****

Fort Clinch, Saturday, June 2

"Okay, I've ordered four banquet tables and thirty chairs, plus chafing dishes and a cooler. Sonny's will deliver the barbecue, slaw, and fixings at five. The wine and beer should arrive by five-thirty. Setup will be complete by six." Judy was clearly determined not to ask any questions about the dustup of the day before.

What did she say? Business is business. "How many servers?"

"None. Nora says the guests will help themselves. Cleanup crew will come tomorrow morning."

Simon wrote it down. "And what do you need from the park?"

She consulted her clipboard. "Lighting—those tiki torches are nice. Porta Potties. Let's see…"

"So you're expecting maybe twenty-five this time?"

"That's what Nora told me. And this time, I got the money up front." Judy nodded in satisfaction.

"I'll get maintenance to deliver the Porta Potties by noon." Simon saw Ellie coming down from the battlements and went to meet her. Making sure Judy had left, he whispered, "Done?"

She nodded. "Monitors set in the cannon to the left, in the room under the walls, and at the entrance."

"How far away can we be and still hear?"

"It says up to eight hundred feet if unobstructed. Not far enough to reach the visitor center."

"Let's test it." He took the other half of the monitor while Ellie went back up to the ramparts. About fifty yards out, he lost the signal. "Damn."

She joined him in the parking lot. "I guess there's too much in the way. We'll have to park nearby." She pointed at a small grove of hemlocks. "That looks good. It'll be dark, and anyway, a ranger truck isn't going to draw any attention."

"Okay. Meet back here at seven?"

"Roger. What are you going to do now?"

"Amos says Maurice is finished with Lisabet's car. I asked to be there for the report."

"Let me know if they find anything interesting."

As Simon entered the impound lot behind Amos and Bobby, the CSI agent slammed the hood on the Mercedes. "We're done here."

"Okay, Mo, let's have it. Anything we can use?"

Maurice held up a checklist. "Interior. We found a couple of the victim's prints on the steering wheel."

"Why just a couple?"

"Most of the wheel was smudged, indicating a second person—possibly wearing gloves—touched it."

"You think the smudging was purposeful?"

He shook his head. "If it were, the second person would have erased all the prints."

Simon muttered, "It could have been Stephanie. She had gloves on when she came in to the station."

Amos nodded. "How about on the keys?"

"Nothing."

"Anything else? Blood? Shreds of cloth, perhaps a long, thin string that could be used to strangle a man?"

Maurice chuckled. "No blood. No garrottes. We did find a black hair or thread on the shotgun side. Sent it to the lab."

"*Hmm.*" Amos turned to Bobby. "What color hair did Neely have?"

"Purple."

"Purple?"

"Cut in a mohawk. Had a ring through his nose, too."

They contemplated this image for a minute without enjoyment. Amos blew out his cheeks. "So it's not his hair. If the black hair doesn't belong to Stephanie, we may have a lead."

"Not much of one. After all, the car belonged to Lisabet, and she has black hair too. Could be hers."

Simon said, "Lisabet was sure Neely had a blonde chickie on the side. You didn't find any blonde hair?"

"Nope."

"All right. Next?"

"Exterior. Dent in front bumper that fits the notch in the tree. Alice dug some chips of white paint from the bark that match the car. One flat tire. Culprit probably a stone embedded in the treads."

"From the fire road?"

"Not sure. It created a slow leak, so it took a while for the tire to deflate entirely. Whoever drove it to the service station may not even have noticed it. Also, left rear taillight broken. Likely happened before the accident."

"Why do you say that?"

"Light bulb dead and fixture dusty."

Simon and Amos looked at each other. "Harvey."

Maurice raised his eyebrows. "Harvey?"

"Harvey Denton. Runs the bait shop at the Panther Point Marina. He thinks this was the car he saw on April 14, three weeks before Stephanie brought it in."

"April 14. The night of the murders."

Amos shook his head. "Doesn't get us much farther. We still don't know who was with the victim."

Simon checked his watch. "I have to get back to the fort. Is Sylvia going to this thing tonight?"

"Yes."

"Good. I want to see how she reacts to MacGregor's latest explanation."

Chapter Twenty-Two
Can You Hear Me Now?

Fort Clinch, Saturday, June 2

"All set, Judy?"

"Yes. I'll be heading back to the office, then home."

"Don't you have to stay for the event?"

"They asked me not to. It's not uncommon. The Masons always close their events." She seemed more than happy to go.

"All right."

Ellie drove up to the entrance. "Everything ready?"

"Yes. If I can get Sylvia alone, I'll ask her about Gregory's latest bit of misdirection. After that, we'll pretend to leave. The truck is already parked in the copse. I'll drive your car back to the station and hike back on the trail."

"Okay. I'll wait for you in the truck."

The first to arrive was his quarry. "We're in luck." Simon sauntered over to Sylvia as she locked her car. "Hi, there. Did you have a nice sail with Amos?"

She greeted him with a blooming smile. "Indeed, yes. We cleared the air and had a marvelous time."

"You're here for the Green Cross event then?"

"Yes."

Simon kicked at a pebble. "Strange. Just the other

day Carson MacGregor informed us that the league's mission is not in fact what everybody said it was."

She blinked. "Not a sister-city exchange?"

"Sylvia, you know that's not true." When she didn't respond, he said gently, "You think the plan is to attack Cuba."

Sylvia's hand went to her purse, but she quickly pulled it back. "I...I did admit it when Amos cornered me. He thinks it will be a bust, but I hope not. It's not like we're talking D-Day. I only want to put a little scare into Castro, so he'll free my cousin."

"The dissident?"

"Yes, Yesenia's been under house arrest for a year. He won't let her out of the country. I...I have to do something. I mean—after all." She gave Simon a pleading look.

He patted her shoulder. "Of course, but armed invasion seems a little extreme." He paused. "Actually, MacGregor told a different tale."

"Oh?"

"He says you're working on a reenactment of the Battle of Amelia Island. Kenny and Mr. Martí agreed."

"A reenactment?" Her eyes grew wide, then slanted off. "Oh...um...darn. I guess our secret's...out." She glanced at him. "It's for Eight Flags Day." She spoke casually, but Simon detected a quiver in her voice. "Carson came up with the invasion story. I mean, really, Simon, you didn't think I was serious? Who in their right mind would believe a motley crew like us could defeat Cuba?"

"I see." He let her go and went back to the car and Ellie. "Sylvia is a really bad liar. I hope she's not captured by Castro's minions—she'd squeal if they look at her sideways. I'll be back in five." He left. In the rearview mirror, he saw Ellie amble over to the hemlocks, then disappear. When he returned, he slid behind the wheel.

"There you are. Did you stop to view the wildlife?"

"On the contrary, I sprinted back." He made a show of gasping for air. "Did I miss anything?"

"Nope." Ellie turned on the monitors. "We're all set."

A minute later, Kenny arrived along with Iggy and Virgil. Iggy parked the truck on the far side of the gravel lot. Lisabet pulled in next to them in a royal blue Maserati. As she was locking her car, Martí drove up in his beat-up Alfa Romeo. They converged on the fort entrance at the same time. Kenny approached Lisabet. The monitor crackled to life. "Hey, Lizzie, I saw a red Bentley that's just your style. Calvin Toomey is selling it on eBay."

"I don't buy my cars on eBay, Kenny."

"Well, gotta keep your collection at capacity. I hear a space has opened up in your garage."

"Where did you hear that?"

"Barnes told me your Mercedes is at the impound lot. Did that hippie manager of yours steal it? I told you not to hire him. Sneaky devil. But no…you've always been partial to purple-haired punks."

"I don't want to talk about it."

"They say he did a number on it. Smashed front bumper, flat tire. I didn't do the autopsy, but Neely must have been pretty banged up himself."

"Not really. After all, he managed to get out of the car."

At that moment, two cars, a Toyota Prius and a

white sedan, drove up. MacGregor got out of the Lexus, and Nathan Hearst and Randall Crowley emerged from the Prius. Ellie and Simon ducked. When the men reached the gate, MacGregor asked, "Where's Farnsworth?"

The publisher answered. "He won't be joining us. A little trouble with the law."

They heard the mayor say, "Damn. I hope he doesn't have to drop out. We need him."

MacGregor sounded worried. "The police don't think it has anything to do with our activities, do they, Hearst?"

"Not as far as I know. It's something about illegal campaign contributions."

"Who from?"

"That's the tricky part. I hear it was money funneled from Cuba."

Crowley groaned. "We can't afford a scandal now. Not when we're so close to announcing the project."

"Not to worry. Lester's got himself a smart lawyer, expert in this kind of law. They met in Washington this morning. He'll be fine."

MacGregor's voice was low. "As long as he doesn't blab about us."

"Why?" Crowley seemed puzzled. "I should think trying to improve relations with Cuba would work in his favor."

There was a short pause. Then Nathan said, "They might try to link the contributions to the sister-cities deal. Make it look like a bribe."

"Damn."

The voices faded.

Simon pulled a beer from a small cooler in the

back seat. Ellie eyed it with disapproval. "Should you be imbibing during a stakeout?"

"This? This is to maintain my electrolyte balance while we wait. You wouldn't want me light-headed?"

"Not right now, anyway." She watched him drink. "Hand me one of those, would you?"

After a bit, the monitor in the small room began to gurgle, replaced by a tapping sound. MacGregor's voice came through clearly. "Welcome, charter members of the League of the Green Cross. I understand Nathan and Randall can only stay a few minutes, so I'll make my report, then we can break for cocktails before the guests arrive."

"Who's coming, Carson?"

There was a pause. "Potential donors. Investors in my other enterprises. I'll do a little presentation for them."

Crowley's deep voice rose petulantly. "You'll tell us the results, won't you? We'd like to see some real movement on this."

"Of course. Let's move on, shall we? First, Julian has feelers out to the appropriate authorities in Havana. They seem receptive to the sister-city idea."

Nathan interrupted. "Who did you contact?"

A heavily accented voice said, "They have asked that their names remain confidential for now. They'll have to broach the idea to the regime. They want a full proposal before they do that."

"And what is the status of the proposal?" The mayor's pompous tones made the monitor rattle. Simon put a hand over it.

"We are working on it. I should have a draft ready in a week. I'll circulate it to the committee then."

Nathan grumbled, "It seems to be taking an inordinately long time. We're into summer already. We need to have something to advertise."

"Yes," said the mayor. "If we don't get onto the travel websites and provide materials to the travel agencies, we'll miss out on the whole tourist season. Who's doing the brochures?"

MacGregor said, "Nora's working on them. Now, I believe you both had to be at the Airport Advisory Commission meeting by seven thirty?"

Ellie and Simon heard shuffling. "They must be out in the courtyard." Soon two figures emerged from the entrance. Hearst and Crowley walked down to their car and left.

A minute later, two more figures hove into view. Iggy's annoyed mutter came through the monitor. "How come he tossed us out *again*? Kenny told us we were equal partners in the League. This pisses me off."

Virgil grunted. "What do you care, Iggy? Kenny's paying top dollar—tax-free—for our cooperation. Me, I don't need to know what I don't need to know." The two men headed toward their truck. They got in but didn't turn the engine on.

Ellie whispered, "Looks like they're waiting for Kenny. Do you think they can see us?"

Simon opened his mouth, but inside the fort MacGregor tapped again. "Okay, now we can get down to business. The police have released the two boats I acquired."

Kenny spoke up. "Did they catch the smugglers?"

"Not that I know of."

A woman's voice interrupted. "You had nothing to do with that, did you, MacGregor? We don't need the police breathing down our necks right now."

Ellie wrote on a notepad. *Lisabet?*

Simon nodded.

MacGregor snapped, "Of course not. I'm not a fool. I heard they found cocaine in another trawler near here as well. Something about Jamaican pirates. Probably thought our boats were unattended and stowed the 'merchandise' in them."

So there's one crime they haven't committed. But what about murder?

"I have the other seven boats on order. They should be delivered in a couple of weeks."

"How much did they cost?"

"Since they were used, I managed to negotiate the price down to two hundred seventy-five thousand dollars."

"Whew! Where did the money come from?"

"Lisabet?"

Her voice came softly. "I found an anonymous donor."

"It's clean money, right, Lisabet?" Kenny sounded dubious.

"Of course," she answered silkily. "I'm not as naïve as…some on our committee."

"Don't antagonize them, Lisabet. We still need them for now."

Martí asked, "Where will you hide the boats?"

Someone—*MacGregor?*—guffawed. "In plain sight. After all, they have to be positioned for the reenactment of the battle of Amelia Island. What did you think of my latest cover story for our activities? It just came to me out of the blue."

Martí's low voice rumbled. "And caught us totally

off guard. Very dangerous."

"No harm done. That idiot of a park ranger bought it. Didn't bat an eye."

Ellie mouthed, "He means you, sweetie," at Simon.

Sylvia's high voice cut in. "Where are the other people? The courtyard is only set up for twenty-five. You promised eighty to a hundred recruits."

Kenny said, "And what about the guns?"

MacGregor answered, "First things first. The recruits are Julian's department. Julian?"

Martí said, a hint of defensiveness in his voice, "I have made my pitch to the Cuban Independence Party. I expect to hear from them any day."

"That's it? We can't make this work without fighters."

"I am hampered by the need to maintain secrecy. Besides working with anti-Castro groups, I am taking advantage of my broadcasts to incite supporters. Based on response, I can follow up with those who indicate interest."

Lisabet said, "Kenny, how many locals have you drafted? Are they coming tonight?"

"My guys have been working hard, but no one's actually committed yet."

Sylvia whined, "Why are we spending money on catering if no one's coming? It's not like we have money to burn."

"Optics, Sylvia. Optics. The medium is the message."

"What's that supposed to mean?"

"I mean, if we build it, they will come." MacGregor's attempt at levity failed even by Simon's standards. "What I mean is, we project an image of a successful endeavor, and people will want to hop on board."

Lisabet groused, "Iggy and Virgil can only do so much without knowing our true purpose. When are you going to tell them, Kenny?"

"I have the same problem Julian has—I can't just march up to my boys and ask them to find men to invade Cuba. You gotta work up to it."

MacGregor interrupted. "Wait a minute. My reenactment gambit may come in handy here. Talk it up to potential volunteers—how they'll get to shoot off guns and dress up in uniforms. You know, war games."

Kenny spoke enthusiastically. "Great idea. Iggy and Virgil can hit the biker bars. And maybe that militia group that meets down by the VFW."

Sylvia added, "Isn't there a club over in Callahan that puts on Civil War reenactments?"

"Uh huh. I'll tell Virgil to scope them out."

MacGregor took the floor again. "All right. We move on to the guns. I spent our whole war chest on the boats, so we'll need more money. Sylvia, where do you two stand on fundraising?"

"Lisabet has been engaging donors before we hold any events."

The restaurateur said, "We have had a slight setback." Her voice seemed very close to the monitor.

The two rangers jumped back. Simon whispered, "You don't think…"

Ellie shook her head and put a hand to her ear. "*Shh.*"

"I had expected a…uh…bundler to deliver several contributions in the last few weeks, but the transactions ran into a slight glitch. My bundler is no longer available."

"Do you have a backup plan?"

Sylvia spoke eagerly. "We're planning a lovely dinner at El Toro for a thousand dollars a plate."

"Will you use the sister-cities project or the reenactment as a draw?"

"No one knows about the reenactment story yet. I think where backers are concerned, we should carry on with the sister-cities approach. I know Lester and Randall are wedded to it."

Martí said, "That won't bring in the money we need. We will require at least a hundred thousand to mount a proper attack."

Lisabet's voice rose a decibel. "I can't help it, Julian. I've had to deal with several issues lately. I do have ten restaurants to juggle you know."

"Oh, for heaven's sake, the taco stands practically run themselves."

"You'd be surprised how closely I have to watch them."

Simon shot bolt upright and knocked his head on the roof of the car. Ellie whispered, "What is it?"

He muttered, "Nothing. Just…um…hungry." He didn't tell her the real reason for his reaction. *I have to think this through first.*

Ellie put a hand on his arm to quiet him. Lisabet was complaining. "Plus I have to find another bundler. You must give me time."

Sylvia chirped, "We can have a bingo night too. I'm sure Debbie Daugherty and her friends will lend a hand."

Even Ellie and Simon could feel the amusement, barely suppressed, that greeted this suggestion. Finally,

MacGregor said, "How about if we take a break and get something to eat?"

Chairs scraped the brick floor and voices faded. Ellie whispered, "I need a break too. I'll be back in a minute."

"Be careful. You don't want anyone to see you."

"I will."

Simon hunkered down in his seat. He'd begun to think everyone had gone beyond the monitor's range when MacGregor's voice bit into the silence. "Martí, you've got to get some troops together soon. This is becoming embarrassing."

"Why embarrassing? No one besides the five of us knows of the plan. We are under no deadline."

"Yes, but that event planner is beginning to suspect we're not exactly aboveboard. Besides, Sylvia's right. We can't afford to keep paying her for nonexistent events."

"Talk to Lisabet. Maybe we can use the restaurant." Their voices faded.

Suddenly, the third monitor blared. Lisabet's voice floated to Simon, faint in the breeze. "Light?"

Sylvia said, "Thanks."

Puffing. They must be sneaking a cigarette on the walls.

Lisabet spoke. "Did Amos give you much trouble about the smoking?"

"Only as much as he thought he had to, but it wasn't fun. You're lucky you don't have to answer to anyone about your cigar habit."

"I should quit."

"No, no. In fact, it adds to your allure—you know, the sultry Latina."

Lisabet chuckled. "All right."

That's right, Lisabet smokes cigars, not cigarettes.

Sylvia was grumbling. "I never did find out who outed me. You were the only one who saw me."

"It wasn't me. When Simon asked if anyone left the fort, I had to tell the truth, but I said I thought you needed to pee."

Sylvia laughed. "And Simon, bless his heart, figured it out. You're a good friend, Lisabet. Say, I believe they found that dead woman on the shore really close to where we stood. How awful to think she might have been out there in the dark!"

Wait... Simon wracked his brain.

Ellie slid into the shotgun seat of the car. "Did I miss anything?"

Simon put a finger to his lips.

Lisabet said soothingly, "I'm sure she washed up much later, dear. Are you finished?"

"Uh huh."

"Shall we go back down?"

"Sure."

The monitor went silent. Ellie clicked it off. "They must be in the courtyard. We won't be able to hear what they're saying."

Simon keyed the ignition. "If they're eating, they'll be there a while. Anyway, I've heard enough."

"Really?"

"Yep. I now have all the threads. I know what happened. We'll gather the suspects tomorrow."

"Where to now?"

"Santa's. And call Debbie Daugherty, if she's not there already."

****

Santa's house, Saturday, June 2

They found not only Santa and Debbie, but Georgia, at the house. "What are you doing here?"

"I love you too." When Simon had made suitable amends, which included refreshing her drink and her plate, she continued sulkily. "I'm down for the weekend. Santa said he had some news, but"—she glared at Simon—"you interrupted him mid-sentence."

"He's free to continue."

All eyes turned to Georgia's father, who stroked his beard in a futile attempt to hide the deep violet blush. "I…uh…" He gazed imploringly at Debbie. She in turn smiled wordlessly at him. "I…uh…that is, Deb and I…uh…"

Georgia jumped up and hugged him. "Oh, Daddy! That is such wonderful news! I'm so happy for you? When did you decide?"

Clueless, Ellie glanced at Simon. He punched Santa in the shoulder. "You old dog, you. Have you set a date?"

"I…uh…"

Debbie took pity. "In a month—if he lives that long. This whole thing is giving him palpitations."

"Oh, but that's too soon! I can't arrange a bridal shower that quickly. And my exams are in five weeks." Georgia turned to her father. "How *could* you!"

Under the onslaught, the poor man crumpled. "I'm going outside for a smoke."

"Don't you dare! You know what the doctor said."

"All right. A breath of fresh air, then. Satisfied?" His shoulders vibrating with resentment, he stalked out.

Georgia clutched Debbie's hands, and they danced a jig. Simon filled a wineglass and handed it to Ellie.

She gulped it down. "Am I right in guessing Santa and Debbie are engaged?"

Georgia trilled, "Isn't it fabulous?" Suddenly she halted and lowered her perfect brows at Simon. "Well?"

"Well, what?" *If she gets on my case, I'll walk right out the door.* He glimpsed Santa on the porch puffing madly on his pipe. *The other door.*

Ellie poured more wine into her glass and spoke in a voice so low the two antagonists had to hold their breath to hear. "Congratulations, Debbie. This is wonderful news. But perhaps we should move on to the purpose of our visit."

Debbie took the hint. "Felix! Come inside. Simon has something he wants to tell us."

Santa rushed in, a look of vast relief on his face. "You too? Oh, thank God."

At this, everyone broke into gales of laughter. Everyone except Simon. He said grumpily, "No, Santa. We're here to discuss the denouement."

"Huh?"

"The conclusion of our mystery. I've solved the murders."

The response to this announcement was rather more subdued than Simon had hoped for. After a minute, Georgia muttered, "Well, it's not much, but it'll have to do."

Ellie had been tapping her fingers on her glass. "What do you mean by solving the murders? We know who killed whom."

"Not all of them." Simon paused. "And I'm still missing a link or two." He rubbed his chin. "Probably not important, but still…"

Debbie sat down on the couch. "What's next?"

Ever the practical one. "I want to gather all those involved and lay out my deductions. Time is of the essence."

Georgia looked as though she wanted to make a snide remark about clichés, but Ellie beat her to it. "The early bird catches the worm?"

"Um…"

"There's no time like the present?"

Simon began to tap his foot. "Are you all quite finished?"

Santa laughed. "For the nonce. When do you want to do this?"

He checked his watch. *Five o'clock.* "Tomorrow."

"But tomorrow's Sunday! How are we going to get all these folks together on a Sunday?"

"And on such short notice? Won't they suspect something?"

Simon scratched his chin. "Since it's Sunday, most of them will be off work. We'll meet at a central location. How about the mayor's office?"

"Closed."

"The police station?"

Santa said, "That's sure to freak everyone out. Besides, we don't want to give Amos a heads-up. He might spill the beans to Sylvia."

"El Toro's?"

"No." Debbie frowned in thought. "Wait—that might work. How about a birthday party or some kind of celebration?"

"Feasible. But what would include all our players?"

"The ex-president's coming through and is demanding the keys to the city?"

Santa snorted. "At least half of them won't see that as a reason to celebrate."

"Okay…" In the quiet, the mantel clock ticked loudly. Finally, Simon said, "How about this? I'll call MacGregor and warn him I'm going to tell the city council about their plans."

"Which plans? The sister cities? The invasion? The reenactment?"

"Does it really matter? The council hasn't been included in any of the scenarios. Their prerogatives have been trampled on. They'll be in high dudgeon whether or not they like the ideas."

Ellie pursed her lips. "But you won't actually do it, will you? That might just throw a political monkey wrench into our plans."

"Of course not. When MacGregor objects, I'll pretend to back down. Then I'll grudgingly offer to meet at El Toro's tomorrow at noon."

"He'll want to bring his posse."

Georgia clapped her hands. "Perfect! They'll all come, if only to defend themselves."

Simon pulled out his phone and walked outside. Five minutes later he returned. "Done. Mr. McGregor was still hyperventilating when I hung up."

Debbie rose. "Who wants coffee?"

Santa said, "Me, please. How about if I make a reservation at El Toro's for lunch tomorrow for…how many?"

"Let's see…" Simon counted on his fingers. "Sixteen? Tell Clarice it's a surprise birthday party."

"Anybody we know?"

"*Hmm.*"

Simon couldn't help it. With a side glance at Ellie,

he said, "Nicole?"

"I have an idea," interjected Georgia with a twinkle in her eye. "Instead of a birthday, let's make it an engagement party for Dad and Debbie. Kill two birds with one stone."

When both Debbie and Santa objected, Simon jumped in. "All right, all right. Santa—tell Clarice it's a birthday party." He picked up his hat. "Ellie, can you let Mother know I'll be a little late?"

"Where are you going?"

"To the movies." He kissed her cheek. "We'll regroup tomorrow at eleven."

Santa grinned. "Should I bring my shotgun?"

"Not necessary, my dear." Debbie surprised them all by pulling out a small pink pistol. "It's a .38 Special." When no one spoke, she said, "What? I have a concealed-carry permit."

"Buckle up your holsters."

As they walked out the door, Simon pulled Georgia aside.

"Hey! That's my new cashmere sweater you're grabbing, mister."

He made sure no one else was within earshot. "Hush. I have a different job for you."

Chapter Twenty-Three
Toro! Toro! Toro!

El Toro restaurant, Sunday, June 3

"Welcome, Simon, Miss Ironstone, Superintendent Barnes. We've put you in the banquet room."

"Thank you, Clarice. And may I say we're all so pleased to hear of your promotion to manager. Well deserved."

"Thank you, Mr. Barnes! It's very exciting. This way, please." Clarice led them through a door to a long table set for fourteen. "You're the first to arrive."

Simon looked over her shoulder. "We're expecting sixteen, Clarice."

"Miss Petrie called to say she was tied up."

"And Lisabet?"

"She sends her regrets, but Ms. de Angeles won't be able to join you for lunch. We're slammed. She hopes to drop in for a minute if she can get away."

Damn. I need all the players here to wrap this up. Simon wandered to the door.

Santa and Debbie were ushered in. "Mr. Petrie. Mrs. Daugherty. This way." They sat next to each other at the far end.

Santa raised his eyebrows at Simon. "Did they all accept?"

"The principals, yes. Georgia seems to be AWOL.

Lisabet's too busy."

Debbie asked cheerily, "Do you have your speech ready?"

Oh my God...a speech? Me? Panic-stricken, he took a step back. "I...uh..."

Inez came in. "Ms. de Angeles welcomes you to El Toro." She turned to Debbie and Santa. "She understands congratulations are in order." When the happy couple stared back at her blankly, she recovered with professional aplomb. "Would you like to order drinks now or wait for the other guests?"

Simon clutched her elbow, pulled her to face him, and barked, "Double bourbon. Rocks. Quick. Go."

"Simon!"

"She'll get yours in a minute." He realized he was panting. *Don't lose control. Don't. Deep breath. In. Out.* He looked wildly around for an exit and realized Ellie was goggling at him, her mouth open.

"What's the matter with Simon?"

Hosea patted her arm. "No way for you to know. He has terrible stage fright. Can't speak to more than three people at a time."

"But how did he get all those graduate degrees? Don't you have to give papers?"

Santa chuckled. "If you check his academic record, you'll discover a pattern—at no time did he take a course that required an oral presentation."

The waitress handed Simon a brimming tumbler, and he knocked back the whiskey. "Thanks, Inez. One more please."

Debbie added hastily, "I'd like a Pinot Grigio, and Mr. Petrie will have iced tea. Ellie?"

Ellie tore her eyes from Simon and muttered, "Jack

Daniels. Neat."

Hosea shook his head. "I'm on duty." He shot a baleful glance at his two underlings.

At that moment Sylvia, the mayor, the publisher, and the judge entered. Hearst caught sight of Simon. "What's going on? You said there was a hitch in our sister-cities proposal?"

Farnsworth surveyed the table. "I thought we'd be only six? This is about the town council, right? Why are you people here?"

"We have other business to discuss."

None of the four responded, but Simon noted that Farnsworth's lids dropped down over his eyes. *Could he be in on it after all? Or is he in fact guilty of the money laundering?* "Lester, how did the meeting with the lawyer go?"

The paunchy man's eyes bugged out. "How did you know about that?" He turned accusing eyes on Ellie.

She shrugged it off. "Of course I told him. We're conducting an investigation after all."

"Not into my affairs. In fact, I'm not sure why you keep pestering our group—shouldn't you be out solving all those murders?"

Simon was saved from answering the question by the entrance of Kenny, trailed by Virgil and Iggy. MacGregor shouldered his way past them. All eyes but Simon's focused on the leader of the group, so he was the only one who noticed Martí sidle in and sit down next to Ellie. MacGregor looked from Farnsworth to Simon. "You didn't start without me, did you?"

"No. We only just arrived."

Simon spread his arms out. "Nathan, Lester,

Randall. I'd like you to meet Carson MacGregor, direct descendent of Gregor MacGregor, master—temporarily—of Amelia Island."

Mayor Crowley gave MacGregor a sharp look. "What's this all about, Carson?"

Farnsworth looked from one to the other. "MacGregor? Who's he?"

"Carson Gregory is in fact Carson MacGregor."

The judge seemed completely at sea. "Wha…I…Randall?"

MacGregor was unruffled. "Yes. As Mr. Ribault knows full well, I use both names depending on which LLC I am dealing with."

"But—"

MacGregor gestured at Simon. "We're here because Mr. Ribault says he's uncovered something he wants to take to the town council."

The judge's eyes narrowed. "This wouldn't have anything to do with the FBI claiming I accepted Cuban money, would it?" He stepped toward MacGregor, looming over the shorter man like a pudgy version of Hulk Hogan. "Did you by any chance *suggest* it to them?"

MacGregor slammed his fist down on the table. "Don't threaten me, Farnsworth." When his accuser flinched, MacGregor made a visible effort to calm down. He laid a placating hand on Lester's arm. "Now, Les, why on earth would I want to interfere with your ability to support our project?"

Farnsworth hesitated. "It just seems awfully fortuitous—the Feds suddenly curious about my campaign contributions. They've found a tie to a Cuban dissident group that's been funneling money to my campaign without my knowledge. You wouldn't know anything about that, would you?"

"Of course not. Besides, like I said, it makes no sense—it would undermine our efforts." MacGregor's eyes flicked to Martí. "We must maintain good relations with the Cuban government if we're to succeed."

"Well...I guess. Well, okay, but..." As Farnsworth tried to extricate himself with his dignity intact, Simon glanced across the room to see Sylvia open the purse on her lap and rummage around in it. She placed the bag on the ground beside her and laid her hand in her lap, an inauthentic look of innocence plastered on her face. The tip of a cigarette peeped out between her fingers.

Must be to calm her nerves. Surely she wouldn't light up. Simon put his glass down. "Why don't the rest of you sit down?"

They obeyed, Farnsworth and MacGregor choosing seats as far apart as possible. Simon took a last gulp of his bourbon. "Many of you are wondering why we've been interested in your activities and not focusing on the murders. It seems a good time to recapitulate everything we've discovered in the last few weeks. Considering the facts, I believe you'll find we were justified in pursuing our inquiries."

Inez stuck her head in. "Are you ready to order?"

"No, we're f—"

"Yes, thank you." Debbie smiled at Inez.

A sigh of relief made the rounds of the table. Sylvia opened her menu. "Inez, dear, I'll have a dirty martini."

The waitress wrote it down. "And to eat?"

"Oh, the Caesar salad with shrimp. And a glass of

Chardonnay to accompany it." She handed back the menu.

The others ordered iced tea and appetizers. Simon refused food. "Don't forget my whiskey." When Inez had gone, he remained standing, but held on to the back of his chair to compensate for the slight buzzing in his ears. "Everybody happy now?" He scanned the table. "Then allow me to begin by summarizing the events of the night of April 14. The League of the Green Cross had scheduled a fairly large event at Fort Clinch, but at the last minute, the entertainment and food were canceled and only ten people attended, arriving about eight p.m. The meeting was still going on a couple of hours later, when a shrimp trawler filled with four hundred thousand dollars' worth of cocaine bricks sailed into Amelia River from the Atlantic. Between there and its ultimate mooring at Panther Point Marina, four people were murdered. One victim washed up just northeast of the fort, one under the walls, and one at the mouth of Egan's Creek—all on Park property. The fourth was found on his boat. Three were stabbed to death. One was strangled."

Someone kicked the table. It shook Simon a bit, but he steadied himself. "The body found at the most northerly point was that of a man named Winston Virtue, a Jamaican undercover cop. He had been tailing Odessa Bonney, the second body. The third victim turned out to be an escaped convict, a Miguel Alvaredo, who was either hired by Bonney or stowed away on the shrimper. The last was Diogenes Goodwine, captain of the boat."

Inez brought Sylvia her drink. Farnsworth looked at it and licked his lips, as though regretting his choice of beverage.

"The three men were stabbed with the same knife. After some deliberation, we believe we have the sequence of events."

MacGregor squirmed on his seat. "What does any of this have to do with the League of the Green Cross?"

Simon didn't acknowledge the interruption. "Bonney was a drug smuggler. Fancied herself a pirate. Virtue had signed on as crew, but she got wind of his real identity and murdered him, tossing him into the river. Alvaredo witnessed the crime and went after Bonney. He managed to wrestle the blade from her, but as he lunged toward her, her foot caught in a rope on the deck and she tumbled backward over the side."

Kenny leaned forward, engrossed in the narrative. "Wait. If she went overboard before Alvaredo did, how did the convict end up with her knife in his back?"

"I'm getting to that. As the boat approached the marina, Goodwine came up from the galley. He saw Alvaredo with the knife and realized what had happened. He must have gone for him, but Alvaredo stabbed him in the side. Goodwine grabbed the knife and, when Alvaredo's back was turned, killed him, leaving the knife in his back. He then chucked him into the water. Goodwine died maybe an hour later."

"That makes no sense." Nathan furrowed his brow. "The police report said the shrimper was found tied up at its dock. If everyone was dead, who secured the boat?"

"According to Kenny, Captain Goodwine's wound would not have been immediately incapacitating. He could have steered the boat home, then collapsed after tying it up."

Inez and a busboy came in bearing large trays. She handed Simon his glass. No one touched the food. *Waiting for my permission?* "Please, go ahead."

Everyone fell to, and conversation lagged. Simon sipped his second drink, allowing its liquid courage to steel him for the imminent engagement. As Farnsworth swallowed the last bite of his empanadas, Simon resumed. "Now let's turn to the League of the Green Cross."

Sylvia took a swig from her martini.

"The public pretext for the league is to establish a sister-city link with Havana. In light of the last administration's lifting of sanctions, our city fathers"— he nodded at the mayor, publisher, and judge—"and Lisabet de Angeles thought to take advantage of new economic opportunities, even though any profits from investment in Cuba would continue to be pocketed by the regime."

Kenny muttered, "Companies are all jumping on the bandwagon. They could care less that their investment goes straight to the military."

Crowley opened his mouth and closed it. "What are you talking about?"

MacGregor jumped in. "The Cuban people will not profit from the new commerce. Those chains so eager to build hotels in Havana? For tourists only. The only Cubans allowed inside them will be the ones who work there. The average Cuban citizen can't go to a foreign-owned restaurant in his own country."

The mayor looked at Nathan. "Did you know this?"

"Sure. But we're in it for *our* economic benefit, not theirs. Who cares if it doesn't actually open up the country?"

"I care." Sylvia's voice was cold. "My family in Cuba cares. They know firsthand the difference between communism and capitalism. Under the Castros, only their cronies get rich. The people have suffered for seventy years. All they want is what we take for granted—the freedom to improve their lot, to provide for their families, to travel. You crush their hopes and dreams with your cynicism and greed."

Nathan looked down at his plate. Simon took the opportunity to light the fuse on his bombshell. "Which is why three of you had an entirely different purpose in mind."

Ellie raised a finger. "But what about Syl—"

Simon cut her off. "I'll get to her in a minute."

Farnsworth checked, his glass halfway to his mouth. "What did you say? Three of us? Which three?"

MacGregor shifted in his seat. "Are you going to tell them about the reenactment?"

"No, I'm going to tell them about the invasion."

Everyone started talking at once. Simon's tenor rose above the rest. "If I may *elucidate*." When they'd settled down, he continued in a near-whisper, forcing his audience to lean forward. "These three"—he gestured at Mathews, MacGregor, and Martí—"have been conspiring to build an army of local people and Cuban exiles, in order to launch an assault on Cuba and liberate its people from the Castro regime."

"*What?*"

Crowley started to pound his chest, but thought better of it. "Martí? But he's just the translator. Isn't he?"

"He's a silent partner." Kenny did not seem happy about it.

Hosea raised a quizzical eyebrow. "Didn't you know, Randall?"

"Gregory never told us. He always referred to Martí as his assistant. We weren't supposed to mention Virgil and Iggy because then everyone would know Kenny was involved."

The judge, who had taken all this in with astonished eyes and an open mouth, turned to MacGregor. "I don't understand. Who's going to translate for us then?"

His question met with an embarrassed silence. Finally, Nathan snapped, "Lester? I don't think that really matters anymore."

"Oh."

Sylvia had been rapping a spoon on the table during this exchange. Suddenly, her hand hit the martini glass, knocking it over. Debbie tried to mop up the spill, but Sylvia pushed her away. She pointed a trembling finger at Martí. "You—"

Martí rose from his chair. "Madam, I suggest you watch your tongue."

Simon, about to lose control of the narrative, raised his voice. "Sylvia, on the other hand…" He waited till she had subsided and Marti resumed his seat. "Sylvia's goal was to free her cousin from house arrest in Cuba." He regarded the woman with compassion before pivoting. "MacGregor, Mathews, and Martí told you they were in it to revive the semi-glorious exploits of their forbears." Simon waited, his eyes on Iggy. *Will he crack?*

Crowley looked mystified. "But…but…how could we possibly find enough weapons? And soldiers? Our little force would be decimated by Cuba!"

"Nothing compared to facing an irate United States."

Nathan cocked his head. "They've got to have a better reason than that. Feats of glory that land you in a Cuban prison for life don't strike me as worth the cost."

Iggy, who had been muttering and grimacing, elbowed Virgil. "Um...Kenny told Virg and me we stood to make a lot of money."

Here we go.

Farnsworth's eyes widened. "Money? How could you possibly profit from a war?"

Santa gave him a disgusted look. "Are you completely out of your gourd or just a moron, Lester?"

Randall snorted. "Yeah, Les. What do you think the words 'war profiteer' and 'mercenary' mean, anyway?"

"They weren't going to make money from the war. Well, not exactly." Simon put his glass down. "Are any of you familiar with the movie *The Mouse That Roared*? Anyone?"

Silence. Debbie spoke up. "I think I saw it when I was a little girl. Didn't it star Peter Sellers?"

"Yes. I happened to notice that the Carmike was playing a retrospective of Peter Sellers movies. I took in the late showing of *The Mouse That Roared* last night. The premise was that this tiny duchy would invade the United States. Of course, they expected to be ruthlessly crushed, thereby earning both the sympathy of other nations and reparations from America. They figured their little plan would enrich them beyond their wildest dreams."

"Let me get this straight. You claim that these idiots want to invade Cuba and, when they're captured, demand ransom money?" The publisher erupted in laughter.

"That doesn't work, Nathan," said Lester. "The ransom would go to the Cuban government, not the prisoners."

"You're right, Lester." *For once.* "No—these fellows had even grander illusions than toppling the Castros. Their names in lights." When no one responded, he said patiently, "Hollywood."

Ellie gasped. "Thad was right?"

Simon nodded, grinning. "Thad learned that some movie people were sniffing around Fernandina, asking about our crazy history. Our trio figured a botched invasion of Cuba would be just the thing to reel them in…Isn't that right, MacGregor?"

Before anyone could answer, Sylvia launched herself at Martí. He fell backward in his chair, and she landed on him, slapping and punching him. Hosea and Ellie pulled her off. She sat on the floor, panting.

"What the hell are you doing, Sylvia?"

"He lied to me."

"What are you talking about?"

"He said if I helped him, he could get my cousin out of Cuba. He said he had a colleague who could sneak into Havana and whisk her out. He even arranged for transport." She threw Martí—who was brushing himself off with irritating composure—a look filled with contempt. "He took ten thousand dollars from me." She spat out, "Pig."

Martí stared at her, unmoved. "You are a fool, lady."

"Sylvia, could you explain?" Debbie was soothing.

She pulled herself onto a chair. Wiping away a

tear, she mumbled, "I gave him the money two months ago. I'd seen an article in the Miami paper that Raoul Castro was going to throw political detainees under house arrest into prison. The paper had gotten hold of a list of them. My cousin's name was on it. I was scared to death. Martí told me his agent would get her out of Cuba and to Miami, where another man was supposed to escort her up here."

Another man? Ah—the last loose end. "You told me your cousin's name was Yesenia. Is her last name by any chance Sanchez?"

"Yes. Yesenia Sanchez. Why?"

"Was the man paid to deliver her named Miguel Alvaredo?"

"No…Wait. You mean the escaped convict who was murdered?" Her mouth opened in shock.

Nathan asked Simon, "How did you know?"

"The news clipping they found in his pocket. The one word Maurice could make out was Sanchez." Simon turned to Martí. "You helped him escape."

He shook his head. "I merely hired him. I didn't ask questions." Hosea said something under his breath. "What did you say?"

"You're going to have a helluva time proving that."

Simon rubbed his forehead. "Whatever hand you had in Alvaredo's escape, you knew he was a criminal. You met him in Miami and sent him on to Bonney."

"I hired him in Miami, yes, but I had no knowledge of this pirate and her filthy drugs. I merely gave him Sylvia's money to find passage on a boat to Havana. That was the last I saw of him."

"Havana!" *Did I get this wrong? Could Martí have been acting on his own?* "Did you give him the

401

clipping?"

"No."

"Then how did he know about Sylvia and her cousin?"

Martí shrugged. "I told him to use the League of the Green Cross and the sister-cities project as a cover story. He must have seen the news article and thought he could parlay it into more money."

"So, if it had nothing to do with Yesenia Sanchez, what exactly *did* you hire him for?"

His tone was scornful. "Certainly not to save some sniveling female dissident who only would have interfered with our activities. No, Alvaredo had ties to the underground—"

"You mean, gangs."

"Whatever. He was supposed to organize a resistance from the inside, to prepare the way for our arrival." He curled his lip. "I should have known not to trust a Honduran. He must have pocketed the money and headed north instead."

"You paid a convicted killer to sneak into Cuba and establish a fifth column there?" Nathan seemed slightly in awe. "Then I suppose you were going to sail in on your pleasure yacht, handily defeat the vaunted Cuban armed forces, and raise the Green Cross over the battlements?"

Crowley's jaw dropped. "Are you all completely mad?"

Even Lester seemed to find this a trifle peculiar. Ellie stifled a giggle.

MacGregor broke his silence. "Julian, are you saying you meant to go *through* with it?"

Kenny wiped a dripping forehead. "This is all your

fault, Carson."

"Me? I—"

"Maybe that explains it." Sylvia did not seem as shocked as the rest.

"Explains what?"

"Why Alvaredo never showed. He did get in touch with me, only he called himself Eduardo. He wanted more money—said he'd spent it all getting my cousin out of Cuba. I agreed, and we arranged for him to bring Yesenia ashore in a dinghy that night. I signaled them with the cigarette."

"So, you didn't leave the fort just for a smoke."

"No." A slight smile crossed her features.

"And you waited outside the fort."

"For as long as I could. Then when Lisabet came out, I had to leave."

Debbie spoke deliberately. "Why didn't you tell anyone?"

"What could I do? The whole plan had to stay secret—even from Amos. Otherwise, who knows what the regime would do to my family? Martí kept putting me off. I haven't been able to get in touch with Yesenia since I gave him the money." Her shoulders sagged. "It was all just a swindle."

"I don't understand." Lester seemed to have lost the thread again. "Did this convict fellow ever rescue your cousin?"

No one seemed inclined to enlighten him. Santa rubbed his forehead. "So, you *weren't* party to the invasion plot, Sylvia?"

"Of course not. When Lisabet first told me about the sister-cities idea, I realized it might work as a cover for my real goal. The night of the event, I overheard

Kenny and Carson talking about an invasion. I thought it was a joke, but when Amos started getting suspicious about my own activities I panicked and blurted it out." She pointed at Kenny. "War on Cuba is the sort of thing only a Mathews would do. The family has always been a little unbalanced. Inbreeding, I guess."

Kenny opened his mouth but, after glancing at MacGregor, shut it again.

Simon reclaimed the floor. "So we know what Kenny and MacGregor expected to get out of it."

"Starring roles?" Hosea couldn't help himself.

"Juicy contracts? A walk on the red carpet?" Ellie laughed.

"I admit I thought Martí was in on it, too, but now…" Simon frowned. "Was it that you wanted to go down in a blaze of glory like your ancestor, the hero José Martí?" Martí said nothing. Simon thought back to Martí's diatribes on the radio and in print. *That's it, isn't it?*

Debbie spoke into the silence. "You've explained the motives of eight of the conspirators. What about Lisabet?"

"Lisabet—"

MacGregor burst out, "De Angeles! No. She—"

A voice came from behind him. "I was happy to go along with their schemes to get what I wanted." Lisabet stood in the doorway.

Simon started to say something when he noticed an object in her hand. *Why, that's a Glock. And it's pointed at my stomach.* Said organ quickly rolled up like a hedgehog and tried to scrabble away.

She waved him to sit down. Her glance swiveled to Debbie, but her pistol continued to point at Simon.

"Drop your little toy gun on the floor, if you please, Mrs. Daugherty." When Debbie complied, she went on. "My plan would have worked if only the Jamaicans hadn't got wind of that buffoon Bonney and her *extracurricular* activities."

Hosea grunted. "Extracurricular. You mean, making a few extra drug runs and pocketing the cash without telling you?"

She nodded. While the rest kept their eyes glued on the gun, she faced Simon. "You thought we were all amateurs, didn't you? Children playing at the game of war, but it is you who are the babes in arms."

"Actually, no. I knew the truth." He hoped that sounded diffident enough. It worked.

Curious, she asked, "What do you mean?"

"I knew you were deadly serious about the invasion, even if the others had different motives. It was you who called the shots, not MacGregor."

The latter bowed his head. Mathews and Martí glared at him.

"You started by funneling money from Cuban dissidents through Lester's campaign."

The judge gasped. "You were my biggest donor, Lisabet. Why?"

Simon didn't let her speak. "But that didn't rake in enough. You needed funds for soldiers, guns, and boats. You were looking at maybe half a million dollars. So you turned to drug smuggling. You laundered the money through your chain of taco shops."

She didn't bother to demur. "It was so easy. A quick trip to Montego Bay and I had smugglers by the truckload. I chose Odessa Bonney because I liked the idea of a woman pirate." Her eyes flashed. "How was I

405

to know she was just as greedy and selfish as a man? Wanted a bigger slice of the profits. Tried to bully me." Her lips set in an angry line. "I told her this was the last run. I was going to find a new mule."

Simon took a gulp of whiskey. "Yes. So back to Saturday, April 14. As the meeting wound down that night you went out for a smoke, just like you did yesterday." He held up a cigar stub. "Alice—our criminologist—found this by Bonney's body. Your brand, isn't it? You saw Sylvia sneaking a cigarette and stopped to chat. When she left, you began to stroll along the shore."

Hosea interrupted. "How do you know she stayed behind? Iggy told us they all left together."

"He was wrong...or rather, his testimony was incomplete. What Iggy actually said was"—he checked his notes—" 'Mrs. Barnes came down the path and got into her car and drove off. Then Kenny came out and told us to go on home.' He said the 'others' were coming to the parking lot as they left. He didn't mention Lisabet by name." He turned to Sylvia. "It was you who gave me the clue."

"Me!"

"Yes. You two were on the battlements smoking last night. You talked about Bonney's body washing up on shore."

Sylvia's eyebrows went up. "And that Lisabet and I were together that night as well. But wait—how did you know about last night?"

"Um...er..."

Hosea jumped in. "We always record events at the fort. Standard procedure." He kept his expression formal.

"Right." *I owe you one, Hosea.* "The pieces fell into place after that. I knew Lisabet had murdered Bonney, but had no proof. Yes, we had eyewitnesses, but—"

"Eyewitnesses! What have we been diddling around for, then?" Hosea half rose, then at a wave of Lisabet's gun, sat down abruptly again.

Ellie said slowly, "Hillary and…Jeb, wasn't it? The teenagers in the boat."

"Yes. Remember, they saw a small light—"

"Sylvia's cigarette."

"And then another, slightly larger light."

"Bonney's lighter."

"That's what we assumed, yes. The second one paused, then disappeared, only to start up again a minute later."

Ellie's eyes opened wide. "Wait, I've got it. There were three lights, not two. The second was Bonney's lighter. When Lisabet appeared out of the darkness, she dropped it."

"That's right. The lighter snuffed out, leaving only the glow from your cigar." Simon shook his head at Lisabet. "Imagine your surprise when you literally stumbled over your partner."

"Took me a minute to recognize her with the dreadlocks gone." Her eyes glinted. "Probably shaved her head so I wouldn't find her. She was going to steal the whole cargo."

"Did she tell you that?"

"Didn't have to. It's typical of double-dealing rats like her. It's all about the money. No vision. No passion." She stood straighter and tightened her hold on the gun. "But the dumb bitch had managed to make a mess of it. She said she'd killed the detective, but that some stowaway fellow had seen her do it and gotten the knife away from her. The boat went on without her. She just lay there on the sand, blubbering. Talk about a sitting duck." Her icy indifference made Simon's skin crawl.

"So you took your scarf—the same lovely black silk one you have on tonight—and strangled her."

Ellie murmured, "The silk fibers Maurice found on the beach."

Sylvia's frightened mewl drew their attention. "I gave you that scarf for Christmas, Lisabet. You were wearing it that night at the fort."

Lisabet ignored her, focusing on Simon. "It was easier than I thought it would be, even though I had to force the material through those layers of fat." She wrinkled her nose. "I can't stand obese people." Shrugging, she said indifferently, "She had outlived her usefulness."

Ellie whispered, "The bobbing…you kept puffing on your cigar while you were throttling her, didn't you?"

There was a general intake of breath. Finally Sylvia spluttered, "Oh, Lisabet, how could you?"

Better move this along. "You knew you had to secure the drugs yourself. You presumed Captain Goodwine would show up at the rendezvous, so you drove down to the dock and waited."

"When Goodwine didn't appear on deck, I got nervous. I thought maybe Odessa had killed him too."

"No. After Bonney went overboard, Goodwine had a fight with the stowaway, an escaped convict." He didn't look at Sylvia.

Lisabet didn't seem to appreciate the interruption. She said impatiently, "I knew nothing about the convict, but I didn't want to wait too long for Diogenes. When I heard the scream, I hightailed it out of there."

"When did you find out he was dead?"

"The Tuesday after. I snuck onto the boat and found his body."

Sylvia gasped. "Why didn't you call the police? His corpse sat there for weeks!"

Lisabet shot her a look filled with disdain. "Do I have to explain that? Honest to God, Sylvia, you're as feebleminded as the rest of them."

Simon resumed. "What you didn't know was that someone saw your car the night of the fourteenth—and noticed the taillight was out."

"Taillight?" She studied the gun barrel. "I…uh…thought it was broken in the crash."

Kenny piped up. "No, Liz. Remember, I told you it was out. Let me see…when…? Oh, yeah, that first event at the fort. The fourteenth…" He broke off.

She turned on Kenny, furious. "You. You told the police about the light."

The poor little man shrank back. "I never!"

I'd better take control before he pees in his pants. "Never mind that. Did Oscar Neely know about your partnership with Bonney? Is that why you killed him?"

Before she could answer, Nathan cried, "Oscar? Your manager?"

"Oh, Lisabet, how could you! He was such a sweet young man."

Ellie and Simon exchanged glances. *Sylvia really has lost it.*

"The prick was a recovering crackhead. He found

409

out I was dealing cocaine and threatened to go to the police. I couldn't have that."

"So you followed him to the woods. You parked on the verge and walked down the fire road."

Hosea interrupted. "That's why we only found one set of tire tracks."

"Yes. You strangled him and hid his body."

Debbie shot Simon a wondering look. "How did you know it was her?"

"Three things—three little slip-ups." He paused.

"Go on." The room hung on his words. Even Lisabet watched him carefully.

"One. When we first informed Lisabet of Oscar's death, she only asked where and when. Not how. It didn't strike me at the time, but later I began to wonder why she wouldn't be interested in the cause of death." He glanced at the Glock. "It could only have been because she already knew how he died."

"That's right," said Ellie slowly. "She didn't ask if it was suicide, or natural causes—she just assumed it was murder."

Debbie stirred. "And the next?"

"She told Kenny Oscar had gotten out of the Mercedes. At the time we informed her of his death, we only mentioned he'd been found in the woods. How would she know that if she weren't there?"

Lisabet apparently decided she could tell it better, waved the Glock at Simon, and began to speak. "Oscar saw me drive into the parking lot. He knew I was angry about his screwing around with that tramp, so he grabbed the keys and took off in my beautiful Mercedes. I jumped in my Maserati and followed him. He turned onto the fire road and barreled down it. I heard a bang. I hoped he'd killed himself, but when I got to him, he was only dazed." She nodded, pleased with herself. "He'd managed to open the door and fall out of the car. It was a simple matter to kill him and drag his body over to the log. The police would assume he'd been fatally injured in the crash and crawled away to die. An accident. I left the keys in the ignition and went home."

"Why didn't you take the car?"

She gave Ellie a withering look. "Hello? How would Oscar have gotten there without a car? And how was I supposed to drive two cars?" She stopped, and a hint of amusement passed behind her eyes. "I confess you threw me when you told me he'd taken it to the dealership."

"Turned out to be a passing hiker who needed a ride."

"Ah."

Santa spoke. "You should have shot him. A person can't strangle himself."

Debbie said matter-of-factly, "But it's her MO, Felix."

He nodded at the pistol. "I think she's more versatile than you give her credit for."

Simon could see the conversation heading off on a tangent and raised his voice. "This brings us to your third error. You told us Oscar had come back after his accident and you fired him the next day. I presume that was to give yourself an alibi." He raised his eyes to the ceiling. "If only Stephanie hadn't taken the car. It tripped us up for a bit, until we realized what it meant. Poor Oscar never left the woods. Which meant you lied."

Lisabet glared at MacGregor. "I was unprepared. I didn't think you'd ever find him, and MacGregor was hounding me about the funding and Sylvia was near hysterics. I couldn't concentrate. It was only a tiny mistake—one I assumed a couple of park *rangers* would miss." She sneered at Ellie.

Shake it off. "So you thought you were free and clear. You started arranging another cocaine delivery. When did you realize someone else was on your tail?"

"You mean that Jamaican policeman."

"Labadie. He came to find out what happened to Winston Virtue. Somehow, he traced it to you."

"He told me how. Just before he died." She said it with a certain relish. "Bonney was indeed a rotten choice—she left all kinds of evidence around, including my private phone number. I guess the first policeman found it. When Labadie called, I made up a story about how she'd contacted me and I was about to go to the police with it. He wanted to hear my evidence first."

"Why?"

"He was in a hurry. He had to get a warrant to search Bonney's house and only had twenty-four hours. So I arranged to meet him at the Ritz-Carlton." She paused, then continued, a reminiscent light in her eye. "What a beautiful kitchen they have! I wish I'd had more time to admire it. The chef's knife collection alone is worth a fortune. I can't get Cecil to maintain his knives in proper condition." She tapped a high-heeled foot. "I may have to fire him."

Absolutely bonkers. "And again you thought you'd gotten away with it."

"He couldn't have had time to report to his superiors. My secret died with him."

"Or so you thought."

She straightened. "Was I wrong?"

"Sort of." *Let's see if she bites.* "He gave the phone number to us the day before he died."

She looked at him curiously. "Then why didn't you ask about it? Or arrest me?"

Damn. "Um…er…"

Her eyes grew wide, and she let out a belly laugh. "Did you believe I'd fall for that? You people are priceless." She looked at Mathews and MacGregor. "And you two were such fine dupes."

"Dupes!"

"Useful, gullible dupes. You didn't think I took your invasion seriously, did you? Certainly not, but while the Cuban military was distracted by your brigade of little rascals, I could have sneaked in and done the deed."

This last was met with bewildered silence. Finally Sylvia asked tentatively, "Deed?"

"Murder my husband, of course. Why else would I want to set foot on that hellhole of an island? Too bad you all failed me. Bunch of losers." The barrel of the gun moved from one surprised face to the next. "It's a shame I have to kill you all."

"Don't be absurd, Lisabet." Debbie was surprisingly calm. "You can't kill fourteen people. One of us will stop you."

She pursed her lips. "I suppose you're right." She surveyed the table. "I guess a hostage would work better. Come here, Sylvia." The object of her attention cringed and tried to hide under the table. "Oh, for heaven's sake, I'm not going to hurt you. We'll just take a little walk outside. Don't be such a wuss."

The woman bit her lip. "Lisabet, you wouldn't."

Lisabet raised her gun. "In that case, I *will* have to shoot you. I can always pick another hostage."

A new voice rang out. "I don't think so. No…I think the jig is up, Lisabet."

The woman spun around to be confronted by Georgia—Amos and Tommy on either side of her acting as flying buttresses. Bobby came through the window. All three policemen had guns trained on Lisabet. Simon snaked a hand around her and snared the Glock. Lisabet stood stiffly while Bobby cuffed her hands in front of her. The rest rose, but Amos waved them back down. "Sylvia?"

His wife bent down, retrieved her purse, and slowly opened it, revealing a cell phone. "Got it all, Amos."

"That's my girl."

Hosea gaped at her. "You recorded the whole thing?"

Sylvia smiled serenely. "As planned."

"Well, I'll be…but how did you know? I thought we agreed to keep our little show from Amos, so he wouldn't leak it to you."

Sylvia beamed at Georgia. "You had a mole."

"Georgia!"

"What? You all think Sylvia's just a pretty face. I happen to know she's one heckuva tough lady. Plus"—she gestured at Amos—"as a future officer of the court, I could hardly shirk my duty to the Law."

Simon patted her shoulder. "Plus I told her to do it."

Amos faced the prisoner. "Elisabeta Zapata Tamayo de Angeles, I arrest you for the murders of

Odessa Bonney, Oscar Neely, and Patrice Labadie." He turned to Bobby. "Read her her rights." Then he walked over to his wife and patted her shoulder. "Are you okay, sugar?"

She straightened her shoulders. "Never better."

Nathan wondered aloud, "Tamayo…why is that name familiar?"

Lisabet burst out, "Orlando Zapata Tamayo was my father! He died at the hands of the Castro regime. My husband Angel Diaz Cartaya—the *cabrón*—turned him in." A tear wobbled in her eye, but she brushed it away savagely. "Papa lost his life trying to rescue the Cuban people from slavery." She waved her manacled hands in the air, her face the color of a ripe plum. "My husband is a monster. I wanted to sneak into that country with an army behind me and march to his mansion. I wanted to see his terrified face up close as I ripped his limbs off with my bare hands. I wanted to grind his evil face into paste and then skin him alive!"

Tommy pushed her toward the door. "Okay, that's enough."

As they carried her out, she screamed, "Viva Orlando Tamayo Zapata! *Muerte a los tiranos!* Angel Diaz Cartaya, you filthy minion. I spit on you." And she did.

In the ensuing silence, Lester cleared his throat. "So…does this mean the sister-cities exchange is off?"

M. S. Spencer

Chapter Twenty-Four
Trials & Celebrations

El Toro restaurant, Sunday, June 24

"I'm going to miss this place." Simon looked around the restaurant. "The *moros y cristianos* were superb."

Georgia put a hand to her throat in mock astonishment. "Does this mean you're now willing to try…let me see, escabeche? Rice with squid ink? Whatever is the world coming to?"

Ellie put down her fork. "El Toro's going to close?"

"No one to take it over. Lisabet didn't have any relatives left. Nor did she have partners."

"What about her ex-husbands?"

"Turns out the last two weren't legal marriages."

"Of course." Georgia nodded. "In her rant, she referred to Diaz Cartaya as her husband in the present tense."

"Their marriage had never been dissolved."

"That's probably a good thing. Murderous soul that she is, they would have all died in their soup."

"Speaking of, are you going to finish the chorizo ragout?" Simon's spoon hovered over Ellie's plate.

She pulled the dish close. "Yes, I am. I suppose having a near death experience has had a salutary effect on your palate. You'll eat anything."

"I still draw the line at mutton."

"Perfectly understandable."

Simon settled for a fifth roll. "One thing I don't get. I thought our excuse for the luncheon was a birthday party, but Lisabet sent her congratulations to Debbie and Santa. I never got a chance to ask her how she knew."

"That was me," said Georgia comfortably. "She wasn't going to join the party, so I told her they were engaged and encouraged her to drop in and make her compliments in person."

Simon kissed her hand. "I was wondering how I'd get her there for the big finale."

"You're welcome." Georgia drained her glass. "Has your mother moved into her new apartment yet?"

"A week ago last Thursday. She's happy as a manatee in warm water. She has a whole floor of the house and all her things around her again. Even the piano fit."

"And she's still doing well?"

"No sign of the cancer."

Ellie kissed his cheek. "It's just so wonderful."

He responded by screwing up his nose. "So, I wonder if we have to have tickets to the trial."

"How ghoulish of you." Georgia raised an elegant eyebrow. "You'll both be witnesses. That ensures a front row seat. Santa and I will be in the SRO section waving green flags."

"Very funny." He hummed a few bars of "When Johnny Comes Marching Home." "One good thing came out of this."

"Sylvia's finally sworn off smoking?"

417

"That too. No, at my suggestion, Crowley, Hearst, and Farnsworth have decided to pursue a sister-city exchange with Suva."

"Suva?"

"Capital of Fiji."

"Ooh, good choice." Georgia grinned.

"Let's see what Nathan wrote about us." Ellie opened her copy of the *Register* and ran her eye down the columns. "Hey, guess what?"

"What?"

"The Hollywood folks? They're definitely interested. There's a little advertisement on page 1A asking for extras."

"Aha. Now we know why Thad tendered his resignation."

"So…" Ellie turned to Georgia. "You never told me how come you weren't at the restaurant for the show."

Simon answered. "I asked her to give the police a heads-up. She, Sylvia, and Amos planned the whole thing, including Sylvia's recording and her '*J'accuse*' moment."

" '*J'accuse*'?" Ellie wrinkled her forehead.

"Heavy sigh. Émile Zola's famous letter to the president of the French republic defending Alfred Dreyfus, falsely accused of treason." He clucked his tongue. "Tomorrow, we begin a rigorous program of reeducation. It will do us both good."

Ellie ignored him. "She's a piece of work, isn't she? Sylvia, I mean."

"Definitely underestimated by all but her loving husband."

"And me." Georgia raised her empty glass at Inez.

"More wine, please. There's a dear." She turned back to Simon. "What about our cabal of greenies?"

"Marti has gone back on the radio."

"He didn't face any legal difficulties for planning to invade Cuba?"

"Apparently, stupidity isn't a crime."

Georgia grinned. "Amos says the police deal with at least one invasion plot a year. It's almost a cottage industry in Florida."

"And our two tin soldiers?"

"Mathews and MacGregor have settled on a parade commemorating the Patriots of Amelia Island and the Republic of the Floridas."

"No reenactment?"

"MacGregor is in charge of fundraising…so probably not."

"A parade, huh." Simon finished his beer. "They'd better have pirates."

Ellie looked up. "Why?"

Georgia explained. "Parades in Florida always have pirates."

"Oh, that's right. Because pirates ruled the waves here, didn't they?"

"Yes, indeedy. In fact, Fernandina Beach had its very own pirate king." Georgia turned to Simon. "Was he one of your ancestors too?"

"Just because he was French doesn't mean he was related to my ancestor, the dashing Jean Ribault, French Huguenot explorer and founder of Amelia Island."

"He didn't found it. He found it."

"Whatever." He rose and took Ellie's hand before bending down to kiss Georgia on the cheek. "Good luck on the bar exam. I'll see you at Santa and Debbie's wedding."

"And may I ask where you are going?"

He curled Ellie's fingers in his. "Justice of the peace."

A word about the author…

Although she has lived or traveled in every continent except Antarctica and Australia, M. S. Spencer spent the last thirty years mostly in Washington, D.C. as a librarian, Congressional staff assistant, speechwriter, editor, birdwatcher, kayaker, policy wonk, non-profit director, and parent. She has two fabulous grown children, a perfect granddaughter, and currently divides her time between the Gulf coast of Florida and a tiny village in Maine.

M. S. Spencer has published eleven romantic suspense/mystery novels.

http://msspencertalespinner.blogspot.com

Thank you for purchasing
this publication of The Wild Rose Press, Inc.

For questions or more information
contact us at
info@thewildrosepress.com.

The Wild Rose Press, Inc.
www.thewildrosepress.com

To visit with authors of
The Wild Rose Press, Inc.
join our yahoo loop at
http://groups.yahoo.com/group/thewildrosepress/

32450942R00239

Made in the USA
Middletown, DE
05 January 2019